CHANGING PLACES

UQP AUSTRALIAN AUTHORS

This is a series of carefully edited selections which represent the full range of an individual author's achievement or which present special themes in anthology form.

General Editor: Laurie Hergenhan,
Professor of Australian Literature,
University of Queensland

Also in this series:

In preparation:

CHANGING

AUSTRALIAN WRITERS IN EUROPE 1960s–1990s

PLACES

EDITED BY
LAURIE HERGENHAN &
IRMTRAUD PETERSSON

UNIVERSITY OF QUEENSLAND PRESS

First published 1994 by University of Queensland Press
Box 42, St Lucia, Queensland 4067 Australia

Compilation, introduction, notes and bibliography
© Laurie Hergenhan and Irmtraud Petersson
The copyright to the individual pieces remain with the author

Typeset by University of Queensland Press
Printed in Australia by McPherson's Printing Group

Distributed in the USA and Canada by
International Specialized Book Services, Inc.,
5804 N.E. Hassalo Street, Portland, Oregon 97213-3640

Publication of this title was assisted by
the Commonwealth Government through
the Australia Council, its arts funding
and advisory body.

Cataloguing in Publication Data
National Library of Australia

Changing Places
  Australian writers in Europe, 1960s–1990s

  1. Australians — Travel — Europe — Literary collections. 2.
  Europe — Description and travel — Literary collections. I.
  Hergenhan, L.T. (Laurence Thomas), 1931–   . II. Petersson,
  Irmtraud.

  Bibliography.

A820.80324

ISBN 0 7022 2615 7

Contents

TRAILS AND TRIALS: THE RITUALS AND CONVENTIONS OF TRAVEL

ORIGINS, HERITAGE, PILGRIMAGES

OUT OF THE COLD:
TESTING POLITICAL CLIMATES

Acknowledgments

We would like to thank Elizabeth Webby and Michael Wilding for their advice. We are also grateful for an ARC research grant.

For permission to reproduce the pieces in this volume, acknowledgment is made to: Allen & Unwin for "Getting around in Europe on the smell of an oily rag", from *On the Smell of an Oily Rag* by Bryan Dawe, 1991; to Thea Astley for "Why I wrote a story called 'Diesel Epiphany'", *Meanjin* 46.2, 1986; to Murray Bail for "Leningrad", from *Homesickness*, 1981; to Roseanne Bonney for "The homecoming" by Martin Johnston, from *The Typewriter Considered as a Bee-Trap*, Hale & Iremonger 1984; to Gillian Bouras for "Stranger in a strange land", from *Made in Australia* edited by Jim Kable, Oxford University Press 1990; to R.F. Brissenden for "Rock climbers, Uluru, 1985", from *Australian Poetry 1986: The Finest of Recent Australian Poetry* edited by Vivian Smith, Angus & Robertson, 1986; to Janine Burke for "Tuscany's talent to a muse," from *Weekend Australian*, 1989; to Chatto & Windus for "Crossing the bridge", from *When I Fell to Earth: A Life in Four Places* by Peter Conrad 1990; to Clem Christesen for "Impressions East and West", from "A Room with a View: Impressions of Germany and the Soviet Union", *Meanjin Quarterly* 24.3, 1965; to Dymphna Clark for "Tramping the battlefields", from "Tramping the Battlefields: In Search of Australia in Belgium and France", by Manning Clark, *Overland* 100, 1985; to Curtis Brown (Aust.) Pty Ltd, 27 Union Street, Paddington 2021, for "London, late 1950s", from "Maybe it's because I'm a Londoner", in *Crossing the Gap: A Novelist's Essays* by C.J. Koch, Chatto & Windus 1987; for "Leningrad", from *Holiday among the Russians* by Dymphna Cusack, Heinemann 1964; for "The return trip", from *Where a Man Belongs* by David Martin, Cassell Aust. 1969; to Dangaroo Press for "Sacred conversations", from *Turning the Hourglass* by Diane Fahey, 1990; to Catherine Duncan for "Rendezvous with the end of an age", from *The Temperament of Generations: Fifty Years of Writing in Meanjin* edited by Jenny Lee, Philip Mead and Gerald Murnane, 1990; to Forest Books for "Plane-journey Momentums" by Katherine Gallagher, from *Fish-rings on Water*, 1989; to Hale and Iremonger for "Europe: A Guide", from *The Stunned Mullet* by John Forbes, 1988; for "Family", from *Absence* by Antigone Kefala, 1992; for "Colosseum", from "The Eating Tree", from *Selected Poems*, 1986; to Marion Halligan for "Aligot", from *Eat My Words*, Angus & Robertson, 1990; to Angus & Robertson/HarperCollins for "Hydra" from *Peel Me a Lotus* by Charmian Clift, first published 1959; for "Youth at Australia House, London, 1973", from *Outer Charting*, 1985; for "Faux travel" from *The*

Obsessive Traveller or Why I Don't Steal Towels from Great Hotels Any More by David Dale, 1991; for "Phigalia" from *Over the Frontier* by Rosemary Dobson, 1978; for "Curriculum vitae", from *The Skylight* by Robert Gray, 1984; for "A Letter to Rome", from *Collected Poems 1930–1970* by A.D. Hope, 1972; for "Australians abroad", from *Clean Straw for Nothing* by George Johnston, 1969; for "Bicycle races", from *A Word from Paris* by Alister Kershaw, 1991; for "Return to Budapest" from *Inside Outside: Life between Two Worlds*, 1992; for "The traveller returns", from *Selected Poems* by Vivian Smith, 1985; for "Maison de la vie" by Michael Wilding, from *This Is For You*, 1993; to Max Harris for "The larrikins in Weimar", from *The Angry Eye*, Pergamon Press 1973; to Shirley Hazzard for "The Tuscan in each of us", from *An Antipodean Connection: Australian Writers, Artists and Travellers in Tuscany* edited by G. Prampolini and M.C. Hubert, 1993; to Graeme Hetherington for "Australians in Crete, 1941–1991", first published in *Sydney Morning Herald*, 4 April 1992; to Hyland House for "Sugar in London" by Mudrooroo, from *The Garden of Gethsemane: Poems from the Lost Decade* by Mudrooroo, 1991; to Dorothy Hewett for "The travellers", *Overland* 67, 1977; to Manfred Jurgensen for "flensburg", from *a winter's journey (1976–1977): diary poems*, Edwards & Shaw 1979; to Alfred Knopf Inc. for "Recharting the globe", from *The Road from Coorain* by Jill Ker Conway, 1989; to Tony Maniaty for "Discovering the world from a cocoon", first published in *Weekend Australian*, 15–16 July 1989; to Norma McAuley (c/- Curtis Brown (Aust.) Pty Ltd, Sydney) for "In the Mirabell Garden" from "Time Given" by James McAuley; to Shane McCauley for "Old City, Rhodes", from *The Butterfly Man*, Fremantle Arts Centre Press, 1991; to *Meanjin* for "Heart of Europe: Prague, 1978" from "Heart of Europe: Letter Pieces" by Leila Rodd, 1979; to Barbara Mobbs for "Greek journeys" by Patrick White, from *Flaws in the Glass: A Self-Portrait*, Penguin 1983; and for "Growing up in Greece" by Martin Johnston from Hazel de Berg tapes, National Library of Australia; to Les Murray for "Vindaloo in Merthyr Tydfil" from *The Vernacular Republic: Poems 1961–1981*, rev. edn, Angus & Robertson, 1982; to Nita Murray-Smith for "German Notebook 1971" by Stephen Murray-Smith, *Overland* 52, 1972; to National Library of Australia for "Self portrait", from *Self Portraits* by Charmian Clift, selected by David Foster, 1991; to Desmond O'Grady for "Budapest, Keleti", from "Keleti & Karizma", *Outrider* 2.1, 1985; to Jan Owen for "Town" from *Fingerprints on Light*, Angus & Robertson, 1990; to Oxford University Press for "Bad Dreams in Venice", © Peter Porter (1992), reprinted from *The Chair of Babel* by Peter Porter (1992); to Geoff Page for "Nuclear plant on the Loire", from *Smiling in English, Smoking in French*, Brindabella Press 1987; to Pan Macmillan Australia

Pty Ltd, copyright © Serpentine Publishing Co. Pty Ltd 1991, for "On the road in Ireland", from *Now and in Time to Be: Ireland and the Irish* by Thomas Keneally; to Penguin Books Australia for "Notebook entries" from *Longhand: A Writer's Notebook* by Murray Bail, McPhee Gribble 1989; for "Irish Customs" from *Memory Ireland: Insights into the Contemporary Irish Condition* by Vincent Buckley, 1985; for "Village life in Greece" by Beverley Farmer, from Ray Willbanks *Speaking Volumes: Australian Writers and Their Work*, 1992; for "Pomegranates", from *Home Time* by Beverley Farmer, McPhee Gribble 1985; for "In Paris", from *Postcards from Surfers* by Helen Garner, McPhee Gribble 1985; for "Memory Crop" by Sneja Gunew, from *Inner Cities: Australian Women's Memory of Place* edited by Drusilla Modjeska, 1989; for "Living in Moscow", from *Serpent's Tooth: An Autobiographical Novel* by Roger Milliss, 1984; for "Crete", from *Poppy* by Drusilla Modjeska, McPhee Gribble 1990; for "Blase in the Land of Swizzlestick", from *Room Service* by Frank Moorhouse, 1985; for "Leaving 1928; returning 1969", from "Another View of the Homestead" by Christina Stead, in *Ocean of Story: The Uncollected Stories of Christina Stead*, 1986; to Jack Porter for "The baggage of memory" by Hal Porter, from *The Extra*, Thomas Nelson 1975; to Peter Porter for "The true country" from "An expatriate's reaction to his condition", *Westerly* 32.4, 1987; to Betty Roland for "Gallipoli: The hills of the heroes", from *Lesbos: The Pagan Island*, 1963; to Isobel Robin for "Freud's backyard", *Overland* 102, 1986; to Leonie Sandercock and *Overland* for "Letter from Ireland" by Ian Turner, from *Overland* 66, 1977; to the University of Queensland Press for "Australian poet c.1988 visits the home of an English poet c.1888", from *Charmed Lives* by Bruce Beaver, 1988; for "The only black woman at Ealing Station", from *No Regrets* by Mabel Edmund, 1992; for "Having a wonderful time" from *Bearded Ladies* by Kate Grenville, 1985; for "Getting away", from *Michael and Me and the Sun* by Barbara Hanrahan, 1992; for "Home thoughts" from *Palomino* by Elizabeth Jolley, 1984; for "Bad dreams in Vienna" from *Neighbours in a Thicket* by David Malouf, 1980; for "After Chernobyl", from "Imagining the Real" by David Malouf in *David Malouf* edited by James Tulip, 1990; for "Searching for the face of Soviet literature" by Olga Masters, from *Olga Masters: Reporting Home* edited by Deirdre Coleman, 1990; for "The Journey with children", from *New and Selected Poems* by Judith Rodriguez, 1988; for "Travel dice", from *Travel Dice* by Thomas Shapcott, 1987; for "Folds in the map", from *Folds in the Map* by Andrew Taylor, 1991; for "Lufthansa" and "Cicada Gambit", from *Under Berlin* by John Tranter, 1988; for "Prodigal" from *The Observatory* by Dimitris Tsaloumas, 1983; to Chris Wallace-Crabbe for "Flat out in the Mezzogiorno" from *The Emotions Are*

Not Skilled Workers, Angus & Robertson 1980; and for "Russia: Lost in Wonderland", from "Lost in Wonderland", *Scripsi* 4.1, 1986; to Ania Walwicz for "europe", from *Joseph's Coat: An Anthology of Multicultural Writing* edited by Peter Skrzynecki, Hale & Iremonger 1985; to Miss Alice Waten for "Odessa" from *From Odessa to Odessa: The Journey of an Australian Writer* by Judah Waten, F.W. Cheshire, 1969; to McKenzie Wark for "East Meets West at the Wall", from *Oriental Geography: Living with Global Media Events*, Indiana University Press 1994; to Tim Winton for "Letter from Ireland", *Overland* 112, 1988.

Introduction

Australians have a reputation for being long-distance travellers. This derives from a tradition of colonialism and post-colonialism; from geographical location, both a deterrent and a spur; from post-Romantic literary tradition, coinciding with the early years of white settlement; and from the universal lure of ideas of travel, never more flourishing than at the present time. "Travel: a word repeated a thousand times in the streets, in advertising; it is seduction itself."[1] Or, as Don Anderson puts it with journalistic flourish: "Travel is to the '90s as sex was to the '60s. Everyone claims to be doing it. Certainly, everyone is writing about it."[2] Travel currently exists very much as writing or "text", as well as, or as part of, "lived" experience. And Australian writing, like travel and tourism themselves, has become part of a global context, with models such as Paul Theroux, Bruce Chatwin and Jan Morris in non-fiction, and with the new growth of an industry of writing "about" travel literature, though this has been preceded by the self-conscious playfulness and deconstructive sportings with travel genres by the "primary" authors themselves, for instance by Murray Bail in *Homesickness*, Marion Campbell in *Lines of Flight* and Kate Grenville in *Dreamhouse*. "I travel in order to write," says Michel Butor, "not only to find subject matter ... but because to travel, at least in a certain manner, is to write (first of all because to travel is to read), and to write is to travel."[3] For Roland Barthes the bourgeois "myth of travel is becoming quite anachronistic ... already, in the *Michelin Guide*, the number of bathrooms, and forks indicating good restaurants is vying with that of 'artistic curiosities' ..."[4] Travel and travel writing, however, flow on regardless, and rather than fading, myths take new forms, as do the semiotics of travel.

Amidst this flow, there is increasing self-consciousness about the ambiguities of travel experiences and ways of representing them. "I love trying things and discovering how I hate them," wrote D.H. Lawrence.[5] "Part of me hankers after domesticity and orderliness. There is also that face which looks towards the wild side," noted Patrick White.[6] And that the true art of writing about travel is not a smooth ride has long been recognised: it "lies less in its narrative line of advance than in the various impediments, interruptions, deflections or 'unforeseen stoppages' that solicit the inventory of the pen and/or eye".[7] Such solicitations can take comic and distinctive forms for writers even in the jet age, for Australian travel has its own rituals and conventions. It also has its own traditions, if one uses the term travel writing not to denote a separate genre, but in an embracing sense (as we have done in planning this volume) to include representations of encounters of various kinds, direct and indirect, with another land and culture, written in various genres and discourses — fiction, poetry, nonfiction, journalism, autobiography or "life writing", interviews, guides, notebooks and so on. Our intention in this selection, however, is to suggest the differences between these fluid divisions rather than to elide difference.

Women's contributions to travel writing are only recently being admitted, in both senses. A sign of the times is *Wayward Women: A Guide to Women Travellers* by Jane Robinson (1991): Women travellers "had been writing about their journeys for sixteen centuries ... All of them voyaged 'over the straits' — not just like Louisa Meredith (from whom I borrow the term), across seas from the familiar to a strange land, but across the boundaries of convention and traditional feminine restraints too."[8] Interestingly enough, Louisa Meredith was a colonial Australian writer and her book, *Across the Straits*, tells of a journey from the east coast of Tasmania to Melbourne. Thus "Australian" works can enter other traditions as well as contributing to an indigenous one. The latter is a rich field, currently being recovered, and it has a double strand: when Australians were not travelling around their own island continent, by foot, horse, camel, looking "through the windscreen", or whatever, they were "crossing the seas" and oceans as "sea-people", as Christina Stead styled them in the prologue of *For Love Alone*.

We have chosen to restrict this collection to the last thirty years because of the richness of material available and because of the interesting changes in that time in the representing of travel experiences, along with changes in generations, outlook and purpose. There is no longer a belief in "the innocent eye" or in transparent language. Australian writers leave fingerprints, sometimes seemingly invisible or hard to spot, on their perceptions of other peoples and cultures, and what they see about this "other" inevitably expresses something of themselves as mediated through their own diverse culture. As fixed ideas of nationality — such as those of Russel Ward's pioneering *Australian Legend*— have broken down and so opened up possibilities, under such influences as the Vietnam protest years, the rise of feminism and multiculturalism, and as the effects of increased migration made themselves felt, so Australians have come to view themselves and others differently. Assisting these changes were changing modes of travel, especially the greater economic accessibility of overseas jet travel in the 1960s, and "the kangaroo route" to London. The Australian versions of the grand tour and cultural pilgrimage were overshadowed by the transitory visit, revisitings and tourism, all using Australia as a "home" base, and less frequently confined to the umbilical route to London. At the same time expatriatism became a less common option or necessity as Australians became more satisfied with their own culture and more confident about it. They went abroad generally to return, they went with different expectations and assumptions, so they saw things differently from previous travellers.

Tourists (and tourism) enter into Australian literature, cutting across their exclusion from definitions of "real" travel writing. "In fact, tourists are often distinguished not by mindless complacency … but by precisely the *angst* about their role and the dislike of their fellows which this formulation expresses."[9] There is ample opportunity for comedy and fellow-feeling here, and many writers have seized it.

Writers as well as tourists keep their eyes on one another. It is more appropriate to look on travel writings as re-viewings than to see them as offering completely new views. This is not a recent phenomenon, though it may have been quickened by postmodernism. Travel discourses freely appropriate one another. As a strategy for writing about the much visited Venice, Henry James began by announcing that it was impossible to say anything new about it, all had been written. In their different ways, writers in this collection are mindful, like John Forbes or Ania Walwicz, of those who have gone before them, whether Australian or not. For example, a post-colonial and conservationist politics informs Geoffrey

Lehmann's haunting poem about the much written-over Colosseum, in a piece which represents more of an imaginative revisiting than the "actual" kind of observation that most of the selections purport to be. It is by writing out of changing times, and by positioning themselves in relation to previous writing and history — and history is "what is told", David Malouf reminds us — rather than in pretending to be "original" or originating that travel writers "make it new".

In selecting material for a collection of Australian travel writing of the past three decades we chose to confine ourselves to reponses to Europe, rather than including the effects of North America on travellers such as Shirley Hazzard, Glenda Adams, Kate Grenville; or the increasing orientation of Australians towards Asian travels. Apart from limiting the bulk of material, such a selection enabled us to concentrate deliberately on changing representations of the allegedly familiar rather than of the "exotic", and on questions of Australian self-definition rather than on discourses of orientalism. At the same time this gives an opportunity of decentring: of drawing attention to the growth of discourses about Europe from other, "newer" centres, rather than pursuing yet again discourses from Europe about the so-called peripheries.

There are parallels between the Australian and the American fictional journey to Europe. The American has been described as "a composite of several distinct patterns of journey narrative — the escape, the pilgrimage, the homecoming, the retreat. It is also, in the twentieth century, a locus of the novel of directionless wandering."[10] There is a distinction to be made between the pilgrimage "as a journey toward a foreknown, fixed goal; [and the] quest, a journey of search for an envisioned but not clearly known or located goal."[11] Australian writers ring many changes, sometimes ironic, on these patterns, often interweaving them. These postcolonial patterns have been seen as expressing classic — or stereotypic — oppositions: between, on the one hand, Australia as "empty" or "unmade" culturally, conforming, derivative and lacking in history, and on the other hand, Europe as representing the original, hallowed cultural source, a touchstone of values and as enabling an individual development not attainable in colonial, or even postcolonial Australia. But the patterns in the best writing are complex and they undermine stereotypes. "It's a complex fate, being an American [we can add post-colonial or Australian], and one of the responsibilities it entails is fighting against a superstitious valuation of Europe," commented Henry James.[12] It is not only the superstitious evaluation of Europe that Australians have had to fight against, but also resentment, animosity, and even superiority, the obverse of the "cultural cringe".

In comparison with America, Australia's relations have been more exclusively with Britain as representing "Europe", rather than with the continental European nations. But this, too, is changing. Britain is no longer the Mecca (though it is still a base) it used to be. There is an increasing tendency to begin and end travel with the continental countries, and also to see them as changing and individual societies. Greece, Italy and to some extent Russia have been centres of attraction, stimulating clusters of impressions, versions of the "same" subjects and sights, so that a richly layered literariness is the result, and the very notion of a "centre", especially a fixed one, is changing. From the beginning of white Australian literature the basic opposition of privileged centre and subordinate periphery was not a simple, "one-way" traffic, but part of a movement towards seeing Australian culture as a centre in its own right, containing its own variety, and capable of relating variously to other centres. This has accelerated since the 1960s.

Christopher Koch, looking back from the 1980s, has seen this change as gradual, as "an intimate evolution", "part of a process that is really a sort of graph of what's been happening to Australia in the thirty odd years since I began publishing my work". From being brought up in a kind of cultural "Plato's cave" living with only shadows of the "real world", "that centre some 12,000 miles away" (here one is reminded of the versions of the Lady of Shalott's reflected world in Australian writing by women), Koch talks about a gradual transition towards seeing Australia as a distinct society and culture to which writers can feel they belong, if not exclusively: "We are no longer a British province; we are a foreign country." A writer "can't finally escape his own country", says Koch, and recently fewer have wanted to.[13]

New directions in some of the autobiographical writing of the early 1960s may have contributed to changes in viewing Europe.

Hal Porter's *The Watcher on the Cast Iron Balcony* helped to stimulate the first volume of George Johnston's trilogy, *My Brother Jack*. Along with the neglected autobiographical work, in essay or journalistic form, by Charmian Clift, both these writers showed a new-found faith in the literary possibilities of individual experience, transformed and structured by mythologising the local, in terms of both place and family — at home and abroad. In Porter's case there was also a drawing on the stylistic resources of modernism and post-modernism, a self-consciousness and adventurousness of language, especially by using the narrating "I/eye" to explore the constructions and instabilities of the self, and of the self as a creator of worlds. At the same time Porter's autobiography expressed a faith and confidence, indeed a delight, in what was locally "given" in terms of his birthright, a specific place and a specific culture. For Porter, Clift and Johnston these works provided a vantage point for exploring "foreign" places: their impact on the self and their uses in constructing selves. A past, specifically an Australian past, thus proved an aid to discovering what was strange or "other", both in another culture and in the recesses of the self. The achievements of Manning Clark and others, in revitalising the writing and reading of Australian history in the 1960s, contributed to this sense that there was a past to build on.

This cultural confidence also shows itself in another way in Charmian Clift's writing about Greece. She puts it to different uses from Johnston's through the different genres of the memoir and essay, but she grounds impressions in a self, and a woman's experience, that have been formed "elsewhere". Such increased travel confidence was in the air as the 1960s developed, showing itself in the way readers responded eagerly to what was essentially a belief in the value and interest of Australian experiences and in the way they could stand up against others to offer mutual illumination. Part of the change arose paradoxically from a more assured treatment of a lack of confidence, an accepting of this as a dramatic subject, not a disability. There is a line of similarity stretching through to the autobiographically based novels of European travel such as Anderson's *Tirra Lirra by the River*, Malouf's *Johnno* and Grenville's *Dreamhouse*, and to the way in which Peter Porter gradually felt free to write of his Australian past as well as of cosmopolitan themes, and in drawing on one to illuminate the other.

Something of the mythic power of an original, or what Malouf has called "a first place", resonant with possibilities often "withheld", is found in Stead's *For Love Alone*, as an impulse to travel and as a touchstone. It is also there in Meroë in *The Aunt's Story*, and is linked with the ironic metaphor of the Odyssey, and Ithaca as providing the impulse for the journey. This motif reappears in Johnston's *Clean Straw for Nothing* and is repeated in Martin Johnston's writing in the allusion to Cavafy's poem "Ithaca":

> Without her you would never have taken the road.
> Ithaca has given you the beautiful voyage.
> But she has nothing more to give you.
>
> And if you find her poor,
> Ithaca has not defrauded you.
> With all the great wisdom you have gained,
> With so much experience,
> you must surely have understood by then what Ithaca means.

What is handed on from Henry Handel Richardson and continues through Stead, White and Peter Porter (it goes back to Marcus Clarke and beyond) is the idea of exile as both colonial and extra-colonial, as not simply a separation from a "home" country, but as a state of mind, of being shut out from some longed-for fulness of spirit. This reappears in Malouf's *An Imaginary Life* and in his poem "At Ravenna": "we are all exiles of one place or another, even those who never leave home". And it appears in Peter Porter's sense of feeling at home nowhere, so that his poems about European art and culture express a permanent loss, a longing for transcendence that is common to modern life.

A "first place" is a starting point and a reference point for travelling in autobiographical works. It is linked with a new emphasis on regionalism, on what Thea Astley calls the "parish" as an originating centre. We see this also in Malouf's Brisbane in *12 Edmondstone Street* and its relation to "A Place in Tuscany", in Anderson's Brisbane in *Tirra Lirra*, in Peter Conrad's and Koch's Tasmania and in Barbara Hanrahan's Adelaide. The powerful presence of these locales, enriched by particular social customs and mores, is something new or "rediscovered" in Australian writing, and it is often sharpened by a journey away to foreign places and by a return. This is also a move away from the powerful metropolitan centres of Sydney and Melbourne.

An increasing emphasis in writings about travel to Europe is on the return home, and one thinks of Eliot's lines about returning to the place you started from to know it for the first time. This raises the question: is it the place we get to know better, or the created self that in turn creates places? For the mind can be its own place and is a transformer of places. In a recent review of a book on Barry Humphries, C.K. Stead quotes Clive James as saying of Humphries: "if he had not had his Europe, he would never have completed his rediscovery of Australia".[14] Stead continues:

> He represents the dilemma of Australian and Anglo-African expatriation — the loss and gain of it. He can only be fully understood at home, but there he's likely to encounter sullenness and resentment, which is overcome, paradoxically, by the irresistible force of fame earned where the comprehension of what he is doing must be less than complete.

One might have some reservations here. Edna Everage, as against some other Humphries characters, has become a creation mainly for consumption in Britain. Bruce Bennett has commented on the useful "bi-focal vision" of talented expatriate writers, but according to Bennett, Clive James and Humphries have been more popularly acclaimed than Peter Porter because each has relied, to some extent, on English-derived stereotypes of the comically naive and uncouth Australian, which complemented their own observations formed before they moved to England.[15]

To return to the cultural confidence of the post-1960s: on the one hand, nationality could be regarded as a disability, a hangover from the cultural cringe, or as a difficult fate one had to rise above (as Patrick White tends to present it); on the other hand, nationality, or more precisely one's national culture, could be regarded as adding a positive and useful dimension to writing about experiences abroad. Frank Moorhouse in his introduction to *The State of the Art* (1983) commented that the story of a journey was currently the most successfully practised short-story form in Australia. "Travel is not only about encounters with foreign ways," he went on, "or the trying-on of foreign styles, it is an encounter with one's nationality ... So before complete personality can cautiously emerge, it is nationality, 'being Australian', which sets the shape of discourse and interaction." Moorhouse exploits this in his own comic stories about François Blase, an extremely "trepid" traveller.

Moorhouse related his views to the changing times in *Days of Wine and Rage* (1980):

> The seventies was a ridge in our cultural history. It was the decade when writers, at least, stopped going away to live in other countries — the end of the expatriate tradition ...
>
> Writers of my age and younger have travelled and continue to travel but do not contemplate permanently living abroad. As Jim Davidson has said, it represents the beginning of the de-dominionisation of Australia.

Moorhouse continues:

> The anxiety still assails Australians working in the arts that Australia may not be a sufficient place for the development of creativity and intelligence, the achievement of excellence. This is because Australia is not worth making art from, or its cultural traditions do not permit the making of art yet, or because the audience or readership here is not sophisticated or receptive enough or, economically, not big enough. Sometimes the deficiency is said to be in our history ... Sometimes it is a fear that to stay in Australia would develop in a creative person an Australian perspective that would be too narrow to appeal to an international readership ...[16]

Moorhouse is too dramatically definite in announcing "the end of the expatriate tradition", but it is changing. Confirmed expatriates like Peter Porter are now almost commuters, via the easily negotiable "aluminium curtain", as he calls it. He is welcomed on his returns and must gain a sense that there is strong Australian interest in his work, instead of facing discrimination on the basis of un-Australian activities. The poet Katherine Gallagher is also a "returner". An expatriate of longer standing and another generation than Porter, Alister Kershaw, who provoked Patrick White's famous manifesto, or diatribe, "The Prodigal Son", about returning to live in Australia, was recently welcomed back on a visit, and his memoirs of living abroad were published.

Moorhouse's views have been echoed by Janine Burke, representing a younger generation: "Attitudes are changing," she says.

"For Hazzard, Italy was the great escape from the aridity of Australian life in the 1950s. Relief marked her arrival, need made her stay. For my generation of postwar baby boomers, the urge was not to flee but to savour, to enjoy and to come home. Home was not such a bad place to be."[17]

This is what the protagonist in Burke's *Second Sight* comes to feel. Tuscany helps to liberate what is in her. The artist Jeffrey Smart left Australia in 1963 when it seemed to him dull and isolated, to live in Italy: "I adored the modernity as well as the antiquity," he said. When interviewed recently he commented: "Australia has changed for the better, Italy has changed for the worse ... now I don't know whether I should live here or in Italy. Actually, there's not much to choose between the two."[18] John Tranter, a spokesperson of the self-mythologised "generation of '68", comments that when he left Australia (for a brief period as it turned out) in 1966, "I felt I was leaving a country that was almost as interesting as Melbourne on a wet Sunday ... Five years later, Australia was a different place altogether, everything had changed."[19]

Peter Conrad's account in *Where I Fell to Earth* of his arrival in London in the 1960s reads at first like a classic account of someone who has escaped the colonial fringes to enter the promised land of the cultural centre, so long and vicariously prepared for through reading English literature. Yet the passage has its ironies. The inevitable recalling of Wordsworth's "Westminster Bridge" as Conrad describes his crossing of Waterloo Bridge when he first arrived, suggests that he is looking back on himself and his near-orgasmic excitement as having the extravagance of the outsider's view, an extravagance which, though "real", can only be followed by diminution. He is hardly coming *home*, as he goes on in his autobiography to show. What he is doing is filtering a "classic" — or conventional — colonial experience through a post-colonial awareness. The passage is celebratory yet has the reservations and self-consciousness of Hal Porter's watcher-narrator observing himself as watcher.

Changes in representations of Europe linked to changing conceptions of Australia can also be traced through the recurrent metaphor of "roots". Whereas the notorious Australian emptiness is figured as a horizontal blankness ("on all sides of me stretched the great Australian emptiness," says White in "The Prodigal Son"), the lack of roots is concerned with vertical space, the supposed lack of depth: the thin layer of native earth as against fertile soil. Henry James commented that "the flower of art only blooms where the soil is deep", and in a change of metaphor from the ecological to the technological, he went on: "it takes a complex machinery to set a society in motion". In contrast to White's celebrated statement about emptiness in "The Prodigal Son", which he felt called upon to fill, is his less quoted much later statement (1980) about the need of native roots, a rationalisation of his decision to return to Australia, having had the advantage of living "elsewhere", and to write out of a continuing love–hate relationship. White's work from the 1950s shows the tension as more fruitful than a comfortable patriotism or isolationism. White recalled an English painter and friend saying: "Even abstract painters can't afford to sever their roots." White went on to make a "plea to artists to cling to the soil from which they grew — even if it is the grit of Melbourne's pavements — or the garbage of Sydney's gutters", images typical of White who instructed that his ashes be placed in one of Centennial Park's more polluted ponds.[20] This is a far cry from Alister Kershaw's comment in "The Last Expatriate" (1958):

> Personally I've always felt that "nationality" — the quirks and tics and prejudices and, no doubt, virtues which one picks up from one's early environment — must be pretty damned tenuous if it's endangered by going outside territorial waters … I'd imagine that one reason why certain people prefer living in France, for instance, rather than in Australia, is quite simply that France feels as though it were *meant* to be lived in. Whereas in Australia it was somehow as if one were hanging precariously to a cliff edge, with the Genius Loci stamping on one's finger-tips.

A less defensive expatriate position is represented by Peter Porter, from a later generation. In his poem "On First Looking into Chapman's Hesiod" Porter questions Les Murray's overemphasis on "indigenous" or "organic" roots. Murray is seen as the assertive, non-metropolitan, local poet, a counterpart of Boeotian art of the countryside represented by Hesiod, whom Porter has recently read in Chapman's translation. In a parody of romantic travel writing

Porter writes that through reading Hesiod's *Works and Days*, a form
of "travel",

> ... I saw, not quite
> The view from Darien, but something strange
> And balking — Australia my own country
> And its edgy managers — in the picture of
> Euboeaen husbandry, terse family feuds
> And the minds of gods tangential to the earth.

What Porter "discovers", too, and asserts is his own individual role
and position as cosmopolitan, and hence as the counterpart of
Hesiod's translator Chapman, and of George Steiner as a "Pente-
costal Silver Tongue", and as one who "feels at home nowhere",
indeed as one who *need* feel at home nowhere because this attitude
of mind is a main source of his poetry. He speaks out of both the
yearning and the positive experience of rootlessness, the sense of
continual displacement of the permanent life traveller.

> Sparrows acclimatize, but I still seek
> The permanently upright city where
> Speech is nature and plants conceive in pots,
> Where one escapes from what one is and who
> One was, where home is just a postmark ...

Porter has commented: "...it becomes honourable to be an airplant
and to live wherever life will support one's imaginative labours."
This is made possible by his attitude to language: the realisation
that "speech is nature" (hence "plants conceive in pots"), that, as
he put it in an interview, "poetry is made of words and not just
experiences", or that words as the medium of writing and reading
— and of travel — are in themselves primary experiences.

This relates Porter to those poets who, like Dobson, Hope and
Harwood, sometimes write out of their sense of European culture,
experienced through books read or paintings viewed (not necessarily in the original). These experiences of Europe transported — or
in Malouf's terms "translated" — to Australia, experiences of
"travel", were not at first regarded by Dobson's early readers as
"real" or "primary" experiences, but rather as serving to remove
poetry from experience. That she, Hope and Porter had to defend
the reality of such experiences — Katherine Gallagher and Dianne
Fahey do not seem to have the same problem — suggests the

limitations of Australian culture, of what could be admitted or rationalised as valid material for literature, and what could not. Perhaps the empiricist tradition and resistance to imported high culture helped to set up these barriers, but they are breaking down. There is now an ever-increasing sub-genre of travel poetry which expresses responses not to landscape, but to artefacts, especially paintings, in European galleries.[21]

The growing self-consciousness in post-1960s writings of representations of Europe involves both choice and treatment of subject matter, including a growing and comic concentration on the conventions and rituals of travel, of its trials and tribulations as well as its pleasures — and also a growing awareness of how travel experiences are processed and mediated through language as culture: through literary and social conventions. Of course the undermining of conventions and myths has long been practised. Puncturing myths and the mystique of Europe has been popular. The more mundane or even "vulgar" aspects of travel or tourism are now fair game. In an age snobbishly bemoaned by Paul Fussell as showing the death of "true" travel writing, they are now sources of comedy. For instance, Kate Grenville can write a story about a coach trip from London to Athens which is a series of unforeseen disasters. Les Murray, internally scorched by eating Vindaloo curry at Merthyr Tydfil in Wales has more revelations forced upon him about his "mortal coil" than he cared to have, and these revelations are expressed in an appropriation of the hyperbole of Dylan Thomas. In a story, "There Were Some Countries", Gerard Murnane, who has never left Australia and whose reputedly most memorable journey was from Melbourne to Bendigo, exploits the post-modern. He shows how we build up ideas about countries we never visit (as well as those we do), and he speculates about the imaginative needs these fulfil. This is indeed ringing the changes on countries of the mind and on exile. Kate Grenville in *Dreamhouse* playfully uses gothic to undercut conventional literary accounts of the idyllic setting of Tuscan villas and countryside. In Patrick White's *Flaws in the Glass*, an unconventional autobiography, he uses a section on travels in Greece not simply for their "travel" interest but to express his love–hate relationship with both

Greece and Australia, and through this to suggest the nature of his lifelong relationship with his partner, Manoly Lascaris.

Developments in women's writing have contributed variously to the sort of travel writings we have been discussing, at the same time creating a useful context for viewing them. Surveying texts by women writers specifically raises questions such as: why do they travel, and what do they expect to find? What do they notice particularly, and what seems important to them? What stories do they tell, and how? Are there any common trends, in subject matter as well as genre, style, tone etc? How have women writers chosen to convey their understanding of European cultures, of foreign surroundings and otherness, and of what their experience meant to them? And — this is the hardest question of all — is there perhaps a noticeable difference to male writing in the ways they represent Europe? Something of the sort is suggested by Jane Robinson:

> Throughout the centuries spanned by this book, men have been setting out for the world with some definite purpose in mind, with reputations to forge and patrons to please, and their written accounts have been dedicated to tangible results. Women, whether travelling by choice or default, had for the most part no such responsibilities: they left the facts and figures of foreign travel to the men, and dwelt instead on the personal practicalities of getting from A to B, and on impression. And now that I have myself hurtled headlong into the trap of overgeneralization, I may as well finish the job properly: men's travel accounts are traditionally concerned with What and Where, and women's with How and Why.[22]

In this collection we have included travel experience told from a female (but not necessarily feminist) point of view in fictional and non-fictional texts. For one thing, fictional travel accounts are usually based on personal travel experience and observation, as writers frankly admit.[23] In other cases, where one would not think of looking too closely for the author behind a fictional character's European experience because of the obvious distancing through irony, comedy, exaggeration or even gothic elements, the uses of place as well as character nevertheless allow conclusions about the cultural consciousness in which the writer is positioned and from which she speaks. And if women's travel writing, as Sara Mills states, has often been "described as trivial because it contains descriptions of relationships and domestic details",[24] this is changing. As well, the deliberate fictionalising of travel experience could be seen as a strategy by women writers to be taken more seriously, by using the mediation of a more accepted and more highly valued genre.

Male and female writers alike have sent their travellers on pilgrimages to places known from art and literature, and it is often through poetry that such "cultural travellers" most effectively respond to place and ambience (for instance poems by Rosemary Dobson, Nancy Keesing, Elizabeth Riddell, Diane Fahey, Isobel Robin, Jena Woodhouse). And many have been drawn by classical Italian civilisation, or by concepts of alternative ways of living perceived in, among others, Mediterranean cultures, either out of disaffection with contemporary Australia or in the hope of finding a stimulus for a more meaningful life.

The most interesting texts, whether fictional, autobiographical or journalistic, involve the traveller, and the reader, in some sort of "learning" process entailing insights or revelations which enable both traveller and reader to arrive at a new understanding of the culture observed and of their own. This may involve finding new models abroad. The questioning, even shedding, of inherited cultural views and values and the transformation that accompanies the acquiring of new perspectives is remarkably outlined in Jill Ker Conway's story of her trip to Europe with her mother. For both mother and daughter the journey "involved the redefinition of our relationship to the past and reconfiguring our sense of geography". For the daughter the transformation involves not only a "recharting of the globe", a "new sense of the world and my new perspective on Australian society", but also the decision to become a scholar, the finding of a new independence and purpose in life.

Travel experience can include a social or political awakening to problems of gender and ethnicity. The Greek experience, for example, of the "temporary migrants" Clift, Farmer and Bouras obviously sharpened their awareness of the problematics of male/female roles in society. More recent writers, particularly Farmer and Bouras, have highlighted the contrasts between Greek and Australian gender roles and positions. Concerned with family issues, both writers feel attracted by aspects of Greek family life such as warmth, closeness, intimacy, reliability. Despite an admiration for some of the strong matriarchal characters they present, ambivalence prevails, with Bouras sometimes subtly questioning the wisdom of letting her sons grow up within Greek male traditions, and Farmer's persona insisting on giving birth to her child in Australia rather than Greece ("Place of Birth"). Being a woman in Greece, Bouras observes, is vastly different from being a woman in Australia. The Greek women in Farmer's stories are emotionally strong and mostly lovable battlers, and they are loyal to their men (though they usually don't get to see them very much). But as a (female) reader one cannot help but sigh with relief at the success of Farmer's Australian character Bell who manages to have her child born in Australia. Though still cherishing her Greek ties, Bell returns to the relative freedom and independence a woman enjoys in Australia and learns to fend for herself (see "Pomegranates" and other stories). "Simply to go away," says Charmian Clift, "is not to effect change. It is what our nomads bring back that is going to count, and how they use the sum of their European experience, even if all they have discovered is some truth about themselves."[25]

A number of so-called migrant writers have, not surprisingly, produced a variety of travel texts which could be classified as "return trip" accounts, centring on travellers who experience a growing awareness of their ethnicity and (often problematic) cultural belonging. Particularly, the more recent pieces on such physical and/or spiritual return trips (e.g. by Sneja Gunew, Ania Walwicz, Antigone Kefala) play with the traveller's affinities with more than one culture. And it is not merely the search for origins, the curiosity about ancestral traits, that seems to inform some of these texts. There is an almost celebratory awareness of the very fact that one has various, diverse origins, resulting in open-ended questions such as: What is it that still binds me to that ancestral culture? What would I be today if I hadn't been taken to Australia? (See for instance Gunew's "Memory Crop".) Perhaps it could be said, cautiously though, that in "return trip" accounts by male writers (e.g. Waten, Riemer, Martin, Jurgensen) the problems of ethnicity are more straightforwardly solved, the outcome or status quo (whether by choice or default) is more firmly, more definitely, accepted.

If the return to ancestral sources provides the motivation for one distinctive type of traveller, and travel writer, the task of a cultural delegate produces another. One early example of this type is Dymphna Cusack, whose political commitment, interest in foreign cultures, close connections and commercial success (particularly in socialist countries) combined to enable her to travel widely, and consequently to publish travel books (*Holidays among the Russians*, 1964, and *Illyria Reborn*, 1966) and travel fiction (*Heatwave in Berlin*, 1961). Cusack implies a familiarity with language, customs, and with social and political conditions of the host countries which allegedly gives her a voice of authority. Cusack's political views may be somewhat naive or, to put it more generously in the words of Christina Stead, "she tends to greatly praise the country (leftist countries); is sold there, makes a profit and is able to go back there again on her earnings! Good idea. (But she would not dwell on the shadows in the picture.)"[26] A major concern in Cusack's travel writing is the situation of women and the depiction of their domestic and personal circumstances. To her progress means, above all, liberation of women and improvement of their (and their families') living conditions, be it in Russia, Albania or elsewhere. (Interestingly, although Cusack was always accompanied by her husband on her European travels, he remains all but invisible in her travel books.)

Such an interest in the situation of women is equally strong in the account of a more recent cultural delegate, Olga Masters, in her newspaper article on Russia, "Searching for the Face of Soviet Literature" (1985).[27] Masters' report of an official tour lends itself to a comparison with that of a male member of the travel group, Chris Wallace-Crabbe's "Lost in Wonderland". Whereas Wallace-Crabbe writes enthusiastically about cultural and literary experience and impressions, Masters' critical account focuses largely on a grey and loveless atmosphere determined by male-dominated officialdom, and on the dire situation of Russian women. Masters sympathises with "the raw deal they were getting".[28]

The earliest travel texts in the period represented in this collection, Charmian Clift's travel books *Mermaid Singing* (1958) and *Peel Me a Lotus* (1959), present themselves conspicuously as personal and autobiographical, and more so than George Johnston's obviously fictionalised treatment of much of the same experience and time span in *Clean Straw for Nothing.* (Both Clift and Johnston, however, changed the names of friends in their books.) The chosen genre with its conventions and constraints demanded a different approach and, as Clift's biographer Nadia Wheatley maintains, Clift's talents find a better outlet in her Greek travel books, "where the writer herself is very much the subject", than in her novels — and stories, one might add.[29] Clift's travel writing provided a novelty for Australian readers in so far as it conveyed the experience of a travelling *family* who had chosen to settle for a considerable period in a place rather unusual for the time, that is, the Greek islands of Kalymnos and, later, Hydra. What makes Clift's travel books and essays such pleasure to read is, on the one hand, her intelligence and style, and, on the other, the personal tone with which she involves readers in an almost intimate dialogue, sharing the ups and downs of everyday family life as well as her opinions on social and political conditions and developments in Greece. But Clift's persona in her travel writing and journalistic column is just as artful, fictionalised, literary a construct as Johnston's character David Meredith.[30] Whereas Johnston's treatment of the Greek period comes across as a self-centred, introspective (albeit agonising) grappling with an existential situation — David Meredith's status as a writer, a husband in a problematic relationship, and a sick man — Clift's writing opens out to more common issues of family, community and culture (Greek and Australian), to general matters of compassion and concern for relationships (traditionally seen as positive elements of "femininity") and, particularly in her essays, to quite courageous political statements.[31] There is one other striking difference in their treatment of their life in Greece: whereas in Clift's writing the children often take centre stage, in Johnston's novel they hardly get any mention.

Clift's views on life on a Greek island in the 1950s and 1960s are ambivalent. There is, on the one hand, an enthusiastic response to the impact of the Mediterranean culture with its mysteries, mythologies and beauty — a response similar to that of later travellers who were drawn by what they perceived as a more vital part of living, a celebration of the sensual supposedly lacking in Anglo-Australia.[32] On the other hand, Clift is also aware of the dark sides of Greek culture: the harshness of life and the poverty, the lack of hope in a better future and, above all, the hard lot of women in a male-dominated, restrained and enclosed society. And the perception of difference between the status of male and female worries her: "I think that here women are never quite regarded as human beings. They are of a different species — the female species, the mysterious Other Ones whose femaleness is derided and despised, but who must be kept under lock and key in case they work a magic."[33]

Reading this, one wonders why it has taken critics of Australian women's writing so long to draw attention to this early feminist voice, particularly since Clift in much of her writing emphasises the importance of creative writing for a woman, in a "room of her own".[34] Clift was aware of her disadvantaged position and objected to it.[35] It is a sad irony that she, the "optimist", couldn't bear life any longer and chose to end it in 1969. The delayed reprinting of Clift's work is a striking example of the changing valuation of both the genre of travel writing and of women's writing in Australia in general.

If Clift cautiously criticised her position as a woman writer, the next generation voiced their objections more clearly. The dissatisfaction with traditional female roles and with male expectations became an incentive to "go somewhere else" (see, for instance, Rutherford's article on expatriation), and this is a theme in much travel writing by women. In her introduction to a collection of travel stories by Australian writers, Rosemary Creswell attempts to classify some of the recurrent themes. The most obvious, she finds, is "sexual adventure": exotic or foreign places seem "to provide the setting, and perhaps the opportunity through cultural freedom or dislocation, for exotic sexual and emotional experience", for unusual attachments, but also for "emotional or sexual expectations which are disappointed".[36] Such a thematic focus indeed applies to stories by many women writers who send their protagonists overseas to overcome emotional crises, or to renegotiate the terms of personal relationships.[37] In Hanrahan's autobiographical retrospective of her time in London, *Michael and Me and the Sun* (1991), for instance, the longing for emotional/sexual fulfilment plays as important a part in the young traveller's consciousness as her artistic education and realisation. However, her "learning" process involves recognising that she neither can nor wants to conform to the traditional values of the feminine: she prefers to be as dedicated, determined and ruthless as the males in her art course; she finally rejects looking after an allegedly sophisticated man and running his household ("I was sick of him being the artist, not me")[38] and leaves him. To give another, more extreme example: In Marion Campbell's experimental novel *Lines of Flight* (1985) the female traveller Rita's emotional relationships are reduced to stages of her "flight", the process of coming to consciousness as a woman and an artist, and finding her own voice outside, and beyond, male discourses (here mainly represented by French theory and culture). Europe then can present a touchstone for self-examination and artistic growth rather than a source of cultural experience and advancement. This is a far cry from the ironic view expressed in one of Shirley Hazzard's novels: "Going to Europe, someone had written, was about as final as going to heaven. A mystical passage to another life, from which no one returned the same ... There was nothing mythic at Sydney; momentous objects, beings and events all occurred abroad or in the elsewhere of books."[39]

With the social changes in Australia in the 1970s, and the growth of feminism, the motivations for European travels also shifted. And, as we have seen, Janine Burke and Glenda Adams turn upside down the conventional view of Australian travel motivation. The figure of the female traveller and her journeys have offered alternative ways of writing about women, a development which manifests itself in the very fact of the multitude of texts centring on women who travel abroad because "nobody can stop them", from Anderson's *Tirra Lirra* to Halligan's *Spider Cup*.

In his study of European travel writing by male authors, *Haunted Journeys* (1991), Dennis Porter maintains that "the traditional question raised, explicitly or implicitly, by male travellers is, as Sir Richard Burton pointed out in his *Personal Narrative of a Pilgrimage to Al-Madinah and Meccah*, 'What are the women like?' "[40] Does the reverse question, about what the men elsewhere are like, also apply to the women's texts under survey? Many of them do profess an interest in men, with varying emphases in writings by, for instance, Roland, Halligan, Garner, or Hanrahan. But it seems safe to say that, increasingly, the significance in women's travel narratives lies less in sexual awakenings or adventures and emotional upheavals in general, but rather more specifically in a kind of stocktaking of the female situation within relationships, on questions of dependence on and liberation from the emotional/sexual partner, and on a woman's need to undergo an often agonising learning process to make her own decisions. It lies in questions of conflicts of power in relationships and thus in societies in general. Frequently European "Culture" serves as a backdrop for revelations. As much as the famous monuments of art and history represent traditional male power and supremacy in society, in personal relationships it is the *knowledge* of art/history, of famous names, epochs, styles or philosophies, that is perceived to be traditionally positioned in the male point of view. From such knowledge the male then derives the power to teach, initiate and thus dominate his lover or spouse (a theme Jolley applies to lesbian relationships, for instance in *Miss Peabody's Inheritance*). It is this well-established social model that many women writers have their female travellers question, subvert or reject outright.

In Helen Garner's story "A Thousand Miles from the Ocean" the narrator, after following her lover to Germany, realises that she has fallen victim to a romantic illusion of Europe as much as to the pretensions of her lover, and she liberates herself from male domination as well as from the veneration of European "museum" culture.[41] Similarly, the female view in Garner's story "In Paris" (included in this collection) highlights the cultural differences between (male-oriented) old-world conventions and (female) new-world practicality. Perhaps the most drastic example of juxtaposing traditional gender roles and European cultural values — and subverting both — is Grenville's *Dreamhouse* where a deceptive, corrupt Tuscan environment immediately expresses the female narrator's disillusionment with her role as the "beautiful" wife of a "cultured" academic.[42] And in some texts by women writers, as in Margaret Coombs' *Regards to the Czar* and its sequel *The Best Man for This Sort of Thing*, place seems important, paradoxically, just because it does not matter, or matters less than gender.

* * *

"To have more than one life is the craft of the actor, and the dexterity of the traveller. It is also the desire and rage of the artist, who no matter what identity he inherits will long to be different, and no matter what portion of the earth is home to him will want to be elsewhere," comments Peter Conrad.[43] Such, too, we suggest, is the desire and rage of many travellers and readers. This selection aims to cater for such desire by presenting some of the rich possibilities. In the arrangement of contents, sometimes views of the same country or place have been gathered into clusters, as with Leningrad/St Petersburg, to invite comparisons. As editors, however, we have not attempted to provide anything like "equal representation" for various countries in Europe, or to include all the writers in the field, but we have aimed to be alert to variety and change. The broad divisions of contents are there to make the fare attractive; it could have been served in many other ways.

"I see eye to eye with such poets as Wallace Stevens (who never left the US) and Ashbery in that I think the poet's true country is his own mind, and that will receive stimuli from anywhere and everywhere," Peter Porter writes. Certainly experiences of Europe — and other places — have come to be accepted as a natural part of the country of the mind of Australian writers and readers, so that it is by no means restricted to home pastures. As with A.D. Hope's migratory bird, going away is also coming home.[44]

Notes

1. Michel Butor, "Travel and Writing", *Mosaic* 8.1 (1974): 1–16; p. 5.
2. Don Anderson, "Peripatetic litterateurs take over the '90s", *Sydney Morning Herald*, 20 April 1991: 46.
3. Butor, op. cit., p. 2.
4. Roland Barthes, "Le Guide Bleu", *Mythologies*. Sel. and trans. Annette Lavers. (New York: Hill and Wang, 1972), p. 76.
5. Qtd. from David Dale, *The Obsessive Traveller* (North Ryde: Collins/Angus & Robertson, 1991), p. 11.
6. Patrick White, *Flaws in the Glass* (Ringwood: Penguin, 1983), p. 192.
7. Richard Sieburth, "Sentimental Travelling: On the Road (and Off the Wall) with Laurence Sterne". *Scripsi* 4.3 (1987): 197–211; p. 199.
8. Jane Robinson, *Wayward Women* (Oxford: Oxford University Press, 1991), pp. vii, ix.
9. Ian Ousby, *The Englishman's England: Taste, Travel and the Rise of Tourism* (Cambridge: Cambridge University Press, 1990), p. 6.
10. Janis P. Stout, *The Journey Narrative in American Literature: Patterns and Departures* (Westport; London: Greenwood Press, 1983), p. 71.
11. ibid., p. 69.

12. Letter to Charles Eliot Norton, in Henry James, *Letters*, ed. Leon Edel. Vol. 1: 1843–1975 (Cambridge, Mass.: Belknap Press of Harvard University Press, 1974), p. 273.

13. C.J. Koch, "The Lost Hemisphere", in *Crossing the Gap* (London: Hogarth, 1987), pp. 91–105.

14. *London Review of Books*, 30 January 1992: 18.

15. "Perceptions of Australia, 1965–1988", in *The Penguin New Literary History of Australia*, ed. Laurie Hergenhan (Ringwood: Penguin, 1988), p. 439.

16. Frank Moorhouse, *Days of Wine and Rage* (Ringwood: Penguin, 1980), pp. 181–83.

17. Janine Burke, "Tuscany's talent to a muse", included in this collection.

18. See extract in this collection.

19. *Yacker 3: Australian Writers Talk about Their Work*, ed. Candida Baker (Sydney: Picador, 1989), pp. 325–26.

20. "Patrick White Speaks on Factual Writing and Fiction", *ALS* 10 (1981): 99–101.

21. These have been recently studied by a European critic, who argues that they "make creative use of European art to examine, question or even undermine the cultural assumptions which inform it, and which Australian society at one time or another may be said to have shared. In doing so, these poems do not necessarily set out to marginalise the outstanding achievements of European culture but rather to use them ironically in order to define a cultural identity which is strikingly different." See Werner Senn, "Australian Poems on European Paintings". *European Perspectives*, ed. Giovanna Capone (St Lucia: University of Queensland Press, 1991), pp. 83–91, p. 84.

22. *Wayward Women*, pp. ix–x.

23. So for instance Beverley Farmer when asked in an interview by Ray Willbanks about the autobiographical content of her Greek stories. See Ray Willbanks, *Speaking Volumes: Australian Writers and Their Work* (Ringwood: Penguin, 1992), pp. 72–86.

24. Sara Mills, *Discourses of Difference: An Analysis of Women's Travel Writing and Colonialism* (London: Routledge, 1991), p. 118.

25. Qtd. Rosemary Wighton, "Clift's gifts: rich imagery and sharp observations". Rev. of *The Sponge Divers*. *Weekend Australian* 11–12 July 1992: Review 6.

26. Christina Stead, *A Web of Friendship: Selected Letters, 1973–1983*, ed. R.G. Geering (Pymble, NSW: 1992), p. 433.

27. See extract in this collection.

28. Considering the official nature of their trip, Masters' allegedly partisan response even became something of an embarrassment to her travel companions. See Julie Lewis, *Olga Masters: A Lot of Living* (St Lucia, Qld.: University of Queensland Press, 1991), ch. 13, and *Olga Masters: Reporting Home*, ed. Deirdre Coleman (St Lucia, Qld.: University of Queensland Press, 1990), pp. 71–74.

29. "Introduction", in Charmian Clift, *Being Alone with Oneself: Essays, 1968–69* (North Ryde: Angus & Robertson, 1990), p. 3.

30. Nadia Wheatley underlines this with some interesting comments by Martin Johnston; see "Introduction", *Being Alone*, pp. 16–17.

31. See Wheatley, "Introduction" to *Trouble in Lotus Land: Essays, 1964–67* (North Ryde: Angus & Robertson, 1990).

32. See, for example, Burke's novel *Second Sight*, or Halligan's *Eat My Words*.

33. Charmian Clift, *Mermaid Singing* (1958. North Ryde: Angus & Robertson, 1989), p. 46.

34. Even Johnston's biographer Garry Kinnane, usually rather critical of Clift's talent, takes up this point in discussing the manuscript of Clift's journals in relation to Johnston's fiction: "Incidentally, there is a pithy epigram penned in Charmian's handwriting on the back of one of the notebook pages that will please feminists: 'She also has a life in the vertical position.' As, indeed, she always had." (Gary Kinnane, *George Johnston: A Biography*, 1986. Ringwood: Penguin, 1989, p. 123) Clift stayed in the shadow of her more famous husband, and she expected — and got — little appreciation as a woman writer, at least before she had her regular column in the *Sydney Morning Herald*. Kinnane reveals that a whole section of Johnston's *Clean Straw for Nothing*, the report on their continental travels "Notes from an Expatriate's Journal", is a slightly edited (but nowhere acknowledged) version of Clift's private journals kept at the National Library in Canberra (Kinnane 123).

35. See her statement about the collaboration with Johnston, in "Self-Portrait", included in this collection.

36. *Home and Away* (Ringwood: Penguin, 1987), p. ix.

37. Grenville's *Dreamhouse*, Halligan's *Spider Cup*, Burke's *Second Sight*, Hanrahan's *Sea-green*, Falkiner's *Rain in the Distance*, Jill Neville's *Last Ferry to Manly* are just a few examples.

38. Barbara Hanrahan, *Michael and Me and the Sun* (St Lucia: University of Queensland Press, 1992), p. 86.

39. Shirley Hazzard, *Transit of Venus* (Harmondsworth: Ringwood: Penguin, 1980), p. 37.

40. Porter, *Haunted Journeys: Desire and Transgression in European Travel Writing* (Princeton: Princeton University Press, 1991), p. 210.

41. Another example is Marian Eldridge's story "Pietà" from *The Woman at the Window* (1989).

42. Grenville's naming of the female narrator, Louise Dufrey, may contain a parodic hint at subverting gender as well as cultural conventions, as it is reminiscent of a more traditional Australian expatriate in a cultural centre of Europe: Louise Dufrayer, the beautiful object of the protagonist's desire, and later wife of the conductor and composer Schilsky, in Henry Handel Richardson's *Maurice Guest*.

43. Peter Conrad, *Where I Fell to Earth* (London: Chatto & Windus, 1990), p. 249.

44. A.D. Hope, "The Death of the Bird" (*Collected Poems 1930–1970*, Sydney: Angus & Robertson 1977), pp. 69–71.

Travellers, Tourists and Expatriates

Charmian Clift

SELF PORTRAIT

We left for England in 1950. At the time I left Australia, I wanted desperately to leave. I didn't like Australia a bit. It had to me that very nasty feeling of postwar, I thought it was money-grubbing and greedy, all the values I thought were important didn't seem to be there any more. Besides, also, I still had that childhood ambition to go further and see more, and whatever the big thing was, it wasn't here in Australia for me, I knew that then.

So we went to England and I was terribly happy to go, and I remember sailing out and waving goodbye to the Harbour Bridge and thinking, I'll never see that again! Of course, I did see it again, but at that time I didn't think so.

I liked England, I was very happy in London, excepting that again there was the feeling of being bound and constrained, held by little children in an apartment or taking them to school or bringing them home or walking them in parks, and I felt that I was an outsider looking in, never part of it, never part of the London I wanted to be part of, because I wasn't free. However, again I did some writing, and collaborated on another novel with George, a novel called *The Big Chariot*. I did very little work of my own because I didn't have time, also in a sort of sense, in some peculiar sense, I felt at that time I was losing my identity completely, I wasn't quite sure who I was; nothing was happening in the way I wanted it to happen, until one day George resigned from the job he had in Fleet Street as a newspaper man and we went to Greece, and this was a big enough thing. It seemed very romantic, very audacious, and audacity carried along for a little bit. We went with a year's living money, two typewriters and the two children, and for a year we got along on the strength of our own audacity, and we lived poor and we lived hard, we lived on beans, we made do with things, and everything was romantic and everything was wonderful, and the Greek light was everything everyone had ever said it was. So the first year passed in this sort of way, and we collaborated on another novel which was called *The Sponge Divers*. Actually, of course, that was a phoney collaboration because I was beyond the stage where I could collaborate any longer, I wanted to do my own work in my own way. This was probably very egotistical but most writers have this. In any case, I didn't have time because I was the one who had to learn the Greek and I was our interpreter and I was our cook, and I had this awful problem on my hands of two small children who were lost and bewildered and lonely in a foreign country, and it took about a year to adjust all that. Then I found that I was going to have another baby, and this plunged me back into a long long tunnel which I thought I'd just got clear of.

Our second year in Greece was very different from the first, because all the brave plans didn't quite come off, it was so much harder than one had ever thought it was. However, with a new baby, we had enough money just to buy a house; this was on another island, we had changed islands by this time. We bought that house and we stayed in it for ten years, and I think that after that second year we began to really build a life for ourselves and it was a wonderful sort of life, in a way. For the first time in my life, apart from the time when I was a very young girl, I found time to do my own writing, I found time for a social life, I found time to look after my family properly. The days are very long there and life is very easy, very wonderful. Of course, we were about the first foreigners who lived on that island, and later, winter after winter and summer after summer, others came drifting in, buying houses, and there began to be established a foreign colony — I don't like that word "colony" very much but I can't think of anything else to call it — a foreign colony composed of people who wanted to write and people who wanted to paint, drifters and exiles from all over the world. I think practically every country, every nationality, was represented there. It was a weird sort of way to live, until finally I think I began to feel like an exile myself. I hadn't until that point, because in spite of the fact that one was alien again, on that island for the first time I didn't feel like an outsider looking in, because I had built something for myself that was mine.

This sort of life is, as they say, fabulous, it is idyllic, it has so many things to recommend it, and of course for the children it was wonderful beyond belief. They never knew they were foreign. They were a little ashamed of us for being foreign but they didn't feel foreign themselves. But eventually one runs out of creative nourishment, I think. We were not taking in so much any more. We'd taken it in. I think we'd given out too much, too. We weren't very capable of giving anything out any more. Also, it never came off in the grand manner as one had so fondly dreamed. We were living precariously still, from year to year. With children growing up, all this sort of thing becomes very difficult, also their education to be considered, and then finally, as costs of living rose and rose because the foreign colony got more and more and more fashionable — more and more people, film stars, all sorts of people, began coming there, and our cheap little island that was ours was ours no longer.

Then we both — and this is quite strange — began to get homesick; that was after about fourteen years away from Australia, thirteen or fourteen years. We began thinking about Australia, I think first for the children and then because George was writing a book called *My Brother Jack* which made us think about Australia and talk about Australia, and try to remember Australian slang and so on, and through my own children I kept going back to my own childhood and my own beach and the sort of happiness I had then.

Finally — in some trepidation, admittedly — not quite sure, thought it was time for us to come back again. By this time I'd written four books alone, two travel books and two novels. I didn't feel that staying in Greece I had anything more to write about and I needed desperately to discover or rediscover something. I think George felt the same way, too.

HYDRA

A fig-tree marks the point where the cliff path turns and plummets down towards the sea. Then, at the bottom of the path, there are twenty descending stairs, three rock platforms cemented over to make sun-bathing levels, an arching cave roof with a jagged hole where the green light slips and slides mysteriously in the sea-smelling purple, an iron ladder for the timorous, and a long, low rock crooked slightly, like a scaly finger around the deep-plunging shelf where we swim.

All down the gulf the islands and islets rise in radiant humps and spires — knuckles and fingertips reaching up from legendary drowned lands. Old things lie under this glass green skin of sea, scaled things, slimed things, crusted things, still potent in the imagination. Who knows what scuttles silently across this sea floor,

or what might one day stir and shake itself and rise, all barnacled
and dripping salty weeds?

I thought today how beautiful my children have become in this
deeply natural world, thin, brown, hard creatures, still unconscious
of their own grace or even of the extravagance of beauty in which
they move and have their being: for them it is no more to be
observed than the number of times their sharp little breasts rise and
fall breathing it in.

The sun streamed over the shelf where we lay watching them,
their arrow-straight naked bodies hurtling from the cave lip thirty
feet down into the water. The sea was so much like glass that the
explosive jets of their impacts were somehow surprising, as though
one had expected the surface to shiver and splinter into fragments
instead. Through the churn we could see them wavering down and
down along the spiny shelf and curving up again to the air and the
sun — the thin scrawl of Martin's legs threshing, the slowly closing
fan of Shane's glinting hair. They broke the surface pearled and
gasping, and scrambled out on the rocks to climb up to the cave
roof and leap again and again.

Sprawled inert under the great warm melting waves of light, I
was glad that we had chosen to live in the sun. To live in the sun is
reassuring. All is open, all revealed. Here are no deceptions, but the
bare truth of things. I think that no beauty has ever been as true
for me as this beauty of rocks and sea and the bounty of mountains
that rush up between the blue and the blue, skirted only with
austere white terraces of houses simplified to the purest geometry
of planes and angles. It seems to me that we have become simplified
too, living here, as though the sun has seared off the woolly fuzz of
our separate confusions: the half-desires irresolutely sought, the
half-fears never more than half vanquished, the partial attainments
half-rejected in perplexed dissatisfaction. Shedding so much we are
stripped to our bare selves, lighter, freer, and impoverished of
nothing but a few ridiculous little self-importances.

Through the hot stillness sounds come distinctly — a splash of
oars, the sharp yelp of the dog Max protesting against a bath, the
children's voices calling away away, and from the village the clear,
bright sound of a single bell. A passing bell again. In these last few
weeks the passing bell has rung often. The old people die in the

resurrection of the year, the old grey women and the old brown men who whiffled and snickered on their doorsteps waiting for the sun to come again; not a church doorway that has not revealed the black box, the sharp, aged profile pointed to the ceiling and clay-coloured against a formal frieze of grieving women.

Here the dead are not hidden away, but carried through the lanes in open coffins for everyone to see. Turned up to the sun the mute, ancient faces go jolting by, exposed for the last time to this clear white light that reveals death as impersonally as it reveals life. Looking down into the dead face of an old grandmother one is reminded that time incises deeply, cruelly, ineradicably, that decay is inherent in all living things. See, it is death, nothing more — an event in life — as significant or unsignificant as being born.//

And now, when it is siesta time for any purposeful activity, summer-time, play-time, easy-living time, lotus-eating time, we must be very purposeful indeed.

The island is wearing its holiday face. The gulf is like milk. There are little motorboats ferrying tourists down the coast to further coves and beaches, there are fishing caiques sliding through their own reflections, market boats skittering across to the mainland to the rumba rhythm of their exhausts, and all the little *várkas* that rested in lanes and sheds for the winter are sprinkled down through the islets like coloured scraps of confetti, or walnut shells painted crimson and cinnamon and lime and yellow and pink; in each an old man standing, rocking dreamily at the oars, and a boy bent over a glass-bottomed tin looking for octopi.//

It had never occurred to me before that there must be a whole nomadic tribe of young men which moves across Europe with the changing seasons on a defined trail where the camping-places and water-holes are fixed by custom and the big-game areas clearly marked. It is clear, suddenly, that this island is one of the summer camps, a stop-over place to rest and exchange stories and information about the year's trail. Something about Sykes Horowitz now becomes much clearer — his odd familiarity with foreign cities and foreign tongues and that gypsyish quality of being at home everywhere and nowhere that used to rather charm me.

For most of these newly arrived young men are also, like Sykes, American — although you would hardly guess it by their accents,

---

// This sign indicates that part of the text has been omitted at this point.

which have the careful anonymity of the expatriate with a sedu-
lously acquired stammer added for interest. Their faces have an
expatriate anonymity also — interchangeable faces — weary,
young–old, vaguely unhealthy under the suntan, and their eyes,
like Sykes' eyes, have that same dreadful centre of purposelessness.

They all speak very good French and have a smattering of Italian
and Spanish and German and Arabic; they have all met Rilke's wife
or Utrillo; they lived next door but one to Wystan Auden on Ischia
or Dali on the Costa Brava; at Majorca one summer they had the
opportunity to work with Robert Graves; they know Picasso well;
they can quote by heart long passages from Gertrude Stein, and
Proust and Racine and Kierkgaard and Nietzsche and Baudelaire
and Mallarmé; they have read the reviews of the latest books and
the latest plays, and talk knowledgeably about action painting,
erotic symbols, psychosomatic disorders, the doctrines of nihilism
and existentialism, and collage.

They have in common a ready fund of scandalously funny
stories involving the great or near-great, and a quick malicious wit
that is usually directed against others of their own kind. These
particular attributes are so ready and so practised, so smoothly
polished, that I suspect they result from long years' experience of
having to sing for one's supper. For although all these young men,
like Sykes, seem to have some small private income or allowance
— they are all, in a way, remittance men — it is never quite large
enough to enable them to live decently but only just enough to
make it unnecessary for them to work for a living.

Their years are spent in following a nomadic trail that leads
them, as far as I can gather, through Greece to Yugoslavia, to Venice,
through Paris to Sweden or down through Madrid to Majorca.
Berlin is on the route for some, and for others Beyrout, Tangiers,
Casablanca. Various Mediterranean islands are summer camps —
Majorca, Ischia, Corsica, Iviza. Capri has been long removed from
the list because it is too banal, they say, and also too expensive: there
is interested discussion about the possibilities of Elba, of Sardinia,
of Pantellaria.

It is quite obvious that this island is gaining in popularity, a
summer camp enlivened by shrill cries of greeting and the sharp
buzz of malicious stories, a swapping of notes, of names.

Australian swagmen on the road used to have a particular mark that they scratched on the gatepost of any house where they had received food or shelter — a sign to their brethren who came after that a hand-out might be expected. These intellectual swagmen also mark doors.//

They haunt me with their young–old, weary, interchangeable faces and their careful accents and their questing, amoral eyes and their scandalously funny stories. We meet them swimming at the cave, sometimes we sit with them on the waterfront at night, or see them drunk in the taverns, dancing a loose parody of the slow, balancing, island dance, gyrating with blind, sick faces on which the good-time grin is stretched and held as though with a strong fixative. It is even difficult to think of any one of them as individual. The boys. The *poste-restante*, interchangeable, culture-addicted, Europe-sick boys, with grey sprinkled through their crew-cuts and little pads of drink-fat around their middles, who yearn for the Europe of Gertrude Stein and Scott Fitzgerald and the "lost generation" of a generation who were losing themselves while they were being born.

They are all more or less of an age with Sykes, the middle thirties and edging over — the war generation who grew up to horror and inherited despair and disillusion. From what they say and don't say around the plastic tablecloth, I gather that they all came to Europe in much the same way as Sykes, carrying their precious little gifts to lay at the shrine. They were to be poets, to be painters, to be writers, come to drink in their culture at the source, the old mystic fountainhead. Perhaps their stomachs weren't strong enough, perhaps their gifts were weighed and found wanting, or perhaps that little private income, the remittance, made it all too easy to put off until tomorrow the actual hard work that might be involved in being the new young prophet.

And now, when they are no longer really young, and Europe is stale old ground, it is too late for them to begin and too late for them to go back. So they go round and round and round, treading the same old beaten track, the clever young men, the witty young men, the careless young men, the oh-so-European young men, the sad young men, who are looking for Gertrude Stein. Do they get frightened, I wonder, as they become staler, and less attractive, and not quite so capable of keeping up with the latest reviews and the latest movements and the screamingly funny stories and the brighter and younger young men? What happens to them when they grow to middle age? When they become old? Is there a special burying-ground somewhere, on Ischia or Iviza or Majorca, where their poor peripatetic bones are laid to rest at last? A sort of secret Elephants' Graveyard?

I suggest this to George and he stares at me thoughtfully for a while, but only murmurs in cold distaste, "The mind *boggles*!"

Thinking of them — and it is impossible not to think of them a good deal — with their tired faces, their fruitless journeyings, their vicarious pleasures, their ersatz culture, their endless self-de-lusions, one cannot help but contrast them with Henry, who started out on his own nomadic trail at about the same time as they did, with probably an equivalent amount of talent. Henry never had time to learn perfect French nor to acquire a European polish. He was too busy painting, all his energies engaged on the thing he had to say, on his desperation to overcome his own technical shortcom-ings, on proving his passionate belief that you can fly for the willing of it.

To accomplish anything it is obvious that a talent is not enough. You need a motive, an aim, an incentive, an overwhelming interest — be it ambition or fear or curiosity or only the necessity to fill your belly. You need a star to steer by, a cause, a creed, an idea, a passionate attachment. Something must beckon you or nothing is done — something about which you ask no questions.

As if in answer to this thought there is a letter from Henry, scribbled in reply to one of ours that must have conveyed all too clearly our misgivings, our mood of hesitation and incapacity. The message of it comes singing and clear, unequivocal, untinged by doubt. Go on then, *fly*!

George Johnston

AUSTRALIANS ABROAD

Waiting in the wintry bluster of the night at Phaleron Airport, Meredith found himself remembering the time on the island a few years before when the Australian Dried Fruits Convention had landed on his doorstep. He had been up in his room wrestling with a book that was going badly when the doorknocker thumped and he had gone down swearing to find the lane choked with staring Australians, sixty-eight of them! They were members of a convention organised by the Australian Dried Fruits Board to study the currant-growing around Corinth and the raisin and sultana industry in Crete and the Peloponnesos, and when they had come off the morning steamer someone had told them that an Australian family was living on the island and they had enlisted a guide to bring them to the house *en masse* so they could check on this.

Since there were too many to be invited into the house Meredith had to go with them back to the waterfront, where they interrogated him closely, particularly one man who seemed to be a self-elected spokesman. He was a small man with a big chin and a thin stern mouth. His eyes seemed short-sighted behind rimless bifocals, and each question he asked was accompanied by a suspicious squint, as if he was well aware that he would be answered by a lie or an exaggeration or at best an evasion. He, and most of the rest of the party, clearly disapproved of the irresponsible way of life which Meredith, a fellow-Australian, had chosen to follow. "But how do you get on living with these bloody Wogs?" the spokesman wanted to know. "Don't they drive you up the wall? And the kids, what about their education? You mean to say they're at school with the Greek kids, not even talking their own language? Jesus, you're taking a risk, aren't you? You ought to get back to good old Aussie, you know." He became proud and expansive then. "You'd never know the old place now. You've never seen progress like it. You'd see a lot of changes. Everything out there's going ahead like a house on fire. I tell you, you don't now, you just couldn't believe, what you're missing. Isn't that right, you blokes?" The rest of the delegation nodded vigorously and vehemently mumbled assent. "You're mad to stick on in a primitive backward little dump like this, when you've got it all made for you out there in your own country. After all, you owe it to your kiddies, don't you? I mean they're entitled to the best, aren't they? It's *their* future you've got to think of."

They went away on the early afternoon steamer, some of them the worse for the *ouzo* and retsina they had insisted on drinking because Meredith had told them that the astringency of the Greek liquor helped compensate for the oiliness of the Greek food, which gave their spokesman opportunity for another homily on "people who live on greasy tucker and always pong of garlic". Meredith quietly pointed out that every Greek in sight had good skin, splendid teeth, and his own hair (which, he added to himself, was a damned sight more than could be said for most of the Dried Fruits emissaries) but nobody paid much attention. Rowing off in the longboats some of the party drunkenly tried to sing "Waltzing Matilda" and "Advance Australia Fair", and old Babayannis, the one-eyed muleteer, who was standing on the quayside next to Meredith, beamed approvingly and said, with real admiration, "They are good people, the Australians, fine people. We remember them from the war. Larissa. Nauplia. Crete. They were our friends. And brave. Very brave fighters. Fine people. The best."

"Yes." Meredith nodded, remembering, and wondered whatever had happened. Their spokesman was right; you *could* see a lot of changes. They seemed so narrow and insulated now, and yet so sure of themselves, so complacent about their small channelled certainties. You could only respond to them by using the instant litmus. Turn pink … Turn blue …

Until then he thought he had forgotten what Australians were like, but this visitation proved to be only a beginning. A new Greek shipping service began between Australia and Piraeus, and troubles with Nasser in Egypt established Athens as a stopover for the QANTAS planes in place of Cairo, and off-season cruise liners from Australia began to call in at Greek ports. So it was not long before Meredith's compatriots were regular arrivals on the daily steamers. Meredith, waiting outside Evangeli's for the mail to be sorted, found he could pick from a hundred yards away an Australian coming ashore, not by their clothing so much, although this was often an indication, as by a way they had of standing and walking and their manner of holding their heads in relationship to their shoulders. There were some who carried identification with them much as their forefathers had carried trade union banners; they would wear Digger-type slouch hats and carry knapsacks sewn all over with the blatant symbols of an aggressive chauvinism, Australian flags and kangaroos and Southern Crosses and boomerangs, or just the simple word AUSTRALIA, although more usually a maroon QANTAS overnight bag with its kangaroo insignia would be deemed identification enough.

What kind of defensive mechanism operated? What were they so anxious to prove?

To these transient visitors the novelty of finding an Australian family actually *living* a foreign life with foreigners in a primitive alien community proved both intriguing and disturbing. Most of them would try to seek out the Merediths, as if they were rare denizens of some exotic zoo. A few of the more sensitive seemed genuinely to envy the — to them — simple enchantments and leisurely pace and undeniable beauties of the island life; the majority, however, were never able to leave without offering some friendly and well-intentioned castigation. The substance of this was always much the same. In actually choosing to live with foreigners, the Merediths were being un-Australian, were missing out materially on the best the world had to offer, were foolishly cutting themselves off from prospects of infinite promise, were precariously enduring discomfort when they were entitled to enjoy surfeits of comfort in the world's highest standard of living, and were being wilfully wayward parents in denying their children their birthright of life in God's own country.

Meredith was never able to find any effective way of countering these charges, for they seldom seemed interested in, or even able to understand, what he had to say about the richer human values and firmer traditions of European culture, the prevalence of historic continuities, the deeper intellectual challenge, the consciousness of being in a mainstream of human conflict and aspiration, not in a backwater or stranded on some remote dry billabong. He thought at one time that he would have a mimeographed circular made, setting out his own manifesto and his answers to the standard questions he was always asked, a copy of which could be handed to each newcomer as a way of saving time; in a still more resentful mood he also thought of printing a sign and nailing it to the front door of his house: BUBONIC PLAGUE — KEEP OUT!

Yet in spite of the shallowness of their attitudes, the naive chauvinisms, the absurdly blinkered prejudice and intolerance, he found himself unable, finally, to dismiss them. Whatever the irritation and impatience and resentment he might feel, he could not keep away from them. There were even aspects of them he found himself approving, admiring, defending — their natural eagerness to be friendly, their simple civilities, their lack of affectations, the rough honesty with which they would look at a matter, as they put it, "without bullshit". And there was something genuinely refreshing in their uncomplicated optimistic vitality after the tired, blasé, angst-ridden attitudes of the world-weary cosmopolitans who had become Meredith's more usual social contacts on the island. Yet the tug of the fascination seemed more profound than this: at times Meredith could feel it stirring him deep down and troublingly, too subtle a feeling to be identifiable, a vague womb-yearning, the dimly sensed wash of foetal tides, or something atavistic and even darker. Not nostalgia. Nor homesickness. But something …

It was only to Tom Kiernan now that he ever talked about these matters.

Kiernan's years of expatriation had served him well. While he had not achieved Calverton's measure of material success or public reputation, he had attained success and reputation enough, and creatively and artistically his stature was a good deal larger than Calverton's; by any count he had travelled much farther on his journey than Meredith. But he was an unattached man — an asexual man, too, Meredith sometimes thought — who drove himself with a ruthless purpose and single-mindedness, endlessly exploring Europe in search of food for his imagination and subjects for his canvasses, haunting the galleries, and painting, painting, painting. He seemed to live for only two things — his work and the few friends to whom he clung with almost obsessive loyalty, perhaps because he allowed himself so little of social relaxation, and needed his few friends for the desperate moments of human loneliness. He painted as he lived, with the energy of a titan, the dedication of a martyr, the passion of a lover. He took prodigious risks, and usually got away with them. He never spared himself, nor anyone around him. "You would have to be his friend!" Cressida once said of him. "If you were an enemy, or even only an acquaintance, he would dip you in pitch and put a match to you if he needed a torch to paint by." He detested any sort of compromise, in himself or in others. "I fly with Icarus, not with Daedalus," he said in a moment of rare boastfulness. This was at a time when Meredith was feeling dispirited about a novel he was writing, and he had confessed to Kiernan his defeatism.

"It won't come out at the end of my fingers," he said, "the way I see it in my head. The reason is simple, of course. The theme is too big and my talents aren't big enough. I've just overreached, that's all."

"I fly with Icarus, not with Daedalus," said Kiernan.

"That's all very well for you. But I'm me, not you."

"Balls! If you *want* to fly, if you think you *can* fly, then all you've got to do is jump off the twig and bloody well *fly*!"

Yet clearly even Kiernan was not sufficient unto himself. The powerful and passionate mystique that drove him seemed centred far away from the trampled arena of his activities; the true wellspring of his inspiration was still located, illogically, in the distant land that had driven him out, so that every few years he would be compelled to return to Australia to, as he put it, "fill up the jug again". He was usually involved in controversy when he got back to his native land and seldom stayed there long, but he would always send off to Meredith a terse report on a postcard, messages like *Europe still has better ossuaries but not bigger ones* or *Something might be cooking here but too soon yet to open the oven and see.* He would always return to Europe renewed and reinvigorated, and go into another furious spell of painting, although anything specifically Australian seldom appeared in his work. He would invariably come back by way of Greece and stay for a few days with the Merediths, and he would tell them amusing or startling tales of life "out there" in the remote southern continent, but seemed more interested in finding out whether there was anything he had missed out on in Europe during his absence. It was taken for granted that nothing would be missed by being absent from Australia.

Once he played the conventional old joke and brought back

with him a handful of Australian gumleaves and threw them on the fire in front of Meredith, and said, "Just sniff that up, man, and you'll be out there like a shot!"

"That'll be the day," said Meredith, laughing. But the odd thing was that the moment the aromatic pungency of the burning leaves struck his nostrils he experienced for an instant a real pang of hunger for something experienced and lost far back in time, and staring into the fire at the darkening curl and shrivel of the scimitar leaves he saw again the blue hazes of hot big distances and brown leaves in a tangle of fallen bark.

Martin Johnston

GROWING UP IN GREECE

Again, I suppose, one has to distinguish between the experience of Hydra that my parents had, and the experience that my sister and I had and … well, Jason, insofar as a kid of one or two years old has. For them there was, to start with, very much the same kind of freedom to write, combined with the fact that there was very little money on which to live while doing so, as they had had in Kalimnos. And at the same time, from very early on, there were the beginnings of what was eventually to become the foreign artistic colony on Hydra.//

For Shane and myself, having had our first year of primary school on Kalimnos, life wasn't so hard on Hydra. To begin with, the ever-precious peanut butter was in fact available there! For another, we'd now picked up enough of the language to get along reasonably happily at school. I remember that both of us in Kalimnos were given, in our final year reports, ten out of ten. Which was a very kind gesture on the part of teachers; we knew about *two* out of ten's worth of Greek, let along being able to do lessons in it. But after a couple more years on Hydra we really were coping pretty well, and pretty much accepted as … well, not quite local kids, a certain exoticism still clung to us, people didn't really know where Australia was or what language we spoke in Australia, if indeed we spoke one at all or if indeed anyone spoke anything outside Greece, it was a very very (forgive the pun!) insular island still at the time.// But all this "specimen in the zoo" aspect of it apart, we made friends, and we settled in and did a great deal more running around barefoot and a great deal more swimming, and lived what I suppose in retrospect was a rather schizoid sort of life, running wild with the local kids on the one hand, but (in my sister's case, at least) scrawling anti-British Cyprus slogans all over the walls of the town and shouting "Death to the perfidious British!". I was much too shy and priggish a young boy to do anything of the sort, although I would have liked to if I had had the courage. All that, all that sinking in on the one hand; and then, on the other, going down to the waterside grocery-shop-cum-taverna (where my parents ran a bill that sometimes ran for a year or two years a time, before royalties came in and they paid it — the grocers were quite happy to run it on this basis), running excitedly down there when school finished (which it did at twelve noon, oh blessed days), and trying to persuade our parents that there were things infinitely more interesting to be done or to be seen than sitting in a frowsy smoky sort of atmosphere drinking that nasty retsina (an opinion which I subsequently revised) and that they should go off and look at starfish with us or something of that sort.

Kalimnos was good; Kalimnos probably would have retained its paradisal aspects, I don't know. But Hydra (for thre first few years, certainly) was closer yet to that promised land, if only because there were these two sides to it and one could switch, more or less at will, from one to the other, even if it did involve a certain amount of dragging one's parents out of the grog shop.//

After a few years on Hydra there would have been, apart from my parents, at any given time anywhere between eight and a dozen or fifteen foreign writers, painters, musicians, more or less permanently living on the island. And this kind of atmosphere of an artistic or creative colony had become very emphatic and very full-time— certainly so for my parents, not so much for us children because there was also our life as virtually Greek children to be lived. Nevertheless the ambience in which my parents lived, which was very much one in which books and, loosely speaking, culture were things that were being talked about and enacted all of the time. This was something that couldn't be avoided. I suppose it would have been at about seven or eight that I began to assume

myself that what one did was write, and I started to write a series
of poems which in style were an imitation of my first poetic model,
Ogden Nash.//

In 1975 it suddenly became possible to go back to Greece again.//
    The Colonels fell. And, even if I had wanted to go back to Greece
in the years between 1967 and 1974, while they were ruling the
place, I wouldn't have been able to, because I had been fairly active
in the Greek community here, I'd made speeches and I read poems
and so forth to meetings of Greeks and local supporters of the
opposition to the Junta. My sister, a year or two before her death,
had acted as interpreter to the great Greek radical composer Mikos
Theodorakis when he was out here, and had in fact smuggled some
documents for Theodorakis between Greece and Australia. As a
family we had been pretty much involved with the Australian
branch of the Resistance. However, they fell. So I presumably wasn't
on a black-list any longer.//
    It was fascinating rediscovering the place. It was certainly fasci-
nating to go back to Hydra. It had been eleven years, just about,
since I had last been there, and the island had totally totally
changed. I made the mistake of going in summer. In the sonnet
"Biography", which I read right towards the beginning of this tape,
I have the line — "and these days the Island supports/ a 'Jungian
sandlot therapist' ". — Now, that's quite a literal description of
Hydra as it had become, it had become so foreign, so wealthy, so
trendified, that indeed it could support a local "shrink" and a local
very trendy "shrink". I've no idea what a Jungian sandlot therapist
actually does, but I would think two things would be true: (a) he
doesn't do any one much good, and (b) he absolutely rakes in the
money, whether across his sandlot or not, I don't know. But Hydra
had become like that, the kind of society that evolved there was
quite frightful. Although at the same time it was rather marvellous
to go back to the old house, the old school, the people of Hydra
who still remembered the family Johnston (as they called it) as
fondly as ever. Apparently over all the intervening years they had
pointed out our house to any and all foreigners as "the Australians'
house".
    Greece in general hadn't changed as radically as Hydra had,

because Hydra, from being one of the most primitive, had become one of the most trendy corners of Greece. And it was still, I found, the place that really I wanted to live in. And I settled, or we settled, for a year in a fishing village on the coast of Arcadia, and for another year in the town of Khania in Crete, both of which were absolutely wonderful in their different ways. And after a long hiatus, in which I hadn't written all that much poetry and what I had written had been pretty depressed and what hadn't been depressed had been pretty bad anyway, I wrote the poems which make up the last section of my book *The Sea-Cucumber*. And suddenly things seemed to be going right again. It was going back to Greece that did it.

THE HOMECOMING

Well, what *was* Odysseus good at? (1) making things (2) lying —
neither a skill I've any use for. Don't talk to me
about subtlety. I've travelled too,
smelt caique-decks' tar and goat and onions in milky dawn
        winds,
snoozed hunched in my fur on offal wharves, and remember
prayer-flagged cairns, moon-priestesses and pig-myths
on steppes beyond the writ of American Express.
And come back betraying nobody — Argo, Argus,
I'm my own device and my own dog: "Beware the Savage
        Cyclops."
Why should *I* lie?
                But for instance I miss
the lobster-scamper down seaweed-stinking alleys,
away from fearful demonstrations yelling
Support Your Local Triple Goddess. — To bed —
I'll give you "sodden toward sundown".

John Tranter

CICADA GAMBIT

[for Martin Johnston]

Exiled by circumstance and inclination
from the land and language of his childhood
and deprived by fate of half his family,
he settled uneasily in his father's landscape.
    From the blue Aegean

he declined to Darlinghurst, exchanging the dialect
of Callimachus and Cavafy for the meat-pie-eaters'
drab vernacular. For this indignity, a gentleman's
revenge: he wrought the vulgar tongue into
    exquisite poetry.

Patrick White

GREEK JOURNEYS

To the Holy Mountain and the Past

We started off apprehensively from the obsolescent Athens railway
station. The train which would meander on through Europe
already smelled of stale air, cigarette butts, excrement and urine.
Obsolescence and fatality loom around each setting forth in
Greece. Manoly is unhappy because he feels responsible for it, as I
am in Australia for all I want to see improved. We have spent our
lives apologising to each other, often mutely, as we catch sight of
the cockroach skittering in the shadow of the skirting-board.
    There are many such moments in Salonika. Ancient ruins and
Byzantine mosaics fail to distract the mind from the air of Slav
menace on the city's northern rim. Our hotel would have accom-
modated the more sinister sequences of some cloak-and-dagger "B"
film. During the night, a French letter in the lavatory bowl refused
to be flushed by either of us. Then in the morning we had our first
glimpse of Olympus through the haze above the curving bay. Any

true Grecophile will understand when I say that the unsinkable condom and the smell of shit which precede the moment of illumination make it more rewarding when it happens.

We set out for the Holy Mountain in one of the cranky Greek buses, checking and re-checking the papers we had extracted from a (holy) department in Athens. Our hand baggage was lumped round our feet, the larger pieces corded to the roof under a tarpaulin. It was not till scaling cliffs to reach monastery gates which close at sunset that we realised we should have come with knapsacks, a change of underpants and socks, and a couple of Penguins. Anyway, here we were, bumping in the rickety bus towards our port of embarkation, a dispiriting village where plastic and the juke box had invaded the *kapheneion.* We settled down to wait.

The caique the pilgrims eventually boarded (you do in fact become a pilgrim) chugged along parallel to this sandy finger of monotonous land. None of the splendours associated with the Holy Mountain reached out to grapple the expectant soul. So we settle down again. (Settling down is a condition peculiar to journeys through Greece; hopes are damped as arrival is postponed; it is a country for masochists like myself.)

At Kariyes, capital of the Church State, we were billeted in concrete dormitories in the equivalent of a hostel. Squalor abounding. Next morning the Church bureaucrats fossick through our papers adding a few more stamps. We stroll around and inspect the souvenir shops at the wrong end of our visit. We buy three little wooden icons like squares of gingerbread carved with saints. Outside an almost deserted Russian monastery, an inflated Fabergé object in chipped viridian, a monk with a look of Verlaine expressed hostility by screaming at us. Time and again we found that Orthodox monks scream like enraged queens. There was nothing we could do to calm this aged Russian, so we walked away, and soon it was time to bring our shamefully superfluous luggage to the mules we had hired to carry it down to Iviron and the caique which would take us on the next stage of our journey — to the Grand Lavra.

Much as the bus from Salonika bumps you over grey, potholed

roads, the caique tosses you on blue waters past cliffs with monasteries attached like the nestings of ingenious birds or insects. What
could only have been projecting dunnies constructed by monkish
spiders added to the grotesque beauty of the Holy Mountain's
architecture. The exception is Vatopedhi, a Byzantine version of a
Harrogate hotel. (The only time I saw Harrogate I was with my
family at the same hotel and historic moment when Agatha Christie
checked in without her memory.) During our stay at the Lavra, we
returned by mule and spent a day at Vatopedhi. The florid buildings
clustered round the main court attempt to exclude the world, but
even serenity is of a worldly order at Vatopedhi. In spite of relics
and the presence of monks, that first impression of Harrogate was
replaced by one of Brighton. We were given lunch on our own in
a private dining-room, a meal in keeping with its comparatively
worldly surroundings, and certainly the only civilised food we
tasted in the time we spent on Mount Athos. We would not have
minded shedding our fellow pilgrims and sinking into the feather
beds and hot baths Vatopedhi must surely have to offer.

As pilgrims we were an incongruous lot: Manoly and I with our
excess luggage; the trumpet-player from an Athens nightclub whose
mission was to bring back a leaf from the miraculous vine at the
Romanian monastery of Hilandari to help his childless wife conceive; a young policeman with progressively smellier socks; a
Jehovah's Witness with a badge in his beret who provoked a quarrel
almost every time he opened his mouth; a restaurant proprietor
from Thebes who expectorated continually, and drove his phlegm
into the Grand Lavra tiles. What we had in common was our
pilgrimage, our exasperation at the slowness of it, and anxiety that
we might not arrive before the monastery closed its gates at sunset.
When we did tie up in the little harbour below the Lavra the sun
was already setting. There began a most infernal scramble up a
precipice, myself wheezing, the Theban coughing and hawking, all
of us by now stinking, ourselves almost ruptured by our suitcases,
the typewriter I never once laid finger on throughout the journey
tinkling feebly as it was mishandled. (The reason for our ridiculous
overloading was that in our simplemindedness — or snobbery —
we had brought along clothes we thought might be appropriate to

Constantinople and Smyrna, something in which to pay tribute to Manoly's Byzantine ancestry.)

To the disappointment of the gatekeeper-monk, we just made it at the Lavra as the sun went down.

In travel anywhere I have discovered you arrive almost always at the wrong moment: too hot, too cold, the opera, theatre, museum, is closed for the day, the season, or indefinitely for repairs, or else there is a strike, or an epidemic, or tanks are taking part in a political coup. At the Lavra we coincided with preparations for celebrating the millennium. Nerves were jittery, tempers ran high as imported workmen attached lath, plaster, and masonite to stone walls which had withstood the ages. Never wanted, but accepted in bad grace, pilgrims were more than ever superfluous to the lives of the monks. One speculated how the Church State would react to the King of the Hellenes, who was expected as its civil guest of honour.

Our first evening started amiably enough with the monk in charge of pilgrims offering thimble-sized glasses of ouzo and squares of *loukoumi* on a balcony outside our quarters. The situation deteriorated as the evening wore on, through a meal of slimy *kritharakia* and naked haricot beans (hadn't we chosen the ascetic way?), the dirty wash-house with broken panes, the expectably filthy lavatories, arguments in the dorm before lights-out, and the policeman–pilgrim's overpowering socks.

On the Holy Mountain, even more than in Greece itself, waiting is a condition you have to get used to. Impatience always let me down. Manoly who is sweet-natured, Greek Orthodox, and a fatalist, came out of it with greater dignity. But whatever our virtues or our flaws, we continued waiting till the monk in charge consented to show us a vestment, a missal, or the relic of his saint.

It would have been more humiliating if the worldliness and bad tempers of some of those holy monks had not matched my own. As we made our way humbly through the stone labyrinth, barely sustained by our ascetic diet of *kritharakia* and naked beans, delicious smells of cooking drifted out of private suites, glimpses of decor offered themselves between the opening and closing of a door, exquisite acolytes tittuped on some errand for an imperious superior. I was reminded of the monasteries of Athos when told of a slogan outside an evangelical church on the South Coast of New South Wales, "Churches are hospitals for sinners, not hotels for saints".

Hotels for the "saints" they house are what some of the less ascetic monasteries of Athos have become, and no doubt the sumptuous Vatopedhi, that Harrogate Hydromajestic-cum-Brighton Pavilion, will end up as an actual hotel for rich, homogeneous tourists of both sexes rather than the assortment of male eccentrics we found ourselves to be during our brief pilgrimage.

And yet, even the most exasperated and temporarily scornful pilgrim can be raised from the slough of his cynicism by the silence of a pine forest, or when, under the blue and gold crag of the mountain itself, an icon in its details of jagged rock, tufts of grass, the florets of a stubborn plant rendered with Byzantine formality, an anchorite of true vocation, looking like a rusty old black umbrella, stumbles down a stony track ahead of his donkey — all contribute to blot out the impression of contaminating luxury in the cells of the hierarchy.

We, the novice pilgrims, are roused from our restless sleep under hairy blankets in dream-infested dormitories by monks whirling wooden klaxons or *semantra* in the alley below to summon us to early devotions. We struggle up and into our clothes. The church still smells of cold wax and stale incense, though live candles are beginning to warm it through. A liturgy is grinding into gear. We took bleary and confused, huddled together in upright self-effacing groups, till giving in to the voluptuousness which lies the other side of asceticism, we dare loll against the wooden supports the walls of an Orthodox church offer those who are spiritually insufficient. As voluptuaries, lulled and lolling, drunk on the fumes of fresh incense and the flow of immemorial words, our souls respond, or so it appears. If I cannot truly claim that the other drunken, bleary, unwashed, unshaven faces share my experience, it is immaterial as my spirit ascends through the branches of the liturgy and loses itself at last in the cloud of bluish smoke.

After several hours of worship, hunger and boredom begin to gnaw at ecstasy. Later that day we bought a tin of Spam at the gateway shop and surrendered ourselves to the sin of gluttony. It was a delicious relapse, equal to those moments in the Western Desert in wartime when you broached a tin of bully or Meat and Veg. Lacerated fingers were not the least part of it.

Lacerations alternating with visions: is this what hooks the more perverse Grecophile? Whether lolling against worm-eaten woodwork in ancient Byzantine churches, lulled by the liturgy he is hearing, or seated on a rush-bottomed chair, seduced by the feminine slither of the sea, its lip extending till almost sucking at his toes, while a golden hen scuffs round the iron roots of the table, and the beads of the *komboloyi* restlessly cannoning off one another draw some of the nervous fever from the hands at play, the Greek is never wholly unconscious of the echoes from a torture chamber in which his psyche is a permanent victim. Initiated into cruelty by Turk and German he is not above torturing his fellow Greek, which rebounds on him as self-torture. Anglo-Saxons who, in general, have not experienced the cruelty of foreign oppressors are more inclined to indulge in games of mental cruelty, while Australians in particular torture their fellows by apathy.//

Towards the Polis

It was dark as we waited for the train which would take us to the Polis. Our Greek nerves had begun playing up at the prospect of Byzantium. Sinister shadows streaked the platform as the train steamed in. At least we had no difficulty finding places. Anticlimax again. Till at Alexandroupolis an American slammed into our compartment, sweating and disturbed. He had become convinced there was a plot to murder him in the hotel where he was staying, and so, had fled in the middle of the night. At once sinister shadows recurred in the badly lit corridors and compartments of the Stamboul Express. Pasty, waxwork faces, but never that of a star in toque and eye-veil, peered at us through the glass.

Once more, anticlimax. During the grey tedium of dawn there was an argument between a customs official and a Greek lady bringing a vacuum cleaner to a relative in the City. The hose was uncoiled endlessly, the plastic examined to an accompaniment of soprano shrieks and bass rumbles. I don't know how the deadlock was resolved. We had begun the approach to the dismal fringes of Byzantium.

In Constantinople (we could hardly bring ourselves to refer to it as Istanbul in spite of the enthusiasm of the British and Australians) we put up at the Silk Palace Hotel recommended by Manoly's father, I don't know why, but he had his unexplained connections, and in his youth, the Romanian mistress with whom he decamped from Alexandria to Chicago. The Silk Palace had the doubtful advantage of being close to the railway station and the brothels. Outside our ground-floor window was a street urinal reeking of ammonia. We were saved from its fumes by a Roman housekeeper who had heard that Romans were checking in. (Constantinople Greeks have always referred to themselves as Romans.) Thanks to this good woman we were transferred immediately to a sweeter side of the Silk Palace, where in spite of the well-meaning housekeper, the plumbing in our bathroom did not work, and the lift which should have carried us up to our room was permanently out of order. (In our first days in the Polis we learned that most facilities were out of order, or else, closed.) But even so, we were grateful for the concern of our fellow Roman, the housekeeper at the Silk Palace.

Constantinople — from which the grandeur and the gold leaf have peeled, leaving the sludge that is Istanbul, the grey-skinned Turks, the heavy, teeming herds infesting the streets and crowding the buses … As practically no average Turk seemed to speak anything but the Turkish language, of which we had about six words, we took to listening for sounds of Greek whenever we were lost or confused. Our fellow Romans always welcomed us as members of what was as much a secret society as an exposed minority. Living from day to day under threat of expulsion, these Greeks were the warm pulse in an otherwise insensitive city.

Numbed by traipsing through squalid streets, dazed by the opulence of bejewelled Ottoman artefacts in museum and palace, we found relief amongst the mosaics of St Saviour in the Fields (Kariye Cami) and in the calm immensity of St Stophia, noblest of churches, nobler even than that other temple the Parthenon. Its spirit has survived Islam's attempts to disperse it by hanging beneath its dome plaques painted the Prophet's green with gold inscriptions from the Koran. This great church is the embodiment of an ideal, none of the finicky Gothic soaring and aspiring towards Heaven, but a balanced statement of conviction that the spirit is here around us on earth. Paradoxically, some of the nobler mosques are inspired by this envied and resented church. We should get the message, but it is difficult when blood has flowed and continues flowing.

We returned several times to Ayia Sophia. Closed doors on some of those occasions only kept us out physically, and I shall continue returning in memory to this supreme church which I first entered as a child through a crude colour photograph in my parents' house in Sydney.

Our other great experience of Byzantium was the Bosphorus, a silken waterway down which we made several voyages. Here at last Byzantine and Ottoman seem to have come to an agreement, old Turkish houses and the ruins of Byzantine walls and gateways reflected in the same placid water. There were small, civilised restaurants serving exquisite Greco-Turkish dishes. Perhaps the voice of the Roman tended to predominate. We felt at home — till the ghost of that English governess marching along the towpath at dusk during a previous century looked down and found herself face to face with a head floating past in a basket.//

The Mainlands

Greece is the greatest love-hate for anybody genuinely hooked. We who are, amaze amateurs by giving them glimpses of what we see and feel. In the same way foreigners who have spent five minutes in Australia and grown sentimental over their superficial acquaintanceship think you have gone off your rocker or that you are another of those Australians with the so-called inferiority complex if you tell them the truth about it. What you truly feel about a country or an individual of great personal importance to you, generally shocks when you are honest about those feelings. If you are pure, innocent, or noble — qualities I don't lay claim to — perhaps you never develop passionate antipathies. But Greece is one long despairing rage in those who understand her, worse for Manoly because she is his, as Australia is worse for me because of my responsibility. There are times when I think that M. in his willingness to forgive Australia must be more Australian than I. But he only came here and joined a club, as those of the first generation inevitably do. He and I won't breed another generation unless those who read and understand my books. I believe that books *could* breed future generations in spite of the pressures on Australian children to choose illiteracy and mindlessness, or if home-bred totalitarians and foreign invaders do not destroy our tentative Australian literature.//

Manoly and I are at our edgiest on Mistra, what with my inadequacies as historian and theologian, and the Lascaris connections, the crumbled palace, the ancestor in the chapel of the Pantanassa, his eyes gouged out by the Turk. So we lose each other on Mistra for fear that our edginess might drive one of us over the edge.

On that first occasion we dripped around in our raincoats, apart, and came together again with our fellow tourists in the convent visitors' room where the nuns got us drunk on ouzo and then sold us embroideries. We still have the little mat in the icon corner in the house in Sydney where we continue living in 1981.

The second occasion we staggered round Mistra was years later in the blaze of summer — the lizard season. We were brought there by our taxi-driver, the elderly Gythion version of the Oz Digger. We began at the top of the mound, separated, lost and found each other among the ruins, sidled past the sign now pointing to the site of the LASCARIS HOUSE, visited the Pantanassa where the nuns had become inhospitable and sharp; they complained that the tourists were using their tap and leaving the water running. But their convent was spotless as ever; the world of plastic had not yet corrupted them.

Looking out from the historic and architectural muddle of this great mound of tumbled stones and drowsy lizards I experienced one of the brief moments of perfection Greece offers the obsessed. Our sweat, our aching feet, the plain of Sparta stretched out in front of us like a dusty carpet under a heavy heat haze, Taygetos puritannical without the snows and violet light of our first visit, were all part of the experience. For the rare glimpse of nobility, the grudging kiss, all you have suffered in the way of caprice, trashiness, a degeneracy of the beloved, is at once acceptable; your passion is justified.

After lunch we drove down into the village and out the other side where a *paniyiri* was warming up. I cannot remember which saint the fair was celebrating, but there were horses, gipsies, "Christians", the jingle of harness, the babble of voices, music from a roundabout, and the first wavelets from a plastic sea. Flowing around and over us this fairing was another instance of the Greek dichotomy of earth and spirit.//

Exhausted to the point of longing for Athens, the Polymeropoulos hospitality, and our rooftop flat in the Street of the Sirens, we would never have seen Pylos and Navarino if our often irritating taxi-driver had not stayed on for reasons of his own and insisted on dragging us for a last expedition the following day.

The painter Brett Whiteley asked us recently which we considered the wonders of the world. It is the kind of question which always strikes me dumb. I could only mumble Ayia Sophia and the Parthenon, without being able to add to them. Till Manoly suddenly united with me in an outburst of, "Pylos! Pylos! Oh yes, Pylos and Navarino Bay!"

At any rate on the evening when we saw it the landscape was the most sublime imaginable, the landlocked bay almost a circular lake. If it had been a lake, the waters of Navarino would have taken on that dead, steely look which seems to distinguish Greek lakes of any size. Instead, as a bay, and in spite of an oil refinery sprouting like a cancerous growth from the inner shore, it has remained alive, a mirror flashing every letter in the code of beauty. The great battle fought in the bay, and which contributed more than anything, if also by accident, to Greece's independence from the Turk, may have added lustre to its eye and my romantic vision of it.

If we did not visit the palace of Nestor (Robert Liddell's "Homeric bore") it was because I am less interested in ancient Greece, property of the fossickers, the professors, and the tourists, than in the Byzantine and Frankish versions of it. We did go as far as Methoni to the south, its magnificent open fortification a stage awaiting some spectacular theatrical event.

On the drive back to Kalamata from Navarino, and Pylos the white, dreamt-of village, we passed peasants returning from the fields leading white house-goats staggering along under bursting udders. The whole landscape was heavy with fulfilment. We too, felt fulfilled, as one does in Greece at moments when earth and spirit complement each other.

Next morning we caught the bus to Athens on a stretch of barren ground beside a dry river, slightly different from the typical Greek bus station, but every bit as depressing. There wre booths selling mummified, fly-haunted food, multicoloured scarves and hand-kerchiefs, and the usual plastic trash.

Then as the bus got under way and mounted the road, a splendid, fertile landscape surged around us on either side. We settled down till at Megalopolis a cement works out of science fiction spewed clouds of dust and fumes over the plains, olive trees, the mountains of the Peloponnese. From Megalopolis to Tripolis I had beside me a small fat grey-haired man in black suit and dark glasses reminiscent of the "great" Austral Greeks. We somehow resented being thrown against each other by the movements of the athletic bus. Our bodies told us we were on opposite sides.

At Tripolis, the prototype of Greek provincial towns, we shed the psuedo-Australian Greek. We ate passable *tyropitta*, and forged on into a distance which drained us of all resistance, and finally life. Our mere bones were jogged, tossed towards the roof, and returned to seat level for further torment. There was a staging post somewhere along what used to be the Saronic Gulf where we were disgorged, and allowed the time to feed if we had the desire. Any appetite left us after a glance at the prospects. While we were standing on a boardwalk above the sadly humiliated waters of that classic inlet, I glanced down, and there amongst the rubbish was a plastic spoon stamped with the word AMERICA.

We reached Athens, and a day or two after our arrival, read of a brilliant government plan to "develop" Navarino by building ship-yards and extending the existing oil refineries. As a *coup de grâce* the planners envisaged a site for the Olympic Games at Pylos. Mercifully the project sank, but during the world crisis of 1980, Greece has again come up with a plan for a permanent site for those renowned trouble-makers, this time at Olympia itself. Rather the death of the Games than the death of Greece. Not only on a plastic spoon casually dropped beside the Saronic Gulf, AMERICA is writ large across its victim. It is tattooed into the body of a goddess turned prostitute, by poverty, materialism, and international politics.

Gillian Bouras

STRANGER IN A STRANGE LAND

I married a migrant: the simple statement masks a multitude of complexities! It has been written that "an emigration is possibly the loneliest experience a man can suffer". For the Greek migrant, pain and guilt are added to the burden of loneliness, for he feels that he has betrayed Greece in leaving her.//

George, my husband, arrived in Melbourne in 1965, worked first as a labourer at General Motors, learned English, studied part-time and by 1980 had become a lecturer at a Melbourne technical college. But he could never forget Greece and the family he had left behind.

By 1980 we were like thousands of other middle-class families. We were both working. Both our sons, then aged seven and five, attended a private school near the school where I taught. We had a pleasant home in a pleasant suburb, which we were generally too tired to enjoy. We saw our friends, both Greek and Australian, fairly regularly, but the weekends were usually a mad rush of preparing for yet another hectic week.

That year we decided to spend six months in Greece, with a view to staying if all went well. "You've got to make up your mind," I remember remarking somewhat bitterly to George. "Get this Greek thing out of your system one way or another." I was prepared to try another lifestyle, but in my heart I believed we would soon be back home in Melbourne.

Even so, early one July morning, I walked across the dew-soaked grass of the Melbourne Botanical Gardens, gazed at the lake and beyond to the trees and the towers of the city skyline. I said goodbye, just in case. I have not seen Melbourne since.

In Greece, everything fell into place. We quickly found congenial jobs close to George's village — Arfara, population 1700 and 18 kilometres north of the southern port of Kalamata in the Peloponnese. Our two sons loved the freedom and the outdoor life; we were all healthier and more relaxed. I remember being quite calm and committed about staying in Greece, until November, 1980, when we went to Athens to register as permanent citizens. After that I realised I was no longer a mere on-looker — I, too, had become a migrant.

Migration is like life itself: so much more and so much less than we expect. For me, becoming a migrant meant having many enriching experiences, but also facing a great number of problems. There was not only a cultural and language barrier, but an educational, class and religious gap which, at times, after the initial excitement of arrival and settling-in, resembled not just a gap but a yawning chasm.

There is a certain satisfaction in being part of a rural scene and a foreign one at that. Instead of seeing yellow trams from my front window, I now see perambulating masses of olive branches, with noses, ears and tails indicating that donkeys are responsible for their movement. There is a sense of continuity missing from any rural or urban scene in Australia. Despite the winds of modernity and change, life here is still very much as it was one hundred or even two hundred years ago: an endless cycle of birth, childhood, marriage, family and death, with little alteration in the conventional pattern.

Activities change with the seasons: planting, watering, fertilising, weeding, harvesting, replanting. In summer, tomatoes are made into paste, and eggs, flour and milk are made into noodles for winter. Autumn is wine-making time; winter is olive-oil processing time. Cheeses are made in spring after the kids and lambs are weaned. Summer and winter, women sew and weave.

Superimposed upon the seasons are the four great religious fasts of the Greek Orthodox year: Christmas, Lent, the Fast of the Apostles in mid-year and the Assumption Fast at the beginning of August. Work is punctuated by Sundays, name-days, feast-days and more fast-days. The steady gaze of the painted saints, the flickering candles, the waft of incense, the ritual chanting, all combine to make even an ordinary Sunday yet another little thread in the tapestry.

A sense of security is another great benefit of village life. True,

Greece is part of Europe, part of NATO, feels threatened by Turkey and by Communism from the north. Yet the village is largely insulated against these tensions — safety on the individual level is what counts here. I leave my doors and windows open all day and night if I fell like it; I can leave the house and know that no vandal or thief will enter. In older houses a stick or a knotted ribbon across the gate indicates that the owner is absent. Then, not even the much-maligned gypsies will trespass.

I have walked through the streets at two a.m. and have felt no fear. My children are free to roam the village lanes and by-ways to their hearts' content. If we returned to Australia, I would have to educate them not to talk to strangers. There are no strangers here, and Dimitrios and Nikolaos, now aged nine and seven, converse exuberantly with anyone and everyone.

Another contrast to the Australian suburban scene is in the Greek attitude to time. A popular phrase in villages here is: *na pernaei i ora* — to pass the time. A dreadful sense of urgency plagues nearly every Australian professional I have known. In the Peloponnese, time is a seemingly inexhaustible commodity to be filled in pleasantly: sitting, talking, sipping coffee, clicking one's worry beads, singing, eating, drinking and dozing, knitting, weaving and crocheting — *na pernaei i ora!*

What is it then, that makes migration such a terrible experience? It seems to me that we are born, we die, and we migrate alone. This last is particularly true for me, for migrants to Australia usually have fellow-countrymen with whom to recollect the past, their childhood and their old selves — I have nobody. I miss so many things: a shared view of life, a certain attitude to work and achievement. I don't say that Australian attitudes are better; I merely say that they are my birthright and that I miss them. I miss familiar sights and sounds. People here are a different shape; they walk differently. I become quite desperate for the sounds of English. The day I met a sandy-haired, moustachioed youth from Wollongong who said simply, "G'day. Where're you from?" I felt a single, dreadful pang of homesickness.

Being a woman in Greece is, of course, vastly different from being a woman in Australia. In Greece, men ride the donkeys to the fields while the women walk. Women wear deep mourning on the loss of a spouse, while men do not. Men are served Communion first in church; men drink coffee in the all-male stronghold of the *kafeneion* on Sunday mornings while their wives are home struggling with the midday roast. I was most affronted when a stall-holder in the market at a nearby town took a heavy parcel from George and thrust it at me, saying that my husband was a good man and should be looked after.

I am thirty-six. My three sons are aged nine, seven and seven months. Many village women of my age are looking forward to being grandmothers. No other thirty-six-year old woman here drives a car, rides a bike or wears trousers. Disapproving male eyes followed me down the street when I first appeared in my jeans; the local priest nearly fell off his donkey when I whizzed past him on my bike one morning. Now he knows I'm foreign — he thinks I'm from Africa!

The migration process has affected my relationship with my children to such a degree that I now understand the particular griefs of migrant mothers in Australia. During my two years here I have learned the hard way that children who are otherwise loving and caring human beings are quite unable to cope with having a parent who is different. They laugh at my funny Greek and taunt me with their accuracy and fluency. It is much preferred that I keep silent while walking down the street with them: they are humiliated at the thought that people might hear me make mistakes in Greek, or worse, speak English!//

Surely this is the main reason why migration hurts. Everything that determines identity is gone: that sense of familiarity and belonging which we only comprehend when it is no longer there. Children, and sometimes spouse, change — not slowly with the gradual accumulation of the years, but often very quickly and with a distressing abruptness.

Lawrence Durrell, that famous philhellene, has said that Greece offers you "the discovery of yourself". I feel, rather, that my old self is lost somewhere, drifting, and I cannot reach it. Even my name has gone, as my neighbours can neither pronounce it nor spell it. They call me "Julie", and a "Julie" I certainly am not. Migration, then, is a kind of death, a death of the old self. But it is also a birth, as the new self struggles to adapt.

By becoming a migrant, I now understand how countless migrants to Australia feel — women in particular.

I now have the split psyche of every migrant. Where's home, Ulysses? I don't know, and neither does George. George misses Australia more than he ever thought possible, the more so as he has finally learned that the past is past and his old life in his homeland has gone forever.

A very wise old man, himself a European migrant, once said to me: "There are no encores in life." Yet a migrant goes back to his old country expecting the playhouse of his life to be the same, with the same audience applauding. The Greek cannot return to the same Aristomeni, Aris or Athens, any more than I can return to the same Eaglehawk, Nhill or Melbourne.

Yet I feel no guilt at leaving Australia. The burden of betrayal is not one Australians assume, perhaps because we have always had a diffuse loyalty. My grandfather, for example, even though he was a third generation Australian, often referred to England as Home, and the capital H was very important.

Perhaps this is the answer: Why have one home, when you can have two? Instead of thinking of the pain of division, I should think of the privilege of being twice blessed: if I returned to Australia now, I know I would miss Greece terribly. Australia is still home because of my roots, because of the letters I write and receive and because of the friendships which are undaunted by a gap of 16,000 kilometres.

But when I sit, as I did yesterday, on a slated balcony shaded by bougainvillaea and honeysuckle, and when I gaze down the mountainside to an impossibly sapphire sea with matching sky above, I know that for me, as well as for Drosinis, Greece has become a "blue beloved homeland".

Beverley Farmer

VILLAGE LIFE IN GREECE: INTERVIEW WITH RAY WILLBANKS

Unlike many foreign brides, I was welcomed with open arms and made much of, loved and tolerated and all that from the very beginning. I'm sure it was because I had some of the language.

You lived a village life in Greece?

Yes. It's not like Greek island life, which is what most tourists are probably more familiar with. The village where I lived is in a comparatively rich farming part of Greece, an alluvial plain in Macedonia where they grow wheat and sesame, barley, cotton, tobacco.

What size is the village?

Nine hundred people. So half the village were relatives of some sort. The sort of all-purpose title was "cousin" and half the village called me "Nyfi", which means daughter-in-law, sister-in-law, cousin-in-law. It really means bride, the woman who married our boy. So everywhere I'd go, I'd hear, "Eh, Nyfi!" and they'd come and ask me to drink coffee or something.

Did you learn Greek stories that you incorporated into your fiction?

Not a lot. The traditional language was a bit of a difficulty in the village because there were two dialects. There was a sort of Slav dialect, which the original people spoke. My husband's family were refugees in 1922 from the massacres in Smyrna and Constanti-nople. So they had been settled there in an exchange of populations arranged by the Turkish government after the cease-fire. Years later they still regarded themselves as strangers. They spoke a Turkish dialect, so the older people didn't speak the sort of Greek I knew. Especially since I had picked up the Cretan Greek to begin with from Kazantzakis, but that was a small hiccup from the Cretan past. I'd miss about one word in ten. Even so, my father-in-law, now ex-father-in-law, has always told me that I should sit down and write the story of his life, and I might do that next year when I go back.

How long did you live in Greece?

Oh, my husband I were there three years straight and then went back for some summers after that, after we'd come back to live here. The last summer I went back was 1983.

Being a liberated Australian female, was it difficult to immerse yourself in a patriarchal situation?

Matriarchal — that was the problem. The household was matriarchal. Especially our house. The patriarch kept well away and didn't
infringe upon her territory at all. But having spent my whole
adolescence in a struggle to liberate myself from my own mother,
it was a bit hard to knuckle down ten years later to my husband's
mother. But because I loved her so much, I tried to do it. She was
a terrific woman to everyone who knew her; she was gallant and
beautiful and strong and brave.

And from your fiction, I'd say generous.

Yes, generous. She had a great sense of humour, so we could deflect
our quarrels by one of us making a joke as an overture and the other
one would respond. So it didn't become the sort of tooth-and-nail
stuff that it often does with daughters-in-law in Greek households.
I got on better with her than did my Greek sister-in-law, in fact
much better.//

*Although you're writing about individuals, individual conflicts, there
are in your fiction implied comparisons between Greek and Australian
consciousness. Would you talk about this?*

I think that's too general a question for my mentality. I pick on
particular instances and moments, I suppose, and focus on them;
it's such a short focus that I can't really generalise. I'm not good at
generalising at all.

*The conflict between individuals is more important than the cultural
conflict?*

Yes.

*What I am thinking of is what you just spoke about — the Australian
woman moving into the matriarchal situation.*

Yes, it wouldn't have been any different, I suppose, what nationality
the matriarch was, or I was. In "Place of Birth", I was observing my
Greek sister-in-law's quarrel with her mother-in-law. I was interested in recording the abrasiveness in someone, people not hitting
it off. I wasn't conscious that I was contrasting nationalities in that
story. I can see that it's there, but I sort of averted my eyes from it.

I think it's like the sleepwalking you need to do when you've found your subject. I wanted the sharp detail to speak for itself.

Could you talk about the web of the Greek family? It's one of the subjects that you deal with often in your stories.

Yes, I do. I suppose in my view of it, it is the women's side that I give, and the male is almost a drone or a parasite. He's uptight, he's at the cafe, or he might be earning his keep at the coffee shop or he might be out in the fields or doing something with the horse or the donkey. But the nub of my life in Greece was the household, and its head was the matriarch, the mother, the strong woman figure. Sometimes I've been taken on by feminists for having no strong women in my stories, and that always stuns me because the mother figures in my stories are so overwhelmingly strong. Maybe the feminists just mean their particular sort of women. It strikes me that they mean role models of their own age, and I'm not in the business or providing role models. But there is a strong woman in my stories, for what that's worth. But I've gone off the subject again. I feel the Greek family is a web of duties and obligations; it is a hierarchy, and although in practice it never works out the way it's supposed to in theory, the mother is the head of the female side of the house and she can give orders to all the daughters-in-law, the sons' wives who live there or who visit. And the wife of the oldest son, whatever her own age, has precedence over the wives of the younger sons in their order. And if, say, the middle brother's wife steps out of line, then the father-in-law might come along and say, "I want you to have a word with so and so about such and such." And if you are me, you say, "Oh, Baba, I can't do that." And he'll say, "You must do that. It's your obligation. If you don't, she'll despise you because you have not exerted your proper authority." So, of course, then I wouldn't say anything, or because it would strike me as ridiculous, I would tell the sister-in-law, "I've been told to tick you off about such and such"; then I would be seen as subversive because I'd colluded with her instead of cursing her, so there would be a lot of difficulty about that.

I've made a list of things you deal with in your Greek stories: jealousy, honor, loyalty, piety, cruelty, anger. All of these explode within your family situations.

Yes, they do. I was brought up in a cold and repressed family in which we didn't say what we felt. If it was anything negative, it was to be suppressed or denied. And we weren't allowed to disagree; we were supposed to be nice and polite. If I was angry, even in my teenage years, I was sent to my room and told not to come out until I could behave myself.//

The images in your Greek stories — flowers, fruit, eggs, wine — suggest a stronger sensual life than the images which dominate your stories set in Australia. Is this an intentional contrast in place, or state of mind?

Yes, I think I was more aware in Greece of the austerity and poverty, where the only extravagance is in the light. Dimitris Tsaloumas says something like this. An orange is something you save for, and a banana is something you fight over, as in "Place of Birth". I actually saw the wine being grown and pressed and strained. I went myself to the hay and picked the eggs out. It was more personal and closer. It wasn't like going to the market and picking a kilo of that or a kilo of this. It was something that was hard won. There could be hail or frost and you would have nothing. What you had was what you'd managed to store up and save and it seemed to me much more precious and sacred. I saw it as sacred. It seemed to me that eating to a family in Greece was a sacrament. I'd never felt anything like that in a family in Australia.

Life itself became more ...

Yes ... Whereas the image of the bread and wine in Christianity had seemed to me a literary one and had no purchase on my mind at all, when I went to Greece, the physicality of it was perfect, it made sense. I was in a world where that image was created.

Physicality is very important in your writing. Let me give you an example of "Place of Birth" and have you comment. "... she hugs herself close to the soomba, *holding the iron door open while she crams pine cones in. She sits with her clothes open. Perhaps the baby can see and hear the fire, she thinks, did he see my hands in there, by the light of the candle? They must have made shadows on his red wall."*

I remember thinking these things when I was pregnant in the village in the winter. It was a very hard house to keep warm and you really cherished warmth. There is a retreat into physicality in pregnancy anyway. This state of mind and body continued when I came back to Australia, the sense that you are somehow a nest and that this egg is making itself in you. And the feeling of repleteness and fulfillment that I felt then, was beginning to feel in the village, I think was a matter of being pregnant. I think one reason that physicality is important to me, especially in this relationship of mother and child, is because we were not a touching family, but with my child there was all this physical contact and that was very important. It was wonderful. Having a child was the single most important thing that ever happened to me.

You sound like Helen Garner.

Yes, I can imagine that she would say something like that. Some feminists we are!

POMEGRANATES

"Your hair's got darker," Kyria Sophia says, "since you came here first. Otherwise you're the same. Your Greek is still all right. I can't take it in, how it's all those yeras since you left our son."

Strolling around the village on a road that has been asphalted past balconied mansions where doughy cottages used to be, she is slow: she who strode laughing and skipped over its ruts and heaps of dung. She is almost deaf. The skin of her face is baked on, her hair dead white. A grey spider like a crab is groping over threads of it; she stands still to let the younger woman flick the spider off, and absently with ridged hands strokes her woven hair smooth again.

Passing a garden, she begs a bunch of marigolds from a young householder whose moustache just covers a tolerant smile. She grabs at running children to ask each one: whose little boy, whose little girl? Outside the bakery they meet a nephew of hers, a man bald as a brass knob who always makes much of her Australian grandson whenever his father brings him here. Merrily she screws two fistfuls off the loaf he has bought. Munching hot sour bread, talking about their boy, they all walk home in the sun.

In barn after barn left open to air, garlands of tobacco are hanging like fur coats. She and the old man no longer grow any. Their barn still has sacks of grain, bales of hay and lucerne; he keeps the old horse in there, and the cow with her calf. Kyria Sophia has her vegetable garden, fenced with beans and morning glories. Her tomatoes hang in skeins among yellowing leaves. She has round peppers and long ones, deep red, and black eggplants curved like horns. Hens scratch and flounce, and two scraggy turkey cockerels. The flowers on her basil are like lilac, white and mauve.

The trees are the same, in the same warm mist as when Bell first saw them, their leaves yellowed, even the cobwebs afloat among them yellowed. Mist-glossy and black, there are the thorny acacias: dented gold pods, green fronds of leaves. Over the doorway the grapes are ripe to wrinkling and hum all day with insects, grapes so sweet that they parch the throat. Along the fence there are trees with round red fruits too bright to be apples and besides they have tails: pomegranates, full of red glass seeds.

It is seven years since Bell was here last; fourteen, since she first came in pomegranate time.

Kyria Sophia picks one now and breaks it open. She and this Australian who was her daughter-in-law sit on stools under the grapevine, nibbling the seeds.

"The boy kept saying when they came this summer that you had made up your mind to come. I didn't believe it. After all these years. And here you are."

"I wanted to come before this."

"I'll pick the pomegranates before you go. You can take some back to Australia for him."

This is the time of year when the earth reddens, and the sun; and the moon, like an egg in a nest of clouds.

"Every summer they come I tell the boy, this or that is his mother's," Kyria Sophia says coyly. "Whenever we use your things." Forgotten things are everywhere. They have just drunk Nescafe from the silver-rimmed Australian cups, with milk from the old blue-and-white striped jug. Today's yoghurt, in the red French casserole, is warm in an Onkaparinga blanket by the wood stove. Kyria Sophia has the earthenware baking-dish — a wedding present — on her lap: under a white crust is tomato paste, dried like blood after days in the sun. She is spooning off the crust of mould.

"All your things have been waiting here for you." She sighs when silence answers her.

"What if I go and see if there are any eggs?" Bell jumps up.

"Go and see."

She escapes to the barn, where the hens lay their eggs in the old mangers. Just inside, the black-lashed eyes of the calf bulge; it stumbles upright, its knees and belly wet with dung. The cow swings her head up from the manger with a snort that stirs the hay warmly. There are four smeared eggs stuck with straw beside the dummy egg.

She remembers the eggs she wrote "B" on.

"She wrote 'B' on the eggs!" Her sister-in-law Chloe's voice. "Why should she hog them? What about my children?"

"Ssst." That was the old woman. "Here she is!"

"So what?"

"Here I am." She saw Chloe grimace. "What's wrong?"

"Nothing."

"Something about eggs?"

"No, no, she didn't say anything."

"I did." Chloe pointed. "That's not fair."

"Because they're hard-boiled?"

"I'm sure it's just a misunderstanding, girls."

"How come you need your initials on them?"

"Oh. The 'B'? I always — it's for 'Boiled'. *Brasto.*"

"Oh."

"So we can tell."

"There! A simple misunderstanding!"

"I still don't see why you had to hard-boil four, when there aren't any fresh eggs."

"I thought there would be. I boiled these for the salad."

"We don't put eggs in the *salad.*"

"No? *Sorry.*"

"They'll do for a *meze* with olives. And Magdalini will have fresh eggs," smiled Kyria Sophia. "Let's all go and see her now."

"Let's go and see Aunt Magdalini?" she is about to call out now, coming back with the eggs. But there is the *papas* fluttering along the road, his coppery hair and beard as if on fire under his black stovepipe hat. "Look! It's the same *papas*! The seaman, the red one who married us."

Kyria Sophia's mouth sets hard. "That's him."

"He's coming over."

"He would."

Both women kiss the red curls of his extended wrist. They all recite the required greetings; then he sinks into the cane armchair with a creak to wait for the cakes and coffee.

Luckily Bell has brought a ribboned box of cakes from the city. She washes her hands and the eggs, pours glasses of water and puts a cake each on three silver-rimmed plates. This *papas*, she remembers, was a wild seaman until his wife made him study theology and give her six boys, burly farmers all. "I ploughed the waves," he boomed. "My boys plough the dry land." Barbarossa.

"He looks like a pirate!"

But the old woman sniffs, stirring the coffee.

"I ploughed the waves. My boys plough the dry land." That time, too, he was having coffee with them both. "Are you still liking Greece, *madame*? Yes? A very different life."

Bell quoted a proverb: "Where there's land, there's home."

"Good, good. Here's the place to raise children."

"I hope to, father. One day."

"Soon, if God wills."

"We'll see."

"Mmm. How many years is it?" Scratching his bright beard, he leaned forward. "You do have contact with your husband?"

"Contact? He lives here!"

"No: contact. She doesn't understand!" He rolled his eyes at her mother-in-law, who shot them both a shifty look.

"Contact? Mama, he can't mean —"

"Of course he does!" hissed the old woman.

"Oh." She felt her red face gape stiffling in a grin. "Yes. I do."

"It's the will of God then, eh?" he said gratefully. Both women glared as he took his leave.

"And what's more, your mother put him up to it!" She was still angry when her husband came home. "What she really wanted him to ask was if I'm on the Pill!"

"Don't start this again," muttered her husband.

"It's *her*. She never stops."

"Ssst. Perhaps it was a misunderstanding."

"Sure."

"Okay, so she wants grandchildren. What's so terrible about that?"

"Like when she took our dirty clothes —"

"She wanted to help you wash —"

"— to see if some disease was stopping me conceiving!"

"You hurt her that night. Shouting, crying, shutting yourself in."

"Asking if I'd like to see a doctor! 'This stain here on your pants — are you sure nothing's wrong?' "

"Oh God."

"Oh yes, God, oh yes. 'The will of God'."

His curly beard is sprinkled with icing-sugar; he rubs his hands and a veil of it falls. "Is it the will of God," he intones now, "that the churches in your country should have women priests?"

"No!" says the old woman. "Jesus was born a man. He wasn't born a woman!"

"Mama, He had to be born one or the other."

"Exactly! And He chose to be born a man. He said woman was born to be man's hostage!"

"What? Hostage!"

"He said so in the Bible. And now the Protestants have women priests! Blasphemers! God will send His fire to Earth!"

"Because of that?"

"The world will end soon in storms of fire. That's the nuclear holocaust. No wonder, when mankind has forsaken His way and let communism and divorce and women's liberation run wild. They worship the Antichrist! May God send the fire to burn them!"

"Well now, Kyria Sophia, time I was on my way." The *papas* sighs. "Duty calls. Have you got the names?"

"I'll bring them, father."

Tomorrow is Psychosavvato, Souls' Saturday, when he will hold a morning service for the souls of everyone's dead. Their names will be read out, and each family's *kollyva* shared among the mourners. Kyria Sophia will be the first one there.

After the afternoon sleep they go to see Aunt Magdalini, who insists on picking all her best roses and presenting them with a hug of welcome. She scuttles in the blue cave of her kitchen dishing out cherry *glyko* on glass saucers, mixing coffee, pouring iced water.

"*Aman*, Magdalini." Kyria Sophia slaps her saucer down. "This cherry *glyko* of yours. Nobody can eat it. Throw it away."

"I boiled it too long," cackles Magdalini.

"Is it *glyko* or glue?"

"Don't eat it, dear, if you don't like it," Magdalini tells the visitor.

"Oh, but it's lovely!" she answers. It's more like toffee than jam. She scoops up the last threads and bites them off her spoon, grinning at Magdalini, who is more than ever a gnome of a little old woman. Kyria Sophia hunches her shoulders and her black brows. Magdalini, as ever, is impervious.

"I haven't boiled my *kollyva*," she says. "Have you?"

"Oh yes," says Kyria Sophia.

"I haven't even cleaned the wheat."

"Bring it here, then."

Magdalini brings in a pan of rustling wheat. The three women sweep it with their hands, picking out stones and husks and seeds. The mist hovering in the doorway turns cool blue.

Kyria Sophia has a bowl of *kollyva* with a lighted candle stuck in it, as if for a birthday; and a little brass incense holder which she stuffs with hot coals from the *somba* before setting in it a bead of red incense like a pomegranate seed. She takes them from room to room. The smoke trails after her muttering shadow.

Back in the kitchen, sighing, she strains the evening milk and puts it on to boil.

The old man comes in cold from the *kafeneion*, hungry for chestnuts before dinner. He smokes with his eyes closed, waiting. Kyria Sophia has to remind Bell where to find the chestnuts. She remembers without being told how to slit them with a knife and shuffle them round on the iron top of the *somba* until they scorch.

Singeing her fingers, she peels them then, enough for everyone; waxen, wrinkled and sweet, they sting in the mouth.

Kyria Sophia cuts bread and cheese and heats up the vegetable stew left over from lunch. The old pots flutter their lids and whistle, now and then uttering a faint crow as of roosters in the distance. The milk, as always, boils over, surrounding the pot with a frill that crackles and burns brown. They eat eggplants and peppers and beans and mop up all the red oil with their bread. The cheese is a salty white honeycomb, the grapes ripening into raisins. To celebrate her coming, they pour what's left of last year's ouzo from the demijohn, and drink it watered.

While Bell washes up, Kyria Sophia decides to inspect the eggbound hen. "I hope she's managed to lay it. If not —" She holds up the knife. "I'm not letting her die on me." Soon squawks and one screech come from the henhouse. A bundle thumps on the kitchen windowsill by the pot of basil: red cords poke from speckled shoulder feathers. Kyria Sophia throws open the window — oil-yellow smoke drifts out among needles of rain — and with a pot of boiling water at her elbow she plucks and cleans the hen.

"Rain at last. Well, we'll eat her tomorrow." She crams the carcase into the refrigerator. (They have one now, and a television set too.) "In red sauce? Or egg-and-lemon, maybe." Her bloody fingers hold up a bright pomegranate: no — the egg that she pulled out. "Pity," she says.

She sits by the *somba* reading the prayer book aloud in her cracked treble, glancing over her glasses now and then. The visitor goes and leans over the sill to breathe in the cold air made lemony by the wet basil. In the mud below, the cat's eyes flash green; it sends up a yowl for more of the tattered hen. Both the old people are snoring.

So many village evenings spent yawning beside the *somba*, to the sounds of cats and snores and night birds. She has put off going to bed, because this is the same old bedroom, and the bed. Those are the two cane armchairs that made up a cot for the baby the first time he was here. These are even the honeymoon sheets that they rumpled and soaked with sweat all the first summer, night and afternoon. Now she opens the window and the hinged shutters:

she leans on the sill. The rain has stopped. Drops fall from the grapes into dark puddles.

On the chest by the bed are old photographs of them all together, here and in the city and on beaches. She is holding one of her boys tossing wheat to hens long since killed and eaten, when his grandmother creeps in.

"Some hot milk?"

"No thanks, Mama."

"All the good times." She points at the photograph. "Don't they matter any more?"

"Everything matters."

"Can a woman just walk out on her man these days, and her little boy? Don't you remember how it was?"

"I remember, or why would I be here?"

"I can't take it in." She turns away. "Hang anything you want in this wardrobe. See, we have a wardrobe now. I'll just take my coat for church, then I won't have to wake you tomorrow." Her voice is still reproachful. Once she would have added: Or will you come with me? She holds up a slim camelhair coat, silk-lined. "Isn't it beautiful?"

"Yes. Let me see it on."

She slips it on and lets her white plait loose.

"Yes, Mama, you look very elegant."

"I'm old." Peering in the dull wardrobe mirror. "Look at me. Is my hair much whiter now? Whiter than when you first saw me? It must be." There are tears on her cheeks.

"No." Bell puts her arms round her. "It's the same."

Anna Rutherford

GOING SOMEWHERE ELSE

Most of us made London our base where we worked and saved for the summer months when we would then "do" Europe. I was no exception. The day after arriving in London I applied to the LCC — the London County Council — for a job as a supply teacher. Several days later I received a phone call telling me to report to my first school. Armed with an A to Z of London and a tube map I found my way to the school where I presented myself to the headmistress and announced that I was the new supply. "Oh," she said, "you're a colonial." "No," I said. "I'm an Australian." But it gave me a shock. You see, I'd never thought of myself as a colonial before.//

In 1966 I went to Denmark.// I wanted to go somewhere else, somewhere different. I applied for a job in Addis Ababa and one in Aarhus. Aarhus answered first. So we might say I didn't choose Denmark, Denmark chose me. It was not until I got there that I was to find out why.

I was employed to give an introductory course on English literature and lectures in one other area — I opted for the seventeenth century. I was reasonably well equipped to do both. What I was not well equipped to do was to teach my own literature.

As I was an avid reader my knowledge of Australian literature and history may have been a little better than that of the "average" Australian but that wasn't saying much. I had read Lawson and Paterson in primary school but those writers and others like them were left behind when I moved to secondary school. Having matured myself I could move on to "mature" literature, and so Clancy was discarded for the Ancient Mariner and Maud replaced the Drover's Wife. In this new era of "maturity" those ubiquitous symbols of Empire, daffodils, ruled supreme. It goes without saying of course that as I reached even greater heights of maturity at university Australia was totally banished. Hanrahan and Saltbush Bill became little more than vague childhood memories. I came to Denmark very ill-equipped for the task which had been planned for me.//

There is surely a degree of irony and cause for despair in the fact that my first real knowledge of Australian literature came not from an Australian academic or Australian institution but from an eccentric Danish academic who had a knowledge and confidence in Australia which was very hard to find in any Australian institution.//

When I arrived in Denmark I was, as I said, nationalistic; I was proud of my country and in no way looked at it as an underdeveloped backwater of Britain. My image of the ideal male (dare I admit to it now) was of the bronzed surfer, clean shaven of course. I regarded anyone who wasn't devoted to sport with suspicion and with a deal of contempt as well. I was confronted by a society where a large proportion of the men were long haired and bearded, dressed in clothing that would have been described as "sissy" in my own country. There was no body cult, good looks were defined differently and were certainly not dependent on physique. There was a high premium on intellectual ability and a relative lack of interest in sport.

The women too were different. There were not so many painted dolls, they were less prey to "feminine" fashion, more independent, not sitting on one wall of the dance floor waiting to be chosen. When Kristen Williamson was in Denmark in 1978 she remarked on the fact that Danish women walked differently from Australian women. This was easy to account for. Instead of teetering along in the instruments of torture that fashion has declared is "feminine" the Danish women wear shoes that are equally as comfortable as those worn by the men. The footwear was symbolic of the greater equality between the sexes. This was also reflected in gender roles which were in no way so sharply defined as in Australia. Not long after I arrived in Aarhus the late John Reid, who was a New Zealand lecturer and critic, gave a series of lectures. At the conclusion of the course he was thanked publicly and presented with a bunch of flowers. Later on I mentioned to one of the Danes that he must have been surprised to be given a bunch of flowers. "Why?" she asked. "Well," I said, "you don't give a man flowers do you?" "We do," she replied.

Of course everyone in Australia connected Scandinavia with permissiveness, and sexual liberty shading into the immoral, an idea that is still prevalent in some quarters. At the time of writing this article there is a picture on Adelaide's buses of a smiling blonde girl with the caption, "Get fresh with a Scandinavian" (an advertisement for Jordan toothbrushes). Well, I found no evidence of the sex orgies that some had predicted were waiting for me. I was surprised (at first) at the number of students from "good homes" who lived together and I remember cutting out and sending home (but not to my mother) some of the bridal photos from the newspapers with the bride holding the baby. I remarked to one of the priests that there was little or no evidence in the church of devotion to Mary. He, like all the other priests at the Catholic church, was not Danish and he shook his head sorrowfully as he said, "No, it's very hard to get the Danes to believe in the Virgin." Whilst I didn't find a society of raving sex maniacs I did find a society with a healthier and more open attitude to sex.

I was being forced all the time to question my "norm", to redefine it, something that has been an ongoing process. It doesn't mean that I have rejected all my former ideals to embrace willy nilly those of another culture. I still can't stand socks with sandals and nothing has happened to change my mind about sport. Where I have changed is in my blind support for a person or a team simply because they are Australian. My interest I believe is no longer a nationalistic one but rather an admiration for skill, though if I'm honest, I still want Australia to beat Britain at cricket.//

Having experienced what it is like to be a foreigner has made me more conscious of "otherness" and for the need of every society to make provision for difference. Even though Danish society is a very racially homogeneous one it does, I believe, provide more room than Australia for other voices.//

I left not because I was rejecting Australia. But I was rejecting a society which by virtue of my sex and my unwillingness to conform to their ideals made me a second class citizen and an outsider. At no point did I not feel Australian, but I did have a sense of alienation and subconsciously I probably chose a country where I was quite literally an outsider. It is possible if the feminist support groups which exist in Australia today were in existence then I may not have left. I don't know.

Peter Porter

THE TRUE COUNTRY

My whole career as a poet has been conducted in England. My setting-out in 1951 was undoubtedly a pilgrimage to the imaginary world of my reading, and, of course, I discovered how different the reality of England was from any idealised portrait of it. Yet, at the same time, right from the start, I did not expect things to go well on a day-to-day basis in London. My earliest efforts at writing were dismal failures. I was thirty-two before I published my first collection of poems, in the same year that I was married. In 1983, Oxford published my Collected Poems, so I should be able to look back on my thirty-six year career as a poet as a melding of myself with my adopted land. However, I do not. For me England (and Britain too) is an agglomeration of friends, colleagues and sites. It is where I raised my children, where my wife died, disturbed and disillusioned in her own country, where I have pursued an uncertain course as a writer. The longer I live here the less I feel I know the place. I am just as expatriated from Britain and Europe as I am from Australia.

This is the chief conclusion I should like to emphasise in any assessment of expatriation. Once, in a poem which has been taken up by Les Murray, I wrote "Some of us feel at home nowhere,/Others in one generation fuse with the land." To someone of my temperament the familiar is always turning into the mysterious: doubt is as generic as breathing. Some critics have described me as a social commentator, an essentially journalistic poet. I see myself quite differently. I have frequent recourse to brand names, surface realities, comic and tragic effusions of the contemporary spirit, but it is all still filtered through books. Life is a dream, but literature is even more so. I must stress that what I have written here is as much an apologia as a confession. I see eye to eye with such poets as Stevens and Ashbery (however differently I write) in that I think the poet's true country is his own mind, and that will receive stimuli from anywhere and everywhere. Stevens never left the States; Ashbery lived for many years in Paris. Both are bookish poets, recognising, Mallarmé-like, that poetry is made of words and not just of experiences. More important, they see that words are experience itself. Thus it becomes honourable to be an airplant and to live wherever life will support one's imaginative labours. Some instinct guided me to London in 1951; this, it seemed then, would be the place to acquire the necessary sophistication and experience of writing which my impoverished apprenticeship had not given me. Had I been making the decision in 1981, I certainly would not have got on the ship: I'd have stayed in Australia, which, by that time, was tooled up to offer any writer material to write about and support in the form of audience and recognition. Not yet, however, support of income, except through grants from the Literature Board. But then there is nowhere in the world where a serious writer, and more especially a poet, may earn a living entirely by his efforts at original creation. He or she will have to have recourse to the academy, journalism or the grant system.//

Perhaps the real point in any consideration of expatriation is choice of subject matter. This lies behind the reactions of Australian critics to the work of their fellow-countrymen who live abroad. Randolph Stow, for instance, continues to write largely about Australia though he has become a citizen of the United Kingdom and lives in Suffolk, where his ancestors hailed from. A multiple murder in Perth can be fitted out with a British background, and Stow is readily discerned as remaining consciously Australian. There is another kind of Australianness on offer: painters such as Jeffrey Smart and Justin O'Brien live and work in Italy and neither employs Australian iconography in his art — least of all, Smart, whose pictures are a powerful collection of imagery from Post-Chirico Italy. But their market is almost entirely back among their fellow-countrymen — the rich collectors of Australia. I have frequently encountered bafflement (at best) and hostility (at worst) in critical notices of my poetry written in Australia, simply because I do not use Australian material in more than a small number of my poems. Even sympathetic critics, such as Vincent Buckley, call my temperament and style English. Less friendly reviewers urge me to remove the cataracts from my eyes with a dose of life-giving Australian sunshine, or attribute gloomy aspects of my work to the occluded English weather. I would be ready to admit that I have cut myself off from a valuable source of inspiration in not having demotic Australian in my ears every day — thus I shall never be able to write as naturally in the voice of my time as Bruce Dawe can. The speech of London is a demotic but it is not quite *my* demotic. It is a natural inheritance of my daughters: for me it will always be something of an acquired tongue. To this day, after thirty-six years' residence in England, I get things wrong when writing about English life. And when Englishmen quarrel with me, they are always tempted to ascribe our differences to my imperfect acquaintance with the English manner of doing things. Viz Tony Harrison saying "Why should I be lectured on English life by a fucking Australian." Yet I suspect I might have much the same problem if I had stayed in Australia, since I have always been attracted to material of a conjectural sort, rather than to social realism.

Returning to Australia has liberated some part of me. It may seem a minor thing, or perhaps all too characteristic an experience, but I now can see the country when I look at it. This was beyond me when I lived in Brisbane. It is not just a sort of Pantheism, but a surprised acceptance of the peculiar beauty and the a-symmetry of the land, especially the trees. One aspect of Nature I enjoyed as a boy — the coastline and littoral of Australia — has been reinforced recently by what I have called "the ecstasy of estuaries". Many commentators have warned of the habit among expatriates of praising the natural beauty of the land, but continuing to excoriate the people. I am tempted only to oppose the automatic anti-Pom rhetoric which is so universal these days. This doesn't hurt the British but does untold harm to Australian sensibilities. Films such as *Gallipoli, Breaker Morant and Crocodile Dundee* not only perpetuate myths of Australian honesty versus British and American deviousness, but do so with one eye cocked on the box office. Flattering Australian self-esteem is far too easy to do. It is just not true that the British were taking tea at Suvla Bay while the Australians were being massacred at Lone Pine. Gallipoli was an appalling disaster, and the British and Churchill especially were at fault, but everyone suffered the consequences, the British infantry as badly as any other body of men.

To sum up: it has never crossed my mind to think of myself as anything other than Australian. Where I live and what I write about is another matter. To paraphrase the Emperor Franz Josef, I am a patriot for me. My true country is my imagination. I wish that modern nationalism would permit that most honest form of the love of country — the expression of doubt and anxiety. Personally, I should like Australia to be a land fit for pessimists to live in.

Christina Stead

LEAVING 1928; RETURNING 1969

All night the sleeper sleeps close to a board, irons rattle, a violin played aft vibrates along the side, the body of the ship rises and falls, the engines beat on through seven hundred sleeps. The first day, yellow cliffs, blue coasts, next day, the steep green island south; a new world. Homeward bound on that ship in 1928, a Lithuanian woman in grey knitted skullcap, fifty-five, short, sour, salty; a tall English woman, eighty-four in black, small hat and scarf, who stands for hours by the lounge wall waiting for the Great Bear to rise; a missionary woman, thirty-nine invalided home, worn by tropical disease, her soft dark skin like old chamois; she is going back to the town, street, church she left eighteen years before, because of a painful love-affair with the pastor: his wife now dead, he has just married a girl from the choir, "Just as I was then," she says. There's an Australian girl, lively, thin, black hair flying, doing tricks with a glass of water, by the big hold aft, and around her her new nation, Sicilians, her husband one — they are playing the fiddle. There's a redgold girlish mother from the Northern Rivers, scurrying, chattering, collecting cronies. Three times she booked for England, twice cancelled; the third time, her youngest daughter brought her to the boat in Sydney. Three unmarried daughters, "Oh, but we are not like other families; we cannot bear to part." Before Hobart, she telegraphs that she will land at Melbourne, go home by train; but they telegraph, "Go on, Mother, please." "They don't say how they are!" She is faded, sleepless, "What are they doing now?" At Melbourne, the women dissuade her and she goes on. Acorss the surly Bight they make her laugh at herself; she laughs and turns away, aggrieved. As we approach Fremantle, she is dreadfully disturbed; the ship may dock in the night and leave before morning. She sends a message to the Captain. At Fremantle, she telegraphs, disembarks, her rose colour all back. "I'm going home! They'll be getting ready! Oh, what a party we'll have!" "What about the presents?" "I'll give them back; I did before."

There's a country minister and his wife, two dusty black bundles who conduct services in the cabin before a number of meek, coloured bundles in Sunday hats. The couple gain in stature the farther they travel, until in the Red Sea, having lost all provincial glumness, the minister shouldering tall against the railing, arm and finger stretched, explains the texts, the riddle of the Pyramids, the meaning of Revelations.

For years, I thought hazily about returning; and like that, it would be, in just such a varied society, myself unhampered, landing unknown, "Poor amongst the poor" (a line of Kate Brown's I always liked) and would see for myself. After I had looked round lower Sydney where I walked every morning and evening of my high-school, college and work life, I would go out and stand in front of Lydham Hill, the old sandstone cottage on a ridge which, from a distance looks east over Botany Bay, straight between Cape Banks and Cape Solander, to the Pacific; and the other way, due west, over a grass patch and the yellow road to Stoney Creek, to the Blue Mountains. That is how it was when my cousin and I lived there with other little ones and played in the long grass and under the old pines.

I knew all that was gone; they had driven surveyors' pegs into the gardens, the neglected orchard, before we left for Watsons Bay; and a friend in the Mitchell Library archives some years ago sent me coloured slides of the house that is. But still I would go and look at the homestead.

The other place — "Watsons"? By a magic that I came by by accident, I was able to transport Watsons noiselessly and as if it were an emulsion or a streak of mist to the Chesapeake; and truly, the other place is not there for me anymore; the magician must believe in himself. And then for long years I had a nightmare, that I was back at Watsons, without a penny saved for my trip abroad, my heart like a stone. It was otherwise. I came by air [1969], the sailor dropped by a roc, Ulysses home without all that reconnoitering of coasts, a temporary citizen of a flying village with fiery windows, creaking and crashing across the star-splattered dark; and looking down on the horizontal rainbows which lie at dawn around Athens, around Darwin.

Unlike the ship, though close-packed as a crate of eggs, we travel with people we may hear but never see. There is only one street in the flying village and in it you mainly see children conducted up and down. Beside me, is a Greek-born mother with her Australian-born son, aged seven, she talking across the alley in English to her Greek-born neighbours, about the good life in Australia, the peace, the prospects, the education. What you hear in her tones is the good news, the rich boast delivered somewhere outside Athens to the grandparents; it is a wonderful country, we are lucky to be there, no social struggle, plenty of work, success ahead, money everywhere, no coloured people. (It turns out she thinks this.) Standing now in the alley stretching, a tall Italian proud that he has been in the country forty-two years (a year longer than my absence). There are fourteen children of all ages, three high-stomached young women hurrying out to give birth in the lucky place. Few get much sleep but all are good tempered, it does not matter; their urge and hope is on, on. "Are you an Australian?" "Yes." I am looked at with consideration.//

As for me, high up, almost lunar, I could not take my eyes from the distant earth, every spine and wrinkle visible in the dry air. There did not seem to be a cloud between Darwin and Sydney. Our firebird lazily paddled (so it seemed against the motionless rush of greater vessels up there) under the broad overhang and what a sight all night! — the downpour of stars into the gulf that is not a gulf. In Australia I never lived in suburban or city streets, but with wide waters and skies and this life expanded was coming home to me; you are nearer there (in Australia) to the planets. Even more now — when we have all got a bit of the astronaut in us.//

It was there [Darwin], over the walls, through partitions, in the women's rooms, that there came in high, tired, bangslapping voices, "Isn't it good to be home?" "Yes, what a relief!" "Better than Europe!" "Oh, yes, I had enough of Europe." And carolling the gladness like magpies singing with parrots, strangers behind doors, "Yes, it is good to be home." (One comes out.) "How long were you in Europe?" "Three weeks — three long weeks. And you?" "Two months." "How did you stand it?" (Forty years of Europe! — I left quietly.)

Novalis said, my friend Dorothy Green remarks, that you must know many lands to be at home on earth; perhaps it is that you must be at home on earth to know many lands. A child in Australia, in the home of an active naturalist who loved the country and knew scientists, nature-lovers, all kinds of keen stirring men and women

---

who found their home on earth, I hearing of them, felt at home; this was my first, strongest feeling in babyhood. I have had many homes, am easily at home, requiring very little. My first novel (before *Seven Poor Men of Sydney*) was to be called *The Young Man Will Go Far* and then, *The Wraith and the Wanderer*, two different novels. (I still have part mss.) The Wanderer, once he has started out in company of the Wraith, the tramp and his whisperer, does not look over his shoulder. He does not think of where to live, somewhere, anywhere; anything may happen, awkward and shameful things do happen; he does not believe it when life is good; by thirty all is not done, neither the shames nor the lucky strikes. He takes no notice, it is his equal but different fate, he marries a stranger, loves an outlaw, neighbours with many, speaks with tongues. So that if he should cross the high bridge of air sometime, going homewards, he is also on the outward path.

Now I am back in shadowy England whose pale streams are sometimes "gilded by heavenly alchemy", they speak of "hot summers" but there is not the pour of gold nor the fire from the open hearth. Here are white cliffs and mornings, white horses on the downs, topheavy summer trees, King Arthur in his mound, gods and Herne the Hunter in woods, green folk, little folk, squirrel-faced elves; and stranger creatures still, Langland, Wyatt, Chaucer, Ford and their pursuit of comets, the English splendour; and all this is in the people, their unconscious thoughts and their language.

Under the soft spotted skies of the countries round the North Sea I had forgotten the Australian splendour, the marvellous light; the "other country" which I always had in me, to which I wrote letters and meant one day to return, it had softened, even the hills outlined in bushfire (which we used to see over Clovelly from Watsons Bay) were paler. The most exquisite thing in my recent life was a giant eucalypt on the North Shore as we turned downhill, the downward leaves so clear, the bark rags, so precise, the patched trunk, so bright. "Look at that tree!" It was outlined in light. It was scarely spring, but the lawn outside the house was crowded with camellias, magnolias in bloom, even falling; at both dawn and dusk the kookaburras thrilling high in the trees, the magpies — I had quite forgotten those musicians and their audacity — //

I don't understand the settled sadness of some intellectuals, artists and academics. The heat mystery, black shadows in the tropics, the long bright road ending in a mirage? Deserts? Not belonging to ourselves? Not united with our nearest neighbours? Smalltowners in the USA leave farm for town, town for Chicago and New York, the capitals for Paris and London. Perhaps it is just *The Beckoning Fair One* singing her faint irresistible "very oald tune" (Oliver Onions). Well, let us be discontented then; it has never hurt art.

Jeffrey Smart

THE FIRST TIME IN EUROPE: INTERVIEW WITH GEOFFREY DE GROEN

When I left Australia early in 1948, I was a little bit known.

How long were you away?

About two-and-a-half years.

What did you get from that experience?

The first time in Europe! That was extraordinary. I was with Jacqueline Hick and we went to London, then to Paris. I didn't like London much, and Paris only a little more. Then I went to Italy and it was like coming home. I was immediately intensely happy and just felt: wonderful country. Then we took a villa in Ischia which we rented for next to nothing. Michael Shannon, Donald Friend, Peter Kaiser came down — lots of painters. In those days it was a completely unspoiled island in the Bay of Naples. Truman Capote was there, Tennessee Williams, William Walton was arriving then, Paul Muni the film star, Sir Alexander Korda and his wife. And so it went on. It was a very select lot of people who were in the know, much like the hippies can find out a place and the general public don't know about it. We found an island with no tourists at all, and it was marvellous. That was a lotus-eating episode, it was so extraordinary of course.

How long did that go on?

About a year and a half. Of course I did no painting of any seriousness. I was just fooling around.

Margaret Cilento came down. All sorts of people. I didn't do any good work there, the living was too good I suppose, and also I was in a very mixed up stage. I'd been in Paris with Léger and I was looking at modern Italian painting and I was at sixes and sevens with myself. I didn't know how I was going to paint or what to do. Later on when I came back to Australia, when I was about thirty-three, I gave up painting for about a year. I couldn't decide — I couldn't see any point in painting.

It was despair at not having any money, because I'd spent it all in Europe, and despair in what to do in painting. What's the point in trying to be a good Rembrandt? What's the point in trying to do another Ben Nicholson? Why try to do a Braque?//

When did you start to live permanently in Italy?

In 1963. Australia seemed to be very dull and isolated, and Italy seemed to be thrilling and modern. It was its modernity; I adored the modernity as well as the antiquity.

Was the religious art an attraction?

No. There's a very strong religious feeling in the Piero della Francesca *Resurrection*, but I'm not sure that Piero was a profound Christian. The greatest religious work is the *Last Supper*, by da Vinci, and yet he was chucked out of Italy for being antiChristian. The religious side … no, that had nothing to do with it. That's just an excuse to paint a picture.

Often the same artist who painted Christian pictures would have painted Mohammedan ones if the Mohammedans had given them a job. An artist has to be like an actor in that he can take on that feeling, *that* mood, *that* thing for that particular religion — in this case, Christianity. Da Vinci's *Last Supper* is a moving work, but I don't think that da Vinci was a Christian. The other thing was that in those days, fifteen years ago, Australia was not the fascinating place it is now. It's much more interesting now than it was then.

What were the problems then?

A general apathy — a naivety. The way everybody embraced

abstract expressionism in the fifties was so naive; I had seen the beginnings of that in America in 1948. With Léger one learnt that there was no such thing as modern art, or new movements, it was all whatever you did. It was naivety. Australian painters at that time were eagerly trying to be *au courant* with the rest of the world and there was a childish eagerness to show: we're not isolated. There's a bit of that still here.

A great deal of it actually.

Think of Patrick MacCaughey and that "Ten Australians" exhibition that toured Europe. That was a dreadful fiasco in Italy; it was all painting of the sixties. It was bad for our image.

What should have been shown?

Tom Roberts, Conder, perhaps some Drysdales, although they're not as good. My own work. Ray Crooke. Brett Whiteley … John Olsen certainly would have been goodo.

Something particularly antipodean?

Yes.

So you went there in '63 …

Yes, but Australia has changed for the better and Italy has changed for the worse. I'm back more or less where I was. Now I don't know whether I should live here or in Italy. Actually there's not much to choose between the two. I feel quite indifferent whether I live here, or there, but I've lived in Italy for fifteen years and I've got all my books there.

Robert Hughes

THE FIRST TIME IN EUROPE: INTERVIEW WITH GEOFFREY DE GROEN

When you hit Europe for the first time out of Australia, you get this flood of visual stimuli which you cannot locate; it's difficult to order your experience of it.

   That's one of the reasons why Australian artists or critics imme-

diately start striking heavy and rather insecure authoritarian pos-
tures when they come back from long spells overseas, I don't know
whether they still do it. Bert Tucker's re-entry into Australia was
one of the great classic examples of that. In 1960 he returned saying:
well, I'm the second most famous Australian painter in the world
next to Sidney Nolan, I'm in the Museum of Modern Art, I'm
known all over the world and now I've come back to get my dues,
my backpay, that was his phrase. And that kind of bluff always
worked. It worked for critics, it worked for John Olsen.

Can you back it up?

I can now, but there was that kind of feeling that you would turn
whatever you could grab to account. I went to Europe for quite
other reasons, I went because I was madly in love with a ballet
dancer called Brenda Bolton, but coming back was a funny business
because you knew that actually you had seen more than most of
the people that you were dealing with, or talking to, but at the same
time you couldn't give them a convincing account of why it
mattered, because to be away for a year is not enough time to
systematise it, to enable you to think coherently and lucidly about
what you had seen.

*In any case it wouldn't relate because the people back there, if they hadn't
travelled, had nothing to compare it to.*

Well yes, except that Australian art is so often based on overseas
prototypes of one sort or another, but these come in a mangled
form by reproduction and so everybody very definitely has something to relate it to. In those days, speaking of the late fifties and
early sixties there was this neurotic insistence upon establishing
one's originality, and it was considered to be a positive insult to say
that an artist comes out of another artist. Of course it's not.//

At that time my mother died, thus freeing me to go to Europe
again, and within a couple of days of her death Alan Moorehead
turned up on my doorstep and said: it's really time for you to leave
Australia. You should take yourself to London because you're not
going to develop if you keep on here. I rather had that feeling
myself.//

I split, and bounced off to London, had a miserable time there, frittered away such money as I'd managed to save up, then ended down in Italy because Alan had said: well, if you run out of luck come down and help me with my grape harvest. He had a house with vineyards near a little fishing village about a hundred miles north of Rome. It has now turned into the Miami of the Mediterranean; in those days it really was rather a nice little fishing village. I had a flat on the port for about £5 a week, and I wasn't really doing anything very much there; I was the town hippy. I suffered one of the crises one sometimes gets; it suddenly struck me that nobody could possibly want to read anything that I had written, not even in Australia, and I couldn't get it up even to write articles to send back.

I had a few Australian pictures, one big Fairweather called *Monsoon* which I sold to Rudy Komon, for the dizzying sum of £800, Christ I wish I had that thing back now. So I lived on that, but the important thing about it was that it enabled me to really get a proper look at Italian art.

I had a little Lambretta and I would simply go off through every hill town that I could, and this went on for about a year-and-a-half. I'd always had a feeling that I was not properly qualified to be doing what I was doing. I didn't have any degrees. My feeling of nervousness about not having proper credentials was actually cured for me by living for that length of time in Italy. I finally realised that one could learn more by looking at the originals, if you did it in a fairly systematic and steady way, than by looking at them in slides in the Courtauld Institute, even though you didn't have a proper educational framework surrounding you. When I got back up to London I found that I actually knew as much, if not more, about Renaissance painting, particularly *Quattrocento* painting, as anybody who was working there as a critic then. I don't mean as any art historian, but I had as much functioning historical apparatus as any regular art critic then working in London. That gave me a lot of confidence.//

One book changed my life and it was not by Joyce it was by Cyril Connolly called *The Unquiet Grave*.

It's a bellestristic exercise. Connolly was the journalistic critic whom I've always most admired. And I set out very consciously to imitate him. I would say the two models in that regard were

Connolly and Moorehead. When I was sixteen my sister-in-law, Joanna, had *The Unquiet Grave* on her shelf and I read it. Here was this threnody for Europe written in 1943 or thereabouts, at the time when Connolly thought, as everybody in England thought, that the cultivated life in Europe as they had known it, was finished, it was over. The Germans had killed European culture forever. There was going to be no way back across the channel. Very pessimistic. Of course we always love pessimistic books when we're sixteen.

It was an extremely pessimistic and beautifully written kind of lamentation for that kind of Mediterranean fishing port, private library, dinners with Bunuel, nodding acquaintance with Matisse: that gorgeous life. The food is good, the melons taste right, the sea is always blue, the people are always civilised, everything is tinged with melancholy, mild ennui, suicidal despair but tempered with excellent *tripe à mode.* Yes, I thought, that's what I want to do, that's the way I want to live. And that was the principal reason I suppose, at the back of my mind when I went to Italy in the first place. Or why I was disposed towards the idea of living on the sea in Italy. It took me years to discover that kind of hedonism is probably only available in Australia. Because the Mediterranean was physically almost a dead sea and terribly overcrowded. And all the time that I'd been fretting by the side of the unmythologised Pacific yearning for the marble and the river gods and Proteus and all the rest of it … it was all there outside Sydney Heads. But of course in one's romantic furies one doesn't realise this. This also predisposed me very much towards Matisse rather than say Nolde or Kirchner.

There's a whole kind of Mediterranean imagery which I've always found extremely congenial. You get it also in some American artists, like Motherwell and Diebenkorn.

That stems from the French tradition.

Yes. It's the idea of the world as a habitable place, not exactly the earthly paradise but something which has paradisical content, and it's the purpose of painting to reveal that, to order it. That's not the whole story about art, but I've just found it's the kind of art that I most like writing about, except you can't write only about that. That predisposed me towards Italian painting too.

Barbara Hanrahan

GETTING AWAY

The cold and the fear — will I find a place to live, will I find a job? Sitting in the Overseas Visitors' Club bus to London, with the black felt Spanish hat that had been fashionable in Adelaide on my lap, and my grey Chanel-style suit with the black braid trim and my frilly white blouse underneath my orange teddy-bear coat. And there's snow outside the window and fences woven like baskets. I am in England, and soon I'll be in London and I'm afraid. The courier on the bus smiles as he says it's the coldest winter for two hundred years and jobs are hard to get, and I keep thinking of the three of them at home: my mother, my grandmother, and my great-aunt, Reece, who can't read or write and wears childsize clothes because she's what people who know call a mongol. I left them for this dream of going to an art school in London, though it's February and the new art school year doesn't start till September. But I couldn't wait — I couldn't keep teaching in Adelaide any longer, saving my money, working at my prints in the evenings and at weekends.//

That summer, just before I'd left, the garden had been full of birds and my grandmother kept tying the tomato plants up higher and her hands were full of their green pinch-leaf smell; the spotted lily was coming up by the buddleia that was out all deep purply by the fence; there was a blackbird's nest in the orange tree that, not long before, had been wreathed with creamy flowers and scent and scrambling bees, but was now hung with hard green tiny oranges. And in London it was Arctic winter with fog and snow, and a similar further outlook was predicted. The newspapers kept telling how many people had died; and firemen were out fighting fires in uniforms frozen like boards, monkeys and pigmy hippopotamuses were being kept alive by oil-heaters. Harrods called the run on hot-water bottles fantastic; sledges, fur gloves, sheepskin mittens, wellington boots and galoshes were also in great demand. Everyone who could was leaving the country on a stay-a-while cruise to places like Casablanca, Madeira, Las Palmas. People were jealous of Mr Kruschchev in his Black Sea resort, where daffodils, irises and primroses were already blooming because of an early warm spring.

In Adelaide I'd gone to the pictures with my mother, and on with the feature was a short about a London where it was always moonless night, and scarecrow old men picked through the dustbins like some giant variety of withered insect. When the pictures came out it was golden afternoon and I walked towards the railway station with my mother and there was Parliament House, all smooth marble and granite, and behind it the City Baths where you saw the shadows of high divers through glass, and behind that the river banks and the rotunda where the Sunday band played, and pleasure-boat Popeye was on the Torrens, and jacaranda trees dropped blue petals, a lion roared over at the Zoo ... It was my city, as familiar as a toy town, and I linked arms with my mother and kept feeling scared, because anything might happen to me in that icy uncaring London world of blizzard winds and treacherous drifts. Though my jumpers were folded up so cosy in my suitcase, and I had the pyjamas and a new candlewick dressing-gown; I had my new teddy-bear coat and the black leather handbag, that looked like a doctor's bag, my mother and my grandmother had given me for a going-away present.

No one in our family had ever been to London. My grandmother didn't want me to go; my mother said I ought to — she would have liked to have gone herself, it was her ambitioin to walk down Bond Street. In London I'd be nobody — in Adelaide I'd been labelled all my life.//

I got sick of pretending, of always being two people. There was the part that made the prints; that cared about the sheets of zinc and copper, the wax grounds, the etching needle, the printing ink with its hot greasy smell. That part of me was at odds with the person my mother and my grandmother wanted me to be — the girl who wore the clothes they wanted her to wear, and put things on the lay-by, and had her hair set. I was two people. One part of me seemed content being the nice girl who just wanted to stay home and be with them, and sit in the garden and pull out the soursobs and weed round the grape hyacinths under the prunus tree. But always, right from the start, there'd been this other person who wanted to be like my dead father — wanted not to care about the little things like — Have you got clean fingernails? ... Are the skirting-boards dusty? That part of me got free when it made the prints, and had made me feel I had to get away.

Peter Conrad

CROSSING THE BRIDGE

I can remember the exact moment of my birth. It happened on
Waterloo Bridge, on a morning in August 1968; I was twenty years
old at the time.

Those previous twenty years were, however, cancelled at that
moment, relegated to a phase of pre-existence. I had spent them in
Tasmania, reading about what my life would be like when I was
reborn in the Northern Hemisphere. I was inclined to see this term
of years as one of those penitential, ignominious lives you have to
toil through in order to atone for crimes in some other incarnation
— except that I was doing my penance in advance, and once I'd
got it over could expect release, perhaps, into a new existence.

The rite of passage from one identity to the next happened in
the middle of that bridge, as I walked out of Waterloo Station,
down a tunnel, up into the air and across towards London. I paused
halfway across, to look at the curve of the river from St Paul's to
Westminster: the dome, the carved range of towers, the ranks of
steeples and columns between them, the growling streets beyond.//

I think I slowed down as I approached it. If this was the
beginning, that meant it was also the beginning of the end. The
years of waiting in the antechamber suddenly seemed precious:
everything was to come; nothing had been risked or expended yet;
all that stored experience was held in reserve, like a heaving,
brimming sea.//

Once on the bridge, with the sun managing to bless the moment, I found that my untimely glimpse didn't matter. It was
simply the last of those anticipatory dreams with which I had passed
the time inside my head for so many years. Here was the truth, to
which I had finally awoken. Light had polished the dome of St
Paul's, the crockets and gewgaws of Westminster were sharp against
the sky. Blackfriars Station and Charing Cross gobbled and regur-
gitated trains, just as Waterloo behind me was doing; all journeys
ended or began here, as mine — both ending and beginning —
had just done. The scene seemed so ancient and thick with life that
Cleopatra might have left her needle on the embankment personally. The gulls swooped after garbage below the bridge for joy not

hunger. The sun, I knew, was out as a personal favour to me. Across the river, the city faintly roared, in what I hoped was exultation.

I didn't walk the rest of the way to that open door alone. My preconceptions kept me company. I knew these things already, because I had fed myself on descriptions of them. To the left of me was Wordsworth's Westminster Bridge, from which London, earlier in the morning than this, seemed as fair and slumbrous as Eden; to the right was de Quincey's St Paul's, whose whispering gallery kept secrets circling in the haunted house of the brain; underneath was the Thames, softly melodious for Spenser, grimly chartered for Blake. For Waterloo Bridge itself my only pretext was a bad old film which Vivien Leigh, having failed to meet Robert Taylor in the railway station behind me, slunk off into the fog to sell her body, before arriving at judgement or redemption under a convenient bus. I recalled Robert Taylor, his hair immaculately aged, leaning on the balustrade as an air-raid ripped the sky and looking down at all the water which had flowed under the bridge since then. I walked on and left him there in his mist of retrospection. I had, as yet, no memories of my own, only hopes.

In front, as the bridge ended and London began, were the streets where Dickens claimed that dinosaurs lumbered through primeval pea-soupers, where Virginia Woolf saw buses dipping on a glittery tide like bright red yachts, and where Henry James, in the squares around the British Museum, overheard the hive-like hum of cogitation. This place had been a many-mansioned house of fiction for its imaginative tenants. Anything could be done in it, or to it; it was the heaped-up sum of human possibility, indexing experience like the volumes of its telephone directory. When I reached the corner of the Strand, the traffic stopped for me (though only because the lights told it to).

I didn't feel any obligation, on that day, to see all the paintings in the National Gallery, or trudge round the tablets in Poets' Corner. If this was the inception of a life, I had a liftime's leisure — I supposed — in which to annex this inheritance. I wandered about aimlessly, making sure that it all did exist: Nelson commanding his flotilla of pigeons, Queen Victoria dourly enthroned in front of Buckingham Palace, the stately battalions of trees in the parks, the rollcall of legendary names outside the theatres on

Shaftesbury Avenue. Everything I saw seemed authoritarian, a reminder of my own insignificance. But that was what I had counted on, in my colonial fantasies about it all. The ancestors on their columns and the ancient trees had to deny any knowledge of me, or of where I had come from. It was only by a haughty act of elimination that they could help me to begin afresh.

My newborn elation lasted until night. I sat at dusk on a bench in Leicester Square, listening to the sparrows squabble for space on the branches above. The metallic jangle of their competition for room to live was thrilling, not yet a cause for fear.

By the next morning, I noticed with a spasm of shame that I had begun to take everything for granted. Yes, of course the buses were red: so what? The long, stealthy, mortal process of diminution was under way. I knew I would probably never be as happy again as I was the day before.//

Oxford was a different matter. I would have to function there, own to an identity and submit to its verdict on me. I had come all this way so it could tell me whether I was any good — or not, as the case might be. I rejoiced in London's indifference, and didn't even mind when a shrewish bus conductress scolded me for pressing the bell to start the bus rather than the cord to stop it. After all, whom was she addressing? Someone she didn't know, someone who didn't know himself. But Oxford was to exercise a more alarming power over my life: disapproval, which meant disqualification.

Crossing Waterloo Bridge, I had sauntered into a place documented in dreams, pieced together from images. About Oxford I had no advance notions. It wasn't really my ambition to go there; the scholarship I had won was simply the first available exit visa from my previous life.//

The addition of Lisbon happened at Easter the following year. I went there to visit a Portuguese friend I had made in Oxford, and to stay with his family.//

I had no advance ideas. I told my Oxford tutor before I set off that I was excited to be going to Lisbon because I'd never seen the Mediterranean; the howler enjoyed a rapid circulation. London and New York I memorised before I arrived there. Actuality was pre-empted by images. My experience of the Northern Hemisphere's notion of the south was confined to Las Palmas, where the boat on which I sailed to England made a last, procrastinating stop. I didn't know where or what Las Palmas was. Impatient for England and its fabled fogs, I wasn't at all curious. I dragged myself around the island — which is what I took Las Palmas to be — for a few hours, and remember now only flies, frying-oil, contingents of operetta cops and the lazy slapping of plastic strips hung in doorways on account of the aforementioned flies. I hoped Lisbon would not be like that.

Nor was it. The road through the city from the airport bobbed nautically over hills which were coral reefs of sunned plaster and shining tiles, pink, orange and ceramic blue, with baroque church domes baked from the egg whites left over after whipping up a batch of angels' breasts; emerged into a ravine over which an aqueduct gigantically strutted on stony stilts, a shanty town clinging by its fingertips to the cliff beneath; looped and twisted through a forest of eucalypts; over the last hill glimpsed the ocean, a plate of shining metal, then veered into a suburb where the streets were powdered with mimosa and jacaranda blossoms; pulled up at a gate, a hedge, a house, another life.

Almost as soon as I was inside the door, Jorge's father — who had phonetically mugged up a welcoming speech in English — produced an atlas and pointed out the bereft speck of Tasmania, so remote that even the navigators who left from the chapel on the bluff nearby had omitted to discover it. Mine was one of the worlds they hadn't given to the world: this hospitality made reparation. I found myself adopted.

Later in the afternoon we went along to the chapel, and stood on the steps looking over the red bridge suspended like a cobweb across the river, the all-embracing Christ with arms spread on the southern bank, the flotilla of monuments to the discoveries, and the cape which was Europe's last western lookout, from where it peered in the direction of America, its other, altered ego. As the view was explained, I had the feeling that it was being offered to me; I accepted.//

I enjoyed belonging to a family, so long as it was someone else's. This one came complete with a grandmother in a black shawl who addressed me at length and refused to understand that I didn't understand the language, and a shaggy mountain dog who by the third day no longer barked at me (except when a haircut made me briefly illegible) and by the end of the week had taken to tugging me round the block on nocturnal missions while I panted at the end of his chain and experimentally asked him in Portuguese not to pull.

I felt, unexpectedly, at home. The emotion meant for me then not much more than being looked after.//

Once, aware that I didn't deserve it, I asked Jorge why his parents were so good to me. "Because they're Portuguese," he said. The smile at the corners of his mouth gave notice of a complicated statement: a shrug, a joke, or a truth whose reasons I would have to deduce for myself? In one sense, he was literally right. Charity in this country entailed the donation of surplus — coins, or affection — to those who needed it. Kindness was the instinctive policy of humankind. They had taken me in, and not because they had to.

In London I was a pilgrim, fervently trusting that the shrine I had come to venerate was not empty. In Oxford I was a candidate, awaiting classification. In New York I had been a vagrant, expecting rejection or exclusion. In Lisbon there were no such insecurities. The place I knew least about, which had not figured on the conjectural map of my future, was the one where I felt safest. Here, in the intervals between being an adult in Oxford and elsewhere, I could catch up on the childhood I hadn't yet had time for, and fill in some of the years before my second nativity on Waterloo Bridge.

Tim Winton

LETTER FROM IRELAND

Ireland was never somewhere I dreamed of, the way I dreamed of Paris and the islands of the Aegean. I planned for Paris, but Ireland just turned up. One evening at home in Perth (that sunny speck in my mind's eye, these days) someone rang and offered me his cottage in County Offaly for five months. I'm glad to say I wasn't stupid enough to knock back five months' worth of generosity, and the chance to have somewhere quiet to write. I'm into the fifth month almost, and now with my wife and son, I'm mentally getting ready to leave. It's a strong place. That's what stays in my mind as I go through the accountancy of settling up, looking back, sorting out — just how strong a presence the Leap [Leap Castle] is.

In the mornings I climb the short hill to Spencer's Cottage where I light a fire and straighten the damp-curling pages of my novel. Spencer used to be the gardener at the Castle, and from his place you can see the whole valley, the gate-lodge where we live, the old estate walls, the ruins of the castle itself, and behind it the quilted wens and bumps of divided fields whose shades of green must all have names in someone's mind. When the mixture of turf, coal and wood burns hot enough to cheer my room up a bit, I get down to the daily business of a thousand words of novel. I suppose for that time I could be anywhere at all, maybe even the places where my novel's set — Perth, Geraldton, Margaret River — but whenever my concentration lapses, or I step out to the stone and slate barn for a pee, my eye will always be drawn to the castle. The sight of it is rarely a neutral thing. It almost always sets off things in my mind. I've discovered it's the same for a lot of locals, and for the Australians, Americans and others who come by or stay awhile. There are innumerable legends and stories about the Leap, and they all compete everytime you look at it. Even for those ignorant of its past, it's often a grim, unavoidable presence. What the effects have been on me and my writing of being in its shadow all these months I can't say, but like all strong places, places of memory, of perversity, beauty, the kind of places I've lived near in Western Australia, I'd be surprised if these effects were entirely negligible.

Places, like the bedrock of most good ideas, tend to attract bullshit, and Leap Castle has brought forth more than a good share of that, but as Sacheverell Sitwell writes in *Dance of the Quick and the Dead*, "The intensity of this strange place exceeds in its details anything that the most dramatic mind could design." And Sacheverell should know. Leap was built by the Ely O'Carrolls in 1380 to guard the pass from the Slieve Bloom mountains into Tipperary. The valley roundabout is dotted with prehistoric burial sites, ring forts, stone remnants. Leap's history is long and depressing (though history itself seems long and depressing), a chain of betrayals, fratricides, tortures. It's hard to imagine the spaces between each "major event" in its history. An event, as always, is some awful deed, a spear in *someone's* guts. The castle's oubliette, the spiked dungeon high in the tower, was cleared late last century and "three cartloads of bones were removed from it and buried in consecrated ground. Bits of several old watches were found among the remains."//

Old men still tell me about the treasure "under the flags" or in the twenty-foot thick walls, and I wonder whether these stories have some factual basis or whether they are created out of some universal story-pool. They seem so recognisable, such familiar territory. Is it because they are archetypal myths or just because they're so damn typical of human behaviour? Regardless, the stories stay with the place and with the locals who have all ingested them since childhood. Certain stories are family favourites. The ones that stick are the ghost stories. Daisy Bates, word has it, once wrote a ghost story set at Leap. When I first arrived, it struck me that the whole valley, the entire farming population was burdened with them. Neighbours would hardly let me in the door before setting off on a familiar tale. To me, the whole business seemed oppressive. People seemed to need to get these stories off their chests. Poltergeists, terrible stenches, moaning — all related to the castle. The later they were told in the evening, the more they were prepared for by endless rounds of Power's and Guinness, the less truly felt and more high-toned the stories seemed to be.// Leap has the reputation of being the most haunted castle in the British Isles, though how one quantifies ghostification is beyond me altogether. Nevertheless, there is a persistent and "well-documented" tradition. "Serious students of the occult" have included one Mrs Jonathan Darby (otherwise known as the author Andrew Merry) whose article in 1908 in the *Occult Review* features Leap and a few things that Steven Spielberg would pay dollars to realise on screen. Mrs Darby also wrote an account of the Sunday in 1922 when the IRA bombed and burned the place to a ruin.

Besides the ghosts, the chief narrative the locals embroider and wonder upon is the burning. Until a few years ago, the IRA man who led the mission was living just down the road. I've spoken with children and grandchildren of the bombers who are all keen to see the castle restored "to bring life back to the area."// One wonders what the Republicans thought they were burning down, the Proddies or the Divil himself. I guess they weren't too keen on that distinction. In any case Darby left the place and gave the castle to the gardener whose cottage I slosh up to every day to light a fire and write my novel in. There's supposed to be a secret tunnel linking castle and cottage, but I've never looked for it. Maybe for fear of finding it.

What I suspect has affected me, as I mentioned before, is the strength of the place, in its physical aspect, its weight of stories, the way it preoccupies people. Here where every field and some trees have names, where walls and cottages have names, where a cluster of houses has a collective name to distinguish it from the cluster five hundred yards down the valley, here place and region are a serious proposition. This is where a Faulkner could borrow a complete world for his own ends. The Irish do not forget. There's a kitchenful of stories awaiting you at every house. Perhaps if I felt they belonged to me I'd stay and take a crack at it, but my mythology was handed down in suburban streets by the sea, stories of fishermen and jockies and superhuman women in Harley side-cars. My reference has been the sea — that's what I saw through my window every day. That was the overwhelming presence in my physical and imaginary world. It was how I gauged my smallness.

Coming up the long defensive slopes near the Hanging Field in the waning light of a spring evening, beneath the whirling rooks and jackdaws, it's possible to know how a human-built structure can have such relentless presence in people's imaginations. Inside at any time of day it's a grim, cold place, even now that the cellars have been cleared of rubble and floors put back into the keep and one Gothic wing. The spiral staircase, where all the sightings of the "elemental" are recorded to have occurred, is not a pleasant place to be in, regardless of the electric lighting and the clearing out of the jackdaws' nests. It's not a place I like to be alone in, though I can't decide why. The weight of story, or the presence of Evil? I'd tend to side with the former, though not out of scepticism. After all, I believe in Heaven and Hell, Angels and Demons and plenty besides. My three year old son is fearless, even without the lights.//

An Australian is renovating the castle, and he'll move in any day. He speaks of "bringing positive feelings" to the place, "healing" the place by living positively in it. His mother was an O'Bannon, a name familiar in the annals of Leap, so he feels connected. He's a generous and intense man. The building obsesses him. He wants to use it, not to restore it. He's not interested in creating a museum. He plans to live there, to write there, to have people stay. A billion things. He's consumed by the notion of continuing its story and, in a sense, I imagine, changing its course for the better. On his fortieth birthday the keep was full of dancing and music and locals, who jigged and sang over their pints of Harp and gnawed chicken bones. Dust rose from the boards and I never heard a single ghost joke. The whole night became another Leap story by morning, and these last couple of months it's evolved a few sub-plots of its own. And nothing awful happened at all.

There aren't many work days left before I leave, but I still go up the hill of a morning with my nose running in the wind. In Spencer's cottage I drag the biro across the page, trying to write this novel, the one full of all the stories I grew up with, the digressions my grandmother managed to slip between verses of Browning, the things I overheard during an insomniac childhood, the things my parents told me, half choking with laughter, while the meat and three veg was still a lump in our chests of a Sunday noon. The rain comes and stays. I get postcards full of sky and water. I look up and that grim old place is there.

Janine Burke

TUSCANY'S TALENT TO A MUSE

The bells woke us. January 26, Australia Day. A bright winter morning in Florence with blue skies and a white sun. We're not here on holidays, we're here to talk culture. It's the Antipodean connection — Australian writers, artists and travellers in Tuscany.

The conference is the brainchild of Gaetano Prampolini and Christine Hubert, lecturers in foreign literature at Florence University. Florence City Council and the Arts Association of the region have funded it, writers and academics are zooming into town — David Malouf from his home in Tuscany, Shirley Hazzard from New York, Peter Porter from London, Desmond O'Grady from Rome, the rest of us from Melbourne, Sydney and the far north.

"I want it to be," says the ebullient Prampolini, "a party."

It's a belated Bicentenary present, the chance to celebrate our love affair with Tuscany. We've lived here, written poems or books, painted the landscape, studied the language, eaten some of the best meals of our lives … the attachment is so strong it's turned into something of a phenomenon.

Prampolini came to Australian writing through his interest in the way American writers treated Italy. The difference, he found, was that the Australian attitude was more open and equitable. Unlike Henry James, we felt in no danger of being seduced. We were explorers — ingenuous, but not prepared to be victims of a sophisticated culture. We were eager to learn and we wanted to stay.

Perhaps this accounts for the number of Australians who now call Tuscany home. There are recent arrivals like Greg Page, who runs artists' studios in the Chianti and who sold his farm to do it, and the expatriate generation like painter Jeffrey Smart, who settled years ago in the region. (Our most famous Australian Tuscan, Germaine Greer, had declined an invitation to attend.)

Then there are the commuters, like Malouf, who divides his time between the village of Campagnatico and Sydney's Chippendale. "I just walk in," he says of his Tuscan home, "and everything's set up for work."

Attitudes are changing. For Hazzard, Italy was the great escape from the aridity of Australia life in the 1950s. Relief marked her arrival, need made her stay. For my generation of post-war baby boomers, the urge was not to flee but to savour, to enjoy and to come home. Home was not such a bad place to be.

Historian Richard White, of Sydney University, points out that air travel and cheaper fares are putting an end to the rites of passage leaving Australia once involved. The long sea journey of the past with ample time for reflection and anticipation must have made Australia seem (thankfully for some) a very distant place indeed.

The point of the conference is that all the journeying is bearing fruit. Writers and artists who spend time in Tuscany these days want to share, rather than shore themselves up. A good example of this is Paretiao, Arthur Boyd's home, generously lent by him to the Australia Council, where artists come to soak up the culture. The work they produce is exhibited in Australia and often in Italy too.

I began my novel *Second Sight* there, which ended as a homage to the transforming powers of the light and the landscape. Painters like Anne Thompson, Dom de Clario and John Neeson have been similarly inspired.

Networks of exchange are forming, barriers are beginning to break down. The Australians who have passed through Tuscany over the years are a weird mob. Around the turn of the century, Randolph Bedford, entrepreneur extraordinaire, discovered the "other" Tuscany, off the beaten track of the guide books.

He decided Tuscany was just like home and the cover of the book he wrote about it shows a swaggie relaxing in front of a classical arch. There was Louise Mack, who wrote Mills and Boon romances while editing Florence's English language newspaper in the twenties. Jack Lindsay spent his time chatting with Norman Douglas about D.H. Lawrence while Marjorie Barnard and Ethel Turner came to see the Renaissance with their own eyes.

But were we overwhelmed by the magnificence of our surroundings? The impish Bernard Hickey detected a cringe-tinge. Perhaps it was the fault of the architecture. After all, the conference was held in the Palazzo Vecchio, the thirteenth century fortress in the heart of Florence, and now its town hall. Outside, workmen were digging up Etruscan ruins while Michelangelo's David looked on.

Amid all the talk, a healthy balance emerged. Hazzard's hymn of praise for Tuscan culture and its humanising effect on all who imbibe it was matched by Malouf's robust account of his first impressions of Florence. Too austere and refined. Give him the chaos of Naples any day.

Porter's lyrical recollections were preceded by White's ironic presentation of that institution of Australian suburbia in the sixties, the slide night after the Grand Tour. (He credited the slides to his in-laws.) O'Grady eulogised Malaparte and Italian academic Francesco Binni castigated the Aussies for not parleying the lingo well enough.

We were pleased and surprised to be there, we were nervous and got headcolds, we ate and drank and talked too much. In the interstices were the glowing moments of personal discovery.

I remember Adelaide Writers' Week last year when Kate Grenville, Joan London and I walked down a long straight road next to a vineyard. Did we talk literature? High art? Mainly we spoke of children, lovers, insomnia, the weather and the little clutch of worries rolled up in our stomachs. It may not have been the weeks' greatest intellectual buzz, but it was certainly one of the warmest.

The Tuscans had been hospitable to us again. It seems we owe them a lot. For writers and artists, Tuscany has played a role in the spirit of their work, providing that necessary dislocation, the long view, in which we see ourselves and where we come from with clarity and detachment. It made us realise our imagination, setting it free.

That, perhaps, was our gift to them. For the capacity audience made up of students and teachers, painters and poets and the amazed Australian tourist who stumbled in and stayed, there was a sense of homecoming, as the long kilometres evaporated and we found what we had in common, rather than what divided us.

Helen Garner

IN PARIS

The apartment was on the fourth floor. The building had no lift. On his day off the man lay on the mattress that served as a sofa and read, slowly and carefully, all the newspapers of his city. The tall windows were open on to the balcony. Every twenty minutes a bus swerved in to the stop down below, and the curtain puffed past his face. At two o'clock the woman came into the living room with her boots on.

"I feel like going for a walk," she said.

"*Bon. D'accord,*" said the man.

"Want to come with me?"

"*Tu vas où?*"

"Up to Sacré Coeur and back. Not far."

"*Ouf,*" said the man. "All those steps." He put one paper down and unfolded the next.

"Oh, come on," said the woman. "Won't you come? I'm bored."

"I don't want to go down into the street," said the man. "I have to go down there every day. I get sick of it. Today I feel like staying home."

The woman pulled a dead leaf off the potplant. "Just for an hour?" she said.

"Too many tourists," said the man. "You go. I'll have a little sleep. Anyway it's going to rain."

Late in the afternoon the man went into the kitchen and opened the refrigerator. He looked inside it, then shut it again. He walked across the squeaking parquet to the bedroom. The woman was lying on her stomach reading a book by the light of a shaded lamp. Her wet boots stood in the corner by the window.

"There's nothing to eat," said the man. "No one went to the market."

The woman looked up. "What about the fish?"

"Yes, the fish is there."

"We can eat the fish, then."

"There's nothing to have with it."

The woman marked her place with one finger.

"What happened to the brussels sprouts?" she said. "Did the others eat them last night?"

"No."

"Well, let's have fish and brussels sprouts."

Before she had finished the sentence the man was shaking his head.

"Why not?"

"Fish and green vegetables and never eaten together."

"What?"

"They are not eaten together."

The woman closed the book. "People have salad with fish. That's green."

"Salad is different. Salad is a separate course. It is not served on the same plate."

"Can you explain to me," said the woman, "the reason why fish and green vegetables must not be eaten together?"

The man looked at his hand against the white wall. "It is not done," he said. "They do not complement each other. Fish and potatoes, yes. *Frites. Pommes de terre au four.* But not green vegetables."

"It's getting on for dinner time," said the woman. She turned on her back and clasped her hands behind her head. "The others will be back soon."

"I don't know what to do," said the man. He moved his feet closer together and pushed his hands into his pockets.

"If I were you," said the woman. "If I were you and it was my turn to cook, and if there was nothing to eat except fish and green vegetables, do you know what I'd do? I'd cook fish and green vegetables. That's what I'd do."

"*Ecoute*," said the man. "There are always good chemical and aesthetic reasons behind customs."

"Yes, but what *are* they?"

"I'm sure if we looked it up in the *Larousse Gastronomique* it would be explained."

The woman got off the low bed and went to the window in her socks and T shirt. She looked out.

"I'm hungry," she said. "Where I come from, we just eat what's there."

"And it is not a secret," said the man, "that where you come from the food is barbaric."

The woman kept her back to the room. "My mother cooked nice food. We had nice meals."

"Chops," said the man. "Hamburgers. I heard you telling my mother. '*La bouffe est dégueulasse*', you said. That's what you said."

"I said '*était*'. It was. It used to be. But it's not any more. It's not now."

The man took a set of keys out of his pocket and began to flip them in and out of his palm.

"Aren't there any onions?" said the woman, still looking out the window.

"No. Not even onions."

"I don't see," said the woman, "that you've got any choice. What choice have you got? Unless you cook the fish by itself, or just the sprouts."

"There would not be enough for everybody."

The woman turned round from the grey window. "Why don't you go out into the kitchen and cook it up. Cook what's there. Just cook it up and see what happens. And if the others don't like it they can take their custom elsewhere."

The man took a deep breath. He put the keys back in his pocket. He scratched his head until his hair stood up in a crest. "*J'ai mal fait mon marché*," he said. "I should have planned better. We should have —"

"For God's sake," said the woman. She leaned against the closed window. "What's the matter with you? It's only food."

The man put his bare foot on the edge of the mattress and bounced it once, twice.

"*Tu vois?*" he said. "*Tu vois comment tu es?* 'Only food'. No French person would ever, ever say 'It's only food'."

"But it *is* only food," said the woman. "In the final analysis that's what it *is*. It's to keep us alive. It's to stop us from feeling hungry for a couple of hours so we can get our minds off our stomachs and go about our business. And all the rest is only decoration."

"*Oh là là*," said the man. "*Tu es —*"

He flattened his hair with one hand, and let his hand fall to his side. Then he turned and walked back into the kitchen. He opened the refrigerator. The fish lay on its side on a white plate. He opened the cupboard under the window. The brussels sprouts, cupped in their shed outer leaves, sat on a paper bag on the bottom shelf. The man stood in the middle of the room and looked from one open door to the other, and back again.

Marion Halligan

ALIGOT

It's a nice conceit, standing on a hill, contemplating a lifetime's nourishment. Only a vegetarian could do it with complete equanimity, and even he not altogether, since Monselet says the fruits screamed when bitten. I was imagining myself in such a position, specially enjoying the prospect of cheeses dotted around like rocks and the cheerful beasts that gave milk for them, when I began to think, where will I situate this hill? In what place shall I stand and gather the ghosts of all these good things around me?

Not in Australia, though I am patriotic enough. I once played South Africa in the Empire Day pageant. Each of us had to wave a floral emblem and recite a verse that summed our country up.

Mine ended, "there blooms my own white heath". The family went for a walk in the bush the Sunday before in order to find something appropriate, by guesswork; in those days not only did the sun not set on the Empire, it was all right to pick native flora. People came home from bushwalks with bunches of gumtips to put in vases: pinkish-olive and bronze new leaves and eucalyptus scents. And being South Africa in the pageant didn't cause any identity problems. You were Australian but you were British too; England was the mother country and all her colonies were your siblings.

Well, we all got older and wiser about that. But when I grew up and went and lived in France I loved its countryside, not simply because it's beautiful but because its civilisation is so sympathetic. I identify with it. In *Spider Cup* a character says that her favourite landscape has at least one Romanesque church in it. I gave her that line out of my own feelings. So I'm going to situate my hill in the Rouergue, a hill whose fortifications though crumbling are stone and not pastry, because not only is it my favourite place in the world for eating, my spirit is nourished there. It's not my home and never will be; I'll always be a foreigner and have no real rights in it, but the locals are kind, they tolerate this affection, may perhaps enjoy it, though you wouldn't want to presume.

Even the French are not always sure where the Rouergue is. It's south of the Auvergne, east of Bordeaux, south-east of the Périgord (abutting that territory of the Lot and the Dordogne that the English have made their own), north-west of Provence.//

The hotel at Conques is named after Sainte Foy. We ate lunch there: chicken galantine, pancakes with herbs, tournedos with artichoke bottoms, cheese, the local strawberries. A fairly standard menu; remember that even in the ninth century the place wasn't well known for its food. That's why they had to steal a money-spinning saint. But the strawberries were good; foods always have special flavour in the places they come from. This lunch was not as cheap as in the secret little villages, for Conques is on the tourist route and knows its own worth. The hotel was one of the dim polished bourgeois establishments. Like the Parisian pâtisseries, strict, orderly, full of the charm of their perfect functioning.

I forgot to mention the church's tympanum of the Last Judgment, best viewed at the setting sun. As usual the most entertaining is the people coming to bad ends: Saint Michael is weighing souls, with the devil trying to tip the scales in his favour; demons, one armed with a tool like a plumber's sink plunger, are stuffing the damned into the jaws of hell, a toothy grinning beast, to be met by Satan and his cohorts with a variety of tortures. Adulterous lovers are gloomily chained together. A hunter is being spit-roasted over a very nicely flaming wood fire. Maybe he shot songbirds. How amusing all this is now. How dull the calm rows of the saved being welcomed to the bosom of Abraham, under the smooth arcades of the celestial Jerusalem. These perceptions must have been reversed once, and that serene dullness devoutly to be wished. And as you gaze at them, their beauty moves you. They have beautiful faces, the saints and the saved, not like the ugly little doll-fetish in the treasure. They are the divine face of humanity.//

The *Green Guide* gives the tympanum three stars. I think it is one of the world's masterpieces. But then I do have a passion for the Romanesque. I see the beauty of Gothic architecture, but it is Romanesque that touches my heart. The little indignant men with egg-round faces on the Eglise de Perse, the capitals where the ordinary lives of people tell Bible stories, the plain round arches and solid walls: I love them dearly. They're all so intelligent.

I've been in Bangkok and admired the temples there, found them amazing pieces of architecture and moving too in an intellectual way, but I don't love them, they don't belong to me, I don't identify with them. I feel much the same about Asian food; it's delicious, I enjoy it very much, but it's not finally important to me. We're always being told to look to Asia, that this is the sphere of influence in which Australia lives, but my civilisation belongs to Europe.//

Pilgrimages were the tourism of the Middle Ages. And quite a flourishing business. (They still are, if you look at Lourdes, but then they had a monopoly of the tourist industry as well.) Those whose sins weighed heavy went seeking absolution; others travelled simply out of holiness, building up a credit balance. They could become a habit. These were difficult journeys, on foot or on horseback, and through inhospitable terrain — not often so easy-going as Chaucer's storytelling progress from London to Canterbury. Monasteries offered shelter at night, from the elements, from cut-purses and cut-throats, so you plotted your route accordingly. Tumblers and juggles frequented the stopping places and provided entertainment for the long nights.

One of the most barren and desolate parts of the route came just before Conques, on the high windswept plateau of the Aubrac, to the south of the Auvergne. Here a Flemish nobleman, having himself been fallen upon by brigands as he made his pilgrimage, set up a shelter in the charge of monk-knights to escort and protect the pilgrims passing through these dangerous regions. The dangers were elemental as well as human. Even on hot summer days when you've been sweltering in the river valleys you can find yourself freezing cold on these windy heights.

At Aubrac you can see remnants of the *dômerie*, a great square tower, a Romanesque church, and a sixteenth century building. It's amazing how young a sixteenth century building seems in the context.

Here, and at Saint Chély d'Aubrac, the great thing to eat is *aligot*. I think this is my favourite dish of the whole Rouergue. I like to imagine weary pilgrims falling upon it, but that's an anachronism. It's made of potatoes, garlic, cream and cheese, which should be *tôme de Cantal*, or of Laguiole; we're not far from those two cheese towns here. If I were condemned to eat only Laguiole and Cantal (they're similar large yellow cheeses eaten at various states of maturity, like cheddars) and Roquefort for the rest of my life, I could be content — especially if occasionally I were allowed a bit of fresh goat, a young Cabacou from Entraygues, say.

The *tôme* is the very fresh cheese, before it is salted and put into moulds to mature. You can buy it in Paris in a couple of shops off the rue Mouffetard which specialise in Auvergnat products, but in Australia you have to make do. And what's called *tôme* here isn't right, it's too soft and creamy.

This recipe will give you some idea of what eating *aligot* is like. Of course, my Aveyron cookbook says it cannot be made with any other kind of cheese than this "still supple" and unfermented Laguiole. But even if you were to buy some *tôme* utterly fresh, and with dangerous illegality jump on a plane with it and get it to your kitchen in no more than thirty-six hours, the *aligot* still would not taste the same. The potatoes, the butter, the cream, the garlic would all be quite different. And even if, with still more terrible illegality, you brought all those things as well, you would not have an absolutely authentic dish; the air, the atmosphere, whatever of *je ne sais quoi*, is against it. So you might as well go in for a bit of creative recreation anyway. Borrow and make it your own.

For instance I find that (I hardly dare write it) mozarella works quite well, and other cheeses could too. This is a recipe my daughter has worked out; she likes *aligot* and doesn't let being purist get in her way.

Aligot

900 g potatoes	*50 g unsalted butter*
250 g mozarella	*125 g cream*
3 cloves garlic, finely chopped	

Peel and cook potatoes, mash. Cut cheese in small squares.

In a large heavy frying pan put butter and cream and the minute they begin to bubble add the potato. Using two wooden spoons mix vigorously. Add cheese and mix, then add garlic and stir thoroughly until *aligot* is thick, stringy and smooth, with no cheesy lumps remaining. Serve immediately. It's not a dish to keep, or to reheat in microwaves; it needs to be fresh.

I think it should be served completely on its own, when you can sit and dreamily scoop it up in thoughtful forkfuls and wonder that something so simple should be so much greater than the sum of its parts. Between say a salad and a main course, a leg of lamb perhaps, with some beans, anyway a single green vegetable, or between some raw ham or salami and a salad. But if you insist on having meat with it serve something like a roast or a steak with a short sauce. *Aligot* is so rich on its own, adding a quite different sauce spoils it. The first time I ate it was between a trout and a thin little French steak, in a small hotel at Saint Chély d'Aubrac, built beside the stream that the fish had probably just come from.//

Aligot is a dish I need to eat from time to time. When I feel a certain edginess, and I think, mmm … an *aligot* would be good. So, when I stand on my hill and survey my lifetime's eating, there'll have to be a field or two of potatoes. And acres and acres of garlic.

My little hill in the Rouerge. My Rouerge. Not exactly the real one, over there in France, though it's similar. Its lineaments are pretty much the same, its topography, its history, its architecture. But the way I perceive these things is different; it's my own. The place doesn't belong to me the way it does to people who have invested their whole lives in living there. I'm no more than a pilgrim passing through, making supplication to its treasures. Bringing back not a cockle shell but a slice of grey slate patterned with moss. But in my head it belongs to me. It's my Rouergue of the imagination. Whatever's happening in the real one, mine's safe.

Alister Kershaw

BICYCLE RACES

Once again that old sick feeling of being unwanted is beginning to creep over me. Normally, we foreigners living in France get off pretty lightly: the natives take us in their stride; they watch us pouring mint sauce over our lamb with an indulgent smile, our inability to use the plusperfect subjunctive is met with a reassuring pat on the shoulder. But it would be a mistake to confuse their tolerance with weakness: there are some things which the French regard as downright provocative and, of these, nothing arouses their hatred and contempt more thoroughly than a disrespectful attitude toward bicycles. Criticise their cooking, their government, their climate or their morals — but, unless you want to be regarded as a real stinker, just lay off their bicycles, and, more especially, their bicycle races.

Well, I know it's all wrong but personally I can very soon be sated with bicycles. I incline to get tetchy when a gendarme orders me to pull into the side of the road and wait for three-quarters of an hour while a long string of cyclists goes trailing past; I decline to go into full mourning because so-and-so has failed to pedal as fast as what's-his-name. I have tried — I alone know how earnestly I have tried — to lash myself into a state of psychotic excitement over the spectacle of one bicycle creeping ahead of another but, deep down, I'm happier when curled up with a good book.

It all makes me realise that I can never truly integrate. Frenchmen can more easily conceive of a world without sunlight than a world without bicycle races. Fortunately for them, they don't have to. The main event — the Tour de France — begins, as nearly as I can work out, around about New Year's Day and terminates in late December. Simultaneously, no local mayor takes office, no village sweethearts get married, no prodigal son comes home without the event being celebrated by yet another bicycle race. Day or night, winter, spring, summer or autumn, somewhere in France a bicycle race is taking place and everyone for miles around is goggling at it — and the chances are that, at any given moment, there are no fewer than *twenty* bicycle races going on throughout the country or, if you include Corsica, twenty-one.

The bedridden and the infirm are not forgotten. Apart from a couple of lines on the back page to the effect that a mixed team of Russian and American astronauts have landed on Mars, the newspapers are virtually given over in their entirety to you know what. On the radio, a first performance of a hitherto unknown symphony by Beethoven is interrupted to bring one the news that a competitor in a race being held in a small Alpine hamlet has just had a flat tire. Not one whit behindhand, the cinema and television provide gripping shots of handlebars and powerful sequences of front-wheel spokes.

It's all very depressing, as I say, for foreigners like myself — not so much because we are oppressed by an hysterical tendency to cry like hurt chlidren whenever another bicycle flashes on the screen of our local cinema as because of our feeling of simply not belonging. Mind you, it's less hard on Australians than on anyone else. The French may not be very clear as to whether Sydney is a sheep station or the name of the Australian President but there isn't one that hasn't heard of Hubert Opperman. I can always explain my reluctance to watch bicycle races by saying that they're not worth looking at since he retired and there's an immediate murmur of sympathetic understanding.

Shane McCauley

OLD CITY, RHODES

Keen for an evening view
Of ancient ocean, we let
The motorbikes nearly skedaddle
Us, used by now to the flurry
Of Greek manouevres, indifference.

The only siege now is within,
Our English words taking on
New meanings, caught here
Like the "Alive Lombsters" advertised
In shops, taking back all
We had said of other tourists,
Realising that any traveller
Is to some extent lost.

Merchants survive conquerors.
Commerce has long sent philosophy
Back to kindergarten. Water-smoothed
Statues as opaque as memory
Here, early hunger subverts
Curiosity, and in these time-dirty
Streets, a remoteness and fear
Settles like a first day at school.

Clouds dim the sea to a grey skin,
A vast stagnant pool. The breeze
Drifts softly to Turkey.

Murray Bail

NOTEBOOK ENTRIES

29.6.70. From Heathrow in the red d/decker I felt myself swal-
lowed by the flat maze of narrow passageways as it closed in behind,
the reddish-brown brick, the blurred edges, grime and slate, and

channelled in a roundabout way into the heart of the city, where I found there was no "heart", no centre. A crowding-in quite different from Bombay and the other Indian cities. The architecture, the people going about their business, and — everywhere — advertisements displaying English words are related to me, though remote.

At the same time, seated upstairs with M. also silent, I felt "above it all" and — adding to the illusion — not being British, not part of all this.

Even the tramps and beggars who sleep out on benches and under bridges here wear a necktie. Usually maroon, dirty and loose. Strange irritation at vestiges of formality. When they ask for money I feel like not giving any.

Here where the water runs out of the bath anticlockwise ...

Some days the stagnancy of the British and everything they've left standing resembles one of those chipped enamel tubs raised from the ground by iron paws. And the water is lukewarm and dirty, grey, with more than a few pubic hairs stuck to the sides, gurgling when it runs out like a tired old man clearing his throat.

Perhaps this irritation at British complacency is only disquiet at my own nothingness here — instead of thinking of people normally (i.e. individually).

There is indifference towards me. From all sides. It can be an advantage.

Often I feel foolish ogling art. Especially after stepping forward and then respectfully back after reading a title. (The way people nearby clear their throats as in a church gets on my nerves.)

There was always a general untidiness about London. Now the garbage strike in its fifth week, producing enormous piles of rubbish in the streets, only confirms the idea that London would smell like any large Third World city, Calcutta, say, if it were in the tropics.

When I think of "Australia" I first see its shape. It is quickly followed by scenes of slow-moving dryness, muted colours, and some of the great white trees. Of people in general, it is often young, flushed mothers in sleeveless cotton dresses yanking or carrying children on the hot city asphalt.

Homesickness: habits of a landscape acquired over time.

29.6.71. One year in U.K. // There is always enough commonsense here to despise it. British gentleness and reason. Complacency.

At least the good sense and dreary stability of England, which extends into literature, provokes in me an opposing, forceful stance, which in turn is so abhorrent to the English it is rejected out of hand.

Living in England I find I am using the semicolon more, as if all statements here are qualified.

Oxford. Strolling through the ancient quadrangles etc. and actively resisting being encrusted with tradition. Blowing my nose, talking loudly.

Paris. 24.12.71. Staggering bureaucracy, an extension of the baroque, like the proliferation of gargoyles and caryatids in French architecture.

A sociological difference between the deck-chairs in London parks and those in Paris of ornate wrought iron: the former are for resting people, the latter for hard and aware types.

Signs in French metro carriages requesting people to stand for (in this order): 1. People injured from war. 2. Civilians who are blind or injured. 3. Pregnant women.

Homeless men lying in rows over the subway gratings for the warm air.

Fairground, Paris. Lifesize photos of strippers in 3-D following me as I walked past. And young Africans from France's colonies happily ramming pimply French girls in the dodgem-cars.

At least Sartre, Debray etc. commit themselves on the streets instead of penning a letter to the *Times*.
Tennis courts filled with snow.

Emerging from three floors of Francis Bacon at the Grand Palais it was the streets, traffic and trees of the bright-aired everyday world that seemed less "real".

1973. White crosses cover the hillside (Verdun) in mathematical rows like vineyards. Soldiers are drilled into disciplined ranks, rows of fighting men. In battle the geometry is violently broken — the regiment gassed, exploded, scattered into chaotic fragments. Afterwards their remains are returned to regimented rows, the military cemetery, to "bear witness".

As if, after all, order came about through war; a return to order.

Even the car junkyards are neat, the wrecks arranged in precise rows (Switzerland).

Milan. Melodramatic motor-cyclists. Histrionic conversationalists on pavements, under columns, seated at cafe tables.

The hearse with coffin doing 90 mph on the autostrada.

Venice. Senses from previous experience are unprepared. The Grand Canal sparkling in the sun carries such a weight of water, a broad curving street flooded to a great depth: not even Turner or Canaletto suggest the mass of liquid — their canals are the surface. And boats instead of cars, pedestrians and traffic lights. Aside from a few footsteps and voices the only sound is the thick chug of boats.

First thing I saw as I reached the top of the Duomo after climbing the 464 steps was the word AUSTRALIA scratched in the marble.

Throughout Italy and France the same faces in medieval and Renaissance paintings can be seen moving about outside in the streets, the markets, behind the wheels of cars. By now only small variations operate within a set of established conditions. Has the Australian face arrived yet? So far it has settled on the long jaw, often with a small mouth, jug ears. A long face, solid bones, strong teeth.

Rome. Wanting to look at every face passing. Short men with deep dry lines running amok. Details pulled the wrong way, stretched, squashed, bloated. Large fleshy noses. Or pale tight faces with eyes unusually close together. Wealthy women in furs: faces guttered with wrinkles, the large roman nose, layers of powder, bold lipstick. Men of smiling ugliness stepping out from corners or doorways with suede coats, colour slides or maps for sale.

And the city itself has its past exposed like old teeth.

The ceiling and end wall (Sistine Chapel) shows what a single man has in his power to achieve.

The Vatican. The grandeur of the centre, a kind of hollowness.

Guide with thin moustache, button nose, bulbous dark eyes and a hat he never took off. Short busy man who learned forward as he walked, kicking back his feet. Every famous object was either a miracle or a masterpiece. He loved Rome; but no superstitious, almost primitive, in a neat suit.

Guide: "Do you all speak English?"
Australian, loudly: "Can you manage Australian?"
    A form of pride.

Vivian Smith

THE TRAVELLER RETURNS

We do not know if gods preside
but I believe in angels seeing clouds
pierced by rays through pencilled distant slopes.
After slow cathedrals, pilgrim towns
Sydney's violent sky can offer this

moment that catches us still unprepared.

Murillo's dark madonna knew such cloud.

Watching the Pacific lick its samples of gold leaf
I voice once more my disbelief aloud.

Trails and Trials:
The Rituals and
Conventions of Travel

Peter Conrad

SIGNS AND PASSWORDS

Society has always seemed to me an idea dreamed up by conspirators. The tribe adheres thanks to shared understandings, which never need to be voiced; it celebrates its uniqueness by the exchange of private jokes, by perfecting a dialect of signals. I used to be amazed, before I could understand the language, by the sight of a whole world which conversed in Portuguese. Everything was unintelligible: I couldn't even read the gestures, and because of their vehemence — having come from the land of laconicism, where only madmen or migrants talked with their hands — I used to assume that people were quarrelling when they were only being exuberant.

These days I know what they are saying, but that's no consolation, since all societies are like foreign languages. You can learn the words and perhaps even manage the grammar, but will never be able to colour vowels as the natives do, or achieve some tiny glottal or lingual effect which defines the difference. I was amazed, when struggling with Portuguese, at the inability of my tongue to roll an r, or to sibillate — as the natives were so properly doing — without a spray of spit. I cheered myself up by remembering that I had the same difficulties with English. I would never (though I admit it was not one of my ambitions) be able to say "Thank you *so* much" in the precise way Oxford colleagues did when a dinner plate was set down before them or taken away, inflecting the adverb with an emphatic squeeze in exactly inverse proportion to the amount of gratitude they were feeling; but equally I could not bring myself to forgo the formalities as New Yorkers did and demand things with an undertone not of threat but of harried urgency, anxious to move on to the next item in an over-scheduled existence. // Every group has its idiolect, unintelligible — or liable to grievous misinterpretation — once you reach the border.

It is a world of small worlds with words as their disputed frontiers. You move in and out of shambolic, accidental places which, like the leaky boxes in the shantytown, are a home to someone. Every speck or spot on the globe is a centre to whichever group speaks its language and knows the stories about it. Since everywhere is convinced of its own centrality, there is no real centre anywhere. But this is a truth, like that of our homelessness, which we would sooner die than recognise. So we reorganise geography and make the map radiate out from wherever we happen to find ourselves.//

The mind is its own cartographer. The maids in Lisbon divide the world into three regions: *terra, Lisboa,* and *lá fora. Terra,* the terra firma of home, is where they are not. It is the village in the mountains they have had to leave, to which they return every summer for religious processions. *Lisboa* is where they have come to work and where they spend their adult lives, but it is never allowed to be home. *Lá fora* is everywhere else, and is of no consequence; it means, dismissively, "out there". The housekeeper Rosalina once asked me what countries Britain had on its frontier. She was merely expressing a polite interest, and I could see was not expecting much from the answer. But when I told her it had no other country on its borders, she gaped. She assumed that somewhere or other it must abut on Spain.

Whenever she notices some extraneous event on the television news — a war or a flood or an earthquake or a royal wedding — she asks — "Is that out there?" As soon as we tell her it is, she is pacified: out there, it is beyond needing to be thought about. We conserve our patch of reality by deeming all the rest unreal.

How do you earn the right to graduate from out there to in here? Usually there are gruesome initiations. The cost of tribal membership is scars.

John Forbes

EUROPE: A GUIDE

for Ken Searle

Greece is like a glittering city
though only in a political speech

but Italians believe in *bella figura*
& mis-use the beach. In Germany there's

Kraftwerk & acres of expressionist kitsch.
Oil-rich Norwegians don't need to ski

they just like it & Iceland is famous
for its past. Doing their physical jerks,

a quiet pride permeates the Swedes.
Denmark is neither vivid nor abrupt

& Belgians have a ring-side seat
to observe the behaviour of the Dutch.

The French invented finesse but it's
their self-regard that intrigues us.

We pity the English, though they get on
our wick, presuming to understand us

& Scotland is old fashioned like a dowry
but unusual, like nice police; mention

Ireland & you've already said enough.
The Spaniards are not relaxed about sex

& tourists are attracted to this. Some
Portuguese exist entirely on a diet of fish

but rich cakes, finance & guest workers
sustain the Swiss. Consult my *By Trailbike*

& Hot-air Balloon Through Central Europe
for details of the Austrians & Czechs

but don't forget Bavaria's Octoberfest
or that Rococco architecture was meant

to be passed out under, pissed, & it's
aesthetically edifying to do this.

For the rest; give Russia a miss,
the Poles will appreciate hard currency

& the latest discs & the fleshpots of
Split will leave you a physical wreck.

This guide stops short at the Balkans,
as it omits the Finns. I don't apologise —

many guides to Australia will include
New Zealand or leave out Tasmania

No doubt some thorough American manual
can give you the lowdown on Europe's margins

But mine, designed for only one traveller
is better written & much more shorter.

Besides, if you remove the art, Europe's
like the US, more or less a dead loss

& though convenient for walking
& picturesque, like the top of a *Caran*

D'Arche pencil case or a chocolate box,
what do you make of a landscape that

reminds you of itself? Is this why
the people are sure they're typical not

standard? I can't advise you on this
but I know how I enjoyed myself: though

knocked out by why convinced me
"Great Art" without inverted commas is

(tho' not because of this) I hung around
with other Australians & hit the piss.

Tony Maniaty

DISCOVERING THE WORLD FROM A COCOON

Travel may broaden the mind, but it helps to be physically small in Catherine Domain's bookstore on the Ile Saint-Louis. In just fifteen square metres of floorspace she's managed to cram at least 10,000 volumes — new and secondhand, exclusively on travel — in shelves stretching three metres to the ceiling. It's something from Dickens: the tottering piles of books, and through tiny windows the world outside.

"Everyone," she insists, "finally comes here. Diplomats and journalists, school children doing projects, authors, company executives and military types. When they want more information on foreign countries, they all come to me."

Publishers too, for advice. Customers write from China and Egypt, others just drift into her shop Ulysse, at 35 Rue St Louis en l'Ile — the oldest quarter of Paris.

"Anything on Brazilian city planning in the early 1960s?" I ask — not a trick question, although it sounds like one.

Catherine Domain directs me to a lower shelf where I find three volumes on the topic. I'm an Australian, writing a novel here, I explain — she smiles at my request, which is not only easy but fairly mundane.

"Once a lady bought a map of South America," Domain says. "She'd lost her son there and wanted to try to find him with a pendulum. I mean, she was desperate …"

"A pendulum?"

"It was very weird, but I gave her the map and she dangled the pendulum over it, trying to find him …"

"And?"

She shrugs, with more pragmatism than hope. Still in her forties, Domain has been almost everywhere and seen both the obscure and commonplace, and some of the most beautiful sights on Earth.

"When I arrived in Kathmandu in Nepal for the first time, in 1966 — it was fantastic, an absolute marvel. But money and tourism have changed all that …"

We sit on the doorstep and watch the passing parade: the local

French clutching their manic poodles, and wealthy Germans and Americans licking their ice-creams.

"Now the economic situation means that young people are very cocooned, they don't just take off like we used to in the sixties. Instead, they go away on vacation for a few weeks — or else they watch television," she sighs, "the world on your plate at lunchtime!"

Domain's travels began early. Born in Algeria of French parents — and educated in England, Europe and the United States — she spent eight years roaming the world, including three weeks in Australia.

"I thought Cairns was fascinating," she recalls, "just like the Wild West. And I saw this lovely beach, and nobody in the water, so naturally I jumped in. 'You're risking your life!' a man yelled and dragged me to the beach." She bursts into laughter. "It was the stinger season, of course."

She found Australians a bit rough, but "true people" and just a little crazy. "Spaghetti sandwiches!" she cries with mock horror. At one stage she even applied to migrate, but in 1971 the Ulysse bookshop took over her life.

"I'd been looking all over Paris and saw this — cute but very small. Then I looked up and saw Ulysse and thought, that's the name for me. They had about five books and a big table, and around it were sitting three men playing poker, and one of them raised an eyebrow and said, 'It's for sale'." The next day she bought the place.

While we talk, the customers squeeze past to browse and buy. "I opened at exactly the right time," Domain says. "In the early seventies, when everyone else in France started to travel."

One man in a crumpled shirt wants a book on cycling in Asia, an Englishwoman in an impeccable suit pays 1500 francs (about $300) for a nineteenth-century volume on the Crusades and a French girl asks for something on trekking in Bolivia and Peru. All leave content.

For my part, I discover thirty-odd books in the Australian section — including a 1911 copy of *l'Australie* for 190 francs, or $38. One illustration features sheep crossing a creek: "Moutons traversant un billabong, district de la Riverina, Nouvelle-Galles du Sud."

Also there: *Sydney Beaches* with photos by some of Australia's greats — Max Dupain, Laurence le Guay, Harold Casneaux and David Moore. One shows a muscle-bound surfer and a girl in a two-piece: "Surfboards, built of plywood sheets, although sometimes sixteen feet (five metres) long, are no great burden from clubhouse to water. They're designed to carry one, but a skilful operator can take a passenger — if she holds tight and doesn't argue."

Last year Domain opened Ulysse II in the same street. It is devoted entirely to travelling in France — for both French people and foreigners. "I try to treat France like a foreign country," she says — which I suspect is a lot easier when you speak six languages fluently.

And I wonder aloud about travellers, as types. In one of Malcolm Lowry's novels, the main character dreads the very thought of leaving. "Travel to him was the extension of every anxiety, which man tried to get rid of by having a quiet home. A continual fever, an endless telephone alarm, perpetual heart attack ..."

But in fact, counters Domain, lonely people are often the best travellers: thrown back on their resources, they learn to mix with the local culture. People in tour groups are definitely the worst, she says.

At this point a black Harley-Davidson comes down the Rue St Louis, and pulls up with the motor rumbling. Domain embraces the rider, a girl in black leather with a black helmet and black sunglasses — quite a colourful sight.

After a couple of minutes the girl roars off, and Domain turns to me with a broad smile.

"That was my sister," she says, "just back from the States."

"Really?"

"Yes, she's much younger than me."

We watch the glistening Harley turn a corner and disappear; together we return to the old shop. Domain glances at her chaotic world of books, and figures it's time to get a bigger place.

"You can't keep travelling forever," she says happily, with a nod back to the street. "It's not a whole life."

Kate Grenville

HAVING A WONDERFUL TIME

There's something about travel that brings on generalisations about the meaning of life. Maybe that's why we do it. Every departure's like a brushing acquaintance with death: getting in practice.

Even at the bus station in Earls Court my bedsitter seems like an abstraction on another planet. Desk here chair there bed here. All the flimsy brown paper makeshifts fall away and leave us shivering. Standing by our bags waiting for the bus we eye each other. At the end of the next three days some of these strangers will have become people, and who knows what might happen? Anything can happen. Three days on a bus is not an attractive prospect, but think of it this way and it will be an adventure. Think of it like that.

Yes John it will be like that. An adventure. Being your second-best woman has not been an adventure. Being your Wednesday woman has only been fun on Wednesdays.

You know what your trouble is, you're too introspective you know that? Snap out of yourself a bit. Travel. Do you the world of good.

There are a lot of Australians going to Athens, like migratory birds. That girl over there with the flat face looks Australian. That low shining forehead, that sharp chin, that lipless slit of mouth. Her huge breasts are contained in a well-upholstered bra like a comfortable armchair. The point of each nipple is grubby where they've brushed against things.

Is it because I'm one of them that I have to sneer?

The colossus in the check shirt looks American. His enormous hiking boots have curved up at the toes and look like cobblestones on the ends of his legs. Great arms like hams, this man's a real meat-eater. Beside him, a dark, dapper little man sits neatly on a neat pack with not a loose strap anywhere, as tidy as a block of butter. He sits and methodically eats a sandwich and makes something in me shrivel.

Is that what you mean, getting out of myself? Seeing how the other half lives?

I've got to get a window seat. Three days and two nights of falling into the aisle will not be an adventure. Or if it is, in my generosity I'll let some other poor bugger have the pleasure. Get the elbows in there. Pretend you don't see them thinking she jumped the queue the bitch. A foot on the bottom step and the bag casually held at the side blocking any bright ideas from the crowd behind me. Okay now. In we go quick. Not too far back, it bounces. Not over the axle where the floor runs in a ridge. This one will do nicely thanks. Now sit back and look innocent.

The man who sits beside me is like a blond Greek god. I imagine his pectorals erect launching a javelin. An adventure! We exchange hellos. We establish that we are both going to Athens. We establish that he is Greek, but studies in England.

"I study to be a pilot."

"That must be interesting."

"It is all right."

We're still in dreary Penge or somewhere but the driver is giving us a taste of Greece. The beginning of our journey coils around and swallows its tail, and suburban London stands amazed, blank windows exclaiming an empty O as the shimmering thump of bouzouki music fills the bus.

"What is your name," I ask.

"Costas. Means King," he explains with a modest smirk.

I think of my collection of conversation stoppers. I knew someone once who lived in that street. I bought this suit five years ago for ten pounds.

"I have a friend who learnt to fly," I say.

That's not much good. I knew a man once who lived in that street.

"He had to learn morse code, do you learn that too?"

Costa leans in impatiently.

"What?"

"Morse code."

I enunciate so clearly that in a moment of sudden silence the whole bus hears.

"Moose …?"

"No, morse, you know, dot dot dash dash. With a little machine …"

I mime the flickering wrist of a morse operator. Costas watches stonily. Dot dot dot dash dash dash dot dot dot. Help I am sinking. Mayday. Costas calls out in Greek and the driver turns up the volume of the bouzouki.

Is it really such a good thing to have quite that number of St Marys and St Christophers and St Whoever-Else and rosary beads and bunches of goodluck garlic dancing against the front window of the bus? And that large efficient-looking clock trying to tell us it's one o'clock at half-past nine? Never mind, it's got to be right twice a day. And we can eat the garlic if we get marooned. We going anywhere near Transylvania?

Here I am. Travelling. Broadens the mind. Maybe I should be taking notes. Look at these houses. Like boxes. Not very original. The hedges. What would I say about the hedges? Very neighbourly way that one is clipped like a poodle to exactly the point where it becomes the nextdoor hedge and then sprouts wildly. Not an inch more. A man is trimming with an electric hedge-clipper, standing back to admire before he hovers in to take off one last errant leaf. Well another day gone, anyway. Yairs, spent the weekend in the garden.

On the boat across the Channel there's a sudden sense of being in the team. "You're on the bus too aren't you," whispers the girl with the grubby nipples. "Do you know what we're supposed to do?" A gangling man in front has reached the tea counter and clutches the top of his head with his arm as he says, "Aaaaaaah, cn Oi ev two cips a coffee? Na tye?"

When we get off the boat there's a long unexplained Greek wait. I decide with profundity that waiting bears the same relation to travelling as matter does to antimatter and fight the suspicion that the bus has left without us. Another Australian girl with a face like Head Nurse, wearing a singlet and tight shorts, follows me around the wharf.

"Then I got the boat to Cairo, only twenty-seven pounds. Then, there was this train down to Khartoum and from there I got the plane to Algiers. Really dirty. The toilets, well you wouldn't credit it."

On the wharf where we stand hopelessly waiting, a group of Americans is also waiting to be saved from the empty glare of this hazy non-place. They stand in a circle talking to each other with their bright backpacks ringing them around, like colourful humped birds. Everyone's on the move.

Keep looking, keep looking. What are you after anyway says John. You want to learn to relax.

France is a blue smog haze. Great tangles of pipes and tanks twisting solidly up into the sky, huge blank buildings the colour of nothing as we speed past. Tall dumb chimneys forever point the way: up there it's up there. Neat triangular heaps of slag rise out of the mist, monumental, lingering. As one is left behind, fading into distance, another takes its place. Or is it the same one fooling us?

Before John there was Jim. My wife doesn't understand me. Before Jim there was Jerry. Baby you're dynamite, see you round. Before Jerry there was Jack. You're a million dollars baby, don't call me at home.

"Then I got the plane to Madrid and from there I got the morning train to Lisbon. That would have been the twenty-eighth of July, no I beg your pardon the twenty-ninth. Then I got a bus to this little place called Ortago, quite nice but the toilets were that smelly. Then must have been the second of August I took the plane from Lisbon to Barcelona."

Electricity pylons walk solidly off into the haze, striding with long praying-mantis legs, unswerving. Some march along with a bundle held aloft in each hand, others like amputees hold only one set of wires. The power must get through.

It's starting to get warm in here. Around me a great rustling of paper bags has begun and in a moment the air is full of orange peel and cheese sandwich. I root in my own bag and bring out an apple. On second thoughts I snap out of myself and get a bit involved and offer another one to Costas. He takes it with hardly a glance. Gotta learn to give a little, give and take, that's what it's all about.

In front of me two more Australian girls with tight shirts and closed smug faces are really getting organised. Long loaves of pre-buttered bread. Salami. Tomatoes and the right kind of knife, no squelchy mess here oh no, these girls didn't come down in the last shower. Even salt, in a shaker with a special lid so it doesn't spill. Paper napkins, I don't believe it. They sit munching while around me others spill biscuits out of burst paper bags, dribble oranges on their legs, and spray exploding drink cans into the back of my neck.

"Gee sorry."

The two young men behind are looking apprehensive and also trying not to snicker.

"That's okay."

They are polite and watch each others' mouths as they speak, watch mine as I speak, although they are not lip-reading deaf mutes. They are a pair of nice boys, off to Athos, they tell me, to check out the monasteries. No women are allowed anywhere on the peninsula of Athos, they inform me, not even female animals. They cannot stop themselves snickering at this. Boats containing women are forbidden to come closer than half a mile to the shore. It's almost enough to give you the feeling women might have something after all. Wonder if they strip you off at the entrance to make sure. And what is it they really get up to in there? Little leather lap-laps like the Masons maybe, standing displaying their paraphernalia at cock-crow.

Afternoon wears on. Are we still in France? Belgium? Luxembourg?

The drama of a frontier: this is Germany. Everyone's important with their passports. Head Nurse with her trembling thighs in shorts shows me her visas. Look I've been here and here and here and the toilets were that smelly. Travel broadens the bum.

Night falls and the Australians in front produce air cushions and blow them up. No doubt about these Aussies they've got themselves organised. How come I didn't turn out like that? A blanket over the knees, snug as a bug in a rug.

Hey what kind of bitch are you? Where's your sense of adventure? Your joy in the rich pageant of multi-faceted humanity? The glowing tapestry woven with a thousand gleaming strands which is Life? Where were you when the smiles were handed out? Huh?

Costas twitches and slumps beside me, trying to sleep. Bugger him if I'm going to offer my seat.

At some dead time of the night we stop for petrol and pisses. Grubby tits is clutching herself between the legs; ooooh a I've gotta go. We line up in the toilet staring at our reflections in a leprous mirror, listening to each other. Unbuckle unbutton unzip. Aaaaah.

Everybody has tried the coffee machine beside the bus. English money doesn't work and nor does French. No one has any German money. When everyone has tried and gone away, the bug twins come over and produce a little bag marked *Foreign Money*. They stand sipping coffee while around them we all blink blearily. Sorry, that was all we had, they say. But here have a sip.

In the morning when we wake we're twisting laboriously through mountains. The Andes? The Alps? The Himalayas? It's raining. Drops streak sadly down my window and on the windscreen huge wipers bend gracefully into each other like dancers. De de de de DAH, de DAH, de DAH.

Around a bend in the road a deep valley spears off into mist, a twisting V weaving between interlocked spurs. Above us the ridges claw the dull sky with serrated edges like a child's scribble. The bus is very silent.

As the valleys flatten out and the rain stops, the bus comes to life. The bug twins squash the air out of their cushions with a rude noise. They tuck the blanket beneath housewive's double chins and fold it carefully. Then they produce little bottles and clean — cleanse — their faces, and settle back without any expectation of surprise for another day. Oh yairs, we did Europe.

The last night with John, before goodbye forever, he said as we got into bed, "I've decided I like the outside of the bed best." Then he told me the one about the condemned man being led to the gallows. Someone offers him brandy. Oh yes he says eagerly. Never tried it before, maybe I'll like it.

Horses and mountains and chickens and cows pass. I discover that by rubbing a finger on my teeth I can make an internal squeaking noise. Locked in solitary confinement, a person could become a virtuoso on teeth.

Boredom's like that. Someone should start a brain bank for when you get tired of your own. Better than shuffling through the tired old pack of Europe.

When we stop again we hover near the bus like nervous children afraid of being left behind. We've lost track now, no one knows for sure what country we're in.

"So anyway then I got the plane to Rome and I went to Florence on the train. Nearly missed it, they've got another name for it. Really dirty train with all these peasants stinking of that garlic.

Rude and ignorant. Not a word of English between the lot of them. Don't talk to me about Italy."

Head Nurse has a voice of such authority it threatens to burst her singlet, but boy she's been everywhere. You name it, she's been there. And the toilets were smelly and the peasants were rude and ignorant. She says to Grubby Tits, who's staring open-mouthed and impressed, "Why'ncha sit next to me, we'll have a real good chin-wag."

Her chin is muscular, the fittest chin in the world, the Mr Universe of chins, from so much wagging. A leathery peasant shuffles past staring at her. His toothless face is like a squashed shoe.

"Wotcha staring at, dumb-bell," she says loudly.

These mountains are rather nice. Silhouetted pine trees walking up their spines, like black paper cut with pinking shears and pasted on a white sky. Orange autumn trees among the dark pines give a stippled effect like trout. The hills hold blue shadows in their laps, their peaks crisp in the sun. Pines as straight as pencils spear up the slopes. We speed through a village while a cracked bell tolls clang clang clang. There's a church of soft ochrous plaster painted all over with small pink crosses. The ambitious sign on the Hotel Moderna is almost too faded to read.

We stop and the man with the neat pack gets out, waves tidily and walks off. There's a man who knows where he's going. Quick as a flash Costas takes the window seat he's left empty.

The border into Yugoslavia seems all guns and stubbly big-jowelled faces and those peaked caps that South American dictators wear. The border guards swagger through the bus, rudely going through everyone's plastic bags full of orange peel and embarrassing crusts. Costas gives them a couple of packets of cigarettes and they leave him alone. No flies on this boy. They thumb laboriously through our passports while we sit waiting and sweating. I promise I'm not a terrorist. Honest, I've never seen a drug in my life.

We trundle off into dusk. Slavic faces stare sternly at us from doorways where kerosene lamps hang, and in the fields wooden carts creak long behind horses. A late worker in a field trudges behind the horse, ploughing, bored, dreaming of soup.

In the early morning we pass Mount Olympus and I remember that this is my adventure. We're nearly there. The mountains sprawl over the plain like vast sleeping hounds lying with their paws towards a fire. The gods are up there on that lumpy mountain, and somewhere not far away is the navel of the world. How feeble and faulty those gods are: Zeus with giant godly prick raised at some poor wee thing in the woods. Maybe I should turn into a tree, this is my chance.

Athens. Hieroglyphics instead of street signs. Not a word of English between the lot of them. My feet are huge as I hobble off the bus. Grubby Tits is moaning, "Ooooooh, me feet are that swelled up."

Head Nurse strides away, map in hand, to the youth hostels. "Then I got the bus down to Greece, nice bunch of people, gave them a few tips about where to go and that."

I'm alone. I think I'll like Athens. The pavements are made of marble but everything smells of shit.

Now drop a card to John. Make it nice.

Dear John, had a great trip down on the bus. A nice bunch of people. Got chatting to a few Australians and a handsome Greek too. Saw lots of Europe. You were right, I needed an adventure. See you round, Louise.

Dorothy Hewett

THE TRAVELLERS

Driving all day
they came into a village
            after dark
& slept under feather eiderdowns.

Next morning
a window full of mountains,
great cones glittering
as they hung over the sill
& all the way home
        like Hansel & Gretel
        begging for crumbs
the blood from his young wife's wrists
            darkened the snow.

In the Metropole
        unemployed spies
        left over from Beria
still occupy the landings,

        the intelligentsia
        toss between bedposts
marked with metal roses.

The Berlin taxi-driver
        in his angst
tries the elevator doors
for his lost interpreter.

On slide evenings
she always has the best still photographs.
Under the blow-up
of Mao-tse-tung's mole
she loves the Chinese Liberation Army.

In Constable's country
she wears green eye-glasses & white muslin;
in Weimar the young Turk
        mends her glass slipper;
on the Orient Express
with a rose between his teeth
        she finds Nijinsky dead.

Dreaming of Popocatapetl
        & a tongueless boy
        crossing the Alps
she cuts till the bathtub's rosy.
(Stalled in a snowdrift
swearing, he cranks the car.)

Not celibate but living alone
        on a waterbed
        with a harbour view,
        her psychiatrist,
        her vibrator,
        her color TV
she's happier now.
(Stoned in a Toyota
he drives over the top.)

In the glass dome
the snowstorm whirls ...

Frank Moorhouse

BLASE IN THE LAND OF SWIZZLESTICK

Hi Chief,
Why did I choose Switzerland for my vacation? The Swiss believe
they can survive a nuclear war. I like that kind of positive, forward
thinking. Also you get more Benedictine abbeys per kilometre in
Switzerland, according to the Michelin *Green Guide*. J-O-K-E. I
don't go in for gothic cathedrals and Benedictine abbeys as much
as I did once.

I really went to Switzerland because the swizzlestick was invented there and I'm something of a cocktail bar cowboy as well as a nightclub roundsman. It comes from the slurring of the word "switzer", the old word for a Swiss. Unfortunately the Swizzlestick Museum was closed.

But also being something of a bushman I did go to the Festival of the Swiss Army Knives. The Festival is held in the village of Zug where the men and women from the village wear giant replicas of the thirty or so different types of Swiss army knife, made from wood, aluminium, plastic. Actually, the knives now aren't so much "army" — it's more the Swiss civilian knife. There is a knife for every purpose: the fisherman's knife, the camper's knife, the waiter's knife, the sailor's knife and so on. There is even a Princess's knife. Well, the people of the village dress up as a knife with their blades and tools and cork screws sticking out and all with distinctive caps or clothing denoting their function as a knife. So the villagers who come as the waiter's knife have trays and a napkin over their arms, as well as being inside the knife replica. With their blades and tools sticking out they look like a procession of hedgehogs. The other villagers come in costume as the objects of the knives' desires, so as to speak, dressed as corks, bottle tops, fish, cans, tomatoes. There were also two or three village humourists who came as cut fingers. One had a large replica of a bandaid around the replica of the cut finger. One had a device which oozed stage blood. The cut fingers received loud applause from the spectators. Then followed nice folk dances and songs including the famous Dance of the Swiss Knives and it's all rather wonderful.

After the parade and the dancing in the village square there is a feast with the usual barrels of beer and casks of wine. By nightfall the knives have got a little drunk and begin chasing the bottle tops, corks and cans and so on. There are some real cut fingers, even cut throats, later in the night.

They have a regional expression, "as mad as a cut Zug". I left. I'd been drinking with the lady's purse knife and it was becoming a little dangerous.

At the festival it is possible to order a custom-made knife. I, of course, did just that. They measure your fingers and palm of your hand so that the knife they make fits well into the hand and has the correct balance. You select which tools you want to have on the knife. I'm having mine made with hollow handles which can be filled with cognac and with two small cups which screw into one end. At the other end there will be a small peanut dispenser. The knife also has an electronic calculator which tells you what a tip in which country for which products and services (and a long, pointed flick blade for bell captains who think they haven't been tipped enough). The people of Victorinox — one of the companies which make the Swiss Army Knives — are going to call it the Blase Disconsolate Traveller's Knife.

Hard work display

In Lucerne I went to the Hard Work Display (*Arbeit macht frei*). The Swiss are very good workers and proud of it and at the display they demonstrate some of the ancient skills and practices of hard work, showing children what it was like to work hard in the olden days before morning and afternoon breaks, the three-hour lunch, cigarettes, lavatories, and personal telephone calls. They showed someone answering the telephone before it had rung thirty or forty times which I found truly amazing. I hadn't seen that done for a long time. There was an automated model of a shop assistant who, when you activated the display by pushing the button, used the quaint old express, "No problems — we'll do that for you while you wait", which I hadn't heard for some years. Some of the children visiting the display were disbelieving. There was also an office without a clock where the workers began work at sunrise and stopped at sunset and automated models of employees who went to the washrooms to get ready to leave *after* the finishing time. Some of the countries where these practices have disappeared organise bus tours to the display. There are other things like specimen jars of sweat. I recommend the display to Australians visiting Europe but I have to warn that it's fairly exhausting.

Medieval watch towers are good value

So far the best travel tip in Switzerland — for guys with tastes like mine, anyhow — are the medieval watch towers. You know, they built them in towns and villages to look out over the countryside for many kilometres to watch for the arrival of tourist carriages so that the townspeople could prepare for yet another bunch of weary travellers unfamiliar with the currency, and hence the olde travellers' expression "they saw you coming". Well, my advice is to find one of these towers — every olde town has one — and climb (good exercise) the hundred metres or so up the narrow spiral inner staircases, but do this at ten am or two pm on a weekday during school term — avoid the school vacation. At about this time you have a very good chance that a bus load or two of school girls will arrive and begin filing up the narrow stair case. You can then begin your descent. Not to everyone's taste, perhaps, but it gave me a buzz. Frankly, it was the highlight of the trip. More fun than being chased by a drunken Swiss arm knife.

Michelin guide inspectors' conference

In Geneva I was fortunate to come in on the last few days of the Michelin Inspectors' Conference. They were arguing over revisions to new editions of the guides. There were those who argued against the emphasis on abbeys and cathedrals and who wanted more battle fields and bullet-riddled, blood-stained uniforms of archdukes.

Readers will be interested to know that the Michelin Working Party on Australia again decided not to put out a Michelin Guide to Australia because there were insufficient Benedictine abbeys and crusader castles and no blood-stained uniforms of archdukes available in Australia to fill a Michelin Guide. The Aboriginal people have a lot to answer for — having failed to construct one single crusader fort or gothic cathedral in the 50,000 years they have allegedly been in the country. The Michelin people were absolutely bewildered about the fact that the Aboriginal people haven't got one ruin. I suppose they could begin making some. That's not a bad idea.//

The free drugs trip

My other Swiss experience was a factory tour of Roche, the drug manufacturer. You are given a fascinating sample kit of their drugs to take away with you. And you get to sample all sorts of mood changing chemicals. You can volunteer to join their drug trials program and get free courses of experimental drugs and at the same time participate in the advancement of medicine. I volunteered for the traveller's drug trial. Roche are developing a drug which purifies water, neutralises harmful bacteria in food, lowers Traveller Paranoia, suppresses anxiety, releases energy, clarifies the mind, inhibits flight dysrhythmia, stops diarrhoea, prevents foot ache in art galleries, and gives the traveller a stable sense of euphoria and confidence, exuding at the same time an aura which repels bores and malaria-carrying mosquitoes and attracts interesting, influential English-speaking nationals in bars.

Of course, the drug is in its early developmental stage. They hope though to get it together in one tablet taken daily. I've begun the trial and will let readers know my reports to Roche over the following year. I'll let you Roche my readers...I'll effect my Roche tests on the readers...I'll...

Thea Astley

WHY I WROTE A SHORT STORY CALLED "DIESEL EPIPHANY"

I should explain, I suppose, that I'm not a very accomplished traveller. Some people are expert at it, but things, awful things, seem to happen whenever I board a plane train bus. Actually, I don't do too much plane boarding because I can never afford to travel more than cattle class. This is the sort of thing that happens when I leave the safe perimeters of my patch: once when I was staying in the Marlborough Sounds and had gone driving with friends in the afternoon, I came back to my motel room at four o'clock and the Ambassador for Lebanon was asleep in my bed. Now I didn't think for a minute that he was one of those courtesy presents they sometimes give you in the hotels like the shower cap and the two pieces of fruit and the mending kit. It wasn't a hotel like that. So I went down to the office and I said there's a very large dark man — and I'm almost sure he's foreign — asleep in my bed and they said oh that is the Ambassador for Lebanon. We have changed your room. And then they moved me to a kind of spare room they used for the gardener. And the year before that there was the moose.

Somewhere between Calgary and Regina our Greyhound bus hit a moose. There we were at two in the morning shuddering in the autumn cold of the prairie caught up for an hour while the driver inspected damage to his headlights and waited for the west coast bus to come through. Anyway, after this hour of half-doze the lights suddenly snapped on and the driver went right down the bus handing out questionnaires for us to fill in: nature of accident; estimated speed of bus; estimated speed of moose; nationality (of moose?), sex, purpose of travel, visit. Signature. Can moose write? There was one of those hissed domestics going on in the seat in front of us. The husband kept saying, Will you forget the goddam moose. The moose is just fine. Why don't you worry about the goddam bus, for Chrissake. You're riding the bus, aren't you? You're not riding the goddam moose. The seat in front of us was full of snivels and as if this wasn't enough we're an hour late into Regina and four passengers crawl in from the bus shelter and there are only three seats and the driver says, Will that woman who got on with her husband mind getting off and the woman who was big and black says, I aint got no husban. Ah'd like a husban. And this snaps the bus wide awake and a voice cries from down the aisle, You get her a husban. And there's a general cackle and then the whole bus starts calling, Don't you get off till he finds you a husban and I hear the woman in front of me say, She can have mine and then this couple sulk all the way to Chicago. I mean you can FEEL their sulks.

I think buses are worse in Australia. Or maybe it's the drivers. There are those bus captains who seem to be training to be sit down comics. They have a mike and a PR system and it's like the breakfast show all night or they play country and western and metal rock or conduct community singing. They crack funnies. There was one driver on the southern run who used to say at comfort stations, Now don't forget the number of the bus. Write it on the back of the person in front and don't let them out of your sight. I remember a party of lady bowlers who sang hearty songs with risque choruses non-stop from Gladstone to Brisbane. And another time on the Gold Coast run a young man behind (what was it Bob Ellis said about the beauty of the monologue?) told his life story loudly to an uninterested grunting passenger. By Surfers he'd covered his life to eighteen, his father's life to fifty, his first six jobs, his father's one job. By Grafton he'd gone thoroughly into four girlfriends and was metaphysically examining the failure of relationship with his fifth when this gentle little man across the aisle from me swung round and snarled, Forget her, son and let me forget her too. I can't stand it, he said. I can't stand it another minute. I'll kill him. I'll kill the driver. I'm seventy-one and I don't have to stand it. The last time I went to the Centre I told the driver either you lower that music or you put me off and I'll walk. Right here in the middle of nowhere. And I started to tug at the door and I said, You ought to be ashamed. When the newspapers get hold of this it won't look too good, an old bloke of seventy put out to walk from Oodnadatta. So then he lowered the godawful music. And then the old man gave up trying to sleep and he told me he had this fantasy about buses that did the Wagner run and the Brahms run or *something*, and he liked to think of all the passengers getting excited when the driver said, Now folks, can we have a bit of hush? I'm putting on the Elgar second and all the Norms and Berts get all worked up and say, Shut up, love, it's the Elgar second. Hey, Ron, did you hear? They're gunna play the Elgar second. Then he stopped talking suddenly and began to wrestle with his ear plugs. I'd like to think he got his dream but maybe he had to ask to be put off. I'll never know, because we got off at Macksville at four in the morning and then the horror began from a different angle. We'll leave the key to your room on the table near the office, the hotel had assured us by phone. There was no key. Maybe they've left it in the door, I suggested. Country pubs do that. So we went upstairs and Jack went down one corridor while I went down another and I found a door with a key in it and I opened the door and felt for the light switch in one efficient movement and the naked bulf blazed down and there was this terrible moaning from the bed and I said oh God I'm so sorry and shut the door smartly and then I realised I'd left the light on so I un-locked the door again and the man in the bed let out a sharp cry that cut right through my apologies so I took my humiliation away to the smoking room and lay on the floor with my head on my overnight bag and after a while, a long while, Jack came back and he said, Hey there *was* one door with a key in it. I guess you heard him shouting.

I really don't want to think about buses. Trains have the personality, the tension, the romance of all travel — of waitingrooms and tearooms and the music of the rackety lurch. And with luck you can sleep on trains. And here's another once. First class this time somewhere between Augsburg and Nuremberg and Germany is in darkness though there are lights across the swept fields and the pruned hedgerows. I have the compartment to myself, my bag's on the rack, my shoes off, and I'm hoping for sleep all the way to Hamburg. But just then one of the attendants comes in to check my ticket and he's an elderly frayed man and despite the pressed affirmations of his uniform he looks tired as if perhaps he has done this run too long. He has little English and I have no German except Lieder titles, but in a major effort to communicate, as we pass through Nuremberg without stopping, I point out a fierce blaze of townlight and neon. *Die Meistersinger*, I say. His whole body seems to awake as if a finger has prodded nerve spots of his nostalgia.

Opera, he asks. You like?

I shake my head and say Lieder. Lieder. I like Lieder. Dietrich Fischer Dieskau, I say hopefully. And then to my surprise he smiles fully, widely and leans forward.

Gerhard Hüsch, he says. Ah.

Elisabeth Schwarzkopf, I offer. It's like a competition.

Hans Hotter, he says.

Irmgard Seefried, I say.

Anneliese Rothenberger, he says. And I laugh.

In Australia, I manage with difficulty, train conductors don't know Anneliese Rothenberger.

Ah, he says. They know the Beatles?

We are filled with mutual delight.

On and on the train goes. On and on go we, offering singers' names to each other like small bouquets of respect.

Wilhelm Strienz.

Lotte Lehmann.

Christa Ludwig.

Gottlob Frick.

I remember the old man on the bus. Ah, I think in my turn. Ah.

Hal Colebatch

YOUTH AT AUSTRALIA HOUSE, LONDON, 1973

What brought them here? Their suffering eyes entreat
an answer to this question whose name is mystery.
Have they the week's rent money? Have they work permits?
Will their souls expand at the touch of History?//

Back to the Mails counter. Tearful they demand
the nonexistent letter be searched for once again,
a talisman to protect them, in this vast wilderland
of overcharging restaurants and gentle rain,

of Grendel-like landladies and menacing West Indians,
beggars with skin diseases and broken pens to sell,
of people with sexual partners, a torment and a dream
who precede them through turnstiles of Tube stations like Hell.//

Once they were complacent. They are not complacent now.
Will there be adequate bathwater? Grimly they fear not.
They have learnt of gasmeters now, and body odour too.
The weaker blench. Dreams fall to freeze and rot.

Yet other things replace dreams. However transient,
this empathy is real, for whatever that is worth.
Waiting indifference, shared poverty, draw them together
digesting bacon and sausages under historic earth.

They arise, broadened enough to be able,
almost like foreigners, to embrace and weep.
The letterless, the partnerless, depart
to landlords, sock-washing and sleep.

Yet tears and introspection pass, for Anzac stock.
Heads lift defiant from weeping, as each jaw firms.
Candle flames flicker upwards. They will yet confront
this first fourth-world country on its own terms.

Bryan Dawe

GETTING AROUND IN EUROPE ON THE SMELL OF AN OILY RAG

Taxi Drivers, Rome

Due to noise regulations in the inner city area, Rome's taxi drivers have been overtaken now by Greek taxi drivers when it comes to making the most noise. Of course they still remain, however, the faster of the two countries.

Beware! Rome's taxi drivers have invented a unique system whereby they assure themselves retirement by the age of forty. If you hire a taxi in Rome the meter starts *before* you commence your journey, at the point where the taxi's last passenger got off. If this happens to have been on the outskirts of Rome and your driver has avoided passengers until he picks you up at the Rome Termini, your five minute cab ride to the Colosseum will end up costing you fifty dollars.

Special note: Do not ring for a taxi from your hotel.

If you do, and the taxi doesn't arrive for an hour (a most likely occurrence) be warned that your taxi is probably coming from Florence and you'll be up for a bloody fortune!

Taxi drivers in Rome also have a unique charge system, unlike anything anywhere else. Though no driver admits it, the following charges do apply, so beware:

Turning left: add ten per cent of total fare.
Reversing: add $2 surcharge.
Answering a question: (in Italian) add $5 to fare; (in English) add $8 to fare.
Getting taxi driver lost: add $10 per minute.
Changing down to first gear: add $15.
Do not ask driver to get out of taxi and open boot, unless you are rich.//

Sonya's Diary:

St Peter's, Vatican Square. 1 pm
St Peter's Square is overwhelming. First thing you notice is how much bigger it is than the postcard. That's true of Europe generally.

Bus tour is way behind schedule and only have fifteen minutes to see the whole of the Vatican and St Peters.//

There are thousands of people here, all staring up towards a tiny figure speaking from a balcony.//

Gee, no one told us that the Pope would be here: this almost makes up for the scaffolding covering up the Trevi Fountain.

Couldn't make out what the Pope was saying: Duane thinks he was talking about everyone caring for the poor a bit more, but he wasn't sure.

Duane, who used to be a Catholic, also said it mightn't actually be the Pope. Apparently, so Duane reckons, if the Pope's sick or busy or something, they just play the tape of the Pope speaking and get one of the cardinals to come and pretend to be the real Pope. Because the balcony's so high up, no one down below knows the difference. Makes sense. Also, as Roly pointed out if anyone tries to pop the Pope off, they'd be knocking off the wrong Pope, wouldn't they?

Suppose it's good waving practice for the younger cardinals too.

Roly's Diary:
Crossing St Peter's Square, Vatican.
Wallopers give us some funny looks, especially Duane: with all his recording equipment strung over him he looks like a terrorist about to set a bomb off.

Have crossed the square in just under one minute and thirty-five seconds: Duane is keeping a tight watch on time. Good going when you consider that the place is full of people. Lot of Japanese tourists: didn't realise so many Japanese were Catholics!

Sonya's Diary:
Inside St Peter's. 12½ minutes before bus leaves.
Inside the Basilica now, and racing against time. Dear God, it's so huge and so holy. There's a mass being conducted and this adds to effect, I think.

In order that we see everything possible in the time, we decide to latch onto one of the Japanese tours: they seem to have the same time problem we do. Pass the Confession and the statue of Pius

VI[1] — by Casanova, but stop briefly to admire The Peter[2] by Michael Angelo.[3] //

European Trains

Dining on board: When travelling by rail in Europe always ignore suggestions that there is a dining car on your European train. Particularly ignore any conductor who insists that there will be a dining car *"after Bologna"*.

There may have been a dining car after Bologna *yesterday*, indeed there is likely to be a dining car after Bologna *tomorrow*, but *today*, on your train, *no dining car will appear after Bologna!*

Always, we repeat, ALWAYS carry at least three days' supply of food with you on a European train, no matter how long the journey!

Train conductors: European train conductors are generally extremely helpful. Many are awarded the annual Nobel prize for patience. The exception is the odd French train conductor who tends to confuse employment on trains with ownership of them.

European railway stations: Most European capitals have more than one main, central railway station. In the case of Paris, it appears to have around sixteen of them. You will notice that these central railway stations are always conveniently situated — normally as far away from your hotel as is humanly possible.

On the positive side, you will observe that the stations are often far more interesting than the city sights you have come to visit.

Getting on the correct carriage: Boarding the correct carriage on a long distance international European train is extremely important, not to mention risky. It is quite easy to catch what you think

1   He was the sixth member of the Pius family.
2   A sculpture of an immortal young virgin with the body of Christ lying across her asleep. Not sure what he was doing there, or why he was asleep. An original. Worth a bit.
3   Former member of the Renaissance. Clever joker, could do anything with his hands.

is a train from Paris to Venice, only to find yourself a day or so later enjoying the delights of Split, in Yugoslavia.

Timetables

European trains always run on time. Australian travellers have no experience of this in Australia, so will need to take particular note. Trains in Europe don't so much stop as *pause* — often very briefly — ten to twenty-five seconds if changing locomotives, less if not.

This means you must be ready to detrain with your luggage long before the train arrives at your particular destination.

As soon as your Euro-train has slowed down, start throwing your personal belongings onto the platform and follow them promptly with yourself. A carefully executed swan dive and somersault onto the platform is usually the best method.

Desmond O'Grady

BUDAPEST, KELETI

You may have seen some grotty railway stations but I am sure they can't match Budapest's Keleti terminal. If acknowledged as a museum piece, an example of industrial archaeology, it might be cared-for but instead it is just run-down, dirty, in need of paint — and I would suggest a change from the favoured hues of shit brown and puke yellow. Take some ancient rolling stock, set it beneath a splintering wood hanger and you have Keleti as it was in the seventies. I don't know if the Hungarian railways still use coal-burning locomotives but when I dream of being trapped at Keleti, with a weird cast I will soon introduce but without Karizma, I catch a mephitic whiff.

Biased? Very likely for because of the shabby station I lost my last chance to see Budapest and much more. I did not recognise this at the time but when I saw what had happened, the pain was linked to Keleti.

With Karizma, twenty years my junior, I had been oohing and aahing around Europe. Everything took on a heightened meaning because of Karizma; she meant the world to me — a trite phrase, I know, but at the moment it was meaningful. Whenever she did not recognise one of my references, perhaps something as banal as a song title, I was achingly reminded of how much separated us. But we were busy building our own memories. In Quattro Coronati church in Rome we had seen a twelfth century mosaic where St Sylvester restores a dead bull to life. I'd told Karizma that was what she had done for me. In Poland there had been painful undertones for, in the 1950s, Karizma's parents had left there for Australia but elsewhere it was usually five orgasmic discoveries a day not to speak of the nights. What's more, Karizma had not been trapped: I feared that, raised on her parents' European memories, she might decide to stay even though I could not abandon my Observatory post. However although so excited by Europe that she frequently rang her parents to persuade them to come over, she saw it all as an Australian who would return with me to set-up house. We had found Budapest livelier than Vienna but the Astronomical Congress had left us precious little time to explore it. We had an appointment in Belgrade but on the last day planned to leave our luggage at the station, then take a long look at both Buda and Pest.

"Oh no," moaned Karizma when we caught sight of the luggage deposit queue stretching twenty-five kilometres or, at least, the length of the interminable platform. We had no warning elsewhere in Budapest that at the station we would again strike queues as in Poland and Czechoslovakia, people's republics where service for people was the last thing to expect. I looked at the cobwebbed canopy wondering how many travellers had perished in this queue, then trekked to its head. In the withdrawal queue, a beefy Canadian was frantic at the inaction because his train was about to leave. The indolent attendant ignored the Canadian's shouts then vainly tried to restrain him when he vaulted the barrier, ran around the stacks, grabbed a white bag and rushed to his train.

We decided to hold onto our luggage. Of course the waiting rooms were locked. Although at that time we preferred each other's company to anything else, we trudged to the self-service restaurant planning to take turns visiting the city; but first we wanted a hate session against the railway administration.

Soon we began to observe our neighbours: leather-trousered

German students; flaxen-haired girls who pored over comics; elderly men who may merely have been seeking refuge from the cold;
youths who listened to head-sets beside mountains of luggage. All
had to order food or drink, under an exotic sign ELOC*ETELEK
*BUFE*ARUK, or be bawled out by a Popeye-like cook who threw
Wiener Schnitzels into a squat earthenware pot where diners fished
for them.

"What's least likely to give us station salmonella?"

I suggested wine and Karizma returned with a Bulgarian "Bear's
Blood" red which tasted as if had been bottled as it gushed from
the animal's jugular. But after a while we forgot Budapest as
Karizma invented stories to match the marooned travellers' faces:
a Hungarian soldier filling a crossword was a chess grand master
not allowed to show his superiority to the Russians; a straight-
backed man with steel-rimmed glasses reading *Der Spiegel* was the
son of a top Nazi who had so developed his father's secret weapon
he could threaten the world; a broad-shouldered, pin-headed Ivan
Lendl-lookalike was a failed tennis pro, now into drug running.

A woman whose skirt, blouse and beret were in the red, white
and green national colours came from the back of the restaurant
and took our unfinished Bear's Blood. We assumed this was the
staff's unsubtle way of forcing us to order again.

"Let's try our luck with the throwaway schnitzels." Karizma
went to fetch them: although not dutiful, she had keen appetites.
I warned her Viennese cakes had added inches to her waistline but
that interested me more than her. She was beaten to the counter
by a handsome fellow with cheek tufts, pigtail and an aura of
violence. A Tartar? Joking with Popeye and his offsiders, the Tartar
splendidly offset Karizma's stave-cheeked beauty. She was blushing
with that hypersensitivity which at times worried me: it could be,
as in this case, a swift stain or a slow burn which brought to mind
"bruise like a peach". Her upslanting eyes signalled to me: you come
and get the victuals but my smile reassured her. As Karizma sailed
back with the schnitzels, she had the thrust of a ship's prow. I knew
her momentary fear had been followed by a surge of excitement.
She could squeak in delight at oddities and the Tartar certainly
qualified. I ate speculating whether he was a professional showman.

The schnitzel was tasty: perhaps Popeye was not bawling us out, but merely advertising his wares. However, as we observed the Tartar who now balanced a beer glass on his forehead, our half-finished schnitzels were whisked away by the woman who seemed draped in the national flag. Karizma lunged too late after the red, white and green.

"I was going to have another, now I'll make it two."

"Make it four for each of us."

"Let's have a schnitzel orgy — if she'll let us."

"Orgy" was one of Karizma's favourite words. And our Keleti station restaurant performance justified her recurrent description of us as "pigging it around Europe". The expression hinted at guilt which was not surprising, I thought, from someone who frequently assessed a place on whether death there would be pleasant (she preferred quiet "rural" spots but within cities as if she wanted to join opposites). Or maybe this attention to a suitable burial place was merely a sign that she was ready to depart ... there were depths to Karizma although few would have credited this seeing her, unconcerned by the Tartar's capers, fishing eight schnitzels from the pot of delights.

"There are compensations in this concentration camp," she said on return with the schnitzels and more Bear's Blood, "despite its demented commander Popeye, its barbarous Tartar guard and Elsa, the sadistic warder, who makes lampshades like crazy."

"Elsa?"

"I've got news for you: Elsa's not an over-zealous waitress."

"I know you've great potential but didn't realise it was as a sleuth."

"Elementary, my dear Ross. From the counter I had a clear view of her. Look!"

At the back of the restaurant, the red, white and green-clad woman and a silver-haired deadbeat were eating from many plates of scraps beneath huge sepia photographs illustrating the pleasures of the Hungarian Railways.//

Katherine Gallagher

PLANE-JOURNEY MOMENTUMS

The danger of travelling is how
it takes you over, caught in
that today-dress you wear
not for frills but for comfort —
in the confines of an air-tunnel
marked by arrows on inflight-maps.

You read, pick up earphones,
settle to a book, tell yourself
that any disasters are swaying outside
this steady balloon
where you balance the day,
maybe humouring your child
who is flying for the first time.

So much for trying to forget
your innate strangeness to this absurd
transitory life you've taken on —
these dizzying heights, circuits of chat,
odd secrets laced with reserve
and everything blended for your newest
neighbour as though you'd been
living side by side for a lifetime.

Thomas Shapcott

TRAVEL DICE

Time spat a capsule of saliva.
It was a plane shining in rare atmosphere.
Now it has landed. The sun did not
turn it to salt
the moon did not drink it
this time.
Though you deny it
you are a prayer.
Reassurance clothes you
now you are home.
To be stuck into place
like a poster
sobers you.
It sobers me.

Andrew Taylor

FOLDS IN THE MAP

Lucid as always
you guide us along the autobahn
until at Exit 43
the map falls apart.

Groping on the floor you fail
to tell me to turn.
Furious I find
no repentance on your face.

We overshoot by 80 k
miss our appointment
arrive to observe ducks tow
rippling arrows over the lake

and hear bells from the Romanesque
church tell us that the hour
is always late. Folds
in the map, you say

weakened the paper and we fell
through. A meal
and a bed in the Gasthaus
and we cancel what's left

of the tour, to stay
by a lake, with ducks, together.
After each Exit, we agree
is another, and the next.

Judith Rodriguez

THE JOURNEY WITH CHILDREN
for Sibila and Richard

You have tickets this time for the children. You mean to be
    known
by them in the seasons and cities of your race —
Europe, that further memory; you draw them a face
of roads, with place-names; ritual, passing on.

Experience nests in the branches of expectation.
You do not expect the places to be the same,
even the museums. And they are not the same.
What has been added is the children. At last your decisions

are upon you: time to remark only the best,
or what calls you again with the true remembered voice.
But your ear is no longer in question. The question and choice
are the children's. Your talk of the journey will be obsessed

with their fascinations. You scarcely can guess their reasons
but you guess. Their eyes are your new museum of taste,
young leaf in ancient gardens. You lean to be embraced
and grow there unnoted in their flowering season.

David Dale

FAUX TRAVEL

The island of Hydra was starting to seem a bit too good to be true
until I saw the donkeys carrying the goats up the hill, just near the
port. It was a strange procession — six donkeys each bearing two
goats confined in bags over the donkey's saddle. Only the goats'
heads were visible, and they were looking around pertly as if to say
"Isn't this a great life — I don't even have to walk by myself."

   Donkeys are the public transport on Hydra (which the Greeks
pronounce "eedra"). While other societies set standards for exhaust
emissions to reduce air pollution, Hydra requires its donkey drivers

to carry plastic bags and to clean the cobblestones after them. The only motorised vehicle on the island is a three-wheeled garbage truck. But I thought it showed quite remarkable tenderness on the part of the goatherder to move his flock around in this way.

I asked my friend Bill, who lives on the island and who was having coffee with me at the quayside, what was going on. "Those goats are on their way to the slaughterhouse," he said. "It's up around that bend." I said: "Can't they walk by themselves?" "Well they could," said Bill, "but when they got close to the slaughterhouse they'd smell the panic of the last lot that went in, and they'd refuse to go any further. It's easier to take them by donkey. Did you notice that the last tour boat left ten minutes ago?"

Hydra is very considerate in that way. It keeps its real life carefully separate from its tourist life. It wouldn't do to let such potentially upsetting spectacles as goats being carried to slaughter happen when the daytrippers were still around.

Hydra's harbour front is a tourist bubble, lined with tavernas purporting to serve fresh local seafood for visitors who have one hour off the tour boat to grab an authentic Greek meal and buy an authentic fisherman's cap. One cafe owner proudly pointed to his range of seafood and told me "that calamari comes frozen from Thailand and that lobster comes frozen from New Zealand". The calamari doesn't have to come frozen from Thailand, but the cafe owners prefer it that way because it is easier to slice and fry. Earlier that day, about a kilometre down the coast from the Hydra port, I had seen a fisherman lovingly throwing an octopus onto a rock to tenderise it. Presumably it was not destined for any taverna. The only locally caught fish served on Hydra these days are little red mullet. But tourists don't order them because they are not enough like the wonderful range of seafood promised by the brochures as part of "the Greek experience".

I enjoy Hydra because you need only walk a few steps from the waterfront to enter a world of real Greeks living a rather grim life as goatherders and fishermen. Behind the port is a maze of white-washed cottages and churches, and then barren hills dotted with occasional olive groves, sudden fields of poppies, and solitary monasteries surrounded by chickens. There are even a few cafes back there for the locals, serving goat stew rather than frozen seafood. The island has no real beaches, but a long way from the port you can jump off the rocks into a clear green ocean that's very cold. This is my idea of the Greek experience.

I had a powerful encounter with another version of the Greek experience when I was trying to get back to Athens and found that all the hydrofoils leaving Hydra were booked out. Rather than stay another night, I bribed my way onto a tour boat that had docked for an hour at Hydra's port to let its passengers buy souvenirs. The boat was nearing the end of a four day cruise of the Greek islands, and for a thousand drachmas the purser was happy to let me slip aboard and sit in the lounge for the four-hour journey to Athens.

I wondered why these passengers ever bothered to disembark, because all Greece was presented to them on the boat, albeit a Greece which existed nowhere else. In the lounge two dancers and a bouzouki band were putting on a performance of folk music. The dancers wore blue skirts and white blouses. As they twirled about, they looked at each other knowingly, with a twinkle in their eyes, as if this performance was a satire on the audience. They were not very good, if judged by the normal criteria of balance, rhythm, gracefulness, or unison. But perhaps in their own terms, they were excellent — high camp, did they think, or performance art? The audience, mostly Germans and Americans, had no way of knowing if this was how Greek dancing was meant to look, so they applauded with moderate enthusiasm. Afterwards one of the dancers took the microphone and sang "Strangers in the Night". It was my first encounter with Faux Travel, a fabrication designed to ensure that the consumer has all comforts and no surprises.

Greece has a lot of faux travel opportunities. On the mainland opposite the island of Hydra are resorts called Hydra Beach and Portoheli. They could be anywhere in the world: big hotels, cafes and sand. The language spoken there is mostly French, because they are designed for French tourists who want to get a tan, enjoy *"l'expérience Grecque"* and eat their own food. They wouldn't be confident of that if they went to Hydra itself. They prefer faux travel.

You may be puzzled by my use of the word "faux" here. Isn't it just a pretentious way of saying "fake"? Yes, and that's just the point. I picked up the word on a train journey from Washington to

Chicago, and I realised it was perfect for so much of what the traveller is offered these days: a pseudo experience that's more expensive than the real thing.

Les Murray

VINDALOO IN MERTHYR TYDFIL

The first night of my second voyage to Wales,
tired as rag from ascending the left cheek of Earth
I nevertheless went to Merthyr in good company
and warm in neckclothing and speech in the Butcher's Arms
till Time struck us pintless, and Eddie Rees steamed in brick lanes
and under the dark of the White Tip we repaired shouting

to I think the Bengal. I called for curry, the hottest,
vain of my nation, proud of my hard mouth from childhood,
the kindly brown waiter wringing the hands of dissuasion
O vindaloo, sir! You sure you want vindaloo, sir?
But I cried Yes please, being too far in to go back
the bright bells of Rhymney moreover sang in my brains.

Fair play, it was frightful. I spooned the chicken of Hell
in a sauce of rich yellow brimstone. The valley boys with me
tasting it, croaked to white Jesus. And only pride drove me,
forkful by forkful, observed by hot mangosteen eyes,
by all the carnivorous castes and gurus from Cardiff
my brilliant tears washing the unbelief of the Welsh.

Oh it was a ride on Watneys plunging red barrel
through all the burning ghats of most carnal ambition
and never again will I want such illumination
for three days on end concerning my own mortal coil
but I signed my plate in the end with a licked knife and fork
and green-and-gold spotted, I sang for my pains like the free
before I passed out among all the stars of Cilfynydd.

Hal Porter

THE BAGGAGE OF MEMORY

This more or less detailed record of segments of earlier trips abroad proposes deliberately to expose some of my attitudes and blindnesses — regrettable perhaps, but not regretted. I accept being a stranger in many camps.

The habit of pernickety inspection's inbuilt; it can't be left at home. It registers factories and telephone poles the camera, working for the tourist bureau, omits from the tempting picture of the quaint village street or ancient ruin. I neither use a camera nor wistfully diarise each night while socks and underpants, wash-basin-laundered, dry out on a bentwood chair-back or, in cold countries on whatever heating contraption a hotel or bed-and-breakfast landlady provides: if one can't remember, unaided, where one's been, what's the use of being anywhere? It's taken a long time to be able to be there.

You just don't appear, new-minted and dewy-eyed, sorcered out of space, halfway up the Champs Elysées or Tokyo Tower, plumb in the middle of Glasgow or Cannes, or in the act of skirting, with new-found callousness, a horrible young woman prone in a puddle of gin — there's the smashed bottle — outside Pennsylvania Station, New York. There've been decades of preparation; much time spent in learning to walk, talk, tie shoelaces, open doors, sign your name, buy tickets, fasten seat belts, beat someone else to the porter, waiter, taxi-cab. There's always another thing to learn, the local custom, for example, of skirting a horrible young woman ... Or to unlearn: at New York Air Terminal, the taxi-driver (who looks like a brutalised Mickey Rooney) hoicks your baggage into the boot. You open the door intending to sit, Australian fashion, beside him. He makes no bones and, without a smile, crakes, "In the back, Mac!"

Although your three pieces of three-dimensional baggage — suitcase, briefcase, umbrella — weigh portable less than the air-passenger's maximum, you your computer self are invisibly tonnes overweight, are a mount of crates, cabin trunks, portmanteaux, hatboxes, great peasant bundles, crammed with olde-worlde information, eternal facts, romantic misconceptions, superstitions, garden-fresh intolerances, historic whimpers and exaggerations from the Past; and memories memories memories. And each memory, like trick Chinese boxes, has another inside the one inside the other to infinity. Not one's inappropriate, as you keep finding out. First time in Paris you stay at the Hôtel Lutétia, Boulevard Raspail. An item from the mental baggage is instantly in use: Jules Verne. There you are in a plushly opulent yet compact suite, panelled, ruddy in tone, intently fiddling with the tricky shutter-hasps and bathroom accoutrements Continental hoteliers have a fancy for — Captain Nemo in *Nautilus*! This impression, fostered by fiction, persists until, a day or so later, a dramatic fact turns up in the impalpable baggage: you recall that, at the end of World War II, the Lutétia was a transit hotel for deportees from Dachau, Ravensbrück, such prison camps. The atmosphere's enriched. The images dissolved into the deeps of the wardrobe looking-glass — jilted Paul Bourget *célibataires:* 1923 Russian émigrés brooding about lost estates, and Crimean holidays over for ever; adulterous and sulky Jazz Age wives whose lovers have stormed out — are joined by images of those to whom the curly velvet sofa, fleecy towels, obese bolster, and extra blankets stacked in the wardrobe can have seemed improbable garniture of a dream they expect any second to wake from to a prison nightmare they don't expect will end. With what fear their eyes must have questioned themselves in the old glass that, in its hotel fashion, gives nothing away, and will never crack from side to side.

To travel thus slyly equipped with orts of history is to spend an intoxicating time even if you're only bumping into shadows. These may have acute elbows, piggy-wig-pink rubber faces, garlic-striped breaths, and voices like those of hinnies or cartoon mice, but they're nevertheless shadows on their way out of your vision to trysts with banality or ecstasy, to houses you'll never know the numbers of in nameless streets on the other side of the ravine, nameless too, dividing them from you. Shadows! — no flesh-and-blood being, Xit-small or Og-big, tripe-guzzler or *Chatons-Citron*-nibbler, has anything like the opacity, avoirdupois and lifespan of, say, Peer Gynt, Mother Goose, a confidence man like Julien Sorel, a fury like Madame Defarge. The shadowiness is never more felt than when you confront, at the season's height, some architectural wonder (let it be in Venice) the felicities of which Canaletto, Guardi, Turner, an army of etchers, painters, and arty photographers have made so familiar you get what you've paid for, actuality keeping pace with art, and, thrown in, convincingly clustered about the base, the gapers you're one of. In and out of the frame they move, effective groups of apparently Time-proof individuals. Though their future's diminishing minute by minute, the centuries have subtracted nothing from their essence. They're still what's been recorded uncountable times: napes, faces, legs disposed in this or that manner, arms held thus and thus. Only the costumes change, headgear, what's held in the hand: stiletto, fan, lorgnette, pomander, walking-stick, Japanese camera, over-priced Muranese glass necklace of a tawdriness specially designed to accord with tastes too general not to be taken advantage of.

Why withhold impressions the opposite of the publicity agents'? You may be expected not to register the host country's cupidities and cynical impostures. You can hardly be expected — or are you? — not to spot examples of squalor, and instances of misery. They're there, no detail lacking, next door to the spectacular edifice, the entrancing vista, some mammoth triumph of human ingenuity as indifferent as Nature itself to the single life.

I don't travel miserably, ready to keen if sties aren't silver, itching for rents in the gorgeous fabric, and with a *faible* for rundown gas chambers, thieves' kitchens, filthy lavatories, and those cheerless notices OUT OF ORDER, EN PANNE, NYE RABOTAYET left like saboteurs' visiting-cards in telephone booths, or on machines intended to emit cigarettes, rectangles of chocolate, paper tumblers of coffee, and underground railway tickets. They're included in the meander among mankind's Sunday-best expressions of its many-faceted nature: its interminable façades, limitless botanical gardens, cloud-puncturing spires and minarets and towers, and its enchanting cemeteries. Indeed, sometimes the cemetery's the one place (the Campo Santo of Genoa, for example) that gives a lift and flavour to what would otherwise be flavourless. Knowing I may have to fall contentedly back on a cemetery, on Bunhill Fields, say, and the graves of Defoe, Bunyan, and Blake when the Vera Lynn nightingale I knew never sang isn't singing in Berkeley Square, I nevertheless travel with a hopeless optimism. A conviction the next halting place will enrapture me between trains too often has little to rest upon. My little finger understands that the drowsy isle full of mineral springs and flushed goddesses nibbling nectarines to the feeble insinuations of an Arcadian shepherd's flute doesn't exist, and that the mark of the Goth's likely to turn up anywhere.

See: in St Peter's, indelible-pencilled on the marble thighs of archangels, PROTTEGIA LA MIA FAMIGLIA. See: on famous walls and the plinths of equestrian kings or rebels, the over-lapping hearts side by side with the hammer-and-sickle and the mock-heroic penes ejecting arcs of pellets. See: on the balustrades of exquisite bridges and the flanks of baroque churches, the abrupt slogans of anonymous bigots who write in the dark — JOIN THE IRA, VIETNAM ROSSO, PAIX AU VIETNAM, LISEZ ROUGE, YANKS GO HOME, REMEMBER 1690, VOTATE DEL PARTITO REPUBLICANO, JOIN SINN FEIN. These disfigurements so lack the La Rochefoucauld touch that, when I see them, part of a grisly nursery rhyme always comes to mind:

> *The girl in the lane,*
> *That couldn't speak plain,*
> *Cried, "Gobble gobble gobble."*

More dashing graffiti do crop up: KEEP THE POPE OFF THE MOON on a wall in Redcliffe Parade, Belfast; and, to be seen from my bedroom window, Hôtel des Nations, directly opposite the Nice railway station, neatly lettered on a parapet, the assertion LA DEMOCRATIE EST LE CACHE-SEX DE LA SUBVERSION ACTION FRANÇAISE — VIVIE LE ROI! My favourite one's slapdashed on the wall of a hilltop graveyard in Kalkara, a poor but visually and socially charming Maltese village which steps-and-stairs up above a glimmering harbour, and looks across it at the detailed baroque magnificences of Valletta. Exactly vis-a-vis this endearing graffito's the door of one of Malta's innumerable pocket-handkerchief bars. It's called the Coronation and, like most bars on the island, is kept going by the British *occupationnaires*, visiting sailors, and expatriates (stage people, writers, painters, *rentiers*) drawn to Malta by its odd beauties, siesta habits, and low income tax. On ardent nights, drinking on chairs outside the Coronation, my friends and I find the mural annunciation takes on a mysteriously uplifting significance. Neither imperative nor political, the author demands nothing, least of all hatred, gives away a delightful truth … and leaves his name.

There it is: FREDO/FUSS/LOVE/LIFE … if nothing else the "inspiration" of a short story, but much else: stimulation for my confidence in the human race.

Michael Wilding

MAISON DE LA VIE

"I've been to the Maison de Balzac and I've been to the Maison de Victor Hugo."

"Ah," he said, "but you must go to the Maison de la Vie. It costs ten francs to enter the Maison de Balzac, ten francs to enter the Maison de Victor Hugo, but the Maison de la Vie —"

"Is free?" I said.

"No, no, nothing is free. But with the Maison de la Vie you have already paid the entrance fee. Now all that is required is the supplement."

"How much is the supplement?" I asked.

He laughed. "If I could tell you that I could tell you everything," he said. "It depends on the hours you travel. It depends on the speed or convenience with which you wish to go. If you want to pass through with minimum inconvenience, then it will be different from stopping at every station."

"What, more?"

"Perhaps," he said. "Perhaps not. It depends. More for which? Which way do you want to travel?"

"Well," I said, "it depends."

"On the price?" he said. "You would determine the course of your life according to the price of the supplement? You are some sort of rich boy? Or a clochard, maybe. Maybe you would rather sleep on the grilles of the metro. Then it will only cost you one ticket. Four francs maybe, less than five francs. That way you can keep warm at night."

"And alternatively?"

"Alternatively? For some there is no alternative. For some it is better neither to travel nor arrive, for some it is better to sleep on the grilles of the metro than walk the banks of the Seine and gaze at the cold waters. You've seen them. Surely even you on your way to the museums have seen them, leaning on the parapets, walking slowly and indeterminately because, after all, there is nowhere they are going except to the terminus. Which the Seine offers but it is a cold way to go. So they look at it. Meditatively, you suggest. Singing strange songs, you imagine, singing familiar songs, would that be preferable? While the current sweeps past. There is no further entrance fee for that. But the exit charges: to die without insurance, that is something else again."

"Exit charges?"

"But of course. You throw away your ticket, how are you going to get out? The Maison de la Vie lies all about you and you are trapped in the tunnels beneath. Or swept past on the current and you see, on the embankment there, everything you ever desired: secondhand books, girls, postcards and pavement cafes."

"Is that all I ever desired?"

"Maybe just the postcards now," he said. "Mementoes of where you might have been. You can scribble on the back and who is ever to know whether you were there or not, whether you intended to go but failed to find the time, or maybe saw from the distance the tower, the windmill, the national costume. Or maybe it was one of those secondhand cards, those pre-owned antiquities of a prelived life. And an inscription in faded ink. 'We met here beneath the pyramids aeons ago.' And who will ever know whether you did or will, whether the pyramids were ever there, or will be. And without the price of the postage you will carry the card around, from Maison to Maison, increasingly crumpled in your pocket, between the passport and the shredded tissues, the address a fading will, the insignia of kisses a dying hope, the address smudging, running, like mascara dissolving in tears. 'Is this,' you will ask, 'a life?' Souvenirs of Victor Hugo holding his head, always his hand on his head, fixed in eternal sadness; or Balzac in his capuchin's robe, eternally ready to write, but the writing table immobilised in the Maison, not to be touched, highly polished and free of ink, free of paper. You will sneak a touch when the attendant is in another room. The tears will flood up into your fingers through your arms and gather in the corners of your eyes: for the unwritten novels, for the unlived life, who can tell you? The attendant returns

and you are asked not to touch. You sniff back the tears. They remain
unshed. In the Maison de Victor Hugo the quills are beneath glass.
The ink, if it had been there, would have turned to powder. Buy your
cards, buy your posters, buy your umbrella in the boulevard to shelter
you from the tears of the sky. It is dry in these Maisons, but even you
will have to walk along the streaming streets when you leave."

Robert Gray

from CURRICULUM VITAE

Or, travelling alone in Europe once, and staying in a provincial city,
indolent and homesick of an afternoon,
I turned, as ever, to the museum.
In such a mood, however, the masterpiece will often no longer serve:
it seems too strenuous and too elevated;
it belongs in a world too far beyond one's own.
From experience, one has learned at these times to follow that
    arrow, *Ecole française*
XIXe siècle. There, on an attic floor,
unnoticed by the attendant, a newspaper crumpled
over his boots, or along the deserted outer corridors,
before tall windows, in the light from which
many of them are cancelled,
hang one's faithful mediocrities — in sympathy with whom
one had thought to be borne through until dinnertime.
Armand Guillaumin, Léon Cogniet, Jules Dupré, Félix Ziem:
no artistic claims can be made for these. Their sluggish or
    bituminous pigment,
greasy sheen, and craquelure,
their failures, so complex and sad, have earned them
"an undisturbed repose".
And yet, even these harmless,
unassuming, and forgotten, as I glanced among them, on this occasion
were forgotten
by their one idle, arbitrary re-creator,
and the landscapes that came far more vividly before my eyes
were all memories.

Peter Porter

BAD DREAMS IN VENICE

Again I found you in my sleep
And you were sturdily intact,
The counsel you would always keep
Became my dream's accusing tract.

Still I dared not think your force
Might even slightly slack my guilt —
This wasn't judgment but a course
Which self not knowing itself built.

It scarcely mattered where I dreamed,
The dead can choose a rendezvous:
You knew that nothing is redeemed
By blame, yet let me conjure you.

And this was Venice where we'd walked
Full tourist fig, first man and wife
On earth, and where we'd looked and talked
Your presence could outlive your life.

But now Venetian vapours clung
To every cold and wounding word —
The spectres which we moved among
Came from the phrases I had stirred.

They could not harm you but they bit
Into whatever had not died;
However we might reason it,
Your face and mine marched side by side.

And those old harshnesses which you
Muttered to me unrestrained,
Like Venice, loved but hated too,
Were all the closeness which remained.

John Tranter

LUFTHANSA

Flying up a valley in the Alps where the rock
rushes past like a broken diorama
I'm struck by an acute feeling of precision —
the way the wing-tips flex, just a little
as the German crew adjust the tilt of the sky and
bank us all into a minor course correction
while the turbo-props gulp at the mist
with their old-fashioned thirsty thunder — or
you notice how the hostess, perfecting a smile
as she offers you a dozen drinks, enacts what is
almost a craft: Technical Drawing, for example,
a subject where desire and function, in the hands
of a Dürer, can force a thousand fine ink lines
to bite into the doubts of an epoch, spelling
Humanism. Those ice reefs repeat the motto
whispered by the snow-drifts on the north side
of the woods and model villages: the sun
has a favourite leaning, and the Nordic flaw
is a glow alcohol can fan into a flame.
And what is this truth that holds the grey
shaking metal whole while we believe in it?
The radar keeps its sweeping intermittent promises
speaking metaphysics on the phosphor screen;
our faith is sad and practical, and leads back
to our bodies, to the smile behind the drink
trolley and her white knuckles as the plane drops
a hundred feet. The sun slanting through a porthole
blitzes the ice-blocks in my glass of lemonade
and splinters light across the cabin ceiling.
No, two drinks — one for me, one for Katharina
sleeping somewhere — suddenly the Captain
lifts us up and over the final wall
explaining roads, a town, a distant lake
as a dictionary of shelter — sleeping elsewhere
under a night sky growing bright with stars.

Origins, Heritage, Pilgrimages

R.F. Brissenden

ROCK CLIMBERS, ULURU, 1985

for Adam

First hour in Athens: jet-lagged, raw eyes watering
In the gritty wind, I stood on the Acropolis
And knew my dreaming. We didn't climb Ayers Rock.
Our sacred sites are elsewhere: Marathon,
Glencoe, Gallipoli — mud and sandhills smeared
With ritual blood. And others: Sinai, Rome,
Olympus, ancient rocks on which we've built
Our church. But none so old as this great rock
Where yesterday snake-man, goanna-man
And wallaby-man emerged to make the world.
The web of tracks is torn, the words are stolen.
High above us, sunlit against blue sky,
Small figures struggle up the red stone crest.
The Pitjantjatjara call the climbers ants.

A.D. Hope

A LETTER FROM ROME

for Dr Leonie Kramer

//In fact
Journeying in the company of the Muse,
I'd just arrived at this hotel, unpacked,
Refurbished, washed my face and changed my shoes,
When in she came all smiles and said: "In Rome,
The thing to do is, write a letter home."

"My dear, good girl," I said, "do you forget a
Theme like this needs eagle wings to soar?
I might just rise to a familiar letter,
News, observations, gossip, nothing more.
Besides, it's all been done and done much better;
I've never tried that sort of thing before.
Australian poets, you recall, prefer
The packhorse and the slip-rail and the spur."

"High time they stopped it then," the Muse replied,
"I never liked that pioneering strain,
The tales of how those mountain horsemen ride —
Today they drive a truck or take a plane.//

So here I am in the Eternal City
The Pantheon itself is just next door.
I might be wise, I might at least be witty
Where bards have been so eloquent before.
Some found her splendid, others thought her pretty,
Some said she was the Babylonian Whore;
But each was vocal, *vehemens et tremens*,
From Roman Virgil down to Mrs Hemans.

Yet travelling poets, even at the best,
Are apt to turn out bores or something worse;
Even *Childe Harold*, it must be confessed,
Is sometimes merely Baedeker in verse,
And for a new antipodean guest
Rome as a subject daunts, if not deters.//

Day after day, with guidebook at the ready,
I've stormed the galleries from hall to hall,
Where headless muse or mutilated lady
Are flanked by god unsexed or Dying Gaul.
Checking my members every night in bed, I
Have groaned, I must admit, as I recall
That on the morrow waits for me a fresh
Mountain of marble chiselled into flesh.

I've contemplated all the types of Venus
Which win the heart or take the soul by storm,
The modest fig-leaf and the shameless penis
In every proper or improper form,
Until the individual is the genus
Is lost and all exceptions in the norm,
And fair and foul and quaint and crass and crude
Dissolve in one vast cliché of the Nude.//

Watching these futile pilgrims in their legions
Who must get home to find where they have been,
I find myself who owe them no allegiance,
Caught in a farce as senseless as obscene,
Asking what brings *me* here from those dim regions
Where Dante planted Hell's Back Door, and Dean
Swift his microcosm of civilisation?
The facts fell short of their imagination

For I am no infernal refugee
And reach a normal height of five foot nine.
Yet there *is* something strange, I would agree,
In those dumb continents below the Line.
The roots are European, but the tree
Grows to a different pattern and design;
Where the fruit gets its flavour I'm not sure,
From native soil or overseas manure.

And this uncertainty is in our bones.
Others may think us smug or insular;
The voice perhaps is brash, its undertones
Declare in us a doubt of what we are.
When the divided ghost within us groans
It must return to find its avatar.
Though this puts things too solemnly, of course,
Yet here am I returning to the source.

That source is Italy, and hers is Rome,
The *fons et origo* of Western Man;
Athens perhaps begot, Rome was the womb;
Here the great venture of the heart began.
Here simply with a sense of coming home
I have returned with no explicit plan
Beyond a child's uncertain quest, to find
Something once dear, long lost and left behind.

The clue lies not in art or history,
Relics or ruins that survive their prime.
The thing I came to find was lost in *me*,
Not in the Forum's dust, the Tiber's slime.
The act which resurrects is just to be
Patient before these witnesses of time.
The graves may open and their dead appear,
But mine is the sepulchral voice I hear.

The efficacy of place, like that of prayer,
Lies in no overt effort of the will;
To keep the mind unquesting but aware,
The heart unmoving but responsive still,
Opens the way to forces which prepare
Answers whose questions lie beyond our skill,
And this, I know, is what I have in view,
As other poets, I think, have felt it too.//

Chris Wallace-Crabbe

FLAT OUT IN THE MEZZOGIORNO

for A.D. Hope

Floating far out on the
Mediterranean
buoyed up on greeny deeps …
There's one gold aeroplane
threading the wisps of my
gauzy confusion.

Full stretch, at one with all,
coaldark or luminous,
watching the god wheel over,
I am, in my fashion,
screwed to the ancient world
close to Brindisi.

Glassed like a ghostling's dream,
double as any heart
and just about as black,
antiquity slowly rocks.
Europe is dying,
but in grand style.

Off to my right there floats
buoyant white fairyland,
a steep town once trodden by
paranoid notables
like the Great Ferdinand,
Stupor mundi.

Silvery olive groves
set me to brood about
Quintus Horatius —
he seemed as bland as you,
half-Presbyterian
magus and rogue.

Always you love to rub
God's nose in further dirt;
nobody more than you
embodied the famous
Cornstalk irreverence,
Furphy excepted.

Here, then, a toast to your
rawhide and stringybark
brand of sheer cheek.
Tailtwisting Alec,
sprawled here, I think of you
thousands of miles below.
On with your preacher's bands,
on with your cap and bells:
Avanti, maestro.

Jill Ker Conway

RECHARTING THE GLOBE

Travelling in England and Europe with my mother proved as trying
as I had expected it to be, but it was filled with sudden wonderful
memories of illumination, and with recognitions of things hitherto
only half-understood. When we sailed on the P&O liner *Orsova*,
in early January 1958, I thought I knew my sixty-year-old mother
well. After we'd unpacked and settled into our comfortable flat off
the King's Road in Chelsea, I discovered a new person.

My mother's reactions to new sights and new mores were strong
and spontaneous. On our first necessary pilgrimage to Stratford-
on-Avon, she announced that she didn't care for the English cottage
gardens she'd always admired when seen on chocolate boxes in
Australia. "Too flowery and fussy," she said definitely. But when I
took her to Syon House, for a Sunday afternoon expedition from
London, she was as excited as a child by the flawless Inigo Jones
facade and the Adam interiors.//

After we had made all the routine tourists visits to the sights of
London, she asked to go back to St Paul's. Thinking her interest

related to its symbolism for the distant Empire during the war, I suggested that we take the time to study Wren's plans, climb to the galleries, and look out over the city to imagine the way Wren had planned the relation of his great monument to the eighteenth-century city. We had the luck to come upon a pleasant and well-informed guide, so that even though the climb was agonisingly slow because of my mother's worries about her blood pressure and her rheumatism, we eventually made the 627 steps up to the golden gallery; we lingered there while the guide described Wren's plans for the great square and colonnades surrounding the cathedral, and pointed out the eighteenth-century buildings which could help one imagine London as he saw it. When we descended hours later and made our way to our car parked in Paternoster Square, my mother suddenly dissolved into tears. Thinking her exhausted after hours of climbing and gazing at great heights, I began to make soothing noises and to hurry her home to our comfortable Chelsea flat. "You fool," she finally got out through clenched teeth, "I'm only crying because it is so beautiful. Why have they destroyed it now with all this clutter of buildings?" From then on I knew the day would be a success if it included a great eighteenth-century building, or a manicured garden in the classical style.

For me, schooled as I was in English literature, my mental habits formed by the relationship to nature expressed in Renaissance and Romantic poetry, actually seeing the landscape was a disappointment. The light was too misty, the air too filled with water. The Cotswold hills, the deer grazing in the park at Knole, even the great heath that inspired Hardy's Egdon Heath in *Tess of the D'Urbervilles* seemed on the wrong scale. I had imagined it on a larger scale, and kept wanting to get a longer perspective on things. It took a visit to England for me to understand how the Australian landscape actually formed the ground of my consciousness, shaped what I saw, and influenced the way a scene was organised in my mental imagery. I could teach myself through literature and painting to enjoy this landscape in England, but it would be the schooled response of the connoisseur, not the passionate response one has for the earth where one is born. My landscape was sparer, more brilliant in colour, stronger in its contrasts, majestic in its scale, and bathed in shimmering light.//

Hungry for sun after a misty English spring, we set out in early April for southern France, Spain, and Portugal. New facets of my mother's character emerged as soon as she encountered Latin culture. She loved to sit sipping tea in an open-air cafe, watching the life of the square, getting into conversation with strangers by means of signs, broken English, and her few words of French or Spanish. I marvelled at the sight of this woman, totally solitary at home, in animated conversation with strangers. Hitherto an adherent of the meat-and-three-vegetable school of English cooking, she cast caution to the winds and ate whatever was the dish of the region. She was less curious about seeing buildings and museums than she was about people. I could leave her happily ensconced at some bar or cafe, and wander through the buildings she thought too cold and damp for her rheumatic joints.

When we arrived at Santiago de Compostela I left her, promising to be gone only an hour or so, to see the cathedral.//

My mother was blind to this beauty, so blind that there was a comic divergence between our states of mind whenever we went together to a great monument of Catholic culture. When we arrived at Seville, the Spanish city she found most entrancing of any of our travels, I told her that the cathedral, where it was claimed that Columbus lay buried, was one of Europe's great monuments, and that the square surrounding it, vast in scale, fragrant with the blossoms of its hundreds of orange trees, was something she should see. We happened to reach it on Friday afternoon, in the season before Easter, when it was the custom for the people from the surrounding countryside to fall to their knees on entering the square and progress across it kneeling while reciting the innumerable rosaries it took to traverse the vast space and progress up the steps of the cathedral's grand entrance. I was struck by the faces of the penitents, their dignity and austere beauty, but my mother's tirade about the exploitation of the peasantry by the Church was an obbligato to my exploration of the building which, more than any other, expressed the high point of Spanish culture after the discovery of the New World.

We could each enjoy standing on the spot on the banks of the Guadalquivir River from which Columbus set out to discover the Indies, and we were each entranced by the gardens which were

Spain's heritage from the Moors. In this dry, hot climate, the Moorish influence shaped the use of water and dictated the pattern of walled courtyards where cascades of greenery and the ever-present sound of water banished all sense of heat. "If only I had seen this when I was making my garden at Coorain, I could have made us all feel much cooler," my mother remarked. "I was trying to copy English gardens when this should have been the model." For each of us, in our separate ways, the journey involved the redefinition of our relationship to the past and reconfiguring our sense of geography. Just as we know ourselves in relation to others, so I knew how beautiful Australia was only after encountering the real rather than the imagined landscape of England and Europe. So also, I could not comprehend the blank spaces in Australian urban culture except by seeing the physical expressions of other notions of urban community. The square, the cathedral, the university, and the palace, all grouped around a public space made for theater and processions, yet all on a human scale, made me aware that the heart of our cities was deader than any arid part of the continent, and that our civic and community life was starved of ritual.

In the late 1950s, the Spanish Mediterranean coast north of Barcelona was yet to be discovered by organised tourism. English visitors had been coming there in high summer since before the Spanish Civil war, but they stayed in one or two small resort towns, leaving the small fishing villages which dotted the rugged and beautiful coast untouched. If one did not mind rutted roads, negotiating one's car across the fords which were the only ways of crossing many shallow streams, it was possible to find one's way into small fishing communities where, because of Spain's poverty, the way of life of Catalonia was relatively untouched. Every English person is supposed to shed inhibitions when exposed to Latin culture, and my mother was surely the archetypal one. She didn't make her customary complaints about the plumbing of the simple inn in the small village where we stayed, and she never tired of walking the beach to see the colourful boats of the sardine fleet drawn up after the catch was brought in. The smell of the pines in the hot afternoons, or the shade of the cork woods which alternated with vineyards during our walks along the high jagged coastline, conveyed a strong, definitive sense of place, juxtaposed as they were with one dazzling view of the dark blue ocean after another. At night when the village was filled with the sound of guitars and people could be found dancing the sardana in every small bistro, she abandoned her iron rule about her hour of retiring and stayed happily watching for hours, entranced by a kind of spontaneity and grace she had never seen before. When I told her that legend claimed that the Holy Grail was housed at the monastery of Montserrat, high in the jagged mountains behind the coast, she did not give her usual snort of derision, but said that perhaps we had better make an expedition to Montserrat because she could believe anything possible here. She liked the simple economy of the region, based on harvesting sardines from the sea, wine from the sweet grapes produced along the sunny coast, and cork from the forests. "You may stay in England, or wherever you like," she said, "but I think I may sell Coorain and settle down here, in one of these stone cottages with geraniums tumbling out the window."

Our days in Catalonia were the most relaxed and pleasurefilled of any in our months of travelling together. We had no news from Australia for months, and it seemed foolish here in this world of long siestas and moonlit dancing for me to be fretting about the future. Our visit to Montserrat, laughingly undertaken, proved another moment of cultural revelation. I had been taught about the romantic notion of the sublime, the sense of the grandeur and terror of nature, in contrast to the more domestic and social quality of beauty. Two sites in Europe, Montserrat and the Grande Chartreuse, appeared and reappeared in discussions of the power of nature so revered in romanticism. So it was with my mind filled with Edmund Burke's phrases on the sublime and the beautiful, and Wagner's imagery in *Parsifal* that I drove up the steep and narrow road to the monastery. It was true that from this high point in the mountains one could see the ocean and the expanse of the eastern range of the Pyrenees. It was a grand extended view on a scale I was used to, but I felt nothing here akin to the mystical sense of oneness with nature I felt alone on the plains of New South Wales. On the other hand, when we went into the chapel at Montserrat and heard the boys' choir singing at the end of mass, the same chants such a choir had been singing for seven hundred years, I was transported by the beauty of the first Gregorian chant

I had ever heard. I realised that the English romanticism I had taken for a universal was a cultural category in which I did not participate. Nothing made it clearer to me that I was from another world and would have to arrive at my cultural values for myself. Sacred music and ecclesiastical architecture expressed real universals which spoke to me whenever I met them. I hadn't expected to be moved by the imagery and sounds of Catholic Europe, but I was.//

When we made weekend visits to the country, I was less certain about our English hosts, hospitable though they were. They could not have been kinder, but I resented their air of superiority toward Australians. I wasn't used to being patronised by people less well read than I, nor to having the history I knew so well explained to me as though I could not possibly know anything about it. I came to wait for the ultimate compliment which could be counted on by Sunday breakfast. I knew the confidential smile and the inclination of the head would be followed by "You know, my dear, one would hardly know you were not English." I couldn't control the irritation produced by such accolades, and would usually begin to tell preposterous stories about life in the outback to emphasise how different I was.

Australia's class system seemed harmless enough when one observed British snobbery and class consciousness at work. I chuckled at overhearing one friend my mother made on shipboard tell her proudly about the dinner party at which she and her husband had been guests the night before. "My dear, we were sixteen sitting down to dinner, and Freddy and I were the only ones without a title." But it was not so funny to see the very intelligent child of the caretaker of our flat taken from school at fifteen and sent to work, so that he wouldn't get ideas above his place.//

As the promised year abroad accompanying my mother wore on, boredom set in. I knew now what I was going to do. I was going home to study history. It was no use pretending that I wasn't a scholar. I could certainly make myself an idle life in London being another expatriate Australian enjoying the cultural riches of the city, but that was to live perpetually by the standards of a culture I now saw as alien. I didn't want to take another degree at an Oxford or Cambridge college either, for that would involve going more deeply into the contradictions of being a colonial in the metropolitan society. I'd made one or two excursions to senior common rooms as the guest of fellow Australians. I found I wasn't interested in the rituals of scholarly one-upmanship which seemed to delight my hosts. Several times, I was outraged by the unmistakable undertones of studied rudeness to women. I wasn't interested in becoming less womanly to avoid that hostility, and I certainly wasn't interested in becoming more English and less Australian. I was going back to Australia to test my new sense of the world and my new perspective on Australian society. So far as my mother was concerned, I told myself I would see her established in Sydney once again, and then break the news that I would not be living with her.//

I heard the broad Australian accents of the Qantas stewards and hostesses with new appreciation, as we listed to the flight announcements before our departure from London Airport for the two and a half days in the air required to reach Sydney by the shortest route home from London across the United States. Once I'd thought those voices a tiresome sign of deviation from standard English speech. Now they were an accent like any other, an inheritance of history and dialect. The flight was long and tiring, but always made amusing by the slangy good humor of the crew, and the friendliness of the other passengers.//

Two days later, I was gazing down at the coastline north of Sydney, waiting for the first sight of the Harbour to appear. I'd always thought Sydney beautiful, but now I planned to look at it on its own terms. It was a great seaport city, lying on the rim of an arid continent, Mediterranean in light and vegetation, its greys and scarlets and lemon scents unique to its native eucalyptus. It looked out across the vast expanse of the Pacific, not to Europe but to Japan and continental Asia. To arrive where we started and know the place for the first time, I thought, as Sydney's golden beaches appeared, strung out like a necklace around the grey-green city, dancing in the morning sunlight. I promised myself I would never speak about the Far East again. It was absurd that it had taken me until I was twenty-three years old to get oriented on the globe, but I was glad that I finally knew where I was.

Shirley Hazzard

THE TUSCAN IN EACH OF US

The anthem of praise raised by foreign writers — and in particular by writers in English — to Italy, to Tuscany, to Florence, has consistently sounded a note of relief. Its theme is that of a heaven-sent rescue: the rescue of the self from incompleteness. We realise that we had always dreamed we might dwell among such scenes and sentiments, and now we find our wish consummated. We celebrate an environment that is both a revelation and a repose to us, a consolation and a home. Like all love, this love of foreigners for Tuscany is easy to mock. Like all love, it is an object of envy on the part of those who feel excluded from it. (And let us remember the observation of Dr Johnson: "A man who has not been in Italy is always conscious of an inferiority.") We are told that it is not original, it is not realistic. It is true that there may be illusion in it, and a lack of what is currently defined as realism. But does it not seem to you, in these times, that in the name of realism we are being asked to mock our very souls?

Illusion is part of civilised power. Wherever there is civilisation, there is to some degree illusion. Yeats says that

> Civilisation is hooped together, brought
> Under a rule, under the semblance of peace
> By manifold illusion.

And Clough, in his beautiful poem, *Amours de Voyage*, reflects on Italy:

> Is it illusion or not that attracteth the pilgrim transalpine
> Brings him a dullard and dunce hither to pry and to stare?
> Is it illusion or not that allures the barbarian stranger,
> Brings him with gold to the shrine, brings him in arms
>   to the gate?

As E. M. Forster's hero Fielding arrives in Italy from the orient, Forster tells us that a "cup of beauty was lifted to his lips, and he drank with a sense of disloyalty … He had forgotten the beauty of form … the harmony between the works of man and the earth that upholds them … The Mediterranean" says Forster, "is the human norm. When men leave that exquisite lake, whether through the

Bosphorus or the Pillars of Hercules, they approach the monstrous and extraordinary."

The Mediterranean, as an ideal, is the human norm. Not a norm as a levelling, nor as *la legge della media*; but an equilibrium in which individual quality can rationally flourish. Comprehensiveness here, and comprehension, have time and again restored our disparate elements to form, and healed us. Winckelmann spoke for many of us when he said that "God owed me Italy, for I had suffered too much in my youth." Release, expansiveness, the nurturing of elements intrinsic but denied — these are the themes even of such a rigorous observer as D.H. Lawrence. We embrace this culture as our own, in the beautiful phrase of Burckhardt, "by a kind of hereditary right or by right of admiration", not so much undergoing a transformation as acknowledging at last the Tuscan in each of us.

That sense of rightfulness has its definable source in humanism. Outsiders have been drawn to Tuscany and to Florence as to the centre and capital of their own civilised values. One might almost say that even those — and they are many — who come to Florence to buy new shoes and table linen do so, in some remote degree, in the name of humanism: for they have heard that Florence matters. Travellers from lands where humanism is unknown respond to the Tuscan phenomenon; and perhaps this refers to the humanist in each of us. In the newer societies beyond these shores I believe that we begin to see the death of humanism; and this is even urged on in the name of that unexamined "reality" and in unchallenged retreat from individualism although none can predict what loss of humanistic values will mean, or what will be the future moral bearing of humanity. These matters already have their strong effects on Tuscan life; but here we are nevertheless made aware that what was so many centuries in the making will not surrender easily. In fact, that sensation of relief that Tuscany has always afforded to outsiders has been re-charged in recent years: for here, as yet, humanism labours under no disfavour, and need not appear self-conscious. Like Machiavelli in his great letter from S. Andrea in Percussina, we shed here much nonsense unworthy of our better selves.

An Australian of my generation grew up in raw ignorance of

humanism, of the Renaissance, of Tuscan art. The themes of Italy were little developed in the Australian literature that came to our hands; and although we encountered it in literature more generally, our own circumstances and those of the globe before and during the Second World War made Italy remote from us. We were given no inkling that the immemorial influences of this land had helped to form the Australian social order; and — to speak generally — Australians of those years were often inaccessible to unfamiliar concepts, and hostile to aesthetic revelation. It is notable that these Tuscan places that played so prominent a part in English and European literature figure only exceptionally in Australian writing of past generations. Even now, I think of rather few strong examples, but rather of passing incidents. In Patrick White's *Riders in the Chariot*, well-to-do Australians are glimpsed in Florence at the turn of the century, in a sarcastic aside drawn from the diary of an unhappy matron: "Norbert *indefatigable*. Italy his *spiritual home*. Only a few nights ago he embarked on a long poem on the theme of *Fra Angelico* ... Now that we are in a villa of our own, hope to discover some respectable woman who will know to prepare him his mutton chop." And in the same novel an English girl writes from Florence to her estranged suitor in England in what the author tells us is a "somewhat literary strain, about the 'little green hills of Tuscany, with their exciting undertones of sensuous brown' ." and we are informed that the recipient of the letter "had no inclination to read any farther". Fortunately, perhaps, I had not read those lines when I first came to Tuscany and quite possibly wrote letters of a literary taint about its green hills — *colline, infatti, di un verdolino luminoso. Sì, cantavo anch'io, come tanti altri, le giornate radiose, i campi curati come un giardino, e i solchi disegnati a calligrafia. E più di tutto parlavo — sempre* "in somewhat literary strain" — *delle gentilezze incredibili di questo popolo.* I lived near Siena in a scene described by a Tuscan poet — Folgore de San Gimignano — looking towards

> *una montagnetta*
> *coverta di bellissimi arboscelli,*
> *con trenta ville e dodici castelli*
> *che siano entorno ad una cittadetta ...*

I too, like so many others before me, sat outdoors in what

Leopardi calls the *"sovrumani silenzi"* in the Tuscan night under the moon, to hear the *gufo* in the cypresses; and woke on brilliant mornings to hear the farmer shouting to the two white beasts that drew the plough. That was another Tuscany, then — though not in time historically remote. The paired white cows that pulled the plough, the close lines of vines beneath the olives, the appearance everywhere of order without uniformity or excessive regularity. For the most part, then Tuscany was a countryside of appropriate and long-established rural buildings. One drove from Florence to Siena on the Cassia; and those two hours seemed well spent. Or once in a while by the Via Chiantigiana, which took pleasantly longer. I was too knowing to speak of Tuscany as my spiritual home; but felt it to be so. And, although I never attempted "a long poem on the theme of Fra Angelico", it was in Tuscany that I became a writer.

I have seen Florence under many conditions, and have known this city in dark as well as golden days. I remember a beautiful June morning, just after daybreak, when, arriving overnight by train from Geneva, I crossed from the station to have my coffee at the Caffè Italia, where a waiter was hosing down the pavement. And I sat there lacking nothing, in a state of perfect happiness I've never forgotten, realising I was again in Tuscany. I remember too, years later, another arrival by train — this time on a December evening in 1966, when for a last freezing hour the train laboured through the mud-laden tracks of the city's outskirts, surrounded by detritus of the flood. In those drastic weeks Florence lay as if stranded along the Arno; one looked upstream through the skeleton of the Ponte Vecchio; the familiar streets were befouled watercourses; and everywhere, indoors and out, the ghastly line was streaked along saturated walls. I remember, in streets and shops, the tears and courage, and the Florentine durability — the Florentine toughness. I saw the great Cimabue laid like a living casualty on a trestle table, and the books heaped up like pulp at the Certosa di Galluzzo. I saw a cat called Gianna who saved herself by clinging for a week to a ham suspended from the ceiling of a *salumeria* in Borgo Ognissanti. I remember that the cold was bitterest in Gavinana and San Frediano, where recovery was slowest, and in the poorer streets near Santa Croce. And I remember the hippies in their hundreds, digging out mud and sewage, sleeping on damp floors, and sitting down to eat in long rows at improvised tables. I recall the experts and museum curators, the art historians who converged on the city from Europe and America and raised funds abroad for restoration — funds that came from all around the globe; for the world was moved, and so was the Tuscan in each of us.

It is said to be a misfortune to be granted one's dearest wish. How many of us, nevertheless — outsiders like myself, achieving our desire to inhabit this peninsula — have been rewarded beyond our dreams. Because beyond dreams there is life itself and the intensity of being. Tuscany has a wealth of healing properties, but Tuscany is not a *casa di cura*. It is not a tame place but a stimulus: in the truest sense, one of the world's great powers. I think of Shelley in Florence in 1819 walking one day along the Arno to the Cascine in a hard west wind and coming home to write an immortal poem. Of that "Ode to the West Wind" he would note: "This poem was conceived and chiefly written in a wood that skirts the Arno ... on a day when that tempestuous wind, whose temperature is at once mild and animating, was collecting the vapours which pour down the autumnal rains. They began, as I foresaw, at sunset with a violent tempest of hail and rain, attended by that magnificent hunder and lightning peculiar to the Cisalpine regions."

This lovely place, in its endless richness and hospitality, has touched many great and lesser minds to emulation in the noblest meaning of the word. It has touched the Antipodes, and Australians who have never visited Tuscany have known it by influence and in imagination. It has moved us to do our best.

Rosemary Dobson

PHIGALIA

Vermilion (cinnabar) was mined in Spain
and later sent for processing to Rome:
and this was done two thousand years ago

so we are told. Pausanias, pushing back
the ivy-leaves that clung about the form
of Neat Wine Dionysos carved in stone,

and noting all as he was used to do,
reports the statue marked with fading red.
His annotator following after him

climbed the same cliffs to reach the level ground
and found the village as Pausanias said
though all those centuries had passed between.

I store the pieces that he found. Am loath
to bring together all to make a whole.
I *like* the broken pieces in my mind.

Thus: hens are pecking in the frescoed church
where grasses grow between the paving-stones —
the newer church built in Byzantine times.

The water-spring the village women use
rises from classic marbles tumbled round,
and in a barn wall roughly held with clay

archaic writing, untranslated yet —
like columns in Themistokles' great wall
hastily built — is fastened upside-down.

And, best of all, in nineteen sixty-eight
the village priest, the annotator says,
sat reading from Pausanias in the shade.

I have no part in this but wish I had:
the earlier traveller and the later one,
the priest, the hens, the water-spring, the words

cut in fourth-century marble, and the trace
of cinnabar from Spain smeared on the thighs
of Dionysos (whom they called Neat Wine

in the old days, Pausanias said) I hold
as precious fragments in my littered mind —
a life-enhancing store for leaner times.

Diane Fahey

SACRED CONVERSATIONS

After seeing Titan's "St Mark Enthroned, with SS Cosmas and Damian, Roch and Sebastian", Venice.

I am tired of all those Saint Sebastians standing there
at the feet of Madonna or super-saint, among other
saved ones all waiting for the next prayerful utterance
while ruminating on eternity. He is always so undressed
yet so aloof, so helpless yet complacent, so wounded yet whole.
I like saints who hide their virtues beneath ample,
jewel-coloured robes, for whom pain is pain, and joy, joy,
not some awful mix-up of the two.
                              Still, this Sebastian by
Titian stops me. Only one arrow pierces his body;
another, fallen from his calf, lies on the floor, abstemiously.
He has a serious, inward gaze, and no blood. But the glory
of the painting is his stance, graceful yet arrogant —
if one could strut while standing still, he's doing it.
My guess is that he was a sixteenth century gondolier,
happy to be gaining money for so little effort, but bored
with standing motionless for so long on *terra firma*.
So he imagines being gazed at by each woman who enters
the church — over four centuries, a tall order,
but time has delivered …
                              Above, Saint Mark is half-shadow;
Moses-like, he holds the book, stares at dark stars;
but this man's face is clear, his body resembles neither
ravaged nor risen saviour's, the knots in that white cloth
can be undone … For those arrows belong to Eros,
and this is not Christ but Dionysus, who has wandered into
a strangely silent conversation.

Bruce Beaver

AUSTRALIAN POET C.1988 VISITS THE HOME OF AN ENGLISH POET C. 1888

We being human poet wife and child
not I but we have come to wonder at
all the bloody fuss
over this old house
that once belonged to a family
which managed accidentally
to throw off a famous poet
who probably remained single and died
incredibly old or young
(the brochure's not too strong on biography)
and made a point of never writing a word
when at home (that is to say, here).
One has to pay to get in now.
Two and a bit times in my case.
And all I can think of is "He's dead
and famous. But dead foremost."
My wife is (I hope) silently
forgiving me for not owning
a place even half as old
with a third of the bedrooms and for her
part you can stuff the poetry bit
with the xmas pud and mistletoe
now we are three and expatriate.
                              The child
wets itself in sympathy as we exit.

Christopher Koch

LONDON, LATE 1950s

For me, the London of fancy became the London of fact at the age
of twenty-two; and by pure chance, my entry was made via the
Strand. Robert Brain and I, penniless after hitchhiking about

Europe, had landed in England at Harwich, having come across by ferry from the Hook of Holland. We caught the train to London, and entered the tube system, to emerge into the city's open air at Charing Cross Station.

Here was the Strand then, on a fine summer's morning, carrying its human streams towards the Aldwych, St Clement Danes and the Inns of Court and Chancery where Dickens's Lord High Chancellor had sat at the heart of the fog, and no doubt sat still. Here were men actually wearing black morning coats, pinstriped trousers and bowler hats, wielding furled umbrellas, whom we examined with joy, until one of them glared at us. Here was a real copy of the *Times*, bought from an actual, cloth-capped Cockney at the entrance of the station, who called Robert "Guv'nor". A man passed us now clad in a suit of green silk, wearing a green top hat and talking to himself. He was an unusual sight to young Tasmanians in 1955, but no one else in the crowd even glanced at him: here was the famous British tolerance of eccentricity. We entered Forte's cafe across the road, where we drank without complaint a grey liquid called coffee which was certainly not coffee; then, in a daze of delight, we wandered on under the promised porticoes and pinnacles of filigreed stone. There was Villiers Street, running down to the Embankment, where we might well have to sleep out, we knew, if we didn't find jobs immediately. And here, reassuringly, was Tasmania House, where we went in to the desk and found our mail awaiting us. This was our club, and London was already our home.

But if it was home, it was a stern and tight-fisted one. For the first time, we understood our good fortune simply in being born Australian. Postwar Australia was carefree and prosperous; postwar Britain was grim and poor; these facts were soon borne in on us, as we contemplated weekly wages which at home would barely have satisfied us as pocket money, and nearly half of which would be needed to rent a single bedsitting room. London was still marked by the Blitz: war-damaged buildings were being repaired, and flowers grew on the gaping bomb-sites. An air of austerity persisted, and people had the manner of cheerfulness in adversity: that style we had become familiar with in wartime British films. Faced with these realities, we soon separated. Robert landed a job in one of the counties, teaching in a summer school; and I found myself alone in London.

At that time, the new Welfare State didn't pay unemployment benefits which made survival possible; nor did one thing of applying for them. I must quickly find work or starve; I had five pounds borrowed from Robert to stave off that eventuality, and my search began. Tramping the streets, gazing up at lighted windows in Charing Cross Road, Piccadilly and the Bayswater Road, peering through the doorways of buildings whose intimidating neo-Greek façades forbade entry to any shabby young colonial, I began to understand what the American writer Thomas Wolfe had discovered here before me: that there were two races in England, the Big People and the Little People.

These were the days before large-scale immigration from India and the West Indies, and the island's two indigenous races were very clearly recognisable; I was seeing, although I didn't know it, the last of the frozen old England which the post-imperial era was dissolving. The Big People, who ate in restaurants in Mayfair and Soho where the prices terrified me, were conveyed past in Jaguars and Rovers and Rolls Royces, and lived in another London than the one I was discovering. My London was the London of the tiny bedsitter in Bayswater or Earls Court or Notting Hill Gate, with its gas-ring for cooking, gas-meter to pay coins into, aged washbasin and shared, freezing bathroom down the passage. "Your bath will be on Tuesdays and Thursdays," my first landlady informed me. "Mr Drummond has his on Mondays and Wednesdays, and Miss Appleby has hers the other days." My London was the London of the cheap caf, with sausages, eggs and chips for two and sixpence, and tea for fourpence. It was a London whose streets were the grey of old overcoats, its buildings of that liver-coloured brick whose hue seems the essence of despair; the districts of *Little Dorrit*:

> Wildernesses of corner houses, with barbarous old porticoes and appurtenances, horrors that came into existence under some wrong-headed person in some wrong-headed time ... Rickety dwellings ... like the last results of the great mansions breeding in-and-in ...

This London, into which I was descending like so many other young Australians, was the London of the Little People: Cockneys and working-class Londoners who received us with the friendliness of fellow-spirits. Cockneys in particular assumed that an Australian was a sort of lost tribal brother, and one felt that this was so. The Little People existed with few creature comforts, keeping their clothes neat and maintaining an unaccountable jauntiness. They didn't own the houses they lived in; they had no cars; they could afford no holidays, except for a few days at Brighton; their only pleasures were a few pints of bitter in the evenings and a seat in the cinema or the music hall once a week. And this life was soon to be mine.

The interview for my first job held a promise of glamour. It was conducted by a pretty young employment officer at Lyons Corner House, where I had applied to wash dishes. She spoke in the accents of the Big People. "Hev you ever appeared before the public?"

No, I said cautiously, I hadn't.

"Do you maind appearing before the public?"

No, I didn't mind; and I was issued with the grey, vaguely Cossack jacket which was the required uniform of a Lyons waiter, and sent out on the floor to what was called a "station". This was a block of tables which it was my duty to keep cleared of dirty crockery, and where my other task was to pour tea and coffee for the customers. The kitchen, reached through swinging doors, was a tiled ante-chamber to Hell; here I fought through a line of other snarling waiters to keep my coffee and tea pots filled at the huge, hissing urns. But outside, on the red-carpeted floor, all was grandeur.

Lyons Corner House at the corner of Tottenham Court Road and Oxford Street, long vanished, was really just a big self-service restaurant. But it provided elegance; it was a place where the Little People could pretend to be Big People, helped by the fact that after they had queued for their meals, their tea and coffee were poured for them by waitresses, or by uniformed men such as myself. A big Hammond organ was played by a man in a dinner jacket in the afternoons, and the whole scene was patrolled by a species of floor-walker: men in frock coat and striped trousers who were our immediate superiors, and who kept us up to the mark. They too, I realised from their accents, were technically Little People, but they were physically large and martial looking and had an air of haughty

menace that was very intimidating, lining us up each morning for
a military inspection.

"Koch, your uniform's filthy. Get a fresh one."

"Sir."

I earned five pounds a week, and my bedsitter in Notting Hill
Gate cost three; it was not really enough to survive, but on Friday,
which was payday, Lyons allowed us a free meal. I had worked out
that by Thursday I could usually afford either to eat or to smoke;
being addicted to cigarettes then, I chose to smoke. Lying in bed
on a Thursday night, my stomach rumbling, dragging deeply on a
Woodbine (the cheap fag of the Little People), I would think about
the free meal in the kitchen next day, which included nauseating
cream cakes. Like many of the Little People, I allowed myself a pint
of bitter in the pub in the evening, a picture show a week, and ten
cigarettes a day; these pleasures being digested with miserly care. I
should have been miserable, but I wasn't; a vast elation would seize
me at unexpected moments. My love affair with the real London
had begun.

I had begun to comprehend that this city of cities, despite its
grim façades and its penny-pinching and its beggars, was strangely
gentle. The gold light of October fell on sooty, golden stone, and
on a hundred gently-frowning little church spires, and I began to
understand too what every newcomer here learned: that it was
really a set of villages, and that one of its great virtues was a fond,
village cheerfulness. Cockney bus conductors impersonated comedians on the double-deckers that took me along Oxford Street in
the mornings; motherly women in shops called me "dear", and I
saw that people smiled at each other far more than they did in any
Australian city. One Sunday morning in that autumn, I was woken
in my room in Ladbroke Square by the sound of a tune, floating
through the window from the street below: "Maybe it's because I'm
a Londoner":

I get that funny feeling inside of me
Just walking up and down.
Maybe it's because I'm a Londoner
That I love London town …

I knew who was playing it: a group of street musicians I'd often
seen trudging along the kerb in the Bayswater Road: a one-armed,

straw-haired trumpeter, an old accordionist with a black Homburg hat; a thin violinist in a long muffler. I had heard this ballad in an earlier life, it seemed to me, and I knew, in my Sunday bed, that in some way I already belonged to the London of my ancestors, and would do so forever.

I had now begun to make friends. My first friends were two show-business men down on their luck: Derek, a Canadian tap-dancer working with me in Lyons, and his friend Buddy, a New Zealand accordionist. They shared a shabby double room in Camden Town, home of Bob Cratchit, where Buddy would cook us elaborate Sunday roasts. Later I would make English friends, but for now, we three outcasts from the old Dominions wandered about London in our time off, sharing our loneliness. Derek and Buddy, I came to realise, had no friends other than me.

"They'll never let you into their homes," Buddy told me, discussing the English. "Never. Just realise that from the start." A bald, stout old man of around sixty, always in a brown felt hat, he had a high, chanting voice and a dolefully dogmatic air, and was very bitter against the world. He was now working on a counter in an Oxford Street department store; it had been some years, I gathered, since he had played his accordion around the music halls, and I suspected that he would never be hired again. He put his troubles down to corrupt theatrical agents who refused to book him.

"Those bloody agents," he would say. "They take bribes. They work their favourites into the halls, and leave better performers to starve. If I could shoot them all, I would; every one of the greasy bastards. The barrel of my rifle would be running *hot*, and still I'd be blazing away." His mouth worked, as he stared into vistas of carnage.

"Now Buddy," Derek would say soothingly. "You're just workin' yourself up." He was a thin, pale, sweet-natured man in his thirties, with thin blond hair, who always referred to himself as a "hoofer". He too hadn't been hired for some time, and I wondered if he would ever hoof again.

Buddy and Derek introduced me to the music halls: one of the cheap pleasures that London then offered the Little People. For ninepence, we could go upstairs at Collins' Music Hall or the old

Finsbury Park Empire and watch jugglers, comedians, dancers, and vocalists like Dicky Valentine. Buddy and Derek would whisper professional comments in the dark, staring down at the lemon-lit stage from which they were exiled.//

Derek and Buddy drifted out of my life, because now I'd found a girl, and had escaped from that London which is the capital of loneliness, where the aged and the lost wander in calm despair. Young, poor and happy, my English girlfriend and I held hands along the Embankment and over Waterloo Bridge; we watched Richard Burton play Iago at the Old Vic; we listened to Hancock's Half Hour on the radio in my bedsitter at night, as the iron, majestic cold of the northern winter closed in, and the pea soupers that Holmes and Watson knew began. We tied handkerchiefs around our noses against the smog; breathing in, we left a yellow stain. But I was not appalled by this winter; it was winter in the city of cities, the grim and gentle old friend I had waited for. I thrilled to its sheer, icy edge, and looked up at the pole star, and discovered what I believed no one had noticed before: that the moon here was upside down. Or rather, I told Patricia, the moon in Australia was upside down; and I now understood why the man in the moon's face, in English nursery books, was shown in pictures to have a mouth like an O. In Australia, the mouth was one of the eyes ...

Thomas Keneally

ON THE ROAD IN IRELAND

My Irish-descended relatives in the bush would, in my childhood, never begin a journey without three Hail Mary's for a safe arrival. I know why that was now. It was the memory of Irish roads.

It is a matter of credit that this is a country lacking in freeways, except for rare stretches like the one near Limerick which sweeps the tourist from Shannon Airport to Bunratty Castle. Bunratty's Disney-esque reputation is such that people believe it was built especially for tourism. The castle is a real castle, built by the MacNamaras in the 1460s. During the Irish uprising of 1641, the one which would bring the Curse of Cromwell down on Ireland, it served as a refuge for planted English and Scots. Now it has been restored. It puts on medieval feasts and has a Folk Park where tweeds and sweaters and jaunty hats can be bought. And a freeway runs there from Shannon airport.

But it doesn't last any further. Even the main highways, Limerick to Killarney, Killarney to Cork, Cork to Waterford, Waterford to Dublin, Dublin to Newry, Newry to Coleraine, Coleraine to Derry — even these are real roads, roads you know you're travelling on. Given that normal mix of stubborn conservatism and debonair recklessness with which various of the Irish drive, even for these main arteries you need three Hail Mary's or any other ritual you feel you can depend on.

Motorists wave to each other in Ireland. This doesn't happen anywhere else except in remotest Australia and in cattle towns in Wyoming. I am sure that no collision occurs in Ireland without a fraternal or sisterly wave preceding it.

The realest roads, the most beautiful and the most perilous are the country ones. Examples of them: there's a high, narrow, awestruck road over the Caha Mountains from Glengariff to Kenmare. Bantry Bay, that is, to Kenmare River. On the right day it will keep you honest. At random: another runs from Ballybofey via Glenties and Ardara down to Glencolumbkille (or Gleann Cholm Cille). Here's another one for those who like to arrive with a sense not of routine but of deliverance: Recess (Sraith Salac) to Kylemore to Letterfrack to Cleggan. The R476 from Ennis to Corrofin in Clare encouraged me to yearn for the lost certainties of the Rosary; a quaking decade would have been a great soother. As it was I had to fall back on humanist assurances that the statistics for brain damage in accidents on such lanes are probably lower than you would expect. I won't bore you with other lists of superb but perilous thoroughfares from Monaghan, Mayo, Sligo, Donegal, Cavan, Meath, Wicklow and so on.

These country roads are roads which you know have been built for pilgrims and cattle. Here, as nowhere else in Europe, you are made to travel at a reflective pace. The men who drive the herds down these narrow ways look as though livestock are very important to them. You don't dare nudge the flanks or shoulders of any beast. Local people often drive through herds with a blackthorn in their window-side hands, uttering thick curses and pushing and thwacking flanks. It's still not fast work to get through. One day over near the cliffs of Mother, I drove in a gale in the midst of an ambling herd for half an hour.

Sometimes the roads are for games too. There have been till modern times few suppositions that traffic is more important than games. Once in a Cork, my progress to Clonakilty was held up by a jovial man who raised his hand and came to the window to ask me would I mind waiting. His hands were full of the enormous Irish banknotes which have since been replaced by smaller, niftier coins. There was, he said, a "bahling contest" on between two local champions. "Fellas have a lot of money on this one if you don't mind sir."

Two contestants sling a ball along a country road for a given number of miles. If the road doubles back on itself, they are allowed to throw cross-country, but there are penalties if they land in the rough. This must be an ancient game, maybe a Celtic version of the principle exploited by American Indians in the game which ultimately became known as lacrosse.

If you want to be strict-minded about it, you could say such a plain thing as that Irish roads reflect Ireland's small tax base. But they also of course reflect something of the Irish spirit. The compulsory wave reminds me of the impulse Australian males have to call everyone *mate* as a means of showing they don't think they're better than anyone. So the Irish driver says, "Just because I'm on the wrong side of the road doesn't mean at all that I'm denying your right to be here."

Irish roads are therefore where citizens of flashier and more arrogant nations go to be reduced to an appropriately human scale of progress. Not only by means of the highways' narrowness and peril; not by means of their frequent black spots — a black circle on white — which mark the places where someone has gone too suddenly to his death. But also by means of their packed detail and their recurring beauty.//

On a penitentially narrow, stone-fringed road in Galway I gave a lift to a small, red-haired woman with a backpack. There are few countries in Western Europe where hitchhiking can be so safely done, at little peril for both the driver and the passenger.

It turned out that this woman was a poet. Her first book of verse was about to be published by Raven Arts Press in Dublin. I was very pleased to be in Yeats' country with his potential successor.

She was intelligent and knew a great deal of the world. So I was very careful not to present her with the normal soulfulness of the dispersed Irish back for a visit; the dogged condolence which is typical of those who have become something else yet believe they are still of Ireland's whole cloth.

I was tentative and apologetic about talking of the melancholy of Ireland. To me though it's so inescapable. The vacancies and the ghosts. You wouldn't even have to know anything about the history to see it, but the history helps. Yet I noticed that the Irish were impatient with you for referring to the melancholy. They were getting to a stage of their history where they wanted to be positive. And besides, it was their sadness, and they'd fitted it into their scheme of life, and they didn't want you coming along and over-balancing everything with the weight of your glib emotion.

I realised that the wistfulness of the returner — as I apologised to the woman — must drive the natives crazy. Here they are, attempting to fit in as good citizens of the European Community and signatories of the European Unity Act and fans of U2. But the roads are crammed with effusive foreigners, their brains a pastiche of bits of ballad, of folk and family memory, all of them determined not to associate Ireland with the future, but to rivet to its past, while at the same time complaining about the narrowness of the roads!

I had noticed the same phenomenon in Israel: honest and practical Israelis are often impatient with fervid New Jersey Jews, or Palestinians with the city intellectuals of Amman or Damascus. For it is true that nothing is owned more intimately by a people than their tragedies, that no outsider should, on whatever grounds, try to horn in.

The poet listened tolerantly to me as I spoke, but she was on to more exciting stuff. She told me about a country house, now an An Óige (Youth) Hostel in Doorus near Kinvara, where she'd stayed the night before. The hostel has once been the country house of the preposterously named Count Floribund de Basterot, who entertained there not only Guy de Maupassant and Paul Bourget, but also the leading figures of the Irish Revival — Yeats, Lady

Gregory, AE (George Russell), and Douglas Hyde, the founder of the Gaelic League. There one afternoon in 1897, when Yeats and Lady Gregory were stuck indoors escaping the rain, they began to discuss the establishment of a theatre likely to perform their work, especially work derived from the Irish folklore of the West. The theatre they pledged themselves to that afternoon was eventually established just after Christmas 1904. It was the Abbey, Ireland's massive gift to the world of drama.

It wasn't quite accurate perhaps to say that a fortuitous shower at Doorus generated the Abbey, but it was nearly so.

And so she accentuated the positive, and the visitor from sun-struck Australia wept over the steering wheel, keeping time with the driving rain beyond the windscreen and telling all the sad Celtic tales to a Celt.

She may not have been a Celt anyway, of course, despite her red hair. Because her home town was Ennis originally, and if her ancestors had spent centuries in Ennis, then it must be recognised that it was a great centre of settlement by the Normans and the English. But I think we'd have to say that this talented young woman was at least a demi-Celt.

So I confessed to her that I didn't know if it was childhood conditioning — whether it was what the St Joseph nuns told me in the room in Wauchope, New South Wales, where on Sunday the priest put his vestments on and which the rest of the week was a schoolroom. Or whether it was sudden fumes of anger from grandparents. In any case, I'd never been able to come to Ireland without feeling that it was haunted by absences. Every little stone enclosure, and every cottage whose roof tree had been broken, spoke to me of evictions and forced emigration. After all, I reasoned with this poet, Ireland is the only EC country whose population has declined since 1841, and not just declined, but been reduced by a factor of two or three.

James McAuley

ii. IN THE MIRABELL GARDEN

from Trakl: Salzburg

Tableaux of lust and violence explode
In grey baroque marble. Bell-strokes pulse the air.
A camera circles round a bridal pair
Married this morning by the civil code.

Wrought-iron fronds are rusting on the gate.
Blond Helen smiles at being lifted high;
A weather-stain has blotched one cheek and eye
Of Paris as he abducts his opulent freight.

You paced this formal garden through and through.
Primroses filled the scrolls of the parterre.
The band played brightly. Ladies took a chair,

And stealthy lovers disappeared from view
In turns of the Irrgarten; which for you
Became the crisscross maze of your despair.

Isobel Robin

FREUD'S BACKYARD

Berggasse IX, Vienna

The doctor's not at home.
For a few schillings you may stroll
past letters, photos, musty souvenirs,
and old confessions
sheened like wax on weighty chairs
(though the body imprint's gone).

Prim, sequential, why do rooms like these
bring on uneasiness?
You find you're listening for dead people's pain.
Perhaps the wallpaper
covers too many secrets, old and mousey,
muttering where they scratch with dingy claws.

Go now, unnoticed — leave discreetly
through the door, then run —
follow your footsteps' echo
down cold stairs.

A dusty window, quaintly scrolled,
exposes Freud's backyard:
a glimpse of shattered psyches spilling from a bin;
libido bagged for burial;
Oedipus howling for his Mum —

all in the mind!
There's no detritus here from dreadful dreams;
the sanely waltzing Viennese
have whipped it stiff and baked it in a torte.

Jan Owen

TOWN

Eisenstadt, Austria

The alliance was uneasy even then.
Close to the border
we found that day
your country as it was
before the war
renamed *Kismárton* Eisenstadt.
Arched doors and gateways, fruit trees,
angular houses, plain or baroque as clouds.
Eszterházy Palace where Haydn played,
and Liszt in the Square,
elegant even in stone.
In the little cake shop where you bought
the cakes of your childhood,
almás rétes, pózsónyi kifli,
they spoke the old tongue still,
only you paid in schillings not in forint.
"*Köszönöm szépen,*" smiled the broad-cheeked woman.
The church was a simple dome,
a beehive of russet shadows and yellow light,
round and warm as a country stove,
homely enough for a child to believe in God.
The sky was open as the *Alföld.*
We sat on a wall to eat.
"Look."
A walnut tree by a barn, a wooden cart,
geese honking through wet grass
and an arc of rainbow in bruised light.
"Hungary."
You could not swallow,
staring along the fault-line of a dream.
Hungary. As close as we ever came.

Andrew Riemer

RETURN TO BUDAPEST

My return was a reverse-image of the way I left Budapest in 1946. On a gloomy November afternoon in that year, my parents and I boarded a decrepit train, pompously entitled the Orient Express, in a soot-blackened and bomb-blasted railway station. We sat apprehensively on the worn velour seats of our compartment. The panelling above our heads still bore signs of a former world in the shape of several faded photographs, behind almost opaque panes of glass — images of the marvels of prewar Europe. As the train groaned through a desolate countryside, our anxiety increased to near-intolerable levels when we realised that we were approaching the border. Would our exit permits be honoured by the Russians? Would we be searched? Would they find the last of our gold coins in the hollowed-out heels of my mother's winter boots? After an interminable delay, the grim-faced border guards left the train. With a clang and a grating of metal we lurched forward, towards Vienna and freedom. Several hours later we were travelling in an open horse-drawn carriage down a broad street lined with the empty shells of apartment blocks and grandiose imperial palaces to our hotel in the Graben, where a small pane of glass set in the boarded-up window of our room afforded a glimpse of that once elegant thoroughfare.

A few days before Christmas in 1990, I set out from another — perhaps the same — small hotel in that street, now a pedestrian mall glittering with affluent brilliance. My elder son sat beside me in a purring Mercedes taxi as we were driven to the station along that avenue down which I had been driven, in the opposite direction, almost half a century before in a state of over-excitement because we were embarking on the great advneture that was to carry us to the other end of the world. At the well-kept, efficient station, my son and I boarded a sleek modern train, also called the Orient Express, though not that essay in nostalgic kitsch which carries the super-rich between Paris and Venice. Whereas the train my parents and I travelled on in 1946 was half-empty, the Orient Express of 1990 was filled to the brim with a noisy and excited crowd.//

Eventually the train moved off, half an hour late, to the relief of the generally animated and in some instances inebriated travellers. A neat, tidy Austria slid past in the gathering dusk. Darkness had fallen by the time we reached the border.//

The crowd fell silent. Something was in the air. It soon became obvious that the border-guards were making their way down the carriage. People began to betray the unmistakably apprehensive look of those who had lived under (or had escaped from) oppressive regimes. I noticed that they were impressed and not a little envious as we got out our Australian passports. We were the fortunate ones; we belonged to that privileged world towards which my parents and I had set out all those years ago, tense with anxiety as we sat in our compartment listening for the approach of the guards. And I, protected though I was by my magic passport, shared the tension and anxiety of my fellow-passengers, while my son sat beside me absorbed in the book he had been reading ever since darkness fell. For him this was just another frontier.

The past should not, perhaps, be revisited. Those days I spent in Budapest were among the most painful experiences of my life, for they forced me not only to remember things long forgotten, but also to recall those other days — in Hurlstone Park, in Epping and in other parts of Sydney — that were the occasion of much humiliation and shame. Walking around the decaying streets of a once graceful city, I continually thought of the dead — of all those people, my father's large family, the much smaller circle of my mother's relations, who had disappeared, vanished from the face of the earth. I recalled the days my father spent wandering those streets in 1945, when he had barely recovered from his injuries, because someone had told him that he thought he had seen my uncle, ghastly and emaciated, groping his way along one of those thoroughfares. I also remembered the terrible day when my father accepted the inevitable, that it was useless spending another day searching for a brother he would never find.//

My memories jumped years and continents.// I recognised the baths where my mother and I had to cart bagloads of money, and still did not have enough for the price of admission. That made me recall the embarrassment of a picnic at Palm Beach on which some well-meaning acquaintances had taken us in the early years of our life in Epping. My mother was an undisguised picture of misery as she sat under the tarpaulin stretched between two cars, swatting at mosquitoes with a rolled-up newspaper in the manner we were taught to disperse the red-backs that infested our dunny. I found the pond where I used to go skating, during trips to the city made precisely for that purpose, under the eagle-eyed supervision of one or another German nanny, and the nearby restaurant where I used to be taken for a special treat. I could not, however, find many places I tried to revisit, having only confused and muddled memories of things that had been suppressed for many years.

In the life of the city I began to discern certain alarming signs that I was to see again a couple of months later in the courtyard of the Hungarian Embassy in Canberra. Magyar nationalism was visible everywhere, mixed with a totally incompatible and entirely irrelevant nostalgia for a Habsburg past. Antisemitic slogans, in a world where, surely, there were few Jews left, were daubed on walls and embankments. A statue of the Empress Elisabeth, after whom generations of Austro-Hungarian girls (including my mother) had been named, was in the process of being elaborately restored. The monument to St Stephen, king and missionary who gave my father his name, displayed once more the royal emblems of the former kingdom. It was as though the previous forty-odd years had never occurred. The wave of nostalgia and sentimentality, in a world of grim economic hardship where a couple of Australian dollars would take you in a taxi from one end of town to the other, seemed at times a distraction, at others almost an indecency. And as I walked among these people I realised that they assumed // that I was a foreigner. They would come up to me in the streets with offers to exchange money delivered in various languages, but never in Hungarian. In restaurants waiters would hand me, before a word had been spoken, the English or German versions of the menu. For them I obviously represented that golden world beyond the Austrian border, where elegant people strolled along well-swept boulevards, where sleek limousines deposited glamorous patrons at the vast portals of a huge opera house, where everyone could afford to buy genuine Levis and wear Reeboks to their hearts' content.

I had nothing in common with this world, I came to realise as the initial impact of return began to wear off. This was not my life;

it had almost no bearing on what I was or felt myself to be. I began to be acutely aware of the advantages of my real life. Sydney, with its sprawling suburbs, its harsh, all-revealing light, seemed a blessed place compared with the murk and grime of this depressing city. I glanced up at a first-floor window; someone was leaning out, staring at the tramlines on the street below. I thought of Sydney — how if I lean out of our bedroom window I can just catch sight of a square of blue water with a headland above it that reveals at night those twinkling streetlights my parents and I saw as the *Marine Phoenix* sailed towards the Heads. In this, my home town, I did not dare to board the clattering trams for fear they would bear me off to places unknown, from which I would have trouble getting back to my hotel. The language that people spoke all around me, though comprehensible, seemed strange and foreign. Their ways were alien and a trifle menacing. I did not know how to deal with the many people importuning me to buy this or that. I got confused about the elaborate rituals governing cafe-life: who served, whom to pay, how to tip, and when to leave. I realised that I desperately wanted to go home.

Elizabeth Jolley

HOME THOUGHTS

The slow dying, which was my reason for the self-healing voyage, seemed to be worse while I was travelling on land. There was no music. On board a ship there is the music of the wind and waves and the voices of people and music for dancing is played every night but there is no real music, just as in Europe there was no real music; concerts and recitals of course, but not music to listen to alone where for example it is possible to give oneself up completely to the cello.//

Music is like mountains covered with snow and valleys of deep meadows sprinkled with spring flowers. If I can't be part of the land then I am tired quickly with just looking at it. It is the same with music, I tire quickly of sitting and watching people perform it.//

Snow-covered mountains patterned with magic light and blue shade rise round Salzburg and the trees are frosted with snow.

Everything the tourist sees charms. There are little churches with gilded steeples sparkling in the morning sun, quiet rivers with grassy banks and men waiting in the water patiently to grab a fish. The little houses are crooked with attic roofs and pink and yellow colour-washed walls. Roadside shrines are everywhere carved and cherished with leaves and branches and the people seem so happy and friendly. When I travelled there I wondered if I would feel the loss of it afterwards and suddenly I was tired of it.

When I get back home I want to walk along the dry creek bed and touch the dry hard earth and break it with my fingers. I want to smell the hot earth and I want to walk between the trees and smell them too.

There is a bird I want to hear again. It is like a lark. While I was travelling the bus stopped at the edge of a cornfield and we listened to the larks' rising song. And once when I was a child walking with my father I found a lark's nest and later that day, when the mist cleared. I heard the lark's song. My bird sings in the heat. It is not my bird really, it sings somewhere above my place; it is like a lark, the song rising in hope and in love, not to hurt anyone. A gentle song from a gentle lark. I want to look at my fruit trees, go round them all to cherish them. It will be the time for cherishing. All life seems withdrawn in the intense heat of the summer. I long for the silence. It seems a long time since I left.

I want to see my horses, Lucy and Charger. They are always stabled and looked after on the adjoining Palomino property. The country across there looks like Tolstoy country, that's how I see it. It seems so long since I crossed the paddocks on horseback to inspect the fences. I love to ride. I would love to have her to ride with me; a companion for riding would be superb if it could be her.

After a time I stopped looking at the world. Somewhere between the terraced vineyards on the banks of the Rhine and a winding road between palm trees and tiny grass, thatched huts on the way to a wide gentle bay, pink and blue in the sunrise in Ceylon, I stopped looking at the world and I am disappointed with myself for not looking.

I went to all the concerts and theatres even the marionette theatre for a performance of *The Magic Flute*, the puppets moving with such ease it was not difficult to forget they were manipulated with strings, and all round me people sighed with the tenderness and longing and love Mozart has in his music, and I sat like a block of wood. All my attempts to restore myself failed. I stared with terrible blankness in picture galleries and yawned through museumes, passed close to fountains without seeing them and, standing before great churches I failed to take in their history and to absorb their mystery and significance.//

Again this evening I come face to face with the gold chain and green jewel. I want to love her, I want to tell her that I love her and while I am feeling this I do not for a minute think what the consequences will be. Tonight I shall sit behind her at the film. It is *Death in Venice* from the story by Thomas Mann. It is an extremely suitable theme and I can continue the delicacy of the film, I have seen it before, and work on the impact it will have on someone like her. If only it was the evening now.

I am glad to be obsessed. All the time I was in Europe I handled all the famous places as if with forceps. And even on the ship I go through the daily conventional movements of the day's eating and washing and walking but now I feel I am once more alive. I am even catching snatches of conversation when before I never paid much attention even when people were speaking to me.

The two vegetarian ladies are called Irma and Hilde. They seem to be all over the ship all the time.

"Wait Irma! I have just to put on my shoes," I hear Hilde's shrill voice, sometimes they speak in German and sometimes in English. They have been lying down for a rest under rugs after lunch and now will walk on the deck for their health. Fortunately I have a cabin to myself, although at first this was not so. By some mistake I was in a cabin with three other women, one of whom even had all her things hanging in my cupboard. I thought I would be suffocated in there and went at once to the Purser to object and to get what I wanted. My cabin now is really very pleasant with two portholes and a writing table and an armchair and I have an attentive steward. All the same I am impatient to be back home and especially if I can take her with me.

Ania Walwicz

EUROPE

i'm europe deluxe nougat bar i'm better than most i'm really special
rich and tasty black forest cake this picture makes me think of
germany make me made me europe made me i keep my europe i
europe this town is just like my polish town where born where is
where am here is europe all the time for me in me is europe i keep
it i got it i get it in me inside me is europe italy warm palms lovely
palace chrome chair street busy alive me my and pier with a little
lamp what i remember i don't forget keep this keep lighter and
brighter now this is it this europe in me in me my only what i have
what i have i keep europe hold on to that i thought i lost what i
didn't had carl's mother said don't get out of bed there are goblins
goblins they eat his white long leg i was so so so jealous jealous of
what he had fresh new young just came two weeks from frankfurt
and i'm too long gone left too quick didn't stay what what what i
could have been exactly like him exactly like him they took my
europe away they took my europe away they took my europe away
they took me they stole me they boat me they float me take me
took me away took but but but but but but but i bounce back i get
back i add ten years to my life i look younger all the time i get it
again the it how look my europe now i look fine i ride in my forest
at night with goblins i look pictures i win i don't lose i always get
another chance and i'm europe again and again and again europe
better than it really is better soir de paris perfume my wrist my
picture paris from photos is perfect i never saw paris i distil i don't
have to travel i'm in europe i'm europe i get europe it comes to me
what she said venice after the railway through door to lagoon i can
just see it i can feel it you can go to europe but you can't be europe
like i am i suck my finger and i taste europe i touch europe i travel
on my map with my fingers in my newspaper floods rhine carl saw
little mermaid carl eiffel tower climb famous people everything
very important just tell me europe come to me now my city crowd
friday could be rome now my europe my my my better than really
better than is could be magic feel and taste carl smells of europe his
coat is europe two weeks just came just came ran away from the
german navy bought this trenchcoat in germany i'm young man

i'm young man got this vest in stockholm beret in berlin i'm young fair strong long tall long tall my europe is best only best only nicest loveliest sweetest creamiest i only want best most kind most marvellous i'm homesick for where i haven't been i miss france and i miss norway i only want what i should have had what i should have been where i now am i come home to that in my europe is europe all green all fresh all green i shot geese with my gun white feathers fell in my eiderdown dear carl i hope everything is well with you i'm young and now new i'm looking forward exciting to i'm twenty-two i'm studying physics i'm young man young man everything is going to be

Manfred Jurgensen

FLENSBURG

this is home:
cobbled streets,
rainy days,
the sound of
living. some-
how my love
alone stays
put. it greets
a memory
which i trace
in smoked eels,
salt and tears.
now it feels
all the years
returned me
to this place.
haunted by
the fog-horn
blowing i
am reborn.

Sneja Gunew

MEMORY CROP

In September 1987 my mother and I revisited Germany for the first time together since we had both left it in 1950 — when I was four years old and she twenty-seven. Separately, in the intervening years, we had returned many times but never together. The catalyst for this event was the death of my grandmother earlier that year at the age of eighty-seven. She had spent the last five years with my mother, north-east of Melbourne, late in her life engaged, like Amalie Dietrich, in mapping the New World through its flora and fauna.//

In between, she told stories of a life which had begun in 1900. She gave substance and continuity to that shadowy German half of my cultural inheritance which, before her advent, I had recreated as a sort of scrapbrook of memorabilia.//

My first memories of landscape came doubly framed through both photographs and narratives. A small black and white photo of myself and my younger brother depicts us in a dark forest. He, preoccupied with examining something hidden within the undergrowth, whereas I stare warily outside the frame. We both wear outfits, with intricate border designs, lovingly knitted by my grandmother. This icon haunts my later encounters with the lost or discarded children who wander through German (and Australian for that matter) folk and fairytales.

Who had abandoned me?

Certainly, I was often separated from my working parents in those first post-war years of turmoil. More to the point, what had I abandoned?

In the first instance, my first language and culture, or, more precisely, I transported them, poor convicts, onto that converted cattle and troopship which brought us here and on which I was mostly sea sick.

When much later, in the eighties, I returned to Germany, there was instant recognition of those matted pine forests interspersed with great stretches of farmland, of their smells and the light. I was moved, but could not focus on the cause and perversely wished to close my eyes against the strange and familiar present in order to see with memory.

In 1987 I discovered that this forest had indeed been the first forest of my conscious self and that here I had lived out Saussure's famous lesson that whenever we encounter the signifier "tree" it is always, for each one of us, a particular tree which springs to mind as the signified.

In the severe housing shortage after the war my parents were only able to secure a series of single rooms. The second of these was on the first floor of a former barracks in Haar, on the outskirts of Munich. Here the new family consolidated its boundaries. Across the road was my first playground, the forest. Since my father was studying for his MSc and my mother was sent criss-crossing the country as an X-ray technician, those first four years were often spent with my grandmother who lived in a small villae, Poltringen, outside Tübingen.

My mother and I revisit Tübingen where I was born. Understandably, for her first birth, my mother had wanted to be near her own mother. We have rooms at the top of the hill near the old castle which overlooks that ancient university town. The view from my window extends across a network of medieval houses (akin to the illustrations in my books of Grimms' fairytales) which enclose centuries of itinerant students. When we visit it, we find the castle ringed with elderberry trees heavy with berries and later sit drinking their juice at one of the outdoor cafes off the town square.

We visit the women's hospital and a sympathetic midwife conducts us to the very theatre where my mother gave birth to me. Of this performance my mother remembers only the view from the windows. We take photos of each other in front of the hospital entrance before proceeding to the Town Hall where we brave the awesome German bureaucracy to obtain a copy of my birth certificate. Many proofs of identity and forms in triplicate are required before this is disbursed. Genealogy remains a touchy area in German culture. I finally discover, forty years down the track, that I was born at nine pm.

The next day we embark on the trip to Poltringen. We are misled about bus timetables and end up taking one to Pfäffingen, the next village. On the bus a woman had recommended an inn where we pause for lunch and regale ourselves with our favourite salad of rapunzel (rocket) and the local white wine. The food releases euphoria and a sense of occasion, without our having to make fairytale promises in exchange for the succulent rapunzel.

Now, writing this, I recall the poignant moment in Christa Wolf's novel about Chernobyl, *Störfall*, where the narrator forces herself to resist collecting her usual handful of tender salad greens on her customary daily walk. The invisible blight may still be lingering a year later but we ignore it. We walk towards Poltringen in the midday heat. On our left the hill is crowned with the Würmlinger chapel which my mother tells me had dominated the views from our window in Poltringen. I am overcome with deja vu at the sight of the tangle of summer flowers and weeds by the roadside: wild hedge roses (is this why I've always loved the Schubert song "Heidenröslein"?) and small white trumpet-shaped flowers. My mother tells me that from an early age I had learnt to walk the road between Poltringen and Pfäffingen. The roadside flowers would have been the right height to form my first landscape.

Suddenly we have arrived. The village is sensibly closed for lunch and the streets are deserted so that it appears like one of those enchanted places encountered in dreams and fairytales, waiting for the hero to bring it back into the natural cycle. Almost immediately we encounter the castle we had been seeking.

An old black-and-white photo I have long cherished shows the small nineteenth-century castle where, in one of the four turrets, I spent a large portion of those first four years with my grandmother. I am not sure why she should have lived in this building but it was certainly fitting. I recall the dark room with bunches of bats hanging upside down in the invisible corners and behind the double bed. My grandmother, always wearing a dark blue dress with a pattern of tiny white flowers, keeps the world at bay for me. Again she is the signified, the material content, for those stories of ambiguous wise women who are encountered at the tops of winding stairs or in turret rooms and who deliver precepts which protect the questing heroine.

The castle has been renovated into expensive units and we are not able to go inside. Outside it has been painted a soft pink instead of the grimy yellow I remember. The moat with stagnant water and the old stone wall remain the same, as does the stream behind it overgrown with trees and weeds leading to the nearby mill which is far older than the castle.

My grandmother tells the story. She and I are walking as usual in a nearby ploughed field. I am only just learning to name the world in a shared language. We encounter a small wayside shrine of the crucifixion. "*Vogelscheuche!*" (scarecrow) I say with authority. My convent-educated, but a-religious, grandmother enjoys repeating the blasphemy down through the years.

Back in Tübingen my mother and I buy a huge book on witches. What would have happened if we had never left Germany?

Antigone Kefala

FAMILY

The garden full of trees in bloom
spring scents, angelica, birds
crying in the still, clean light.

In the dark house behind the shutters
they were waiting
with the bread and the olives.
Marble dusted, ancient faces
with eroded eyes,
shell eyes of statues bleached by time.

At night, their shadows
on the white-washed walls
breathing in silence
the scent of the white lilies
blooming in the moonlight
as if consumed with longing.

Dimitris Tsaloumas

PRODIGAL

Fanatical mosquitoes and persistent fetid stench
  hold absolute dominion
over the twilight swamps. Evening comes early
  full of mutterings. Our days
were never rich — but now!
  The ox is skin and bone and the goat
barely yields enough for the baby. Therefore
  make no rash decision.
The other day Eros was seen in the marketplace
  unrecognised in cast-off clothes,
grown old. Come of course since you insist, but
  whatever you remember, now forget.

Drusilla Modjeska

CRETE

In the autumn of 1961, Madeleine took Poppy to Crete. Cecily
went too. Cecily lived with her children at the end of a lane on the
other side of the main road from the village. Her husband was
usually abroad. She was a family friend, not yet a rival. She was
going to France and said she'd take Poppy with her. Poppy had come
back from Pilsdon for the school holidays and was still *weepy*,
Richard said, *and not herself.* Another break was suggested from a
routine that was both familiar and not; so Richard wrote to
Madeleine, and Madeleine said Crete. She had never approved of
Poppy's romance with France. She wrote to her about de Gaulle
and Algeria. That is France, she wrote, describing for Poppy the
internment camps of North Africa which had been reported in the
French press while Poppy was in hospital, and the young Arabs
she'd seen loaded into police vans in Paris. That is France, she wrote,
but for Poppy Paris remained the city of Victor Hugo and Colette.
Of Crete she had no opinion. She went where she was taken.

    Poppy, Cecily and Madeleine arrived in Heraklion by boat on a clear morning at the end of September 1961, just before Algeria's independence. When they had left Piraeus and Poppy could no longer see the coast of the Peloponnese, she stood at the stern where sea birds flew above the foam. It was the first time she'd seen the sky meet the horizon in a clean curve. Like a new moon, she wrote. It was also the first time she'd left England since she'd visited France with China.

The three women took rooms in a small hotel above a covered market. Poppy lay on her bed listening to sounds from the street below, as strange to her as the bright slats of light in the room, and while Cecily looked at the shops, Madeleine read her an account of Sir Arthur Evans' excavations at Knossos; but Poppy's attention was on a small, almost transparent lizard that was basking on the edge of a slat in the shutters that accounted for the strange arrangement of light and shade. All she remembered from Madeleine's reading was that Sir Arthur Evans was looking for an early Greek script, and found the ancient palace by chance. Looking for the origins of a culture we recognise as a foundation of our own, he stumbled on evidence of an earlier lost world.

"Read me that bit again," Poppy said to Madeleine, and she did. When Poppy turned back to the light, the lizard had gone.

Before Poppy died she told each of us there were two things she wanted us to be sure to do with the money she left. The first was to buy a washing machine; the second was to visit Crete. May already had a washing machine, and now Phoebe and I do too. Poppy was right; apart from the work it saves, there is the satisfaction of order that hanging out a load of washing can bring to domestic life. As to Crete, only May hasn't been. With young children she hasn't had the chance. But Phoebe has, and so have I.

The April after Poppy died, Thomas and I took a cheap flight from London to Heraklion. As a consequence our first sight of the island was of mountains and a small perfunctory airport, not the Venetian fortifications and long harbour wall that Poppy saw from her boat. But we had dinner that night on the terrace of a cafe overlooking the harbour, already seduced by the grace and hue of Crete.

Like every other tourist, we collected our guides to the remains of Minoan culture and went to the Archaeological Museum. Unlike Poppy I had already read about Minoa, not only because of her, but because it has become part of the iconography of contemporary feminism. I was already interested in the riddle of a culture that is hidden under the acknowledged history of our own, almost as long before Christ as we are after, a culture about which we know little, but in which women were priests and acrobats and, it would seem, where there were no defences or equipment for war. But I was not one of those who claim Minoa as a matriarchy, suspicious of a tendency to validate the present struggles of women by an appeal to past rule. In this frame of mind, and having taken measured preparations, I was not expecting the shock that made me sob out loud when I stood in front of the figurines that Poppy had described so well: the agile, the squat, the working women of Minoa: mothers, priests, animal handlers, acrobats, preparers of food. *Where do such women come from*, Poppy had written. Where indeed? Their images are quite unlike any we are used to from Hellenic Greece, the idealised classical feminine. I sobbed, as Poppy did, out of shock, and also recognition, as if in those figurines and frescoes, still singing with life three or four thousand years later, there was something I already knew; and that something ran counter to everything I'd learned.

In his work on the puzzles of female sexuality, Freud writes that the early pre-Oedipal attachment to the mother by the daughter, which lasts much longer in girls than it does in boys (the model for his *normal* Oedipus complex), *comes to us as a surprise, like the discovery, in another field, of the Minoan-Mycenean civilization behind the civilization of Greece*. This first attachment to the mother in girls, which Freud admits to finding hard to grasp, *so grey with age and shadowy and almost impossible to revivify*, would seem to be the foundation of a femininity which is subsequently overlaid by another order, as Minoa was by Greece. These are thoughts I've had since. At the time I simply stood and looked, reminded perhaps, as Poppy must have been, though neither of us knew it, of something every daughter once knew, a dim region, an ancient possibility that has long been surpassed, and yet lives on, shadowy and grey with age, and yearning to be revivified.

The next day Thomas and I took the bus to Knossos, the palace excavated by Sir Arthur Evans and said to be the site of the labyrinth where Greek legend placed the Minotaur that Ariadne and her thread gave Theseus the power to destroy. Why was this Hellenic myth of an insatiable monster built on the traces of a culture, apparently peaceable, which the Greeks defeated or at least superseded, possibly as early as 1300 BC? Did terrible things happen there? There is some evidence of ritual sacrifice. Surely the Greeks wouldn't have been squeamish about that? What was so powerful about Knossos, about Minoa, about the feminine, that a monster had to live in a maze at its heart, appeased only by the sacrifice of Athenian youth, seven boys and seven girls fed to him every ninth year? Was the monster already there? Is there something monstrous at the heart of femininity? Or did Hellenic legend put it there for us?

With no answers to these questions, Thomas and I hired a car and drove across the island to Phaestos, the southern palace of ancient Minoa, where Poppy had gone with Madeleine when Cecily had returned to the mainland, bound by some other itinerary. Like Poppy, I sat at the top of that wonderful citadel, looking out across the plain to mountains that still had snow on their peaks. But unlike the parched grass and bare rocks Poppy had described in her diary, I saw a hillside covered in flowers; and on the altars of shrines and tiny churches along the road there were bunches of small red Poppies.

It was on Crete that Madeleine told Poppy the full story of Ariadne. She knew that Theseus, the son of the Athenian King Aegeus, was among the shipment of youths who'd arrived on Crete for sacrifice to the minotaur. She knew that Ariadne fell in love with him and gave him the ball of thread that would guide him to the monster and bring him back from the labyrinth to her. Theseus killed the monster, and claimed Ariadne as he promised, escaping with her from Crete and her cruel father, King Minos. But Poppy hadn't realised the significance of Ariadne being Cretan, coming from the same island as the minotaur, and she didn't know that Ariadne never reached Athens. On their triumphal way home, the Athenians put in at Naxos where Ariadne fell asleep on the beach. When she woke Theseus had sailed without her. Some accounts said he loved another, others that Dionysius ordered him to abandon her so he could marry her himself. Whatever the reason, Ariadne was left behind and Theseus, distraught with loss, or shame perhaps, forgot to raise the white sails to signal his success to the waiting Athenians. His father, King Aegeus, saw the black sails, presumed the worst and threw himself off the rocks, giving his name to the sea that Poppy had crossed by ferry, watching its colour reflected in the sky.

"When Madeleine told me that story," Poppy said, "I cried at the distance between those sturdy Minoan figures which I understood without knowing how, and Ariadne holding the thread for a man who abandoned her. Madeleine said the myth of Ariadne came later. We don't know what her own myths were, or her songs, or her prayers. No one knows her story."

Something moved in Poppy on Crete, and something moved in me. I don't know how else to put it. As if for a glance, or a moment, future and past lost their separation. Poppy took the story of Ariadne as emblematic of her own, a gesture I first understood simply as a tart comment on her life as mother and wife, and I'm sure that's part of what she meant. But on Crete I could see there was more to it than that, for underneath the Ariadne of Hellenic legend lay the girl who was heir to a silent and mysterious world.

Poppy went back to England and a situation which required her continued attentions as mother and wife. One could say it is unreasonable to expect that a brief visit to a Greek island as one of thousands who pour there every year searching for renewal could change anything, and I don't suppose it did. The daily round exacts its toll, and there were six more years before the rift that had opened between her and Richard was acknowledged in separation. But that visit gave Poppy a way of imagining herself. Or maybe it's only me who is given that, for my task is to find pattern and shape in her life; hers was to live each day.

Betty Roland

GALLIPOLI: THE HILLS OF THE HEROES

It had not occurred to me that I would be very near the Dardanelles, and that Gallipoli was only a few hours sailing time away from Lesbos.

I can recall one particularly wild and blustering night when the wind buffeted the shutters and the sea lashed at the rocks as I sat alone in my room and read till the lights went out at midnight and then sat on in the darkness.//

In such a place, at such an hour, sitting alone in the dark, it was easy to create a mood and it called for no great flight of fancy to imagine there were voices in the wind and to conjure up a vision of ghostly figures standing on that lonely headland, peering through the darkness, wondering why the mates who went away that long-ago December night had never returned to break the silence of the endless years.

Hardly anyone ever visits them.

To me, those words did not suggest the well-kept cemeteries with their neat rows of headstones, but the men themselves, the wild Colonial boys who had come whooping out of the bush to join in what they felt convinced was going to be the greatest lark of all time: a dinkum war with no holds barred, no referees.

They were of my blood, my race, and I felt very close to them that night and told myself that on next Anzac Day there was going to be at least one Australian on Gallipoli to let them know they were remembered.//

The previous day had been overcast, with grey clouds and a melancholy wind that whipped The Narrows into angry waves, but April the 25th was bright with sunshine and the wind had died.

I had carefully considered the clothes that I should wear this Anzac Day. In Australia it is a day of solemn dedication and I was going to the place where men had died, yet I could not bring myself to dress in black.

The men who had died in 1915 had been little more than boys, and youth flowed hotly in their blood. They were not of the breed to relish mournful faces and funeral clothes, so I had packed my prettiest and most becoming dress and was grateful that the day was warm enough for me to wear it.

I took special pains about my make-up, using lipstick and mascara, feeling sure that this was how they would have liked it, and I added perfume. I wished that I was younger but felt sure "the boys" would understand.

Captain McMann and his interpreter John were waiting on the wharf. Mac had got the necessary permit for me so we lost no time in boarding the launch that was to take us across The Narrows. This is a regular ferry service and plies back and forth between Chanakale, on the mainland, and the Gallipoli Peninsula at half-hour intervals all day. It took us no more than ten minutes to cross and we landed at the tiny settlement of Echiabat with its heart-shaped fortress, built, so Mac informed me, by a love-lorn commander long ago as an expression of his yearning for the damsel on the far side of the Straits. Not far away Leander swam the Hellspont, but this less daring lover was content to express himself in stone.//

For the first mile or so we passed little farms and scattered houses. Then we began to climb the hills that run like a spine down the entire Peninsula and we could see the true nature of the country. It is so barren and so desolate that not even the land-hungry Turk has tried to cultivate it. No trees of any size grow there, just low scrub, thorns, and a stunted shrub called prickly-oak.

The road is a fairly recent addition, laid down by the War Graves Commission to give easy access to the cemeteries. John drove rapidly and we were soon at the top of the ridge. Behind us lay the Dardanelles, with Chanakale across The Narrows.

John paused to let me look, and then continued for another mile or so along the red dirt road, stopping before a low wooden gate in a thick screen of pines. Mac got out and held it open for me.

"This is Lone Pine," he said. "I thought you'd like to come here first."

I looked around. On every side the silence and a brooding sense of loneliness. "Am I the only one to come here on this day?" I asked.

"Aye lass, you are," said Mac. "The only one." And then he turned away, leaving me alone.

Inside the screen of pines were flower beds and rosemary, shrubs and lavender. Square white plaques engraved with the name and rank of the men who had died there lay in neat rows along the ground, and, at the far end, a tall obelisk. In front of this, the massive Stone of Remembrance with the words THEIR NAME LIVETH FOR EVERMORE cut deep in its marble face.//

For what then, had they died? That is the inevitable question which one asks, standing alone on Anzac morning with the sigh of the wind in the pines, the soft call of a pigeon the only sound that breaks the silence that has reigned there since the last retreating footfall left the dead alone to keep their endless vigil through the years.

I stood there for a long time mourning for them, then remembered that they would not like to see me cry, so dried my tears, walked softly up and down between the rows of stones, reading the names, the ages — nineteen — twenty-two — twenty — twenty-five — brushing off a stray leaf that had fallen, pulling out a weed, thinking of the wives, the mothers, sons and daughters who were not there with me, wishing they had come.

Mac was waiting for me at the gate. He held a sprig of rosemary, a rose, a purple pansy in his hand. "I picked these for you to take away," he said. "I thought perhaps you'd like to have them."

Rosemary, I thought, that's for remembrance. A pansy, that's for thoughts, and a red rose, that's for love.

I have them now, pressed between the pages of a book, their colours still preserved.

Graeme Hetherington

AUSTRALIANS IN CRETE, 1941–1991

for Michael Winters

Your drawings catch the cutting light
To show the Greeks as too relaxed,
Reclining carelessly in streets
As full of twists and broken lines

As their long history's fractured with
Duplicity, mistrust and war,
Or leaning in stone doorways wrenched
And bent by time into all shapes,

Against warped windows crucified
As though it were their natural right,
Your lone Australian soldier raw,
New-looking in his uniform

As tripping on the cobblestones
He sheepishly looks round, exposed
As out of place beneath the slouch
Set stiffly on his youthful head.

Manning Clark

TRAMPING THE BATTLEFIELDS

My companion and I had come to Europe for different reasons. He wanted to see the areas of rural France which provided the setting for *Swann's Way* in Marcel Proust's *The Remembrance of Things Past*. I wanted to see the battlefields of the first world war in Belgium and France. I was hoping they might help me to find clues to explain things that puzzled me in the history of Australia since the 1890s — why, for example, the suburbs of Australia had never acquired a soul, and why the horrors experienced by Australia in the Gallipoli campaign and in Flanders and Picardy strengthened conservatism in Australia, prolonged the power of the Australian-

Britons, and elevated Anzac Day to the "One Day Of The Year" for so many Australians.

It all began at the Menin Gate. The landlady of the Hotel Continental in Ypres (Ieper) had said to us as soon as we arrived by car from England: "You will want to hear the playing of the Last Post at the Menin Gate at eight pm. They have sounded the Last Post at eight pm every night since the King of the Belgians performed the opening ceremony in — I think — July 1927." So fortified against the cold of early April — the cruellest month of all — with the landlady's excellent soup, served from a huge silver soup-tureen by a beautiful young girl, followed by fish, meat, vegetables, ice cream, cheese and tea ("You will have more — Yes — I know Australians like their food"), we walked along the cobblestones, the footpaths of the ancient city of Ypres reduced almost to rubble between August 1914 and November 1918.

On the way we saw the punks flirting, jostling, laughing and chiacking each other in the street. When we got to the Menin Gate the punks were there in force, their uproar reminding me of the cries of the corellas at sunset on Cooper's Creek when they are having their brief squabble about perches for the night in the dead branches of the coolibah trees. While my companion read out some of the names of the men commemorated on the Menin Gate memorial — the men whose remains were never found — I began to think about the role of the punks in our society. We had seen them and heard of them in England. I wondered whether, if Karl Marx were to rewrite the Communist Manifesto, he would change the first sentence to read: "A spectre is hanging over Europe, the spectre of punkdom." But, as so often, my reverie was on the wrong track. The experiences of Ypres were stronger than punkdom. At eight pm the traffic through the Gate stopped. The human uproar fell to whispers between the bystanders. The punks were quiet. Two men in uniform, and a woman, and an Englishman stepped into the middle of the road. The Englishman declaimed the words:

> Age shall not weary them, nor the years condemn.
> At the going down of the sun, and in the morning,
> We will remember them.

The men and women near my companion and me wept: the faces of the punks briefly expressed awe and wonder. Then the two men and the woman sounded the first note of the Last Post, the middle C which is so difficult to get right when the lips are cold, and the fingers frozen. As it soared upwards to the overhanging arch of the memorial, and was followed by a solemn E, the bodies of those around us shook with some powerful emotion.//

Walking back to the hotel my companion and I were silent. The punks had stopped their rowdiness. I wondered why we had all wept, why we had been carried into the high places. Perhaps we were weeping for the dead — but probably no one there knew any of the dead, any of those who had no memorial, no final resting place except their names carved into the stone on the inside walls of the Menin Gate. Perhaps we were weeping for all of us. But then most of us do not like everyone — most do not rise to universal compassion, or the universal embrace. Perhaps the Australians present were weeping for their fellow countrymen caught in such a trap, all those victims of human madness and folly. Perhaps in the twentieth century, with God high up on the list of Missing Persons, such secular ceremonies are all we have left to arouse pity and tenderness in all of us.

The following day, after driving through the Menin Gate along Hell Fire Corner to cross what had once meant death or some terrible injury to the body, and staring vacantly at the green fields where so many Allied and German soldiers had drowned in the mud, they being too weak to stand up again after falling in that miry sea, we stood for a moment on the mounds of Hill 60 where the Allies and the Germans spent three years trying to burrow their way to victory, but ended so often in knowing only the victory of death.

Then we drove to Passchendaele a few kilometres away. I expected to see a hill of the height of Mt Ainslie or Red Hill in Canberra, but saw only the slightest rise, for the occupation of which hundreds of thousands were killed or wounded.//

It was a cold and windy day. On another rise, perhaps two hundred metres from the mound over which the brave men from the British Isles, Canada, Australia and Germany fought during October and November 1917, the Belgians have built a memorial in stone to Christ the King. Christ looked so sad in the lemon-coloured sunlight — I wondered whether He was sad because so few were now answering the church bell's summons to the people of Passchendaele to come to Mass, or whether He was sad because of what had happened there so many years ago. My companion was impatient to see the battlefield. But neither there nor in the nearby Tyne Cot cemetery did I receive any enlightenment on what it was all about. Perhaps what had happened was like the words composed by Rudyard Kipling for the headstones of the soldiers who could not be identified: "Known unto God". No human being would ever know what these men had been through — or why, when the survivors got back to Australia, they should become the backbone of the King and Empire Alliance to suppress and expel all anti-loyalists, all Bolsheviks, Sinn Feiners and "Wobblies". I thought, too, of the role of Passchendaele in the Hughes decision to hold a second referendum on conscription, and wondered, as I was to wonder later at Pozières and on the Somme, why Hughes had been so obliging, what had driven him to put his career, the judgment of his colleagues in the Labor government, and the judgment of posterity at risk for the monstrous idea of gaining victory at such a price in human lifes.

After two days with my wife's cousin in the village of Booischot, where my companion learned much of what had shaped him in life, he having been till then like a man who had not seen the first act of his own drama, we set off for the battlefields of Picardy. On the way we by-passed Lille, my companion nodding sagely when I tried in vain to interest him in driving through it by telling him the story of how that most lovable man, the correspondent and war historian Charlie Bean, had heard just after 11 am on 11 November 1918 a boy blowing a tin whistle, and knew there must be an armistice. When that failed I told him Lille was featured in the works of Zola, but not even that would shake him. He was making for Pozières where, I had told him, Australian soldiers had fallen more thickly than on any other battlefield of the war.

We walked slowly to the memorial which immortalised the event as skylarks ascended, and sang, and the long stalks of grass waved in the chilly wind. We also stood before the memorial to the first tank which went into action on 15 September 1916, Haig, Lloyd George, Foch, Hughes and others believing the new invention would bring victory swiftly — but they, too, foundered in the mud, and the slaughter went on.//

At dusk we came to the cemetery at Villers Bretonneux, where thousands of Australians lie in graves lovingly tended by men and women, first of the Imperial and now of the Commonwealth War Graves Commission. The curator, sensing our interest, kindly offered to re-open the memorial on the crest of the hill in which there was a stairway leading to a balcony from which we could see all the battlefields of Picardy — the Somme, Pozières, Bullecourt, Villers Bretonneux. He pointed out that the trench line was marked by a change in the color of the grass.//

That night as we lingered over yet another excellent dinner in a French country hotel I wanted to know answers to many things. Why Australians, unlike the English, the French and the Americans, have been relatively inarticulate about the Somme and its significance in the history of humanity — I did not know then some of the comments made by Vance Palmer. Australians were so caught up in the conscription barney that they did not essay the broader view. They were not stirred to discuss the effect of the Somme on belief either in God or in the Enlightenment. Again I wondered why the surviving Australian rank and file provided numbers for reactionary movements, while survivors in Germany, France and Russia became part of a revolutionary movement — why the war chained Australia to her colonial and provincial past.//

As we drove on in the late afternoon there was still so much to think about. What, for example, went on in the mind of Haig? After the slaughter at the Somme and at Pozières why did he go on believing in the breakthrough? What went on in the mind of Billy Hughes? Why were the Australian soldiers, notorious for their cheek and bounce, so suspicious of all radicals, so uninterested in dreamers and visionaries? Why did the age of progress end with the horrors of the Somme and Passchendaele?

Perhaps that was why the cathedral of Notre Dame at Chartres made such an appeal. I remember I stood a long time in the gathering dusk in front of the Black Madonna, hoping some things would be made plain. My companion walked around the huge cathedral, his mind being by then on Marcel Proust. So off we went across the plains where the grass was green, the sky close and intimate, and the spires in each village a reminder that men once had answers. As darkness descended the waiter in the hotel at Illiers (Combray in *Swann's Way*) was already bringing us the soup. Out of the corner of my eye, through the steam rising from the hot soup, I could see a reproduction of a portrait of Proust. I wondered then as I had often wondered before whether *The Remembrance Of Things Past* was not simply a magnificent record of a self-discovery, but a tapestry of a doomed world. The man had a painted face. The tormented have both understanding and wisdom — but no one in the New World or the Old had come up with an answer to Verdun and the Somme — to 1917 — that year when Robert Gordon Menzies and John Joseph Ambrose Curtin both saw themselves as men of destiny. But what did they have to say, what did anyone have to say to stifle the memory of what had happened at Ypres, Menin Gate, the Somme and Passchendaele? Have those experiences left the soul of man in the suburbs?

So I wondered as we drove to Quiberon on the French Atlantic coast, from where, in between fruitless attempts to hear what the Bretons had to say about Tristan and Isolde, and love, my companion and I drove on to Tréguier, the birth place of Ernest Renan, the author of the *Vie de Jésus*, a book almost as central as the works of Dostoevsky, Newman and Carlyle for authors who want to portray the life of humanity in a kingdom of nothingness. Then on, ever on, to Montreuil, yet another of Haig's headquarters, where my companion and I walked round the equestrian statue of Haig, and made one last, almost despairing attempt to see whether the artist had penetrated what no historian had succeeded in piercing — had seen what went on in Haig's mind. By then it was time for my companion to face up to working with English doctors. And I must go back to Canberra, back to the blank page, to see whether I now had anything to say.

Out of the Cold:
Testing Political Climates

David Malouf

BAD DREAMS IN VIENNA

for Judith

Past midnight turning east at Deutsches Eck, a shallow corner
where the first legions broke out of the wood. A little ice-age
settles in, like Charlemagne's iron crown its fierce grip tightens

from Aix to the Pyrenees, Belle Ile to where the Danube swinges
its tail to lash the Balkans. It is the shadow of empire falls
to mark the shaky boundary of dreams. Old verbs contain

the anarchist's plot, there are fingerprints all over. A province breaks
away but can't shake off the small clerk's passion for gold braid,
gild saints, diminished sevenths and *Schlagobers*. Nightmares
     drag us

back to the same address. Sweating in snowfields of white sheets
tonight at the Hotel Graben, a million dead turn in my sleep
as the great wheel in the Prater turns on the breath of children
     sleeping

at Döbling, Rudolfsheim, the Freudian suburbs. Over garden
tables of rustic wood, black ironwork angels creak, dark exiles
gather, gunfire rattles the canal. Snowclouds come lowering

in off the Polish plain, a new invasion from the east.
Flakes drop their dark — fat ashes. In frozen pipes typhus bacilli
wait, dreaming of heatwaves. The Turks are always at the gate.

Blind hands poke over scrapheaps in the wind: a begging letter
of Mozart, the slum where Hitler mooned, worn shaving
     brushes, gold-
rimmed spectacles, gold fillings, the foul breath of a death's-head
     party

whistling *Wiener Blut*. I wake towards morning and look out
on the snowbound square, the Graben, grave or ditch. The great
     Pestsäule
a column of white worms writhes out of its pit, and touched by
     winter

light the long dead wrestle, wave upon wave, hard heel on
   shoulder
surge upward, choke for breath. The survivor's warm breath
   freezes. Here
bad dreams have monuments. Their agents yawn and lick the
   moon.

Catherine Duncan

RENDEZ-VOUS WITH THE END OF AN AGE

They fought all night under my windows, and I stood shivering in
the cold May darkness of the balcony watching the battle sway up
and down the street.

On the opposite footpath I could see the CRS, booted and
helmeted, with shields to protect them from the missiles, and the
sinister grenades of tear gas hanging from their belts. At the lower
end of the street the students made forays, individually or in small
groups, hurling paving stones and insults.

"*Salauds!*" "*Assassins!*" And the supreme charge: "*Charonne!*" This
the name of the métro station, doubly accusing in its assonance
and its associations, where five people were killed by the police
during a demonstration against the Algerian war.

The students looked terribly young and vulnerable under the
street lights, but the police were wary, hugging the doorways, or
crouching behind cars which had been slewed sideways across the
road to form barricades.

Suddenly the shutters of one of the windows opposite opened,
hands shot out dumping some heavy object in the middle of the
police, the shutters closed again in the same movement.

A CRS ducked. "Look out for your heads!"

I reviewed my flower-pots, but my youthful prowess as a baseball
player suggested I'd be more likely to lay out one of my side than
hit a policeman. And as if suspecting my intentions, one of the
CRS raised his rifle and fired a tear-gas grenade in the direction of
the balconies.

The air became unbreathable and I began to cry, the involuntary,
stinging tears that seem to leave a bad taste in the lungs.

Momentary retreat to close the windows and listen to Europe I, the commercial radio station which had mobilised all its forces to cover the street fighting.//

Reports from the thick of the battle — Europe I served as a headquarters for information and instructions, a field map in sound which covered the whole of Paris from the Elysée, where de Gaulle received three of his Ministers before seven am, to isolated telephone calls offering help or asking for ambulances. At only one point did the musical punctuation seem hysterically funny: "I'm in the mood for love, dear."

The moods of love nevertheless changed that night from a certain impatience with these unruly students and rebellious schoolchildren to an almost unanimous sympathy. Doors of private apartments opened to receive the hunted. An old maid of seventy summers unfolded the lavender-scented sheets of a far-off trousseau and spread them over dirty tennis shoes and blood-stained sweaters. Other boys found themselves in an elegant Louis XV salon where a gentleman in dressing-gown reviewed them with military brusqueness.

"Nobody seriously damaged? Fine. Then, to work!" and led them onto the balcony where they were astonished to find a positive armoury of missiles arrayed. "Start throwing!" ordered the gentleman.

A colonel's wife risked arrest and her husband's reputation by hiding sixty students outside the service entrance while police ransacked her apartment.

When the sick grey dawn came, the Students' Unions gave the order to disperse, and one by one the exhausted, hungry students went home.

The Boulevard St Germain from the Deux Magots to the Place St Michel was closed to traffic. For days afterwards workmen would be repaving the road in the Rue Gay-Lussac. There was blood on the stones of the Rue St Jacques.

One hundred and eighty cars — those status symbols of a materialist society — had been burnt down to their metal skeletons, and nothing so clearly expressed a whole generation's grand Refusal of the degraded values of that society. In a grocer's shop next morning I heard a man, shaking with rage, say, "If they'd done that to my car, I'd have killed them!"

But on Saturday morning there were few Parisians or provincials who were ready to defend the values of violence with a clear conscience.

By some miracle it seemed that nobody had been killed. Partly perhaps because the students were the sons of the bourgeoisie and the police had received orders to pull their punches. At Charonne the dead had been workers.//

"Contest" is the key word of action, and Herbert Marcuse, rebellious philosopher of *One-Dimensional Man* and adopted as theorist by the students, has at least elucidated the direction of the struggle: against a society which is a productive combination of consumer goods and war; against a society which allows the "free" election of masters, but which implies the continuing existence of masters and slaves.

Marcuse demands a refusal of all complicity with a society riveted in immobility between more cars, the wasteful and destructive methods of production and the "clean bomb", a technology which turns out condensed classics and Bach in the bedroom; a context of received ideas which excludes the logical processes of thought. And because thought, the conquest of a private space where man can reintegrate his life and be himself, is the only hope of replacing false needs by the real needs of liberty, the intellectuals have taken the lead in the new revolution.

Can they succeed? Not alone, certainly. Nor was this ever their objective. From the first they made every effort to integrate their movement into that of the working class and to overcome the traditional suspicion of workers for the intellectual. If they have been prevented from doing so it is not their fault, and one is entitled to question the accusations levelled against them to justify the *"cordon sanitaire"*. Are the students really an "irresponsible element", or are the attempts of the government and trade union leadership to isolate them based on the fear of contagion?

For the students the only valid aims in a highly developed industrialised society go far beyond claims concerning salaries, conditions of work and social insurance, and set out to attack and transform basic structures.//

But whatever the immediate outcome, there can be no doubt that the May revolution demonstrated the fragility of present structures, and that the means exist for young workers and thinkers to control their future and to fashion the kind of society in which they choose to live. For this reason the bloody nights of May will go down in history as a rendezvous with the end of an age.

Vincent Buckley

IRISH CUSTOMS

You tend to remember your arrivals in Ireland, perhaps because none of the points of entry, even Dublin, has anything of the huge, maze-like, heavily industrial, impersonal quality of great airports such as New York or Heathrow. Instead, it has a smalltown, even rural character, and is not divorced from its natural setting. I am not aiming to endorse sentimentality, or create an odour of ecstasy; but it is a fact that arrival in Ireland is apt to be, at first, reassuring, even if it is found later to be slightly offputting.

In any case, we may as well avoid the selective and sentimental way of the important German novelist Heinrich Böll, whose *An Irish Journal* tells of his long love-affair with Ireland. His account of his first visit opens with a girl smiling on a windowsill in the early morning as she takes in her jug of milk — that heavily symbolic milk. Ireland, we register at once, is a pastoral country, a dairying country, a land given to cattle. James Joyce's *Ulysses* also begins with a milkwoman, but somewhat older. Milkwoman, the window, the sea. Like Böll I too first arrived in Dublin in the early morning, and saw sights such as he saw. But context is all. Dublin, sleazy at the best of times (whenever they may have been), was then crammed with unemployment. It was the mid fifties, and workless men stood everywhere, as on a smaller scale they did for Böll, in O'Connell Street, along the docks, outside Westland Row station, all along Clanbrassil Street and the South Circular Road. Not so much gathered as left. Hawking and spitting. Talking and smoking. Spitting. Crying "fecking" or "fockin". Murmuring from the sides of their mouths. Making their parts of Dublin which, for the visitor arriving by sea, are also his first parts, unbearably comfortless, sweat-caked and cold.

Phlegm capital of the world.

On the first or second trip, in the mid fifties, coming from Liverpool, we had a lot of luggage roped under tarpaulin on the open deck. All promises delivered in England about how and when it could be got off were obviously null and void. No uniformed person knew or would say. It was time to turn to the non-uniformed ones, the men of no property, the hawkers and spitters. On Dublin docks I approached a group of idlers, who considered my case most politely, indeed with a deference mounting to pity, before deciding whether they would release the secret. "Go down there, turn left, then left again, and ask for Sean." Sean! the most common name in Ireland. Still, I did, and there was a Sean, or someone pretending for the moment, and he did get it off for me: as a favour, using brazenly uninstitutional methods, and refusing a tip. He had seen my daughter Brigid's five-year-old face, and was captivated.

On that or the next visit, we faced the customs men. Book censorship at that time in Ireland was a wonder of generalised bigotry; but I had forgotten that, and when the customs man tapped the brown paper carrier bag in my hand and demanded, "What's in that?" I answered; "Books!" he half-shouted, looking up sharply. "Not banned books!" "I've no idea," I said. "What books are banned here?" He was a large ageing man with a fire-red face, like the parish priest of some child's nightmare. "Give us a look. Give us a look," he yelled. The top exhibit was a copy of *Masses Ouvriere*, a French leftwing Catholic journal. "What's this? What's this?" he carolled, scenting a winner. "Well, it's a French …" I began, but he had already thrown it on the counter and was facing the next. This said in firm gold capitals on a black ground *Holy Roman Missal*, and I could see his mind clicking from disappointment to renewed suspicion to resignation; but he knew when he was licked. Into Ireland, fly as you please, with the help of Sean and of some unlikely Providence.//

Many years later, entering Dublin by air from Canada, I met another customs man. For some reason, I was through the arrival gates long before anyone else, and the customs man seated at the small desk seemed surprised to see me. Again, I was carrying an open carrier bag, this time full of small carvings and other Indian and Eskimo artefacts. "Anything to declare?" "No." "What's in the bag?", and I produced the objects one by one, to exclamations of wonder and pleasure from the youngish functionary. "Well, isn't that grand now!", and so on. As always, I became immediately intoxicated by the whiff of simple human feeling that you get in Ireland, and expatiated light-headedly on the provenance of the articles, Cree Indians, Vancouver, and sacred ceremonies, all to the accompaniment of "That's a lovely one now" and "Is that a fact now?", ending with, "Welcome to Ireland. And God bless." In any other country you might have expected a question about value or price. The Irish are generally too courteous and, whether they are wearing a uniform or not ("Sure, it's just a job, after all"), delighted by whatever diversion comes their way. Eye to eye contact is also important, as are rhetorical and lyrical sayings, sounds and devices.

All these are features of the national temperament and value-system, but they also reflect social fact. Dublin and its airport only play at being cosmopolitan: or, perhaps I should say, they are cosmopolitan in everything but ambience. They are regional, a smalltown entry to a largely sequestered delight. The visitors for whom they are prepared are returning emigrants and casual friendly strangers: people who come to remember or to savour. They are not geared up for dignitaries, big businessmen or millionaire hedonists, although no doubt many individuals approximating to these types have passed through their doors. Air fares are now so high that at least half of each flight consists of business people.//

You can almost always smell the grass and the sea through or behind the creeping reek of benzine and diesel which afflicts the inner city, all the more savagely since Irish petrol contains a lot of lead. That is miles away, and at the airport, close though it is to the main Belfast road and the stupefied highrise flats of Ballymun, you are smelling a small rich pastoral earth, very far from the mixture of benzine, stained cloud and door varnish which gets to you at Heathrow. Bord Failte should call Dublin Airport "The Airfield of the Cows", which would go well with the ethos of Ireland in its heroic age, based on the ownership of cattle. It is always a joy to arrive by this means, even though you notice straightaway that the familiar shabbiness and aimlessness are still there: from the wandering look of the cleaners to the jaunty flat-footedness of many of the cabs, which look as if too many returning bums have sat on those springs. Then, if you have sent luggage ahead, and have now to get it out of bond, the dealings with Customs come to seem endless; more than once I have engaged in the hopeless defensive ploy of demanding to know what is happening. Nothing, that's what! On one occasion I said, "If it's not ready in ten minutes, I'm going," and after ten minutes set off resolutely towards the defeat of departure, only to be called back, "Hoy there! Hoy!", and to be called "Sir", and to receive the stuff. They had been testing me: "If you go, we'll have to send it out to you." "That's all right." "It will be at your expense." "Don't you believe it." I think this slowness is a device to give the impression of busyness, to preserve jobs in a rapidly shrinking market, where nothing very much, after all, is now coming into the Customs store at Dublin Airport. We did, on two occasions in 1981, have stuff delivered. One of these deliveries turned out to be by way of a courtesy trip. One rainy evening in Rathfarnham, a small van pulled up, a cheerful Dubliner handed over some goods, and refused payment. "On the house, is it?" I asked. "I was in Sydney for two years, so I thought I'd bring it meself." He was evidently a foreman, and Australia was often in his thoughts. "Wish I was there now."

Such people have the adventurous disposition of minor entre-preneurs; they are not mere functionaries. The airport employee who usually has charge of luggage lost in transit is highly efficient: the expert operator of an inefficient system, which is inefficient largely because of the cumbersome transfer arrangements and the prevalence of theft at Heathrow; cases get lost (or "lost") in the rush. It is surprising that so few disappear entirely; after all, there is nothing posh about the Heathrow arrangements for Irish flights. On the contrary, as you are beckoned, searched, and led, you feel shuffled into some corner of unimportance; you are being trained to accept some menial role and status.

For one thing, the searchers and the searched almost never speak to one another; this is depressing but inevitable, for whereas no one wants to be bombed, no one wants to be demeaned, either. Once I saw a jolly Irishman, slightly jarred, attempt a joke to two Englishmen who were interrogating him; but the demeanour of the searchers is that of guardians of virtue, and they insist on an inscrutability not to be broken through by Celtic irresponsibility; the unyielding superiority is shared by all searchers, men and women, English, Scots, blacks and Asians (not that they exactly proliferate). When trade is slack, they turn this to an equally inscrutable casualness, and "joke", gutturally among themselves. The jolly Irishman could not face this threatening system of signals, and actually failed to take the flight.//

Anyway, it is foolish to send large quanitities of luggage ahead, because then you will have to go through Ordeal by Customs, with its base in manana-thinking and its aim of testing your detachment, a virtue of which some Irish people have a lot, most people have some, and I have none at all. The rule on Irish visits is travel light, and be responsible for yourself; then Customs and Immigration will hardly concern you. In fact, immigration officers don't even meet the flights from Britain.

Now that the struggle in the six northern counties is so advanced, and the ties between Irish and British governments so strong and complex, if rarely visible, coming into Ireland can be fraught with prohibitions. In 1981, when I had been living there already for seven months, and had paid three months rent in advance to live in marvellous working conditions in County Kildare, I set off to go to an international writers' conference, organised for Amnesty International, in Toronto; there I was to give two papers and a poetry reading. My chosen route took me through Heathrow, my contact with English soil being limited to the bus ride from Terminal 1 to Terminal 3. Trouble arose only when I passed through the immigration desk to catch the Canadian flight. The smart young interrogator wanted to know where in England I would be living on my return and, when I told him I would be going straight to Ireland, became very "concerned", consulted a book on the desk *(How to Look Concerned? Keep Them in Their Place?)* and a computer list of terrorists, prohibited persons and, no doubt, Irish-Australian poets, suspended under the desk. Then, in spite of my growing impatience, and not meeting my eyes, he stamped the passport briskly and said, "Report to the Irish authorities in Dublin." "What does your stamp say?" I asked. "I have given you permission to stay in the UK for twenty-one days," he said.

"But what has that to do with Ireland?" I asked. "It also entitles you to stay in Air for twenty-one days," he said; and then the row started, and he had to meet my eyes.

But it was all legal, as in my furious astonishment I found out; because of those barely visible ties between governments, an English immigration officer can determine the length of my stay in Ireland. I was told the same thing by a much nicer version of the original interrogator as I passed through immigration at Heathrow on my way home to Kildare. "What Irish authorities?" I said. "I'm living in Ireland. You've had a fortnight to check up with the Kildare police on whether my wife and children, my rented house and my unpaid bills, are where I said I left them. Just whom are you asking me to see, and why?" "The Irish immigration officers," he said. "Have you ever flown to Dublin?" I said. No. Of course not. "Immigration officers don't meet English flights," I said. "They're rarer than hen's teeth at the airport." To the "authorities" in Dublin Castle, then; he would give me a phone number. Special Branch, is it, I said. I imagine so, he said.

I prepared myself to "report" to the Dublin interrogators in that seat of ancient foreign (English) power, Dublin Castle, now an administrative centre for the Irish Republic, which itself is known incorrigibly to British bureaucrats as "Air". Eventually I did; and I was put in touch with a superintendent whose sense of the drama and urgency of my case was so underdeveloped that in the end he seemed more interviewed than interviewing. When asked what legislation it was that required me, an Irishman born in Australia and an Australian national, to accept Irish residence at the say-so of an Englishman, he courteously murmured something about "alien registration". "But almost all my forebears were Irish," I said. "I can't possibly regard myself as an alien in this country." "Yes," he said, for, unlike the Englishman, he could see some humour in it all, and thought Necessity the mother of Procrastination. "I can see it makes you sound like a little green man." "I *am* a little green man," I said.

None of the Irish seemed to feel any sense of urgency about my registering with them, but I came to the conclusion that I had better do it if I were to have a clear passage into England later that year; when I came to register, the grain of conscription in the Irish casualness came out, and I was asked for our passports, which would be returned to me later. "When?" "About six weeks." "How?" "By mail." "Certainly not," I said, for I had started to have weekly confrontations with the Irish mail system, "nobody will be given possession of my passports. If you want to register me, do it now." And they did, with as much ungracious impersonality as they could muster, which was not much, for the Irish may make you wait for an hour, but it upsets them to have you sitting there for a day (unless they have forgotten all about you, that is).

Ian Turner

LETTER FROM IRELAND

I think I must have caught the Irish Disease — along with other Good Causes — at the university. The infection didn't invade me as totally as it did many of my Irish–Australian–Catholic friends and acquaintances, whose sentiment (then and now) seemed to me akin to that of Henry Lawson's father and the father's mate, who "talked low, and their eyes brightened up, and they didn't look at each other, but away over sunset, and they had to get up and walk about and take a stroll in the cool of the evening ..." // There was nothing of Ireland in my blood, but there was something of her in my heart. So going to Ireland was like visiting a half-remembered and half-recognised home.

A childhood home. The cottages of the small farmers of the west coast were made of stone, mostly stuccoed and white-washed and thatched; but the shape was familiar, and they clung close to the ground. The buildings of the country towns, the advertising signs, the shop fronts, the dress of the men and the women in the streets, were reminiscent of the bush towns I knew forty-odd years ago — the more so because the superficial prosperity which has coloured the Australian countryside is not yet apparent in Galway and Clare and Limerick and Cork. The pubs had a furtive air — still the kind of places where the men sank their (and Ireland's) sorrows, while the women and children waited in resignation, outside. And there was one instantly recognisable symbol. Scattered throughout Ireland were statues of soldiers in slouch hats with the left-side brim

upturned. It was some time before I recognised that they commemorated the men of the Easter Rising, and not my father and
his digger mates of World War I.

Ireland is a country which lives closely with her past — because,
of course, the past refuses obstinately to leave her alone; it is still
there in the border which divides the Republic from the seven
counties of the North. The streets and squares of Dublin bear
witness to the recent past. Leopold Bloom's house has disappeared,
but his front door is enshrined in a central Dublin pub. The
martello tower, through which stately plump Buck Mulligan carried his shaving bowl and from which Stephen Dedalus set out for
his school, still stands, and alongside it is the rock pool, still with
its enigmatic sign, "Forty Foot Gentlemen Only". (The memory
is so recent that, when I returned from Dublin and told a London
friend that I had visited James Joyce's tower, she said, sharply, "That
was not Joyce's, it was Gogarty's!") The Liberator stares proudly
along O'Connell Street. The Post Office still carries some of the
bullet-scars of 1916. A twelve-foot Wolfe Tone stands on the edge
of Merrion Square, in aloof yet passionate bronze, backed by rough,
erect stone pillars which cannot envisage defeat. In Parnell Square,
three cranes soar over the women who are fighting — and some
dying — for the liberation of Ireland. In the courtyard of the
Customs House, a defiant woman holds the sword of freedom
while she supports a wounded soldier. I found these more moving
than any public memorials I had seen (though I have a twenty-five
year old memory of the Warsaw Ghetto memorial, and a more
recent memory of the stark simplicity of the Paris memorial to the
victims of the Nazi prison camps, to challenge that judgment).//

Faith is one — perhaps the most important, and certainly the
most long-lasting — dimension. Imperceptibly, it merges with
politics. My most moving experience in Ireland was to attend, in
the Abbey Theatre, a performance of Sean O'Casey's *The Plough
and the Stars*. Like Ireland, O'Casey seems to have been with me
for ever. I read a part in his play, *The Star Turns Red*, in 1947. //
More recently, I had remembered O'Casey, in the years after 1956,
as a stubborn, intransigent Stanlinist, who seemed unmoved by the
events in Poland and Hungary and by Khrushchev's secret report
to the Twentieth Congress of the CPSU. I had forgotten his plays.

The Plough and the Stars was a rediscovery. Here, once again, was all the ambivalence which Irish writers characteristically express when they confront Irish nationalism: patriotic fervour balanced against irresolution, cowardice and idle rhetoric; the strength and humanity of the women counterposed to the windy nothings of the men. And, for me the crowning irony, the figure of "Young Covey" who circled around the tragedy of the Easter Rising, quoting Jenersky's *Thesis on th' Origin, Development an' Consolidation of th' Evolutionary Idea of th' Proletariat.* (As was to be expected, the Abbey company turned in a brilliant performance.)

Mabel Edmund

THE ONLY BLACK WOMAN AT EALING STATION

In the middle of 1982 I accepted an invitation from the International Biographical Centre in Cambridge, England, to attend an Arts and Communication Congress at Queens College, Cambridge. I had to pay my own way and all expenses while over there. I shall never regret having made that decision to go, because I met some wonderful people there. Some lasting friendships were formed at the college and in London where I stayed a while with friends of my Canberra friend, Professor Audrey Donnithorne. I also spent some time in Dorset and Oxford. The congress is a great opportunity for delegates from around the world to meet and get to know each other better through the art of communication. Each year it is held in a different country. The time that I spent at Cambridge was very valuable to me. I learnt so much in the discussion groups and plenary sessions that were held every day.//

There were over three hundred delegates from forty different nations and they all had letters after their names or titles. I checked the list of names and I think I was the only one there without a degree. On the last night a large banquet was held, and in his speech the director general said that for the first time the congress had the honour of having a descendant of the original Australians attend, and he invited me to stand and everyone acknowledged my presence. You don't have to have degrees to be important, you just need to be yourself! People accept you.

Catching a bus from Cambridge to London, I asked the driver if he went near the station. He said yes, but I meant the railway station, and he meant the bus station. I was left about a mile from the railway station. I picked up my heavy suitcase and started walking the longest and most humiliating mile I have ever walked. About every six steps I would have to stop for a rest, my arms felt like they had been pulled out of their sockets. I had to get to Ealing to phone Mike and Kay, the people I would be staying with.

Halfway there, I sat on the suitcase and burst into tears. I didn't have a clue where I was, I couldn't see a railway station in sight. Then a young West Indian girl came along and stopped and she told me where to go. She said if she were going the same way as me, she would have carried my suitcase. I asked a cab driver if he could take me there and he said the station was just around the corner and he did not want to lose his place at the front of the taxi rank. I battled on and made it to the underground platform, bought my ticket to Ealing and waited for the train to come flying along out of the darkness. A young girl helped me throw my suitcase in when the doors flew open and dragged me in with her. I tell you, you have to be fast, the doors just open and shut again so quickly then the train is gone again. When we arrived at Ealing, I grabbed my suitcase and went to throw it out on to the platform and I lost my balance and fell out of the train and rolled over the suitcase on the platform. As I picked myself up, a lady asked if I was hurt and I told her, no, just my dignity, that's all. By now I was thoroughly fed up with the suitcase, but I dragged it up the stairs to ground level and rang the number my Canberra friend had given me. Mike answered and said he would be straight down to pick me up, but what colour dress was I wearing, so he could recognise me?

I started crying and I told him I did not know what colour my dress was, but "I am the only black woman waiting at Ealing station!"

We had a great week together, every day I caught a train and went out to explore London. I watched the changing of the guards at Buckingham Palace and all that. The only problem I had while there was that my bed had satin sheets on it and nearly every night I fell out of bed! Another surprise was the thousands and thousands of West Indian people living there, all spoke with "plums" in their mouths. They held jobs in high positions and no matter where you went there were West Indians working there. This was very different from Australia, where only the selected few Blacks got good jobs and only then because their relatives ran the committees.

Mudrooroo

SUGAR IN LONDON
London, July 1988

We all come here, one time, many times, all times
Staying on in a never ending debate of going home,
Though never going home, dispossessed, brought down,
Left here, abandoned in free will to say on,
Overstay, becalmed, refugeed, overthinking
Our being, creating our stand, denying our ground,
Braiding our hair, matting our inner emptiness,
Filling and overflowing with our imported sorrows,
Or joys, or take your pick, or return for a deposit,
Deposited, once more or never more, over-staying, over-here,
Over-bearing, losing out, emptying out any inclination
To go home, to be the prodigal, the old-new
Returnee with gifts, with knowledge, with terminology,
With harshness, with toughness, with a for rent sign,
Having lost ourselves to the hungry streets,
To the desolation of our private spaces and absent evils,
Vacant of any reason for ever belonging here,
Always of just being here,
A shadowy presence not quite legal,
Though never quite illegal or breaking free of constraint,
Or breaking loose to construct, to build, to centralise,
To remake our being into a fullness of our lives
Forever in this city.

* "Sugar" in the title refers to the production in London of Jack Davis' play *No Sugar*.

Judah Waten

ODESSA

I was born in Odessa but I was only fourteen days old when I left in August 1911. My mother was still in hospital when she made the decision to leave Russia. Father didn't agree; Odessa was his city; his family lived there, his parents, sisters and one brother and dozens of relatives. But Mother prevailed.//

My parents never saw Odessa again nor any other part of Russia. We went to Palestine and then at the beginning of 1914 we set out for Australia. I was then two-and-a-half years old. My parents lived out the rest of their lives in Australia but to the end they never forgot Odessa. From the dawn of my memory Odessa was with me, an exciting, colourful place I would have to go to one day.//

Odessa was unquestionably a great city of culture, greater than Warsaw where Mother had done her midwifery course. Out of Odessa came music as well as literature, she said. Famous composers wrote their music on the banks of the Black Sea; they were an even more romantic lot than the writers. // No other city in the world produced as many celebrated string players and pianists. Then there was that large body of Klesmorim (Jewish strolling players) who played at weddings and other jollities, walking from village to village and town to town. A song had been written about them "Yidel mit dem fiddle, Berel mit dem bass". And as if the Klesmorim weren't enough there was a veritable regiment of Gipsy fiddlers from Moldavia and Bessarabia. The Gipsy players and the Klesmorim filled the hearts of the people with music, Mother said. So much so that Odessans gave their sons violins as soon as they were old enough to hold them.//

Yet Odessa had a flaw. For all their music and culture the Odessans weren't really a refined lot, not even the Jews. So she said. They were not like the Jews in her native Minsk region; they were refined people with clean bodies and minds. To put it charitably the Odessans were an earthy people with a fondness for vulgar jokes.

Out of Mother's hearing Father often talked with his men friends about the Moldavanka, that part of Odessa where the thieves and the whores lived as well as the very poor. He would be so carried away with his recollections of bars, teahouses, dancehalls and brothels that he quite forgot the presence of youngsters listening to him wide-eyed.

According to him the Odessans bubbled over with the joy of living despite the Tsar and his regime. In summer they ate luscious apricots and watermelons and they loved eggplant, salty moist cheese, olives and fish. And they got sloshed on Bessarabian wine, the Odessa Jews being the only Jews in the world who drank heavily and liked getting drunk. He said he felt a pity for the austere Jews from Minsk because they only took sips of wine, and then only on the Sabbath and other Holy days.

He said Odessan women were dark, plump and lusty, the most ravishing in the world. And he boasted that Odessa turned out the most talented thieves in the world, certainly more ingenious, dexterous and brazen than the Warsaw ones.

His plausible yet brightly coloured stories made me dream of writing a novel which began in Odessa. This was when I was in my last year at school. I set out to read everything I could find on Odessa, every story with an Odessan setting. I wanted to be immersed in Odessan colour.//

Odessa, my birthplace. I didn't experience any strong emotions when we stopped out onto the railway platform, only curiosity. All night I had been thinking of our arrival and now we had arrived I was quite calm.

The station was on the site of the station my parents had known so well. Postwar, it looked prewar, Edwardian pre-1914 grand. A young lady from Intourist had met us and was taking us to a car outside. Now I was walking over the same ground my parents had walked when they were young, eager, ambitious, my mother anyway. Yet the station wasn't how they had described it. There were no beggars, no enormously fat policemen, no pickpockets, no whores, no young boot blacks and not much clamour. No Odessa dandies either, in fact few well dressed people. But plenty of healthy faces and healthy bodies. Everybody seemed so decorous, so law abiding. Only loud emotional voices remained. You could hear the hearty reunions and the loud smacking kisses.

Only the Intourist lady spoke in a quiet, prim voice, almost

English, prim, circa 1914. The car was driven by a handsome young
man who might have been a Georgian.

It was pleasantly cool but not cold, actually the warmest we had
experienced since our arrival in the Soviet Union. We drove down
quiet, handsome, tidy boulevards between rows of acacia trees
lining the roads.

"White acacias in Odessa and horse chestnuts in Kiev," Irene
said.

Our hotel was in the Maritime Boulevard, not far from the top
of the long Potemkin staircase that led down to the quay, the
staircase immortalised in Eisenstein's film, *Battleship Potemkin*, the
same hotel my mother had seen Chekhov entering. We could see
ships in the harbour when we stepped out of the car. To our right,
at the end of the boulevard was a beautiful eighteenth-nineteenth
century colonnaded building in yellow and white. It was the Town
Hall, said the Intourist lady. In Tsarist times it had been the Stock
Exchange. This was where Sholem Aleichem had lost all his money
on absurd speculations and where my father had thought he'd make
his fortune but he could not make a start as he had no funds and
he had to content himself with reading the quotations on the board
outside which only proved that he would have made a fortune if
he'd had the funds. The whole boulevard suddenly came to life for
me. As it was exactly nine o'clock the Town Hall musical clock
played a pretty tune from an opera called *White Acacia*, by an
Odessa composer, Isaac Dunayevsky. Every hour the clock played
the tune except between eleven pm and six am.

The hotel foyer was old fashioned, dim and cavernous. Gorky,
Bunin and Kuprin as well as Chekhov had stayed in the hotel. I
don't think we passed any writers as we walked up the imposing
staircase towards our rooms. Just tourists with bored American
faces.

Our rooms were roomy and comfortable and we had a wonderful view of the Black Sea and the wharves and the ships and the
exquisite long narrow park that runs down the middle of the
boulevard.

The Intourist lady gave us an hour to shower and change and
then she took us for a drive through the city, a beautiful drive.
Although much of the city had been destroyed by the Nazis there

were very few traces of war damage to be seen, anyway not from a moving car. It had been rebuilt to the original pattern.

We could not help saying that it wasn't a Russian or Ukrainian city in the way that Moscow was or Kiev. Even Leningrad was more traditionally Russian than Odessa. There weren't any ancient Slavic churches or monuments like the famous remnants of the eleventh century, the Golden Gate, or the St Sophia monastery in Kiev.

Not surprising of course. Odessa was quite a young city as Russian cities go. It was founded in 1794. Until 1789 it had been a fort in Turkish hands. In some of the distinguished eighteenth century type buildings you could see French influence, due to the fact that the Duc de Richelieu, a refugee from the French Revolution had been Odessa's first Governor. We passed his statue just above the Potemkin staircase.//

I felt sure that many of the people I passed were of Jewish origin but none of them looked like Sholem Aleichem's Jews or the kind of Jews Babel had described.//

I could have sworn not one cook at a circumcision passed us. More likely a ship's cook or a cook in a sanitarium kitchen. Such respectable family men they looked and there was a neighbourly atmosphere in the street.

I kept staring at the passing faces; not even a descendant of Benya Krik and his colourful Jewish bandits. This was not the Odessa of my father, the Black Sea Baghdad of the Odessan Thousand and One Nights. Neither was it the city of violent pogroms, the city where as Babel said, Jews were kept strictly "to one side of the street, chased away by policemen from the other".

My father's stories, the writings of Odessa were entrancing, colourful, but that was all. Man doesn't live by literature and tales alone, Brecht once said. First food, then thought. First good housing. The rest is to be read about. Odessa had a new set of priorities now.

Dymphna Cusack

LENINGRAD

Whenever Leningrad is mentioned someone present is sure to go into romantic rhapsodies about "the Venice of the North". Someone else sighs ecstatically about its ballet. Still another demands a comparison between Leningrad and Moscow people. And, according to age and taste, the names of Pushkin, Dostoevsky, Pavlova, Chaliapin, Ulanova will be reverently breathed.

It seems as though in some mysterious way Leningrad's history has been translated into myth. As though the formal perfection of its planning where past and present blend harmoniously; its exquisitely proportioned bridges linking the hundred and one islands on which it is built; the classic beauty of its buildings along the Big Neva and the Little Neva and the many canals connecting them; the aerial grace of its slender golden spires; its domes — all this, to many people, appears to have destined it to static enchantment.

Leningrad will cast its spell over the most hardened globetrotter. Second largest city in the Soviet Union, it is one of the most beautiful cities in the world. Wherever you seek your enchantment — in its parks, its historical monuments, its galleries and museums, its music and drama and ballet, in its bewildering variety of scientific institutes — you will find what you want.

Leningradians are polite, charming. They will do everything they can to help you. But they reflect reality, not myth. The dynamism of its founder, Peter the Great, a colossus, physically and mentally, is not only indelibly stamped on the city of his conception, but beats still, like a giant pulse that gives it, as it has given it for over two centuries, its peculiar individuality.//

If ever a city was built in blood and sweat it was this city "built on bones" which took fifteen years to build. In those yeras, it has been estimated, a quarter of a million serfs conscripted from all over Russia died to realise their royal master's dream. Yet the impression it gives is one of serene loveliness to which the newcomer instantaneously reacts, whether in its magnificent squares, its long avenues, its palaces or its parks.

I do not know how many of the 80,000 foreign visitors who were there the year of my first visit carried away from it a memory of more than its gracious beauty and the magic of its midsummer nights, but from the first moment Vera and I stepped out of the express from Moscow, I found that the "White Nights", which I had timed my visit specially to enjoy, had for Leningradians a significance other than their poetic charm. On these, the loveliest nights of the year, the bombers of the Luftwaffe had droned overhead knowing that the city would lie revealed to them in all its beauty. The 900-day siege which it suffered is written into history as one of the world's heroic feats of endurance and courage. It won for Leningrad the title of "Hero City". It left on her people a mark that still burns like an old wound. This was the first thing I learnt from the two friends from the Writers' Union who met me: she a writer who has written many stories about the siege; he, in those days a war correspondent, who each morning walked to "the Front".//

A "road-of-life", as it was called, was laid across frozen Lake Ladoga. The whole Union came to the city's aid, sending food for the besieged population, material for the factories and troops to reinforce the fighters.

50,000 civilians were killed in the bombing; 632,000 died of starvation.

What those stark figures meant in human terms is revealed in the unpretentious Museum at the Memorial to those who died in the siege. I cannot understand why Leningradians do not make a point of showing it to tourists. Perhaps it is too dear to them. Perhaps, as my young Intourist guide said, "because foreigners don't like to be reminded of unpleasant things."

It is a simple memorial. The inscription reads: "A grateful Leningrad will remember you for ever." A figure, symbolic of the Motherland, grieves over the graves. All that is formal enough, but the photographs in the little museum, the pitable relics, all the evidence of ordinary people lifting life to heroic levels, is unbearably poignant.//

Early in 1944 military salvos marked the lifting of the Leningrad blockade. Though the war still raged elsewhere, money and material were immediately allotted to rebuild the city.

Sixteen years later its beauty enchants the visitor, whether in winter with its snow, its frozen rivers and canals, or during autumn and spring with its flower-decked squares, its glittering spires and domes, the magic of the long summer nights.

As I sat in my window recess at three o'clock in the morning reading Dostoevsky's *White Nights* I thought my American from the Middle West probably would not be surprised to see Peter the Great and Vladimir Ilyich Lenin go arm in arm across the square, mutually congratulating themselves — for all their difference in temperament, politics and time — on their joint work.

Murray Bail

LENINGRAD

Yes, I went to Russia late February 19—. I was in a group. I was in the party. Fifteen thereabouts in all, well-educateds, in woollen tweed jackets, mainly British. The American schoolteacher — something wrong with him — his plaited Southern wife and kid were always the last to board the bus. Something wrong with him — built into his forehead. I remember that tall thin Englishman from Norwich who had almost no lips, very small eyes, forever looking over everyone's heads, complaining about the absence of tea. The lecturer in Russian from St Andrews University was pale, bald and boney: a living example of how a Slavic language can enter the convert's features. A plucky bulldog surgeon very neat in silken scarves and royal blue: she had a glued-on nose, stout rubber-capped walking stick, result of a car crash. I forget her name too. For the first few days she and her husband who was taciturn and from Hampstead, I seem to remember, sat at a separate table with the Professor and his French wife — it was she who told me he was a Mallarmé specialist and a friend of J-P Sartre. Such behavioural patterns emerged after the first sit-down meals and excursions. A natural sorting process took place. Initially our group sat dispersed in the plane, concealed from the other passengers and even from itself.

The cold exhilarated us all. So did the expanse. Both sharpened our sense of proportions, of what things are or can be, as the Ilyushin crossed the northern border of Germany.

The land below became wide open, bare, all grey ice, emptiness, the same colour as our accompanying clouds and the dripping alloy of the wing. The jet went on and on labouring and labouring, as if it worked against a headwind. It was hard to know if we were making progress. It was the sensation of endlessness ... that this extraordinary, barely coloured expanse can never end ... which gave the impression. The ice and snow barely changed; villages were few and far between; forests were eaten into, clogged up with snow; the occasional long empty road looked like a line stretched into the metal wing; and so the simple fact of Russia's expanse and harshness signed itself into our minds. I thought of the madness of Napoleon and Hitler, the tail of long armies. How many boots and weapons must be buried under the snow? Other examples of platitudes (obvious truths?) abounded.

I remember the landing. I was taken to one side by a stone-faced officer. His longcoat was grey. He didn't mind the Penguin *Secret Agent*. He was concerned about my hardback on their revolution picked up secondhand. Curiously empty of colours and airport movement, the bare terminal caused the passengers to go quiet, more obedient than usual, a kind of confusion. He kept turning the pages and reading a paragraph at random, turning back, then forward. Trying to determine ... I don't know. He saw the photograph of Trotsky in uniform and stared at me. Speckled green eyes: I saw the forests of Russia there. Eyes of a similar fractured perspective belonged to the guard in the buttoned overcoat checking each face — and mine — in the line at Lenin's tomb, close to the wall and the ashes of Reed and the cosmonauts.

This was Leningrad. Our hotel was that modern one alongside the Neva. Each floor had its samovar and an officious woman at a small table. She held a pencil over papers, keeping track of our keys. The ground floor had a purple carpet and a long enquiry counter. A row of wide-cheeked women there spoke patient English. A strange enquiry counter, looking back. The staff remained seated and since the counter stood almost chin-high we had to stretch on tiptoe and look down, while they looked up. I suppose it's still there. The Professor of French demanded to know if our freedom was being inhibited by the itinerary of the tour. He seemed to be making a point, insisting. I had to interject and tell him not to worry. In Leningrad you are free to go anywhere. Silver-haired and

transparent-skinned he moved his lips as if he was chewing something small; not out of nervousness, I confirmed later — out of
age. First impressions can be very interesting but are often mislead-
ing. He was a gentle, reflective man; impressive the way he had fun
travelling with his wife. They were forever laughing. And delegations from Mongolia stood around, looking lost.//

The Neva — like so many pieces of jigsaw on the map — was
dramatically clogged up with broken ice, small icebergs, most of
all under the bridges, and Peter's canals were frozen solid. Down-
pipes on many buildings had their water suspended a foot or more
out, frozen in midair. Taking a stroll by the river I noticed condoms
evidently flushed from various hotel rooms preserved in the ice like
bloated toad fish, for all to see. A small unnecessary detail. The
cold, not soggy like London's or Dublin's, was the true biting cold
of insects swarming around the mouth and ears, especially as I
walked along by the river. And the Russians kept saying how warm
it was, much warmer than usual. Leningrad has more than forty
bridges.

A loaf of bread cost forty cents. Taxis could be hailed only at
designated ranks. Rent for an apartment was nine dollars a month,
approx. Five cents on a bus can take you anywhere in the city. The
streets were clean. Women were seen repairing the bridges. Others
were climbing along steel scaffolds — plasterers. A sense of clean-
liness, of emptiness, made some in the party complain it was drab.
Few bright colours in the clothing, and no advertising signs. I was
told that in Old Russian "red" is the same word as "beautiful". Was
it the lecturer in Russian? The three single English women travelling together, led by a particularly loudvoiced slide photographer
reported how they were each fined ten roubles for jay-walking. In
Leningrad it was oddly gratifying to see people crossing casually
against the red light.//

As in any foreign country there was the instant impact of the
local people's faces. For several days these were as constantly curious
as the windows on the buildings which all had deep double-glazing
to keep out the cold. I found myself staring at them: at the tundra
hairlines of the men, their cheekbones, eye-sockets and pallor.
Being surrounded by such faces underlined my visitor's status. That
is, in the streets I felt conscious of my foreignness, of that definite

separation from the nearby faces. As a further reminder they seemed to take no notice of me or the group. We didn't exist. I remember sensing that in a crowded bus.//

There is no doubt being in a foreign country rejuvenates the powers of observation and sense of wonder. In Russia I felt that wherever I turned my "experience" was being broadened. I think Russia, especially, does that. It gives that impression. I said to the American schoolteacher ...

I noticed among couples a conspicuous amount of arm-holding: wives with their husbands, and pairs of men too. Someone in the group merely put it down to habit, a result of the cold. I don't think so. I sent an inordinate number of postcards to show friends ("Dear Comrade") that I was there in Russia, and they were not. The best was a colour photograph of Lenin's blue Rolls Royce, a Silver Ghost in a Moscow Museum. Skis had been fitted under its front wheels, and a caterpillar-track grotesque but no doubt practical replaced the elegant back wheels.

Many reasons can be given for visiting the Soviet Union. The dark-haired Brazilian (in our group; I forgot about him), always laughing, wanted to see Communism for himself. He wasn't impressed. I think we all wanted to "see Communism", a Communist country. Certainly that was a large reason for going. Outside an enormous shop for children the tall Englishman nudged me, "You know what that building is next door? The Lubyanka." He nodded significantly. Next to a toy shop: ironical, you see. But there are other reasons for Russia. The Professor of French was interested in the art collections and early Russian architecture. "My husband," his wife said, "knows much about Manet." He kept asking to see a wooden church. Churches I was told are called *Pokrov,* meaning "covering" or "protection". Again this must have come from the lecturer from St Andrews. He asked questions for us in Russian and sat up front with the drivers enjoying conversations.

For anyone interested in the history of the Revolution, Leningrad has many landmarks. It can feel eerie standing at these places. In Russia you can sense the force of history: the spot opposite the old Singer Sewing Machine building where the Czar was assassinated; the terrible open space before the Winter Palace; the Finland

Station and Lenin's preserved locomotive; and so on. Russia. Doesn't expanse and tragedy exist in the word?

Yes, there is much evidence, remaining from the Second World War, traces of the siege of Leningrad. Shrapnel-marked walls and chipped corners, and German bunkers near bus-stops, the cemetery and the reconstructed villas, have a profound impact. Such marks must mean something or have a constant effect. I found myself searching the faces and again noticed the wives holding the arms of the men. No city in Australia, none in America for that matter, posseses such scars. Two pudgy New York girls (in the group; I clean forgot them) went to the ballet and the renowned theatre for children. The language, the climate, the foreignness, the sense of drama, of past events: quite a panorama. Absurdly, too, I think many of us had the vaguely thrilling feeling of being in forbidden territory. And there was the food: the different soups, borscht, their smoked fish and so forth. Vodka, not Smirnoff's either. In a foreign country there is always the cuisine.

Roger Milliss

LIVING IN MOSCOW

The Australian coterie was smaller still, even allowing for the six or seven hapless souls trapped in the diplomatic compound cursing the day they ever got a transfer to the god-forsaken place, graded by Canberra as a **hardship posting** like such dreaded limbos as Rangoon and Ankara. The only others there when I arrived — though later more lobbed in — were Rex, the *Tribune* correspondent, and his wife and two young kids, despatched the year before as an earnest of our re-admission to the Soviet fold after our embarrassing liaison with Peking. A colourful expansive fellow with a little clipped moustache and acid turn of phrase, he was a first-rate journalist who'd served the Party faithfully through thick and thin, and not without his share of persecution in the process: at the espionage commission ASIO had tried to fit him as the biggest cuckoo in the celebrated **Nest of Traitors** they had conjured up. For all his cynical exterior there'd never been the slightest trace of deviation in his whole political career or any tiny sign of doubt about the shining virtues of the workers' fatherland — until he actually came to live there. When I looked him up as soon as I had settled in I was amazed to see how soured and bitter he'd become by eighteen months' first-hand experience of Soviet power. It wasn't just the queues and shortages, the lower living standards, the dead weight of bureaucracy, the gap between the propaganda and the truth, but anything and everything about the place he'd come to hate, even the language which he couldn't get a centimetre of his tongue around, not to mention the abominable weather. His disillusionment was best summed up by a story he took special pleasure in recounting: *Some thievin' bastard stole me blinkin' door-mat, so we put a new one out and fuck me dead next morning it was gone as well! That's New Soviet Man for you, he'd even pinch the mat outside your bloody door!* He found some consolation in the position of the Chinese upon the burning issues of the day, and we used to argue fiercely from the comfort of his flat on Prospekt Mira, Peace Avenue, about the liberation struggle, coexistence and the ending of the arms race. *The masses of the world don't want disarmament!* he shouted, brandishing a tea-towel in the kitchen as we were washing up one evening after dinner, *They want fuckin' guns!* At last his two-year tour of duty ended and he went back home, presumably to carry on the fight on *Tribune,* but it appeared that Rex has other plans. He strode into the office of a leading functionary in Market Street, flung his Party card down and announced, *That's it — I've had it!* turned on his heel and exited, to melt into obscurity in a suburban press producing weekly throwaways. *Sic transit gloria,* I thought more than a little sadly when I heard the story on the grapevine some weeks later. In the meantime I was trying to put my own impressions of the place into some sort of order, more especially through my day-by-day experiences of life immediately around me. // My block was // functional and adorned in single brick, though still set around a pleasant garden square where pensioners sat out the day playing draughts and chess and preschool youngsters romped on swings and slippery dips under the watchful eye of *babushka,* or grandmother. *Babushka,* that archetypal Russian institution, fascinated me especially. Time, it seemed, had passed her by, with her thick-boned peasant features dense with lines on which the centuries of ignorance and superstition were inscribed, her long dark coat, her heavy boots and woollen scarf wrapped firmly round her throat: summer or winter, she would not allow the sun to visit more than a few square centimetres of her face or hands. *Dedushka,* her husband — if she was fortunate enough to have one, for many of the menfolk of her age-group had obviously perished in the war or maybe in some earlier carnage — was her male equivalent, with his bushy white moustache, his trousers stuffed inside his leather kneeboots as he slumbered in a corner of the courtyard in the sun or strolled in patriarchal contemplation down the street, his hands clasped regally behind his back. // If I needed any further proof this [Russian] miracle had not quite worked itself out yet, I very soon received it in my first encounters with the Soviet shopping system. The language barrier was difficult, but not impossible to overcome — survival was a great incentive to enlarging one's vocabulary, and I soon picked up the words for basic foods and how to order them. Nor did the absurd routine of lining up to order, lining up to pay and lining up again to take delivery bother me unduly: *When in Moscow* was my motto and if the locals could endure it I could too. And even the interminable queues themselves were something I could cope with. You had to queue for everything and everywhere, in shops or at the stalls that sprang up in the street when something unexpectedly came on the market. I hated it — it meant you often had to spend three times as long as normal just to get your simple daily needs, and was bad enough in summer but an utter misery in deepest winter — but I somehow learned to grit my teeth and freezing feet and bear it like a trueborn Muscovite. But the incessant, inconsistent and impenetrable shortages were something else entirely, worst of all when staple foodstuffs suddenly went off. There seemed to be no rhyme or reason to it. One week, or even day, there'd be a plethora of something, and the next week, or next day, a virtual drought. Eggs would arbitrarily disappear, or milk or butter for a day or two even in the shops that specialised in them, or oranges, or bacon, or potatoes, this last a sore blow not so much to me but to the Russians, to whom the darling little *kartoshki* — how they used to rhapsodise about their unique quality and beauty — were a prime necessity of life, along with cabbages and bread: anything beyond was almost luxury. Part of the cause was obviously shortfalls in production *(What is Comrade Khrushchev's hair style called?* a common joke the following year asked cheekily: *Harvest Nineteen Sixty-Three!)* but just as much the fault of failures in the creaking distribution system, with the situation varying from shop to shop: sometimes a line that one store hadn't seen for days was flowing in abundance somewhere else. // So off I'd trudge along the street and try the next one, maybe meeting with success and maybe not, which meant another trek up to the outlets on the distant avenues until I got the item that I wanted, making a sixty-minute circuit of the suburb in the process. I soon acquired the local knack of never going out without a string bag in my pocket — an *avoska*, meaning *maybe*, it was called appropriately — to have on hand if something suddenly materialised upon an *ad hoc* footpath stall. But I adapted to the hassles and survived quite adequately, knowing my neighbours on the average wage or less would find it hard to do as well. There was another area in which I didn't realise at first how fortunate I was compared with those around me, or how they must have envied me my privileged set-up. If I thought the feverish building programme had done any more than scatch the surface of the housing problem, then I had a lot to learn. Yura had told me something of the massive overcrowding still existing: he and Ella lived in a five-roomed flat in the old part of the city with his mother and three other families, ten or twelve people overall sharing the bathroom and the kitchen, and they were lucky, he maintained: there were many families, not just of parents and their children, but a set of in-laws too, crammed in a single room. Priority was given to the grimmest cases, so he said, but the waiting time for new accommodation was several years. And the people I was working with were little better off, it happened, if at all. They might have seemed a fairly privileged lot, sophisticated, highly educated, hovering somewhere on the fringe of the *élite*, their incomes maybe double the prevailing norm — more for the translators if like Gans they also freelanced on the side — but in western terms their perks were only marginal and certainly did not extend to housing. I'd told myself before I came that I had no illusions left, but I was completely unprepared for some of the conditions that I witnessed at first hand: five or six people eating, sleeping and God only knew what else all in one room so cunningly disguised by folding daybeds, moving screens and sliding curtains I could only marvel at their ingenuity and talent for survival. Nor was it something that applied to just the older areas. Even my fairly recent-vintage building, I discovered, was a virtual rabbit-warren. The flat next door to mine contained a pair of Chilean journalists, but otherwise the residents were ordinary Russians, mostly factory workers judging from appearances. The other two apartments on my landing were of three rooms each, and at first in my naivety I thought that they housed separate families, the lucky beneficiaries of progress, but as I saw the constant stream of people trooping in and out I gradually realised that they were in fact communal set-ups, home to some twelve and fourteen souls respectively. And I couldn't fool myself they weren't aware of how well off I was by comparison. *Vy zhivyotye odin v svoyey kvartire — do you live alone in your flat?* someone would ask me in the lift, wistfully rather than aggressively. *Da, odin*, I'd guiltily reply, and try to switch the conversation to some other topic such as my lack of words allowed. But apart from the odd muttered comment which I maybe fortunately couldn't understand there was never much resentment, let alone antagonism, towards me that I could perceive at least: they were a friendly and expansive people once the ice was broken and in time I got to know them fairly well, starting with stumbling observations on the weather — *Sevodnya kholodno, cold today —* *Da, ochen kholodno, skoro upadyot sneg, vy predstavlyali nashu zimu? Yes, very cold, it'll start snowing soon, have you heard about our winter?* — and eventually exchanging names and other simple intimacies. The *babushka* next door befriended me quite early in the piece, maybe for less than noble reasons — she used to borrow money from me just before her pension day, though always scrupulously paying it back — but asking me in occasionally to the room she shared with her daughter, son-in-law and swaddling grandchild whom she doted on adoringly, for a cup of tea or even, taking pity on my bachelor condition (the French girl never did eventuate) for a bowl of *borshch* or *shchi* for lunch or sausage fried in omelette mixture, quite unembarrassed by the crowded quarters, as she told me tales I barely understood about the war and more especially of the Revolution when, on one unforgettable occasion, as a young girl she had marched across Red Square one May Day only a few steps from the leaders viewing the parade: *Ya videla Lenina!* she declared, *I saw Lenin!* and crossed herself devoutly as if it was the other Vladimir she'd glimpsed. I made my first big breakthrough with the other people in the block after I'd been there six or seven weeks when I saw a notice in the entrance for what seemed to be a Sunday working-bee — *Subotnik*, as the Russians called it — to plant trees in the courtyard. So that morning I went down to find some forty other civic-minded volunteers already hard at work with spades and garden forks. It was a biting cold October day when autumn was already giving way to winter with the first faint flecks of snow beginning to drift down. Someone handed me a shovel, and I dug a hole or two and filled them in with shrubs lying on a heap nearby, feeling a bit left out of things until a friendly ten-year-old named Misha, living the next floor down from mine, came up to lend a hand. A little heartened by his overture, I went across to join the rest of the brigade busily digging up the centre of the yard. Between the saplings that we set into the clayey soil — poplars and silver ash, as far as I could make out — we swapped cigarettes and introduced each other in a farrago of extremely elementary Russian, a word or two of German someone had remembered from the war and an elaborate pantomime where language failed. They were mostly youngish workers, friendly, cheerful coves — Sergei, I remember, a mechanic of some sort, Andrei doing something in a textile plant, and another who had spent a year in Indonesia on a Soviet aid scheme and kept trying to speak Bahasa to me. By early afternoon we'd filled in almost every vacant spot around the yard and done some other basic gardening when suddenly the mercury slid down another few degrees, the solitary specks of snow began to form into a heavy soggy sleet and we were forced to call it quits. If it never actually produced a deep or lasting friendship, the episode at least ensured that I was known around the block and generally accepted: it was good to bump into Sergei on the stairs and hear his hearty *Privyet, Rodzher, kak dela? — Hi there, Roger, how're you going?*

Chris Wallace-Crabbe

RUSSIA: LOST IN WONDERLAND

When you set out to travel to the USSR you have, not so much bureaucratic difficulties, but a veritable Himalaya of clichés to overcome. These blocking clichés are massive. They include everything from the Kremlin, the KGB, an impenetrable bureaucracy (it was far easier to get my visa, in fact, than it had been going to the USA twenty years earlier), gerontocracy and a powerbroking Writers' Union through to caviare, drunkenness, uproarious merriment and antisemitism. Such caricature elements are so powerfully reinforced by the media that they sink in firmly. Like most clichés they are sometimes true and sometimes not; it would be hard to shake them out in a fortnight.//

There was lots of snow around Moscow. We landed at Domidirova, back of Woop Woop, instead of being allowed to fly into the international terminal. We stayed on the tarmac for three hours, looking at snow and birches. Out there the fox says good morning to the hare. Finally we took off again and flew into Cheredmetova, where they left us next to a Libyan plane at the edge of the airstrip to look at more snow. Arriving at last, I was whisked through customs by our interpreter, Natasha, immediately noticeable in her bright pink parka.//

Those first two days I walked the streets and avenues a lot, growing used to the contrasts between a large physical scale and the narrowish range of consumer goods. Disparate things caught my attention: the rush of women to buy a couple of crates of limes from a fruitstall when it opened at eight am; kids on their way to school tormenting one another with an exact Russian equivalent of "Cowardy cowardy custard"; the many big sweet shops helping to use up the Cuban sugar cane harvests; newspapers stuck up on noticeboards, along with posters for a monologue about Tsvetaeva, another by Okhudzhava and an exhibition of Arvi Aalto's architecture; and more people than I had expected in stylish winter clothes.

By now I had met up with my fellow travellers who had flown in, Olga Masters from London and Tom Shapcott from Belgrade. Olga and I had stravaged around the Kremlin and down the shopping displays of Kalinin Prospect, looking at women's clothes and fur hats in a department store. But it was time to get down to business.

Serious matters began with our morning visit to the Writers' Union in its rabbit-warren of an old mansion, sprawled out around a garden with Tolstoy's statue in the middle. The format of our meeting was one that would soon become familiar to us: sitting around a table, three or four a side, solemn introductory speeches gradually leaching down to more relaxed conversation, Natasha usually kept on her toes translating, although many of our counterparts (if that's what they were) proved to be at least bilingual. General briefing, solemn greetings, much cultural exchange talk, the scent of hierarchy in the air. After this we went on through passages, tunnels and staircases to lunch (with beer and soft drink, for the new semi-prohibition laws were taking effect), laughter and jokes, along with some speculations about the coming millennium of the Russian Orthodox Church. Questions were asked about the intellectual climate in Australia, and Kuznetsov, one of our hosts, smilingly said, "The Italian delegates told us about their interest in structuralism and literary theory. I told them that we had been through all that, and had gone beyond it."

The Writers' Union building is an expansive sort of club. After lunch we struck some eccentrics. One was a primitive expressionist painter who was exhibiting his pictures in one of the reading rooms; he showed us round garrulously, and then gave us copies of little children's books which he had illustrated. Then a very sozzled young woman, seemingly a poet, took a fancy to Olga and Natasha, proving quite hard to shake off. Upstairs we went, past Lenin and photos of a round hundred male notables of the Union — and one female. We did see a show of paintings then by a woman artist. "I think her drawings are good," I commented. "Oh, yes," came the reply. "She is a qualified artist." Nervously fingering my poet's diploma, I went on.

For some combination of reasons we met a number of artists during our time in Moscow. There was one who painted a mixture of mystical paintings and Breughelesque bawdry: his art mainly appealed to people on the embassy circuit. Another, the jovial Yuri Vasiliev, restored icons and made etchings of old churches in their landscapes. Another illustrated children's books. And another,

Boris Messerer, produced paintings and lithographs of wonderfully bold construction, sometimes making use of the fluted patterns of old gramophone horns; he works as a stage designer and showed us several maquettes of theatrical sets, intricate sculptures in their own right. We did not meet any artist who practised in the social realist manner. Indeed, in some large art gallery one of our guides peeped into a room and said to me, "Oh, it's only social realist art in there. Let's go to another room where there's real art."

Jokes are a major genre in the USSR. Everybody makes use of them: everybody enjoys them. My favourite was the one about the man who is arrested by a militiaman for handing out pamphlets in Red Square. "But they are all blank!" he protested. "Why on earth do you hand out blank pamphlets?" asked the stupified militiaman. "Because the people already have everything." Other jokes turned on the gerontocracy in the Central Praesidium, on the Iran–Iraq war, on prohibition, and on historical paradoxes at the end of the second millennium: "The Jews are soldiers, the Germans want peace and the Russians are sober."//

It was a time of energetically busy days, of colourful dreaming, waking in the night, and writing until I was tired again. I even wrote a dramatic monologue spoken by a girl, one night when I could not get back to sleep.

Sleep was not a serious problem on the overnight train to Leningrad, although it came and went in waves. We were woken in our sleeper by recorded birdsong, which gradually modulated into music. The countryside was snowy and twiggy. The train pulled into Leningrad on time, and we were met by "Alexander the Second", a short, helpful man from the Writers' Union, who whisked us off through the city's large Pieran perspectives, past rococo facades washed yellow, blue, green-white, to our hotel, the comfortable Astoria, where Esenin hanged himself. The city is soaked in literature, saturated with culture; one reads it through books: Pushkin, Dostoevsky, Gogol, Akhmatova, Mandelstam, they have overdetermined all our responses. It was hard to take it on the spot that the longed-for Hermitage was *also* the Winter Palace, that art and history inhabit the same site, that Matisse nudges Eisenstein aside. And is it really true that Kerensky missed out on a job in the Russian Department at Melbourne University?

Years ago Jim Davidson had typecast Sydney and Melbourne as Tinseltown and St Petersburg. While I was in Russia I often felt he had it wrong. Moscow was the place of power, politics and the reality principle; Leningrad stood for aesthetic pleasure by comparison, despite all that the war cemetery recorded. At a party in Moscow, one writer said to me, not without a hint of approval, "You know, Nabokov is the typical Leningrad writer." And a Leningrad official of the Writers' Union said that "Moscow writers are more interested in politics. We are more interested in literature." However, we did talk a little, dilute, politics with journalists from *Novy Mir*.

Apart from the war cemetery, suitably stark under its coverlet of new snow, so much was striking or imposing about this city. Little older than the European settlement of Australia, it seemed to bear an almost intolerable weight of history. It is peculiarly moving, even alarming, to think that the Soviet authorities gave such priority after the Patriotic War to rebuilding the palaces of Peter the Great, Catherine the Great and the eighteenth-century gentry. Aristocratic and bourgeois greatness underwrites the visible beauty of this peculiarly European Soviet City. Even the incomparable Matisses and the historically crucial Picassos pay silent tribute to the bourgeois taste of Schukin, who bought them for his walls.

On St Isaac's Square I was moved to a grossly-rhymed tercet about this city of inordinate display:

Snow lashes the Marinsky Palace,
The Admiralty is a golden phallus:
I am lost in wonderland like Alice.

But for all I say about display, there was a modesty, or informality, of personal style, especially when compared with the visible elite of Beautiful People in Moscow ("Dangerous, easy, in furs, in uniform," as Auden puts it). The people we spoke to in the northern city struck us as much more matey. There was even an unbuttoned air about the Astoria, where young, blond, stonkered Finns could be seen swaying along the corridors, ready to rage on in a mate's room, vodka bottles clinking.

It was here in Leningrad that we first saw sunshine, the custard-yellow facades abruptly glowing, the patterns of light and shadow underwriting Peter's honey-classical perspectives. On the radio in my room I could hear bad rock from Radio Riga, such blare curiously out of kilter with my serene prospect of St Isaac's Square, the only public space where I ever saw the statue of a Czar. It was impossible to feel any truth here in the accusation I heard later from a Muscovite that the USSR has become "one great museum of kitsch". Not even in Tashkent would I feel this — despite its unspeakably wretched Museum of Literature. At the farthest extreme from kitsch, we saw the Kirov Ballet doing a new piece, a compelling ballet on the life and death of Pushkin. I had been told that the Kirov was far more impressive than the Bolshoi, and so it proved.//

Things inhere in the memory for very different reasons, in very different modalities. In some cases the mode is spatial, as for example with my clear memory of the glittering Hall of Mirrors in the Catherine Palace at Pushkin, pure sculpture of air and light and glass, or with my recall of the distinctively stuffy, reconstructed rooms of Dostoevsky's house in Leningrad. Sometimes they attach to a face, like that of the merry, blond, boyish young man who came along as a photographer from *Novy Mir*. Sometimes an utterance gives focus to the whole gestalt, as when we were having afternoon tea with the Rector of Zagorsk monastery and I began discussing Soviet Islam with Alexander Koriakin ("Alexander the Great"); we moved onto the dangerous territory of Afghanistan and he suddenly remarked, "The anti-progressive forces recently launched a rocket attack on a mosque that was full of people worshipping." There was no accessible answer to that. Another patch of recollection turns on Boris Messerer, Bella Akhmadulina's husband, taking me to an upstairs window from which we looked out over the modernist shopping complex on Kalinin Prospect and remarking that this was the new Moscow; he then led me further upstairs, to the very top of his studio, and opened another window, which gave onto old tiles, decaying chimney stacks, rooftop grass and a small birch tree growing in its patch of accumulated dirt, high above the centre of the city. "And this is the old Moscow," he said. "Which do you prefer?"

Some things vanish entirely. I have not a single memory trace of the return train journey from Leningrad. Where do lost memories go? *Où sont les neiges d'antan?* This sense of lost things keeps turning me back to the lovely beginning of Mandelstam's poem,

> We shall meet again in Petersburg
> As if the sun was buried there
> And proclaim for the first time
> The immaculate and meaningless word.

Perhaps our lost things are not in the lunar sphere, but clustered around that primal, immaculate word. We struggle towards it, of course, using the old familiar set of shopworn signifiers.

Olga Masters

SEARCHING FOR THE FACE OF SOVIET LITERATURE

In Russia we were shown somewhat briefly, for time did not permit long and searching looks, the face of Soviet literature, circa 1985. Or, perhaps we should say, the one face of Soviet literature with many expressions.

The stolid, the cautious, the inquiring, the alert, the eager, the glimpse of friendliness, the tragic.

The face, whatever other expression it wore, never failed to reflect courtesy of the highest kind, whether it was the Soviet Writers' Union the hosts, magazines or newspapers, their table spread most generously with grapes, apples and matchless Russian chocolates with close attention to our teacups.

The message was clear. Our visit was of great importance.

At these arranged meetings of Soviet Writers' Unions (in Moscow, Leningrad and Tashkent) we saw, or rather I felt I saw, the closed and stolid face.

They were without exception elderly men. Grey men. No women. On the wall of the Writers' Union Club in Moscow more than one hundred photos of male writers. Few young or even youngish faces. Only one woman's portrait in a corner. No look of triumph having made it to this male dominated sanctuary, but a sort of pained nervousness there, like a guest a party by mistake.

Rightly or wrongly one is made to feel that this panel of men run a tightly controlled (literary) ship, kept sternly on course.

In an exchange of information on writing and publishing in our respective countries we asked about opportunities for and encouragement of young writers in Soviet Russia. We were assured such programs were operating.

But nowhere was our attention drawn to any named young and exciting new writer perhaps with an award (we were told they were given quite liberally) for poetry or prose.

Have you a Kate Grenville or a Tim Winton? I longed to ask.

Nowhere did we hear, for all the Russians' devotion to the theatre — opera, dance and drama — of any new experimental writer whose work was performed and acclaimed.

There may be a healthy growth of youthful writing being nurtured. We may have missed the nursery in our tour. Perhaps it was like an old-fashioned visit to relatives where the adults entertained and the children were kept out of sight.

In Leningrad in the Writers' Union building we were shown a quite curious Soviet expression. I mentioned with sympathy the obvious gaps through the Nazi siege of 1941–45. We saw the memorial to thousands who died, the little building with a scant collection of photographs depicting the deprivations of those terrible times. A glass case enclosing a stub of candle and a crust of bread. The beautifully kept grounds were a common grave. Countless dead.

But the spokesman said no, no writers were lost. They worked as journalists, correspondents and in allied (and protected) occupations. What? No talent decayed there under that sheet of snow? None with their tales yet to tell? Is Soviet thinking generally as closed at that? Would post-Revolution writing be akin to it?

Another curious expression, stubborn, part-scornful on the face of Moscow radio interviewer George Murzin, who described Mayakovsky's poetry as "early revolutionary stuff".

"He died before the revolution really matured," he said.

We discovered for ourselves Mayakovsky's statue of giant proportions outside our hotel. Our attention was not drawn to it.

Nor were we shown the Chekhov museum, although the ever-alert Chris Wallace-Crabbe tracked it down.

But we were shown in the Dostoyevsky museum, the first-floor flat where he lived with his family. Full credit must go to those responsible for the careful restoration of the trappings of the life of the author most famous for his *Crime and Punishment.* //

I believe I found the healthiest side of Soviet literature on the faces of the women we met. Of course none were established women writers taking part in the formal meetings. They were translators, interpreters, secretaries, organisers of the project in which we were involved. They hummed in the background, seeing to our needs. One or two ventured to murmur they wrote a little poetry and short fiction. They sounded as if they were clumsily trying to imitate a Pavlova.

I thought many of these women splendid. Anna Martinova was one. She was a journalist heading the international section of the *Literary Gazette* in Moscow. Behind her flood of questions on the status of women's writing in Australia I detected an urgent appeal to Russian women to make their mark on Soviet literature. She gave over a page of her newspaper to extracts from our books. She came to the hotel with photographs for us taken by the newspapers. She seemed as if she wanted to talk forever.

Again we saw women in action for the cause of better understanding between our two countries through published and translated works at the office of *Soviet Literature*, the monthly magazine available in Australia. There seemed a dominance of females producing this magazine of poetry and prose.//

Around the table were the daughters of this generation's women, their spirit reflected on those gentle womanly faces, words the weapons they were seeking to use in their quest for peace.

The tragic face of Soviet literature was that of poet Bella Ackmodolina. We are indebted to Chris Wallace-Crabbe for this meeting, her address given through a mutual colleague in Australia. She lives with her husband Boris, a theatre designer, on the top floor of a derelict Moscow building.

We met the pair with Bella's fellow writers, whose work is turned down for publication by the Writers' Union. Their collected works appear in a handsomely bound book, *Metropole*, and is banned by the Writers' Union.

What excuse is offered for this treatment of Bella Ackmodolina, once recognised as one of Russia's finest poets? The answer would be, we were told: She was a good writer once. Now she is a drunk.

Literary history is peppered with such people, their works legendary.

The pity of the scene was the conflict of loyalties. All of these people loved Russia with a similar passion for one's own country as that expressed by our writers — Lawson, Katharine Susannah Prichard, down to the moderns.

Their cultural starvation contrasted with the food they spread for us. Russians have a reputation for spending a week's salary on the best caviar, smoked salmon and grapefruit for their guests and eating frugally for the next six days.

The decor of the room spelled out their message. On one wall was a huge stone crucifix, Jesus with bowed and sorrowing head. On the other, so close by there was room for only two people between the two, a bear skin of similar size. The teeth were bared and sharp, as were the unrelenting eyes.

As the night wore on, Bella's unaccepted verse read aloud, the gloom deepened and it was hard to believe the face of Jesus did not droop lower and the lips of the bear lift in a more cruel snarl.

The tour program, to the credit of the organisers, included visits to galleries, museums, and exhibitions, apart from those of a literary nature.

We saw behind the restoration of such palaces as that of Catherine the Great in Leningrad the sacrifices of the people to allow the billions of roubles to be spent this way.

On the other hand, at Tashkent, there was the well-designed Museum of Economics, and here we saw proof of the industry and dedication on the people's part to contribute to world markets as well as self-support.

The spirit of the people seemed indomitable. You saw them as strong and honest. What a triumph it would be to be able to say the same of post-Revolution writing.

But we need an increased flow of translated works to see for ourselves what is being said or written. We need to increase the current somewhat tentative flow of Australian works for them to see what we are up to.

They readily dropped the names of Prichard, Alan Marshall, Dymphna Cusack, Judah Waten, most of whom had visited there. It is fairly easy to become familiar with writers met. We need to show them the works of our moderns, including those of our budding young.

They might then be encouraged to expose more of theirs.

Everywhere we went our Aborigines were mentioned. I think we all shared some embarrassment that interest expressed in their culture was greater than that of many of our near neighbours at home.

This piece would be incomplete without reference to Natasha, our interpreter. She looked like a ballerina with her white skin, black hair parted in the centre, slim and shapely figure, giving lie to the theory that Russian girls are frumpish and unattractive.

She lived with her widowed mother in a two-roomed flat and no matter how late the hour when our official engagements were completed she took the last train home with amazing good cheer. "If I miss it, I'll sit in the waiting room until morning," she said.

She had no phone and shared her bedroom with her mother. She spoke fluent English and has just about mastered Italian. Between stints as an interpreter she works in an office at a job she hates. Her dream is to one day set foot in France, Italy or America. She said, with her wide and aching smile, her chances were slim indeed.

Perhaps I could also add that we were in Moscow for Revolution Day on November 7 and had tickets to Red Square to see the parade. Thousands watched, thousands took part. The city closed its doors for the celebrations. We tried at the Australian Embassy to make telephone calls to London and Australia but were told, although it was early the previous evening, we would need to wait until life returned to normal the day after.

The militia marched with such precision their overcoats rippled as evenly as if a breeze ran through them. Guns boomed, smoke swirled and missiles and other warfare grew larger and more menacing as the parade reached its climax. Then the people surged on to the ground carrying paper carnations big as young trees.

Where did they store them in their tiny flats massed in a huge housing development on the outskirts of the town?

"By 1990 everyone will be housed," we were told.

It sounded as if the people were akin to those wooden Russian dolls that unscrew to fit more dolls inside.

Will Natasha's daughter, if she has one, carry a carnation, too, on Revolution Day? Will she stand in the cold as thousands of children did that day mouthing the words that came over the public address system, faces nearly as still and stern as those of the marching soldiers?

Will she be content with a shared room, no car to drive, a goodbye to an American boyfriend she will never see again?

Perhaps it's there, in those multi-storey flats, that the real Russian army is in training for a new revolution.

Leila Rodd

HEART OF EUROPE: PRAGUE, 1978

Our hotel —

a traveller's repose
a tourist's refuge —
is classified C
as compared to a night in a B
and has one hard pillow
and one lumpy quilt
on single beds in separated corners.
No double-bed rooms.

Or hot water in our hot-water tap or heating during the day nor during the night. There are the evening showers, to wash and get dry underclothes and hair. Mixed. Cubicles without curtains. And you have to write down your name and pay extra to be given a key for twenty-five minutes, performing balancing tricks with towel by the on-or-off heater and with toes over the ice-block space between. Other people's hair on the tiles. I meet women cleaning every morning but there's a limit to what muscles and rags can do without what "cleans cleaner that clean". When we came back to our room our things had been touched. We don't use it much except for sleeping and we'd sleep in except for the girls' giggling team along the corridor, for it gets light very late. After breakfast — a ritual of boiled water served in a glass with a silver-plated handle from long-ago, teabag and lemon slice on its saucer — we only return if in need of the toilet: with its roll of toiletpaper threaded on a chain padlocked round a pipe. Usually our beds go unmade, not this time. Though our sheets were still unchanged, the hand basin uncleaned, and our things had been touched. Our radio wasn't quite the same on the shelf. We'd covered the telephone with a cushion, now moved ... we'd been told it listened, and we'd heard: "Please Sergeant (to us: they're not sergeants at all you know but it flatters them), please Sergeant don't cut me off it's my mother's birthday", shouted by Jaroslav over long-distance. We looked for other possible listening devices ... we'd been told someone'd found one in their ceiling light. We found nothing. Apart from labels: numbers stamped on aluminium rectangles screwed underneath every piece of furniture or fixture. We suspect a search. We could have something worth finding, books. Two nuns we met on the way warned us about bibles and prayerbooks but this is nothing subversive ... there's no banned list we've been told. We also have packets of Douwe Egbert's coffee and Drum tobacco. It makes our suitcases heavy. We whispered possibilities outside our room by the worn wooden bannisters, panelled mirrors of a past elegance. Xavier walked down to the hall to ask had somebody been up to our room. A man was sitting there on well-matured mahogany, waiting. Our porter, who speaks an English faded with age and disuse, wasn't on duty. Of pre-war politeness, he's the only one who understands us. When we'd arrived late at night we hadn't booked, couldn't guarantee a departure date: not booking's not normal, hotels claim to be full in the middle of January; in the country we'd spent a Russian-novel night on a railway station; in the city in a tourist office upon enquiries about hotels a uniform had appeared with a notebook to copy down all details, so we'd got on a tram — even a night in the car in the snow is preferable for the freedom of it. Our soft-eyed porter hadn't minded, had left blanks in his ink writing in filling-in his forms, and we'd laughed our relief into the lift after he closed us and our luggage in with a "Cheerio" and a key to a room. Xavier wasted his time on the German-speaking porter who has a defensive look in his eye for us. He wouldn't understand. Much later, when we check out but have to come back he'll know nothing, either, about my Norwegian greasy-wool socks left drying, or of our soapbox forgotten in a shower with a film inside (for somewhere to put it); Xavier posing with aluminium hammer-and-sickles with red stars and ribbons in the snow. And even later we'll remember a man sitting on matured mahogany, waiting; and a man, that last time, leafing a telephone book by the counter.//

Somewhere a tram screeches along its slippery tracks. On the other side of the road a gaslight shimmers blue as we step out onto rain moist cobbles to find a place to eat. A coatless man is standing there, smoking. We talk a bit. Xavier runs back as though something is forgotten. The cigarette drops and goes out. I move quietly away. The man, not smoking now, deliberates before also rushing inside. Underneath the lamp post the pink patterned pavement glistens: river pebbles in sun-filtered water or autumn colours floating in a puddle. That Man and Fur Hat hurry up the hill, see me see them, slacken; I turn towards them, our hotel in between, they almost stop but continue and pass and go on up. Xavier rejoins me, alone. Alone we set off again. Not always. A woman and a man holding arms enter an exhibition of scenographists ahead of us and linger with us beside the best, Svoboda; I'm surprised by the woman and try to get close to her reaction to me and therefore they're already gone when we leave. In an ice-cream parlour at a table opposite a sad small man with his hat still on sits and stares without any ice-cream. We don't always see the same: some person pacing nearby corners, car chases, a control of who's meeting whom at the theatre. Imagined or real. We study faces. "Paranoia?", we ask ourselves eating dinner of brown sauce poured on a slice or two of the meat and dumplings, what we get every time no matter how we try our dictionary. The grams of the meat are marked on the menu. Some order only dumplings with their brown sauce. Some have potatoes instead. These places to eat are not easy to find till you learn to recognise a thick curtain in an entrance. We can sit for hours after the cream cakes stay tasteless-sweet on our tongues, it's warm here to do things like read or write.

David Martin

THE RETURN TRIP

When we had crossed the border the sun had come out, but now it looked as if we might be in for another shower.

"Nach Hause," I said. "Coming home."

"At last," said Paul. "How does it feel?"

I made no reply. I was staring at the thick grey china cups with the entwined initials of the German railways, at the bottle of *Selterswasser*, at the white bread rolls with their twin ridges of crust, at the flowers in the narrow vase, secured to the table by a metal grip. The conductor passed noiselessly. I looked at him. He was as I had known he would be, as was the *bouillon* in our cups, with the little eyes of fat, the tablecloth, the polished woodwork and the square serviette rings, dented and with spots of black showing through the silver coating. I had loved all this. Trains: Charlottenburg station at night, the gritty taste of engine smoke, porters handing in the luggage, the cries of food vendors, *Warme Würstchen, warme Würstchen*... And later, rolling up the blinds, the darkness of Rübezahl's forest. Osnabrück, Bentheim. On the way to Scheveningen, the sea, happiness. To wake up at the frontier, in the *wagon-lit*, my half-sister sitting up in the other berth, and Greta kissing us good morning in a new country. Heaven was a train, a *D-Zug*, and God an eternity of travelling.

The couplings were clanking together, we were beginning to move. The crowing of the cock was cut off in the middle. *Mein guter Hahn*, are you crowing for me? And you, boy on the bicycle, do you too love trains and dream of travelling to the sea?//

The train was not my train, the trolley not my trolley, the sparrows not my sparrows. Because they were not they had never been: the past is possessed only in the present.

To say I had not been afraid would be a lie, but I had kept the fear at bay. // It had been with me, too painful to be denied, since we had come on the boat at Harwich. I had slept little during the night. I had hoped that Holland would take the edge off my forebodings, but we had crossed it in a few hours, and when we reached the border I had been as nervous as a smuggler and felt slightly feverish. The official who had entered our compartment had been friendly and polite. Handing me back my passport he had addressed me in English, and I had answered in German.

"I see you have visited us before."

"I went to school in your country." (I often said I went to school in Germany, rarely that I grew up there.)

"I trust you'll enjoy your stay."

He had stamped Paul's passport, and I had been left to brood over my dishonesty.

The eyes of the travellers in the dining car were without curiosity. The waiter came up with the menu, which Paul was trying to decipher. He hesitated, and with intense concentration pronounced a word. The man looked at him and back at the card. Paul repeated his order and the waiter looked at me.//

"Communicate by signs."

"Easy for you. If I had the nerve I'd get off at the next stop and take the first train back."

"Oh, everything is easy for me. I have no problems."

"Well, nobody forced you to come. Your problems are the ones you've made for yourself. You should be in your element, a German among Germans. Do you notice much that has changed?"

"Only myself."

"Then wake up and look around you. Pull yourself out of the past."

When we came back from lunch our compartment was no longer empty. In the seat by the door sat an elderly priest in a black cassock, and facing him a girl of about eighteen or nineteen, dressed in a light-coloured suit. She had taken off her gloves, and on her lap rested a travelling draughts board.//

The priest took off his pince-nez and asked if Paul would like a game.

"My niece will be very glad to give you one, and I promise to stay neutral."

As Paul was setting up the board, the other explained that they were going to Hamburg. They had joined the train at Osnabrück, where she had been working in an optical laboratory and where he had been attending a seminar. She was a skilled technician, but her career was being cut short — before the end of the week she would be married. He was fetching her home, very conveniently for them both. Were we going to stay in Germany, or were we only passing through?

I told him that we had come from Australia, but that I had lived in Germany, as he could probably tell by my accent. My friend, an Australian, was here on holiday, but I had not yet decided how long I would stay. Looking at his soft, mobile features, and visualising him gesticulating from some pulpit, I was wondering what might happen if I were to be so incautious as to open my heart to him. Could he guess that I was a Jew? Older than I by fifteen or twenty years, he must already have been a priest when I had left the country. Curious to know where he had learned to speak English so well, I asked him. It turned out that he had taught at Oxford, and that he still frequently wrote for English church publications.

Here Paul interrupted him to say that I was also a writer. The priest, accepting this with a respectful nod, wanted to know whether all my work was done in English. I replied that it was.

"If it's not too personal a question, may I know if you have ever written in German?"

"A few stories, when I was young."

"In what journals did they appear?"

"You probably don't know them. A couple came out in a magazine of the emigration, whose founder was a Nobel Prize winner." I mentioned his name, which he said he knew.

"He died, I think, during the war?"

"He was caught and perished in a camp."

"Yes, very tragic."

But his smile discounted tragedy. In deference to his niece whose attention was divided between her game and our incomprehensible conversation, I switched to German. "They were the usual beginner's stories, and have never been reprinted."

He explained to her that I was a writer, and went on:

"The first work of a young author is sometimes his most revealing. He usually begins by freeing himself of his childhood, perhaps his parents. In this way one prepares the ground for true individual experience."

"You could be right, but mine certainly had nothing to do with my parents. Would you like to hear what the very first one was about?"

"With pleasure, of course." But he sounded surprised.

(Why was I trying to push it on him? He had not demanded it. What meaning could it have for him?)

"It was a kind of love story."

"Aha. A natural choice. And the setting?"

"Quite prosaic. A boarding-house in a small mountain spa."

"In Germany, I suppose?"

"As you say. There was a woman, no longer young, one of those spinsters come down in the world, daughter of a minor functionary, a plain, respectable body."

"I once had a governess like that," the niece threw in, *"ein sehr nettes Fräulein."*

"She could have been a governess, but I'm not sure. Let us say she was. In the boarding-house she meets a man, another holiday maker. Very quiet, very sober, like her a lonely individual, well-spoken and well-preserved, keeping himself to himself. He always sits at the same small table, doesn't talk much, takes long walks on his own. Once or twice they accidentally meet in the woods, to exchange a good-day and pass on. It is autumn, the off-season, and only a few people are about."

"An autumnal love story," the priest murmured, folding his hands over his compendious chest. "As we grow older we prefer our stories to take place in spring or summer."

"Then the inevitable happens. She becomes fascinated, falls in love after a fashion. The reader can see that they would suit each other, these two left-behind, loveless people. Gradually, without any dramatics, they strike up an acquaintance. I think it is she who has to take the first step. // What most draws her to him are his hands, which are slender and finely made, like a musician's, but he claims not to be interested in music. He prefers the open-air life, a student of birds, nature ... She gathers that he is some kind of a public servant, not exactly well off, but not penniless. His leave ends before hers does, and they have not come to an understanding, but they have exchanged addresses, and she believes that he will write. She feels that she has made an impression. He goes home. A day or so after he has left she finds out who he is. Somebody tells her, a forest ranger, if my memory serves."

"Please, let me guess," the niece said, with sudden animation. "I know: those sensitive hands. A murderer? He has killed his wife!"

"You have a nice intuition."

"Or a murderer innocently convicted, or, better, a kind of Bluebeard from whom the poor soul had a narrow escape."

"I am afraid not. He was the hangman of Magdeburg."

For perhaps twenty seconds neither of them spoke. Paul shifted restlessly. "What a dreadful tale," she said at last. "I wonder why you wrote it."

"He wrote it," her uncle spoke up, "because youth has to come to terms with death before it can come to terms with life, and because those were the years of the hangman. It's a father and son story, all the same."//

Without having used it, he put away the little piece of chamois which he had produced to polish his glasses. "Our friend has been away from Germany for many years. Perhaps he does not realise that things have changed since his time. We are not all executioners, for example. The death penalty has been abolished."

"I have heard."

"And I can vouch that not every German was a monster, not even in those days."

"I don't doubt it. Not all my early stories were of this kind, of course."

"I hope not. Could you tell me whether your pity extended only to the woman, or also to the hangman?"

"To neither, as I remember. Pity did not play a great part in it." He said, in English, "Mine is the vengeance, saith the Lord."//

The priest stretched himself and pointed to the window. "Do you know the district we are passing through?"

"Barely at all."

"We are now getting near Neuengamme. Does that convey anything to you?"

"Only a name."

"You have heard of Bürgermoor?"

"Vaguely."

"Do you know the song of the *Moorsoldaten*?"

"The one about a concentration camp?"

"It was written at Bürgermoor, where the prisoners from Neuengamme were sent to dig peat. The fiancé of this young lady had a cousin who was killed there. He was a Catholic, incidentally."

"And the man who killed him?"

"A Fleming, they say, not a German. I am taking the liberty of mentioning it, because it might give you material for another story. If you should ever write it, please send me a copy."

Soon after we entered the suburbs of the city, and Paul helped them to carry their luggage to the door. The priest had already left the compartment and was waiting by the carriage exit, but just as we were pulling into the station he came back. I thought that he had forgotten something, but he merely said that he could not leave without wishing me God's blessing. I thanked him for his kindness.

"Good-bye, then, and *shalom*."

"*Shalom*, Father."

"And *Mazal Tov*, as you people say."

Stephen Murray-Smith

GERMAN NOTEBOOK 1971

Munich-Nuremberg

DACHAU on the sides of the trains and on some street signs.
Strong feeling of self-satisfaction, and conservatism. The beer cellars and somewhat selfconscious folksiness are apparently allied to this — what should be gay is somewhat sinister.

Fine sense of style — superb, original, modest street fountains — many of them. One of a little child with a wolf. It reminds one of the dear little children fed into the gas chambers by these people or their parents or relations. I wonder if it ever reminds them of that. Even with Emil, my self-possessed, cool, human guide and helper, I didn't know how far to go. I mentioned a visit to Dachau, but didn't press it. He raised the matter again once. Neither of us took it further. Yet if the new Germany *is* new, should I not assume that they don't flinch from Dachau, that they want this in their consciousness? Or is it perhaps Germanic of *me* to demand this degree of logical self-assessment?

At the light opera — Strauss's *Gipsy Baron* — nice piece of genre corn. Second row from front.// *The Gipsy Baron* — charmingly romantic, these gipsies. I wonder how many in that theatre thought of how the Germans exterminated the European gipsies. Udo, at Nuremberg, tells me later that no one would have had the same thoughts as me, and neither would he: people go to the theatre to forget the world, not to remember it. Udo is (like Emil at Munich) another mid-twenties "permanent" university student — the mature-age aspect partly a function of the late *Abitur* (18–19) and of military service, and also perhaps of the liberality with which scholarships are given and renewed.//

Udo works with the Christian youth though he doesn't consider himself a card-carrying Christian. He won't vote Christian Socialist (Bavaria) or Christian Democrat (Federal) because the Nazi fringe voters have swung to them. He fears the youth wing of the SDP — considers them too close to communists — doesn't like the label slung from the university left as such as he — *Scheissliberalen* ("shit liberals") — doesn't like disposing of others' opinions in this "certain" way. On the whole admires best the FDP — the Liberals — but quotes the saying: "There are three parties to vote for — Pestilence, Gangrene and Cancer."

This seems to me, as indeed it did in Eastern Germany in 1950 ("Because I know people I love animals" — the slogan I saw on an office wall and quoted to my communist hosts, to their chagrin, though I suspect they would never have noticed it themselves), to be part of the Freudian memory-hole protection-against-trauma bit. Udo says that you can't reflect on what you haven't known. Those who have not known freedom don't know what they are missing. Those young people like he, who have never known Nazism, cannot identify themselves with the moral issues arising from the Nazi era. They do not ask their parents, of course: and are constantly surprised at how it is impossible to find anyone who held his hand up in the Nazi salute in the Third Reich photos with which they are familiar.//

I'm depressed partly by loneliness and a sadness at being parted and at being so far from home in London and home in Australia. But the other part, and more immediate part, of the depression is really this country. Nuremburg is, superficially at least, a far more attractive city than Munich (and less than half the size). The rebuilding from almost total destruction of the centre is of course impressive. It's good that only two per cent of the art treasures and only six thousand people were lost in the great raids (especially the US raid of 2 January, 1945). But for me at least there was not much impression of joy, not much of humour, not much of intellectual behaviour or thought. How much can one learn in a day? I think I can get a pretty good idea of a place in a day — particularly a day questioning an intelligent man like Udo who believes fascism could return to Germany, who would either leave Germany immediately or fight it from within if it did, and who went off tonight after the ceremonial handshake at the train to his planning meeting for his church youth club — though he despises many aspects of church life.//

Nuremberg — the place of the *Parteitags* — the grass-grown steps of the stand of honour; the plinths where the searchlights stood, and the flagpoles; the avenues for marching men, with railway stations at each end. A used ticket on the ground — for the recent Germany–USSR soccer match in the stadium nearby! The drums and trumpets and crunch of boots and shouts and salutes seems long away when you see the dilapidation of the whole arena and the Führer rostrum. There is no menace here. The remarkable, novel film show, multi-projected on swinging screens, at the Castle has some good anti-Hitler feet in it — but Udo tells me it was devised by Ludwig Svoboda of Prague (Lanterna Magika) and that a German wouldn't have given the Hitler era ("only thirteen years in our long history") such prominence. I suggested to him that (a) the Hitler era started long before Hitler, and that its roots must be sought, inter alia, in nineteenth-century romanticism and the lack of a liberal tradition; and (b) that thirteen years or not, Auschwitz was in human, moral terms, the most important world event since the birth of Christ. He didn't argue.

I suppose what depresses me is the sense I get that to these people the past is irrelevant — the memory hole here is on a national *and* individual level, especially the latter. In the USSR it's a purely state matter. Here in Nuremberg, history is important if it's about Dürer. But if it's about yourself, it didn't happen.//

Frankfurt

Joan says she was so depressed at the immanent cruelty in Europe and Germany when she first came here from Australia two years ago that she would sit in tramcars weeping. But she questions whether the Germans, however many are fascist in the heart, should have the monuments of the *Konzentrations- und Vernichtungslager* about to harry their consciences.

Germany is a rebuilt nation. To an historian, or an antiquarian, depressing (again that word!) — nothing is as it was — except, Erika tells me, a small town called Rothenburg, or some such name, south of Würzburg. (And surely Bamberg, which we visited on our way to Prague, too?) The rebuildings are no doubt faithful, but don't carry much conviction, even in Nuremberg — they lack a complete dimension of veracity, they carry a Disneyland effect. Once the dust of the centuries has been disturbed, the old bricks carried off to the *Trümmerhügeln*, it seems a sad exercise in pretending it didn't happen. But that's the German theme.//

Joan agreed this afternoon that Europe is full of a cruelty that Australia doesn't know, that it is covered in blood, as our writers have so often said. But, she said, she would stay here because, on the whole, she saw this as the necessary lot of man. I said that, on the whole, I would return home, both because I couldn't stand it (the present, and the weight of the past), and because I don't concede her point.

I suppose the problem is to stop becoming righteous. *Because* one is Australian it is easy to be righteous in terms of communist and fascist bullies and executioners. But, shit, there's got to be a bit of righteousness around. Would the world be a worse place if we asked more rude questions and made more uninvited interventions? If we don't do this while we are safe, we won't be able to after the deluge.

Berlin

My new interpreter and guide in Berlin is Gerda. These interpreters make interesting contrasts. First Emil, the cool young operator, who will make the system work for him (his word for himself is "detached"); intelligent and very generous; with his record collection of nearly a thousand discs and his disgust at the piggery of the student flats in which he lives. Then there was moon-faced Udo, the man with a conscience. // Then Minna in Frankfurt; again, a kind girl, but with a smooth, efficient, tight-lipped, knowing-where-she's-going, quality about her. // And now Gerda, whose husband teaches history at the Free University — older than the other guides, lively, small, with a good sense of fun, plenty of self-possession, and giving the impression of being able to talk about the bigger issues without any particular hang-ups. A lot of what she says rings true, too: "I never spoke to my aunt again after she divorced my uncle (by marriage) because he was a Jew — after she married him because he was a doctor."

Gerda goes, it seems to me, with Berlin: lively and of life. The despondency which has affected me throughout Germany has lifted here: it is the only German city, of those I have visited, that I could possibly live in. To walk down (or was it up?) the Ku-damm last night in the dusk, shopping, as the lights came on and the dark storm clouds of an autumn evening drifted over, and as the Berliners pressed past and around and ate and drank in the sidewalk cafes, was the nearest I have had to an exhilarating experience for a long time. Of course I was on my own, and that helped. And spending money on myself, and on presents, which I like doing. *And* perhaps I like Berlin because to be here means I'll soon be home, to London and Australia. But I still think I like it for good reasons of Berlin's own.

But I was really depressed on return from East Berlin yesterday — David and I went over for the morning. The border inspection, the delays, the inhuman spaces of the Alexanderplatz, the queue in the post office where we bought stamps — all these and other things made me say to David, walking wearily back to the Schweitzerhof from the S-Bahn station, how badly I wanted to be at peace again among my own trees and friends.

Clem Christesen

IMPRESSIONS EAST AND WEST

The cancer eats on and on, also troubling the sleep of Berliners. On one side of The Wall is a brash, garish architectural monstrosity of a city, with smug porcine faces bilious-green beneath the flickering neon lights; on the other side the faces are constantly turned to the west in apprehension. In envy too? I wonder. Drab by comparison with West Berlin, East Berlin is at long last generating its own forward-moving dynamic force, and there is now a feeling of confidence and hope; at least of hope, among the many. Where there was nothing but utter desolation and devastation twenty years ago, a new city-state is now in the making; and not before time. The growth-rate during the past year or so has been remarkable. Can a "new man" also be shaped by new ideologies? Have East Germans, to put it bluntly, been purged of all remnants of Nazism? I gained much evidence to support such a claim. In West Germany there is no such evidence; on the contrary.//

Earlier this year [1965] the twentieth anniversary of the defeat of fascism was celebrated in East Germany. The occasion seemed to cause some embarrassment in West Germany, where it was finally decided to invite Queen Elizabeth to help ease any feelings of guilt which might still twinge the conscience of the Good German. If I were an Englishman the ineffable cant and mockery and sham would have made me vomit, or commit an act of extreme violence. In East Germany the generals also gathered, and the politicians, and speeches too were made; but at least those speeches made some sense, retained some elements of decency, even if the dead remained mute.

And there was also held in East Berlin and Weimar, from 14-22 May [1965], an internationales Schriftstellertreffen, to which (by a happy accident) a "delegation" of Australian writers was invited, together with writers from fifty-two other countries. (Chinese and Albanian writers regretted they were too busy to attend.)

It was an oddly assorted group of twelve Australians. One spoke German fairly fluently, another had retained a meagre knowledge of the language; for some it was their first visit overseas; one arrived very late, another turned up on the last day of the meeting; most were scandalised when told by a Berlin publisher that their work was provincial, old hat — and incredulous when he urged them to write like certain Americans; one wrote a well-turned poem for public offering, others sold stories to more charitable publishers; not one was a subscriber to *Meanjin Quarterly*, some knew scarcely anything about the contemporary Australian literary scene — and even less about foreign literatures; one had never heard of Weimar; all had a ball, and all voted it was a grand experience.

And so it was. At first we gathered together in the Hotel Berolina, a modern glasshouse; visited the Wall, the University, the Brandenburg Gate, the Treptow Memorial, the Pergamon Altar; met other writers, danced at nightclubs, attended plays, took part in a seminar conducted by Helene Weigel and the Berliner Ensemble and over cognac discussed the finer points of Brechtian theatre.

Later we went to Weimar, "the heart of German culture", where the main business of the meeting was conducted. Weimar can no longer be thought of apart from the monument on the Ettersberg: admonishment and memorial, designed and built by Germany's foremost artists in honour of the heroes of the Resistance, and to warn against neo-fascism in any of its forms.//

In the Goethepark or in the Schillerhaus, in Tieffurt or Dornburg Castles, in our hotels or in the Klub der Intelligenz, we talked with other writers, tried to communicate through interpreters — if we were unable to speak Turkish, Arabic, Danish or Uzbek! But it is amazing how effective can be a smattering of a few languages, plus ability to mime.//

If most of the Australians missed visiting the famous Thüringian library, the Franz Liszt Academy, Wittums Palace or the many other places of historic and cultural interest in and around Weimar, we all attended a fabulous banquet at the Wartburg, near Eisenach, where Luther translated the New Testament. The Wartburg, a palacefortress dating back to before the eleventh century, is a traditional symbol of German independent thinking. Here we mixed with writers from Mali and Honduras, Paraguay, Iceland, Bulgaria and the Lebanon — from across the world from Cuba to Mongolia. The Cranach paintings, the tapestries, mosaics and frescoes, the cross-vaulted ceilings, the castle moat, drawbridge, keep, watch tower and massive battlements — here was a fine place for drinking champagne and eating Pökelrinderzunge nach "Art des Hauses", Hasenrücken "orientalisch", Gefüllte Kalbsbrust "kaukasisch" and Langustenschwänze "Havanna" auf beleuchtetem Eisblock, while listening to works by Händel, Ricciotti, Mozart and Bach! Those among the wild colonial boys who looked around for steak and eggs were persuaded to settle for Roastbeefröllchen mit Sahnemeerrettich Creme. All in all, an unforgettable experience.//

Australians are scarcely ever invited to literary functions in foreign countries. Some individual writers (who happened to be in London) took part in the great Paris conference thirty years ago; other individuals have attended occasional PEN conferences, or literary celebrations in India and Romania; and during recent years two small delegations were invited to the Soviet Union. To my knowledge no group of Australians has ever been invited to an international meeting of writers in (say) England or the United States. Thus the Berlin-Weimar invitation was unique; and for that invitation the Australians were profoundly grateful.

But I can still hear the tolling of that great bell on the heights of the Ettersberg — tolling its pity, and its warning ...

Max Harris

THE LARRIKINS IN WEIMAR

From all directions they converged on East Berlin — three hundred writers, Africans in flowing regalia, impassive Mongolians, impeccable Cubans, noisome Americans, West German poets looking youthful and ill-at-ease, plus the gregarious and omnipresent band of Australians. Where the guffaws were loudest there they were.

But it wasn't basically all fun and games for the hosts from the "unstable city-state of East Germany" who had spent an astronomical sum in organising an International Meeting of Writers as a cultural counter-measure to the royal visit to West Germany.

It was a deadly serious matter to them that the cause of East Germany should be understood aright in the light of the perpetually damaging mystique built up in the West around the Wall and Checkpoint Charlie. And, for that matter, the East Germans needed desperately to change the view in other socialist countries

that East German communism is the most puritanical and formal-
istic of all.

The East German organisers played their cards wisely and well.
They prepared only one formal meeting, no guided tours or
compulsory itineraries. The writers were offered a fistful of drinking money whenever they required it and allowed to attend discussions or not, as they saw fit. Manifestations of propaganda were
suppressed in favour of the subtle and disarming technique of
saying: "Here we are, take us as you find us! Most of you writers
are far from being communists, and you will have your own views
about our society. This doesn't matter so long as you depict our way
of life as truthfully as you can. For our part we are concealing
nothing."

These methods are nothing new as a cunning way of converting
the liberal mind which believes in the spirit of open and unpreju-
diced enquiry.

Did these ingenious non-directive methods work to brainwash
the ingenuous band of literary boys from the Australian bush?

If ASIO keeps dossiers on political loners, then they'd better start
one on me. I'll gladly give them a hand. It's not that I, or any of
my writing colleagues from the Australian contingent to East
Berlin, have been brainwashed by the Mephistophelian sophistries
of East European communism, but rather in my case that a direct
experience of Western Europe makes one realise with a shock of
shame and dismay how much of the propaganda and manifestly
untruthful guff of our own side has rubbed off on us as we luxuriate
on the beaches of the Lucky Country.

West Germany for instance. Here we have a country besotted
with affluence and self-assurance, the streets of Frankfurt and
Wiesbaden more bepoodled than any in the world; citizens fighting
to pay £5 a seat to see the Italian Opera; the shops gluttonous
mountains of decorative carbohydrates.

And the West Germans themselves? Not bitter and still arrogant
as they were when I last saw them a decade ago, but suave and
possessed of an all-embracing self-assurance. It is the unpretty
affluence of a discreetly powerful emerging middle-class, dressed,
young and old alike, in the uniform of current fashion and with
the omnipresent expensive leather briefcase.

They were to a man much amused by the royal tour of West Germany, much amused in a tolerant way that Britain's desperate need to secure a better economic toehold in the Common Market in the face of de Gaulle's capriciousness had led to such an elaborate act of flattery on the part of Britain. Being obedient Germans they took their little flags, lined the streets, and benignly accepted the decorations that were strewn over Germany like confetti from the royal fingers.

Nothing shameful in Britain using its royal paraphernalia to strengthen its hand in Europe: it demonstrates clearly the value of a monarchy as a device even in modern political psychology.

But this was not the story reported in Britain or Australia. Day by day, hour by hour, the BBC, the popular Press, even journals like *The Guardian*, which should know better, reported endless vistas of jubilant Germans transported at the thought of being finally forgiven their past — "their queen is now our queen too". This nauseous guff of old Bavarian women saying to children: "Now we really belong to the free world again" saturated the British and Commonwealth mass media so that one was aware of a compulsive "party line" on this event — that it symbolised to the Germans British forgiveness of their Nazi past.

But it was just untrue! And dangerously untrue. The West Germans know their commanding strength in the Common Market, that 1,000,000 Italians have been absorbed into their work-force like a flash, and that they can well afford the luxury of old hard-core Nazis in their new army and to hell with ancient remorse.

And they can increase their pressure and intensify their manoeu-vres towards a German reunification (which wise editorialists, like those of *The Sunday Times*, see as historically unrealistic and politically dangerous in a period that hopes for American-Soviet rapprochement).

One sees present history falsified and this leads one to wonder about past history and to worry how far one has brainwashed oneself in one's own environment, where free and unimpeded intellectual enquiry is the greatest merit of our social order.

For my part, out of laziness I had become attuned to a Hopalong Cassidy goodies-and-baddies image of the division of Berlin and the lethal terrors of the Wall. As I flew up the Corridor to Tempelhof I began to suspect with some shame that I had become habituated to seeing the world in terms of over-simplifications just as stark and untrue to reality as the views of the West that prevail in Iron Curtain countries.

In fact there probably only exists a world of confusing, diffuse and kaleidoscopic greys.

West Berlin, a vital, vibrant city of work and happy fleshpots set against the grey, dazed poverty of communist East Berlin, bleak and rubble-strewn over the impenetrable Wall?

Not a whit! My mind had been filled with two half-truths together constituting a dangerously viable untruth. West Berlin is as sad as East Berlin in a different way. The vestiges of war destruction are less evident; the true sadness of the town lies in the crass vulgarity of its modern architectural splendors, often donated by an over-grateful United States, and the weary effort to affect the gaiety of Americanised affluence. Your true Berliner, East or West, is invariably sardonic rather than gay about his world.

East Berlin? As quiet and repressed as Melbourne on a Sunday — in fact a bit like that noble if uninspiring city. East Berlin now proffers a variety of splendiferous restaurants that still manage to purvey amateurish and down-at-heel variants of Western culinary luxury.

But you can wander into the remotest shrub of East Berlin and the citizenry eat as well and as modestly as they do in any unpretentious London pub (German beer's better) and they are clothed as well as the suburban Britisher. If they have lived twenty years under the most puritanical communist yoke of them all, then they must have come to terms with it in some way, for they do not appear to move under any obvious shadow.//

What dreams the East Germans have had about the Day of the Fleshpots have long since gone, and reconciliation of a sort to the historical realities has taken place.

Those of us attuned to meetings in the style of the Congress for Cultural Freedom, sodden with motions, speeches and heavy intellectuality, were ill-prepared for the East European new style of handling such affairs.

After luncheons of some substance one proceeded at will to

meetings on themes of poetry or literature or films which were held around a banqueting table.

It is a fearsome European custom to begin a meeting with cognac all round. Then, while the first and only speaker unburdens himself of his brief remarks, flunkeys circulate with fruit and light Hungarian wines.

The discussions begin to warm up — and the flunkeys are in action again with massive arrays of hors d'oeuvres and Hungarian champagne to make sure that the discussion doesn't dry up. That moods should be finally mellow, coffee and cognac circulate, and the meeting breaks up in amiable and inconclusive disorder so that visitors may prepare for the massive parties and orgies of the evening.

The scale of the hospitality ensured that political overtones would be impossible and that our impressions of a communist social order would be ones of the utmost urban normalcy broken by ancient conventions of high life.

This worked to perfection in Weimar, the town of Goethe, Schiller and Bach, a town corrupted from its ancient peace by neither tourism nor commercialism, as is a town such as Heidelberg.//

If the East Germans had called for the literary whirlwinds, they had received only the sunset zephyrs of early autumn.

But West Germany, with American assistance, is maintaining the barrage of propaganda on the theme of the "suffering" East Germans, and the East Germans respond bitterly to an image of themselves that is blandly untruthful.//

Here was a national climate — in which criticism, not only of literary ideologies, but even of beer and beds, is disposed to stir up silent pain close to the heart, rather than hearty discussion.

From our antipodean burrows, Australians are disposed not to be over-sensitive to a national climate in which criticism, not only of literary ideologies, but even of beer and beds is disposed to stir up less hearty discussion than silent pain close to the heart.

How then did the Australian larrikins fare in an environment calling for a hypersensitive response to realities we have been traditionally disposed to praise or rubbish at will? Not too badly.

They did appear to me to have some of the appropriate quantities of vigorous and enquiring young nationhood in their participation.

It was not inept, even if politically ludicrous, that the rumbustious Russians, the quicksilver Cubans and the ratbag Australians seemed to form one of the many enclaves of human affinities that had developed by the end of ten days.

Now, retrospectively, I wonder how many of my Wall-climbing mates feel the weight of a cloud of intellectual unknowing as the outcome of it all? Australia and Australians are so well insulated from the labyrinthine realities of Western Europe and communist Europe, that we don't see through our glass newspapers darkly. The values of the world we inhabit are clearly defined for us.

McKenzie Wark

BERLIN WALL

Dateline: 16 November 1989. The ruling party in East Germany announces that henceforth all East German citizens will be allowed to pass directly to the West. In Berlin thousands rush to the border posts to cross the threshold. By Sunday night four million East Germans have crossed the border into West Germany. West German authorities in Berlin hand out maps and shopping money to the Easterners. The Mayors of East and West Berlin push through the crowd on the Postdamerplatz to shake each other's hands, while many thousands climb the wall; champagne and music are in the air. The *Guardian Weekly* comments: "Europe seems to be a different place this week." //

East Germans may have run westward, provoking a crisis, but they were running in the direction from which images of the good life came. The wall notwithstanding, there was still what Stefan Heym calls "the vision on their screens evening after evening of a richer world, a world without boundaries and which is said to belong to the industrious … No wonder that the people of the country run off at the first opportunity." The platform on which Kennedy made his famous *"Ich bin ein Berliner"* speech was pulled down, leading Timothy Garton Ash to comment: "Europe's *Mousetrap* had ended its twenty-eight year run. Clear the stage for another show."

The oppositional East German churchman Werner Krätschell recalled that, after he drove thought the breach in the wall, his wife wanted him to stop the car in the West. "She wants only to put her foot down on the street just once. Touching the ground. Armstrong after the moon landing. She has never been in the West before." It is appropriate that the pathos of this remark stems from its evocation of the moon, from the austere image of another place, the "other" place, supposedly conquered once and for all when Armstrong put his foot on it. Though it wasn't his *foot* that touched down, but an airtight boot. Armstrong travelled many thousands of miles and still didn't touch the moon. The other is an uninhabitable place, a mirage; even when one travels to it, sets foot in it, one still does not quite touch it. There is something there to touch, to be sure, but it is not quite the other that one has already mapped out in advance.

Krätschell and his wife might feel like actors on a real terrain, touching strange earth, but the theatricality of the act of making that small step gives a clue to the imaginary travelogue mixed in with this border crossing. Viewed from a distance, preferably from the other side of the world, they look more like actors on a set. Just like Kennedy on that platform we have all seen in television documentaries, like Armstrong on a moon that we can only imagine, the Krätschells appear to be acting on a map of imaginary identities. One notices something else: in Krätschell's metaphor of touching the moon, it is as if the two halves of Europe have become the whole universe, and nothing else exists. From a certain distance, however, the whole of Europe looks like another place, a tiny speck somewhere over *there*. A place that holds a mirror up to itself, sees the other in itself, and does not notice the rest of us at all. One thinks of 1989 as the opening night at a theatre where the curtain goes up and the audience comes face to face with another audience. Each thinks the other is the spectacle, themselves the real audience. One has to be outside the theatre to see it as a double game.

Starting with the East Germans who stepped into the West like astronauts, these actors are within a *double* spectacle. One is the external spectacle on our TV screens — the breach in the wall, the champagne spray, the pickaxe chipping the old wall away; the other spectacle is the one that the East Germans experience as interiority, that they are reacting to from within. Rather than simply crossing a border, they are also starring on *two* separate screens, each a lopsided mirror of the other. In the imaginary of the West, the West itself figures simply as everyday existence. It seems the most natural thing in the world for the East to want to climb through the looking-glass to join it. In the imaginary of the East, the West does not appear as everyday existence. It appears as something other, an image juxtaposed to those the East makes of itself. In the domain of images, the administration of the referent so common in the spectacular world of the East is no match for the inventiveness and proliferation of the spectacle of the West.//

In geographical space there was a wall, no doubt about it, a physical constraint on movement. But, as Ash remarks, in the psychogeography of East Germany, on the specular map of places and spaces, "the Wall was not round the periphery of East Germany, it was at its very centre. And it ran through every heart." The wall did not only partition one set of people from another; it interpellated individuals, structuring their sense of who they were, particularly in the East. Although the physical wall was ever-present, it could not halt the flow of information that blew through it like radiation. East Germans, the bearers of oppressive social relations, were also the bearers of an unbearable contradiction between the rudimentary divide in physical space imposed by the architects of the Cold War, and the spectacular shopping-arcade landscape beyond the mirror of West German television. Whereas to West Germans television held up a specular mirror to the social relations of capital and those who bear them, to East Germans it was a mirror to pass through into an enchanted land. They imagined a real world behind the mirror, which Westerners "know" is just an image. So they passed through the mirror and redrew the map. The remaking of the real has yet to catch up.

Geoff Page

[NUCLEAR PLANT ON THE LOIRE]

Avoine-Chinon
on the Loire
has spun its power
since sixty-three.
The vines approach
the fence as if
drawn by
electricity

which steps away
across the farms
swooping through
the gentle weather.
Two reactors
and barbed wire
hold the patchwork
all together.

David Malouf

AFTER CHERNOBYL

What I want to describe is what I observed recently of how a whole community's attitudes were changed, immediately and I believe irrevocably, by a frightening *actual* event; the appearance of the nuclear cloud from Chernobyl over a village in Italy that I happen to know well.

The village consists largely of peasants — not a word we like to use in English but we have no other for people who live on the land, usually in villages, by farming a plot in which they grow a large part of their own food. These are intelligent people. Not well educated, but lively, witty, and sharply sceptical — a vigorous scepticism rather than passion being the leading characteristic of most Mediterranean minds. They care deeply about politics; but what they mean by that is a lifelong loyalty to a sectarian political party. They follow blindly, and the parties, which are highly organised associations of power-brokers and ideologues, treat them to little more than hard-line directives, either of the right or left. For the most part they are concerned with local matters — as most people are. They are not, and so far as I can see never have been, Christians, except in name; their religion, which is very strong, has to do with the land and its generations, with olive trees, vines, the vegetables in their seasons; with the passage of the land from hand to hand down a family; with close-knit family ties. This religion is a daily affair — not a Sabbath one. It is practised in the fields and in the little kitchen gardens in the village where men work late in the evening, and where women may work as well, growing at different months of the year broadbeans, artichokes, a dozen or so varieties of salad vegetables, several kinds of cauliflower and cabbage, and, after a good cloudburst, gathering snails in plastic bags. This daily ritual reaches its climax when the whole family comes to the table at midday, eats what the fields and the little garden have produced, and drinks its own wine. The church's sacrament, of course, is based on this meal and draws for its deep spiritual resonance, in some part, on the ordinariness and sacredness of this shared meal and its relation both to the land and to labour.

What I am asking you to imagine is the depth of shock these people felt when they were told, one day last year, that a nuclear accident had occurred some five thousand kilometres away and that a cloud had come that would poison their crops, make the vegetables they had grown for their own table inedible, and worst of all, that the effects of all this — which was already in the food chain — would touch most powerfully their children, especially those under ten, causing diseases that might not be apparent for many years.

The nuclear age dawned for those people — right then and for the very first time.

They had heard about Hiroshima. They had seen the horrors of nuclear war argued on their television sets, and the pros and cons of whether missiles should be stationed in their territory argued to death by the political parties. But here it was. A cloud, that had nothing to do with them, moving back and forth across their land

— its movements, and the levels of daily fallout reported in the newspapers and in bulletins on the television. A cloud. Poisoning everything above ground that had been planted weeks before and which they expected to bring to their tables. No spinach or any other leafy vegetable, no salad, no fruit. What were you supposed to eat? No hay for the cattle, or for the sheep or rabbits. No milk for the children. Worst of all was this unseen threat to the children — to the one thing, for most people, that gives them a grip on the world, on history — and the doubt sown that the invisible evil might already be in their bones.

I cannot express to you the anger those people felt, of helplessness, of betrayal. The conservation movement, which was till then a middle-class intellectual affair, became explosive and universal at that moment in Italy. People understood its issues in their blood. The unimaginable had become immediately present and real with the vagaries of that cloud — a cloud that had nothing to do with them but revealed at last that they were in the nuclear world and could not escape. They were at last as fully informed on this great issue of our times as anyone can be. It had entered their imagination in the most physical terms.

We have had no such immediate demonstration here — I hope we never do have — which means that only an act of the most extraordinary imagination can make us feel the full physical danger of the world we live in. What Chernobyl revealed, in one shattering moment to a huge number of Europeans, is that once one of those clouds starts moving there is no stopping it — it does not respect borders or iron curtains, or places that have taken a decision to keep nuclear reactors out of their country, or signed anti-nuclear pacts, or those who have declared their cities nuclear-free-zones, or declared themselves special respositories of Grace. We are all citizens of the one moment and the one place.

Mark O'Connor

COLOSSEUM

Tourists are fooled. Locked in the human world
they hear who built the wonders, not what plucked
them down. The mighty walls, deforested and clear,
conceal what wrenched great tiers in ruin
or ground the marble into brick-size clods.

Yet Shelley saw it wooded: heights bedecked in myrtle
and wild olive, haunt of thrushes, and the arches such
as elephants might choose to den their young;
while from the heights, long after rain, there ran
brisk streams from thickets high above.

　　Amazement asks
what plant could set its hero hold at first
on such a height of stone, severe and nookless
as the primal Earth. In summer drought the wall
casts heat off like an oven. Yet from the toppling
inane rim, further than workmen risk, a brown
and fruiting fig still waves the answer.

Geoffrey Lehmann

COLOSSEUM

They did not wait for this, the crowds:
Two men with a wheelbarrow in the dusk
Collecting the mess.
The muscles of a lion not quite dead
Contract as if shuddering in sleep.
The last life stops on a gently inserted knife.
Patiently, courteously the two workmen
Lift each body into the barrow
And wheel it away.
They rake the gore into the sand
And talk in undertones,
Not of Europe's vanished fauna,
The mountains which have no lions,
Birds twittering in grass amongst the empty lairs,
Africa ransacked for elephants.
They do not talk of this,
But of women and the high price of food.
And they dump the bodies
In the foul, rancid pits in the foundations,
So foul that workmen digging two thousand years later
Sickened by the smell will lay down their spades.

Plants die cleanly
In stationary impersonal conflicts
For light and water.
But the death of animals appals.
They grow legs to run from death
And death as quickly grows legs to hunt them down.
The manure of grass eaters is mild,
But the shit of man and the carnivores is corrupt,
For what they eat resents being eaten,
And when man and the animals die
The stench of the carcass
Is our last silent protest at death.
But they are not talking of this,

No, certainly not of this, our two workmen
As they come out from their underworld
Of monstrous corpses decaying in half-light.
Perhaps they wish that the pleasure seekers
Should have to go down there with them,
The frivolous children of serious fathers,
Gaudy with expensive gold and more expensive silks,
Women admiring themselves in metal mirrors,
Eating sweetmeats amongst cushions on stone tiers,
While death-yells drown in the roar of the crowd
And the florid music of hydraulic organs.

But now in the dusk as the last blood is soaked up,
There is even a kind of peace here
With the lonely rumble of an iron wheel
Across the empty arena.

Notes on Authors

THEA ASTLEY (1925) is a short-story writer and prolific novelist who often focuses on the "misfit". Her most recent novel is *Coda* (1994). Humour and irony are among her strengths.

MURRAY BAIL (1941), novelist and short-story writer. His novel *Homesickness* (1981) is an ironic account of Australians abroad and of the phenomenon of tourism.

BRUCE BEAVER (1928) is a poet who lives in Sydney and was one of those writers who turned in the 1960s to American models. His *New and Selected Poems 1960–1990* appeared in 1991.

GILLIAN BOURAS (1945) is an Australian expatriate who lives in Greece. Her books of these experiences include *Foreign Wife* (1986), *Fair Exchange* (1991) and *Aphrodite and the Others* (1994).

R.F. BRISSENDEN (1928–1991), poet and critic. He taught at the Australian National University and at some overseas universities and was a previous Chair of the Australian Literature Board.

VINCENT BUCKLEY (1925–1988), poet and critic. Born in Victoria of Irish-Catholic parents, he identified strongly with Irish culture and its presence in Australia. He wrote an autobiography, *Cutting Green Hay*, and his *Selected Poems* were published in 1982.

JANINE BURKE (1952), novelist, critic, and writer about art and artists. Her novel *Second Sight* (1986) draws on her experiences of living in Italy.

CLEM CHRISTESEN (1911), editor, fiction writer, poet, journalist. He founded the influential magazine *Meanjin* in 1940, moving with it to Melbourne from Brisbane in 1945.

MANNING CLARK (1915–1991), historian and nonfiction writer. For many years he was Professor of History at the Australian National University, and his major work is *A History of Australia* (6 vols, 1962–1987).

CHARMIAN CLIFT (1923–1969), journalist, essayist, novelist. With her husband George Johnston and their children she went to London in 1950 and to Greece in 1954 where they lived mainly on the island of Hydra. They returned to Australia in 1964. Her accounts of her experiences in Greece are included in *Mermaid*

Singing (1956), *Peel Me a Lotus* (1959) and the essay collections *Trouble in Lotus Land* (1990) and *Being Alone with Oneself* (1991).

HAL COLEBATCH (1948), journalist, editor, poet. Many of his poems are set in Europe. His most recent book is *The Earthquake Lands* (1990).

PETER CONRAD (1948), critic and novelist and author of autobiographic and travel books. He writes about his experiences of living in England and other countries in *Where I Fell to Earth* (1990).

JILL KER CONWAY (1934), critic and prose writer, has had a distinguished academic career in the USA where she has resided for some time. Her best-selling autobiography is *The Road from Coorain* (1989).

DYMPHNA CUSACK (1902–1981), novelist, travel writer, dramatist. She was politically active and her novels were popular in Russia and Eastern Europe where she travelled widely.

DAVID DALE (1948), broadcaster and journalist, specialising partly in travel writing, for example *The Obsessive Traveller* (1991) and *Australians' Guide to Italy* (1991).

BRYAN DAWE (1948), writer, including radio comedy, and performer. He created characters Roly and Sonya Parkes who are comic, sometimes burlesque representations of Australians abroad and who appear in *On the Smell of an Oily Rag* (1991).

ROSEMARY DOBSON (1920), poet, editor and translator. Her poetry often draws on Europe and its art as well as on places and myths. She has published *Collected Poems* (1991) and recently has written many poems about Greece.

CATHERINE DUNCAN (1915), playwright, stage and radio actress and film maker. Born in Tasmania, in 1945 she joined the Australian National Film Board.

MABEL EDMUND (1930), with South Sea Island, Aboriginal and European forebears, was born in Rockhampton. She has lived on remote sheep stations in the bush, became a shire councillor, founded a black legal service and began a career as an artist and writer. Her recent book is *No Regrets* (1992).

DIANE FAHEY (1945) is a poet whose work draws frequently on

experiences of Europe and on Greek mythology. A recent work is *Mayflies in Amber* (1993).

BEVERLEY FARMER (1941), novelist and short-story writer who has spent three years in Greece. She draws on these experiences in her short-story collections *Milk* (1984) and *Home Time* (1985) and in *A Body of Water* (1990).

JOHN FORBES (1950), poet. His *New and Selected Poems* appeared in 1991.

KATHERINE GALLAGHER (1935), poet, has lived in England since 1982. Many of her poems concern her experiences there and her travels in Europe. Her most recent book is *Fish-rings on Water* (1989).

HELEN GARNER (1942), novelist and short-story writer who has lived in Paris. Her first novel was *Monkey Grip* (1977) which was made into a film, and her most recent novel is *Cosmo Cosmolino* (1992).

ROBERT GRAY (1945), poet and editor. His *Selected Poems* was published in 1986.

KATE GRENVILLE (1950), novelist and short-story writer. Her novel *Dreamhouse* (1986) and some of her stories are based on her experiences abroad.

SNEJA GUNEW (1946), critic and editor. Born in Germany and now a teacher at a Canadian university, she has done much to promote the recognition and criticism of multicultural writing in Australia, including editing a number of anthologies, for example *Striking Chords* (with K. Longley, 1991).

MARION HALLIGAN (1940), novelist and short-story writer. Her latest award-winning novel was *Lovers' Knots* (1992). Her book on travel and food, *Eat My Words* (1990) draws on her experiences of living in France.

BARBARA HANRAHAN (1939–1992), novelist and printmaker. She lived and studied in England in the 1960s and wrote about these experiences in *Michael and Me and the Sun* (1992), her posthumous book.

MAX HARRIS (1921), poet, critic, nonfiction writer, journalist. He was co-editor of the avant-garde journal *Angry Penguins* (1940–1946) and has written on a range of cultural and literary issues.

SHIRLEY HAZZARD (1931), short-story writer, novelist and essayist who has spent most of her life abroad, based in the USA, but with frequent trips to Europe, particularly Italy. Her best known novel is *Transit of Venus* (1980).

GRAEME HETHERINGTON, poet, was born in Tasmania and grew up in the mining towns of Tasmania's west coast. He has lived for a considerable time in Europe, mainly Greece. He has published *Remote Corners* (1986).

DOROTHY HEWETT (1923), poet, novelist, dramatist and short-story writer. Her most recent books are her autobiography *Wildcard* (1990), *Selected Poems* (1930) and *The Toucher* (1993).

A.D. HOPE (1907), poet and critic, was for many years Professor of English at the Australian National University and has travelled widely in Europe and elsewhere. His *Collected Poems* appeared in 1972 with later reprintings and he has continued to produce individual volumes.

ROBERT HUGHES (1938), art critic who has travelled widely and lives in New York. His books include *The Shock of the New* (1980), *The Fatal Shore* (1987) and *Culture of Complaint* (1993).

GEORGE JOHNSTON (1912–1970), novelist and journalist. With his wife Charmian Clift and their children he spent ten years in the Greek islands, mainly Hydra. These experiences formed a basis of his novel *Clean Straw for Nothing* (1969) which is part of a trilogy, also including *My Brother Jack* (1964) and *A Cartload of Clay* (1971).

MARTIN JOHNSTON (1947–1990), poet, novelist, essayist and son of George Johnston and Charmian Clift. Poetry collections include *The Sea-Cucumber* (1978), *The Typewriter Considered as a Bee-Trap* (1984), translations of modern Greek poetry, *Ithaka* (1973), and *Martin Johnston: Selected Poetry and Prose*, edited by John Tranter (1993).

ELIZABETH JOLLEY (1923), novelist and short-story writer. She was born in England, and her mother was from Vienna. Her fiction often moves between Europe and Australia, as in her comic novel *Miss Peabody's Inheritance* (1983), and in *The Georges' Wife* (1993).

MANFRED JURGENSEN (1940), poet, novelist, short-story writer, critic, academic, and editor of *Outrider* (1984–). Born in

Flensburg, he came to Australia in 1961. His *Selected Poems* were published in 1987.

ANTIGONE KEFALA (1935), poet and prose writer. Born in Romania, with Greek parents, she has lived in Romania, Greece, New Zealand and Australia. Her most recent publication is *Absence: New and Selected Poems* (1992).

THOMAS KENEALLY (1935), novelist, dramatist and screen-writer. His prolific and widely-read fiction and nonfiction have settings and themes drawn from many corners of the world. One of his latest works, *Towards Asmara* (1988), concerns Eritrea.

ALISTER KERSHAW (1921) has spent much of his life in France. His is a poet and critic and journalist. One of his most recent works is his autobiographical *Heydays* (1991).

CHRISTOPHER KOCH (1932), novelist. Born in Hobart, Tasmania, he has lived in America and Europe and has also travelled widely in Asia. His essays *Crossing the Gap* (1987) drew on some of these travel experiences.

GEOFFREY LEHMANN (1940), poet and anthologist. His work embraces Australian subjects, as in *Ross' Poems* (1978) but also a range of European reference as in *Nero's Poems* (1981), *A Voyage of Lions* (1968), and *Selected Poems* (1976).

JAMES McAULEY (1919–1976), poet, critic and editor. Born and educated in Sydney, he became Professor of English at the University of Tasmania in 1961. He was keenly interested in European writers, especially Georg Trakl. His *Collected Poems* appeared in 1971.

SHANE McCAULEY is a well-known poet from Western Australia and his latest publication is *The Butterfly Man* (1991).

DAVID MALOUF (1934), poet, novelist, short-story writer, critic, dramatist, librettist. Born in Brisbane, he lived in Europe from 1959 to 1968. He has divided much of his time between living in Tuscany and Sydney. His most recent novel is *Remembering Babylon* (1993).

TONY MANIATY, Brisbane-born journalist and screenwriter, was the Paris-based correspondent for SBS Television in 1991–92. He has published two novels, *The Children Must Dance* and *Smyrna*, and his Brisbane boyhood memoir *All over the Shop* appeared in 1993.

DAVID MARTIN (1915), novelist, nonfiction writer, journalist, critic. Born into a Jewish family in Hungary, he was brought up in Germany which he left at seventeen. He settled in Australia in 1949. He has concerned himself with political causes and with people who move between different cultures. *My Strange Friend* (1991) is his autobiography.

OLGA MASTERS (1919–1986), short-story writer, novelist, journalist. Her stories often concern small-town life in Australia as in the autobiographically based collection, *A Long Time Dying* (1985).

ROGER MILLISS (1934), nonfiction writer. His writings often concern political injustice, as in his recent book about Australian suppression of Aborigines, *Waterloo Creek* (1991). He lived for a time in Moscow.

DRUSILLA MODJESKA (1946), critic, prose writer and editor. Born in the United Kingdom, she has worked in Australia as an academic teacher and publisher's editor. Her recent work is *Poppy* (1990).

FRANK MOORHOUSE (1938), short-story writer, novelist and much-travelled journalist. His essays and stories *Room Service* (1985) are comic representations of an Australian abroad, and *Grand Days* (1993) is a novel set in Geneva..

MUDROOROO (previously Colin Johnson, Mudooroo Narogin, Mudrooroo Nygoorah), poet, novelist, critic, is one of the leading contemporary Aboriginal writers and spokespersons. He is well-known for his novels, including *Wild Cat Falling* (1965), *Doctor Wooreddy's Prescription For Enduring the Ending of the World* (1983), *Doing Wildcat* (1988), and a critical book, *Writing from the Fringe* (1989).

LES MURRAY (1938) is a poet, critic and essayist who maintains his rural ties, from which he gains much of his inspiration, but he also travels abroad for readings and lectures. He has published *Selected Poems* (1986) and *Blocks and Tackles: Articles and Essays 1982–1990* (1990).

STEPHEN MURRAY-SMITH (1922–1988), editor, essayist,

nonfiction writer. He founded and edited the influential magazine *Overland* and played a prominent role in Australian cultural debate.

MARK O'CONNOR (1945), poet, anthologist. He has spent considerable time in Europe and both his essays and his poems often deal with ecological questions. *Firestick Farming: New and Selected Poems 1972–1990* was published in 1990.

DESMOND O'GRADY (1929), short-story writer, novelist, journalist. Born in Melbourne, he has lived most of his life in Italy. His books include *Valid for All Countries* (stories, 1979) and *Raffaello Raffaello* (1985).

JAN OWEN (1940), poet, born in Adelaide. As well as travelling widely, she has published in overseas and Australian journals. A recent volume is *Night Rainbows* (1994).

GEOFF PAGE (1940), poet, novelist, anthologist. He lives in Canberra and his *Selected Poems* were published in 1991. He has also edited a collection of Australian travel poems, *On the Move* (1992).

HAL PORTER (1911–1984), short-story writer, novelist, autobiographer and avid traveller. His autobiographical triology comprises *The Watcher on Cast-Iron Balcony* (1963), *The Paper Chase* (1966) and *The Extra* (1975).

PETER PORTER (1929), poet and critic, was born in Brisbane and now lives in London. His *Selected Poems* appeared in 1989 and his latest volume is *The Chair of Babel* (1992).

ANDREW RIEMER (1936), critic and nonfiction writer. Born in Budapest, he emigrated to Australia with his parents as a child and has published an autobiographical account of this experience, *Inside Outside* (1992). His recent book *The Habsburg Cafe* (1993) looks at contemporary life in Central Europe.

ISOBEL ROBIN (1924), poet. Born in Sydney, she has lived in Melbourne since 1939, working as an advertising copywriter and as a secretary.

JUDITH RODRIGUEZ (1936), poet and editor including of the Penguin Books Poetry series. Her collection *The House by the Water: New and Selected Poems* appeared in 1988.

BETTY ROLAND (1903), dramatist, fiction and nonfiction writer. She lived in Russia and England and draws on these and her

Australian experiences in her autobiographical works, including *Caviar for Breakfast* (1979).

ANNA RUTHERFORD, an Australian who lives and teaches Commonwealth literature at the University of Aarhus in Denmark. She edits the international journal *Kunapipi* and is publisher of Dangaroo Press.

THOMAS SHAPCOTT (1935), poet, short-story writer, novelist. As writer and as previous director of the Literature Board he has travelled widely and often writes of European–Australian connections. His *Selected Poems* appeared in 1978 and 1989.

JEFFREY SMART (1921), painter. Born in Adelaide, he did much of his study and painting overseas and has lived in Italy for many years.

VIVIAN SMITH (1933) is a poet and critic whose travels in Europe and knowledge of European literatures are reflected in his writings. His *Selected Poems* appeared in 1985 and his *New Selected Poems* in 1994.

CHRISTINA STEAD (1902–1983), novelist, spent the greater part of her life abroad in Europe, the United Kingdom and North America. Her best known novels are *The Man who Loved Children* (1940), and *For Love Alone* (1944). Some shorter pieces, including travel, appear in *Ocean of Story* (1985).

ANDREW TAYLOR (1940), poet and critic. He has written frequently of European experiences, especially in Germany. His *Selected Poems* appeared in 1988.

JOHN TRANTER (1943), critic, editor and poet. His *Selected Poems* were published in 1982 and his latest poetry volume is *At the Florida* (1993).

DIMITRIS TSALOUMAS (1921), poet. Born on the Greek Island of Leros, he came to Australia in 1952. He has published several collections both in Greece and Australia, including *The Observatory* (1983) with translations by Philip Grundy, and *Selected Poems 1972–1986* (1987).

IAN TURNER (1922–1978), historian, nonfiction writer. He taught History at Monash University and was active in radical political causes. His posthumous essays are *Room for Manoeuvre* (1982).

CHRIS WALLACE-CRABBE (1934), poet and critic and director of the Australia Centre at the University of Melbourne. He has published *Selected Poems* (1973) and many volumes of poetry. Latest essays: *Falling into Language* (1990); poetry: *Rungs of Time* (1993).

ANIA WALWICZ (1951), performance poet and prose writer. She was born in Poland and her writing often features comic and satiric representations of Australian–European connections. Her latest work is *Red Roses* (1992).

McKENZIE WARK is a regular contributor to *Australian Left Review* and lectures in Mass Communication at Macquarie University.

JUDAH WATEN (1911–1985), novelist, nonfiction writer, essayist. He was born in Odessa, Russia, of a Jewish family which settled in Australia in 1914. A dedicated communist, he was active in political causes. He is best known for his autobiographically based stories, *Alien Son* (1952).

PATRICK WHITE (1912–1990), novelist, short-story writer, dramatist and Nobel Prize winner. He travelled extensively in Europe and wrote about his experiences in Greece in his autobiography *Flaws in the Glass* (1981).

MICHAEL WILDING (1942), short-story writer, novelist, editor and critic, born in Worcester, England, but has lived most of his life in Australia. He has been influential as an experimental writer and also as a publisher (Wild and Woolley). His latest volume of selected stories is *This Is for You* (1994).

TIM WINTON (1960), novelist, short-story writer who lives in Western Australia. His most recent, award winning novel is *Cloudstreet* (1991).

Sources

Travellers, tourists and expatriates

Charmian Clift. "Self portrait" from *Self Portraits*. Sel. and intr. by David Foster. Canberra: National Library of Australia, 1991.

———. "Hydra" from *Peel Me a Lotus*. North Ryde: Angus & Robertson, 1989. First published 1959.

George Johnston. "Australians abroad" from *Clean Straw for Nothing*. London; Sydney: Collins, 1969.

Martin Johnston. "Growing up in Greece" from Hazel de Berg tapes, National Library of Australia (tapes 1165 and 1166).

———. "The homecoming" from *The Typewriter Considered as a Bee-Trap*. Sydney: Hale & Iremonger, 1984.

John Tranter. "Cicada gambit" from *Under Berlin*. St Lucia: University of Queensland Press, 1988.

Patrick White. "Greek journeys" from *Flaws in the Glass: A Self-portrait*. Ringwood: Penguin, 1983.

Gillian Bouras. "Stranger in a strange land" from *Made in Australia: An Anthology of Writing*, ed. Jim Kable. Melbourne: Oxford University Press, 1990.

Beverley Farmer. "Village life in Greece" from Ray Willbanks. *Speaking Volumes: Australian Writers and Their Work*. Ringwood: Penguin, 1992.

———. "Pomegranates" from *Home Time*. Fitzroy: McPhee Gribble/Penguin, 1985.

Anna Rutherford. "Going somewhere else" from "Not One of the Jacks". *Westerly* 32.4 (1987): 10–21.

Peter Porter. "The true country" from "An Expatriate's Reaction to His Condition". *Westerly* 32.4 (1987): 43–47.

Christina Stead. "Leaving 1928; returning 1969" from "Another View of the Homestead". *Ocean of Story: The Uncollected Stories of Christina Stead*. Ringwood: Penguin, 1986.

Jeffrey Smart. "The first time in Europe" from Geoffrey de Groen. *Some Other Dream: The Artist, the Artworld and the Expatriate*. Sydney: Hale & Iremonger, 1984.

Robert Hughes. "The first time in Europe" from Geoffrey de Groen. *Some Other Dream: The Artist, the Artworld and the Expatriate*. Sydney: Hale & Iremonger, 1984.

Barbara Hanrahan. "Getting away" from *Michael and Me and the Sun*. St Lucia: University of Queensland Press, 1992.

Peter Conrad, "Crossing the bridge" from *Where I Fell to Earth: A Life in Four Places*. London: Chatto & Windus, 1990.

Janine Burke. "Tuscany's talent to a muse: Australia meets Italy in Tuscany. Janine Burke reports on a conference in Florence". *Weekend Australian* 4–5 March 1989: Weekend 7.

Tim Winton. "Letter from Ireland" (extract). *Overland* 112 (1988): 37–39.

Helen Garner. "In Paris" from *Postcards from Surfers*. Fitzroy: McPhee Gribble/Penguin, 1985.

Marion Halligan. "Aligot" from *Eat My Words*. North Ryde: Collins/Angus & Robertson, 1990.

Alister Kershaw. "Bicycle races" from *A Word from Paris*. North Ryde: Angus & Robertson, 1991.

Shane McCauley. "Old city, Rhodes" from *The Butterfly Man*. Fremantle: Fremantle Arts Centre Press, 1991.

Murray Bail. "Notebook entries" from *Longhand: A Writers Notebook*. Melbourne: McPhee Gribble, 1989.

Vivian Smith. "The traveller returns" from *Selected Poems*. North Ryde: Angus & Robertson, 1985. First published *Southerly* 38.4 (1978).

Trails and trials: the rituals and conventions of travel

Peter Conrad. "Signs and passwords" from *Where I Fell to Earth: A Life in Four Places*. London: Chatto & Windus, 1990.

John Forbes. "Europe: a guide" from *The Stunned Mullet*. Sydney: Hale & Iremonger, 1988.

Tony Maniaty. "Discovering the world from a cocoon". *Weekend Australian* 15–16 July 1989.

Kate Grenville. "Having a wonderful time" from *Bearded Ladies*. St Lucia: University of Queensland Press, 1985.

Dorothy Hewett. "The Travellers". *Overland* 67 (1977): 30.

Frank Moorhouse. "Blase in the Land of Swizzlestick" from *Room Service*. Ringwood: Penguin, 1985.

Thea Astley. "Why I wrote a story called 'Diesel Epiphany' ". *Meanjin* 46.2 (1986): 193–96.

Hal Colebatch. "Youth at Australia House, London, 1973" (extracts) from *Outer Charting*. North Ryde: Angus & Robertson, 1985.

Bryan Dawe. "Getting around in Europe on the smell of an oily rag" from *On the Smell of an Oily Rag: Roly and Sonya Parks' European Odyssey*. North Sydney: Allen & Unwin, 1991.

Desmond O'Grady. "Budapest, Keleti" from "Keleti & Karizma". *Outrider* 2.1 (1985): 201–06.

Katherine Gallagher. "Plane-journey momentums" from *Fish-rings on Water*. Intr. Peter Porter. London; Boston: Forest Books, 1989.

Thomas Shapcott. "Travel dice" from *Travel Dice*. St Lucia: University of Queensland Press, 1987.

Andrew Taylor. "Folds in the map" from *Folds in the Map*. St Lucia: University of Queensland Press, 1991.

Judith Rodriguez. "The journey with children" from *New and Selected Poems*. St Lucia: University of Queensland Press, 1988.

David Dale. "Faux travel" from *The Obsessive Traveller or Why I Don't Steal Towels from Great Hotels any more*. North Ryde: Collins/Angus & Robertson, 1991.

Les Murray. "Vindaloo in Merthyr Tydfil" from *The Vernacular Republic: Poems 1961–1981*. Rev. ed. North Ryde: Angus & Robertson, 1982.

Hal Porter. "The baggage of memory" from *The Extra*. Melbourne: Thomas Nelson, 1975.

Michael Wilding. "Maison de la vie" from *Outrider 90: A Year of Australian Literature,* ed. Manfred Jurgensen. Brisbane: Phoenix Publications, 1990.

Robert Gray. "Curriculum vitae" (extract) from *The Skylight*. Sydney: HarperCollins Publishers, 1984.

Peter Porter. "Bad dreams in Venice" from *The Chair of Babel*. Oxford; Melbourne: Oxford University Press, 1992.

John Tranter. "Lufthansa" from *Under Berlin*. St Lucia: University of Queensland Press, 1988. First published *Weekend Australian* 13–14 October 1984.

Origins, heritage, pilgrimages

R.F. Brissenden. "Rock climbers, Uluru, 1985" from *Australian*

Poetry 1986: The Finest of Recent Australian Poetry. Ed. Vivian Smith. North Ryde: Angus & Robertson, 1986.

A.D. Hope. "A letter from Rome" from *Collected Poems 1930–1970.* Sydney: Angus & Robertson, 1972.

Chris Wallace-Crabbe. "Flat out in the Mezzogiorno" from *The Emotions Are Not Skilled Workers.* Sydney: Angus & Robertson, 1980.

Jill Ker Conway. "Recharting the globe" from *The Road from Coorain.* New York: Alfred A. Knopf, 1989.

Shirley Hazzard. "The Tuscan in each of us" from *An Antipodean Connection: Australian Writers, Artists and Travellers in Tuscany,* ed. G. Prampolini and M.C. Hubert. Geneva: Slatkine/Centro Interuniversitario di Ricerche sul "Viaggio in Italia", 1993. 75–81.

Rosemary Dobson. "Phigalia" from *Over the Frontier.* Sydney: Angus & Robertson, 1978.

Diane Fahey. "Sacred conversations" from *Turning the Hourglass.* Sydney: Dangaroo Press, 1990.

Bruce Beaver. "Australian poet c. 1988 visits the home of an English poet c. 1888" from *Charmed Lives.* St Lucia: University of Queensland Press, 1988.

C.J. Koch. "London, late 1950s" from "Maybe it's because I'm a Londoner".*Crossing the Gap: A Novelist's Essays.* London: Hogarth Press, 1987.

Thomas Keneally. "On the road in Ireland" from *Now and in Time to Be: Ireland and the Irish.* Sydney: Pan Macmillan Australia, 1991.

James McAuley. "In the Mirabell Garden" from "Trakl: Salzburg". *Time Given. Poems 1970–1976.* Canberra: Brindabella Press, 1976.

Isobel Robin. "Freud's backyard". First published *Overland* 102 (1986).

Jan Owen. "Town" from *Fingerprints on Light.* North Ryde: Angus & Robertson, 1990.

Andrew Riemer. "Return to Budapest" from *Inside Outside: Life between two Worlds.* Pymble: Collins/Angus & Robertson, 1992.

Elizabeth Jolley. "Home thoughts" from *Palomino*. St Lucia: University of Queensland Press, 1984.

Ania Walwicz. "europe" from *Joseph's Coat: An Anthology of Multicultural Writing*, ed. Peter Skrzynecki. Sydney: Hale & Iremonger, 1985.

Manfred Jurgensen. "flensburg" from *a winter's journey (1976–1977): diary poems*. Sydney: Edwards & Shaw, 1979.

Sneja Gunew. "Memory Crop" (extract) from *Inner Cities: Australian Women's Memory of Place*, ed. Drusilla Modjeska. Ringwood: Penguin, 1989.

Antigone Kefala. "Family" from *Absence*. Sydney: Hale & Iremonger, 1992.

Dimitris Tsaloumas. "Prodigal" from *The Observatory*. St Lucia: University of Queensland Press, 1983.

Drusilla Modjeska. "Crete" from *Poppy*. Ringwood: McPhee Gribble, 1990.

Betty Roland. "Gallipoli: The hills of the heroes" from *Lesbos: The Pagan Island*. Melbourne: F.W. Cheshire, 1963.

Graeme Hetherington. "Australians in Crete, 1941–1991". *Sydney Morning Herald*, 4 April 1992: 43.

Manning Clark. "Tramping the battlefields" (extract) from "Tramping the Battlefields: In search of Australia in Belgium and France". *Overland* 100 (1985): 6–9.

Out of the cold: testing political climates

David Malouf. "Bad dreams in Vienna" from *Neighbours in a Thicket*. 2nd ed. St Lucia: University of Queensland Press, 1980.

Catherine Duncan. "Rendez-vous with the end of an age" (extract) from *The Temperament of Generations: Fifty Years of Writing in Meanjin*, ed. Jenny Lee, Philip Mead and Gerald Murnane. Carlton: *Meanjin*/Melbourne University Press, 1990. First published *Meanjin* 3 (1968).

Vincent Buckley. "Irish customs" from *Memory Ireland: Insights into the contemporary Irish condition*. Ringwood: Penguin, 1985.

Ian Turner. "Letter from Ireland" (extract). *Overland* 66 (1977): 49–51.

Mabel Edmund. "The only black woman at Ealing Station" from *No Regrets*. St Lucia: University of Queensland Press, 1992.

Mudrooroo. "Sugar in London" from *The Garden of Gethsemane: Poems from the Lost Decade*. South Yarra: Hyland House, 1991.

Judah Waten. "Odessa" from *From Odessa to Odessa: The Journey of an Australian Writer*. Melbourne: Cheshire, 1969.

Dymphna Cusack. "Leningrad" from *Holidays among the Russians*. London: Heinemann, 1964.

Murray Bail. "Leningrad" from *Homesickness*. South Melbourne: Macmillan, 1980.

Roger Milliss. "Living in Moscow" from *Serpent's Tooth: An Auto-biographical Novel*. Ringwood: Penguin, 1984.

Chris Wallace-Crabbe: "Russia: lost in wonderland" from "Lost in Wonderland". *Scripsi* 4.1 (1986): 163–71.

Olga Masters: "Searching for the face of Soviet literature" (extract) from *Olga Masters: Reporting Home*, ed. Deirdre Coleman. St Lucia: University of Queensland Press, 1990. First published *National Times* 20–26 December 1985.

Leila Rodd. "Heart of Europe: Prague, 1978" from "Heart of Europe: Letter Pieces". *Meanjin* 38.4 (1979): 411–21.

David Martin. "The return trip" from *Where a Man Belongs*. Melbourne: Cassell Australia, 1969.

Stephen Murray-Smith: "German notebook 1971" (extract). *Overland* 52 (1972): 14–20.

Clem Christesen. "Impressions East and West" from "A Room with a View: Impressions of Germany and the Soviet Union". *Meanjin Quarterly* 24.3 (1965): 390–400.

Max Harris. "The larrikins in Weimar" (extract) from *The Angry Eye*. Potts Point: Pergamon Press, 1973.

McKenzie Wark. "Berlin Wall" from "East Meets West at the Wall". *Virtual Geography: Living with Global Media Events*. Bloomington: Indiana University Press, 1994.

Geoff Page. "Nuclear plant on the Loire" from *Smiling in English, Smoking in French: A Journal*. Deakin: Brindabella Press, 1987.

David Malouf. "After Chernobyl" from "Imagining the Real". *David Malouf*, ed. James Tulip. St Lucia: University of Queensland Press, 1990.

Mark O'Connor. "Colosseum" from "The Eating Tree". *Selected Poems*. Sydney: Hale & Iremonger, 1986.

Geoffrey Lehmann. "Colosseum" from *A Voyage of Lions and other poems*. Sydney: Angus & Robertson, 1968.

Selected Bibliography

Alomes, Stephen. "A Distorting Lens? Australian Perceptions of France and the French". *Island Magazine* 23 (1985): 35–37.

Anderson, Don. "Peripatetic litterateurs take over the '90s". *Sydney Morning Herald* 20 April 1991: 46.

Ariel 21.4 (1990): special issue "The Literature of Travel".

Australian Cultural History 10 (1991): special issue "Travellers, Journeys, Tourists".

Australian Studies 5 (1991): special issue "Europe and Australia".

Bader, Rudolf. *The Visitable Past: Images of Europe in Anglo-Australian Literature*. Bern: Peter Lang, 1992.

Barnes, John. "Australian Pioneers in Europe". *Meridian* 3.2 (1984): 181–88.

Barthes, Roland. "Le Guide Bleu". *Mythologies*. 1957. Sel. and trans. Annette Lavers. New York: Hill and Wang, 1972. 74–77.

Brydon, Diana. "Buffoon Odysseus: Australian Expatriate Fiction by Women". *Aspects of Australian Fiction: Essays Presented to John Colmer*, ed. Alan Brissenden. Nedlands, WA: University of Western Australia Press, 1990. 73–85.

Burke, Janine. "In the Light of Contradictions: *Second Sight* in Tuscany". *Island Magazine* 39 (1989): 63–67.

Butor, Michel. "Travel and Writing". *Mosaic* (University of Manitoba, Winnipeg) 8.1 (1974): 1–16.

Commonwealth 6.2 (1984): special issue "Australia and Continental Europe".

Creswell, Rosemary, ed. *Home and Away*. Ringwood: Penguin, 1987.

Culler, Jonathan. "The Semiotics of Tourism". *American Journal of Semiotics* 1.2 (1981): 127–40.

De Groen, Geoffrey. *Some Other Dream: The Artist, the Artworld and the Expatriate*. Sydney: Hale & Iremonger, 1984.

Dodd, Philip, ed. *The Art of Travel: Essays on Travel Writing*. London: Frank Cass, 1982.

Fussell, Paul. *Abroad: British Literary Travelling between the Wars*. New York; Oxford: Oxford University Press, 1980.

Granta 10 (1984): special issue "Travel Writing".

Granta 20 (1986): "In Trouble Again: a special issue of travel writing".

Hassam, Andrew. " 'As I Write': Narrative Occasions and the Quest for Self-Presence in the Travel Diary". *Ariel* 21.4 (1990): 33–47.

Hergenhan, Laurie. "The 'I' of the Beholder: Representations of Tuscany in Some Recent Australian Literature". *Westerly* 36.4 (1991): 107–14.

Higham, Charles, and Michael Wilding, eds. *Australians Abroad: An Anthology.* Melbourne: Cheshire, 1967.

Horne, Donald. *The Intelligent Tourist.* McMahons Point, NSW: Margaret Gee Publishing, 1992.

Jurak, Mirko, ed. *Australian Papers: Yugoslavia, Europe and Australia.* Ljubljana: Edvard Kardelj University, 1983.

Kershaw, Alister. "The Last Expatriate". 1958. Rpt. *The Vital Decade,* ed. Geoffrey Dutton and Max Harris. Melbourne: Sun Books, 1969. 153–55.

Kröller, Eva-Maria. "First Impressions: Rhetorical Strategies in Travel Writing by Victorian Women". *Ariel* 21.4 (1990): 87–99.

MacCannell, Dean. *The Tourist: A New Theory of the Leisure Class.* New York: Schocken, 1976.

MacDermott, Doireann, and Susan Ballyn, eds. *A Passage to Somewhere Else.* Proceedings of the Commonwealth Conference held at the University of Barcelona, 30 Sept.–2 Oct. 1987. Barcelona: Promociones y Publicaciones Universitarias, 1988.

Martin, Gillian, and Ged Martin. *Waltzing Britannia: A Guide to Britain for Australians.* Sydney: Hale & Iremonger, 1989.

Meanjin 49.3 (1990): special issue "Unsentimental Journeys" on tourism and travelling.

Mellick, J.S.D. "The New and the Old: Responses to Translocation". *Commonwealth* 6.2 (1984): 29–34.

Mills, Sara. *Discourses of Difference: An Analysis of Women's Travel Writing and Colonialism.* London; New York: Routledge, 1991.

Nisbet, Anne-Marie, and Maurice Blackman, eds. *The French-Australian Cultural Connection.* Kensington, NSW: University of NSW, 1984.

Ousby, Ian. *The Englishman's England: Taste, Travel and the Rise of Tourism.* Cambridge: Cambridge University Press, 1990.

Page, Geoff, ed. *On the Move: Australian Poets in Europe*. Springwood, NSW: Butterfly Books, 1992. Intr. ix–xii.

Petersson, Irmtraud. *German Images in Australian Literature from the 1960s to the 1980s*. Frankfurt a.M.: Peter Lang, 1990.

Pierce, Peter. " '… Turn Gladly Home': The Figure of the Revenant in Australian Literary Culture". *Island Magazine* 38 (1989): 62–68.

Porter, Dennis. *Haunted Journeys: Desire and Transgression in European Travel Writing*. Princeton, NJ: Princeton University Press, 1991.

Raines, G. "Travellers' Tales". *Australian Studies* 6 (1992): 68–80.

Robinson, Jane. *Wayward Women: A Guide to Women Travellers*. Oxford; New York: Oxford University Press, 1991.

Senn, Werner. "Australian Poems on European Paintings". *European Perspectives: Contemporary Essays on Australian Literature*, ed. Giovanna Capone. St Lucia, Qld: University of Queensland Press, 1991. Special issue *ALS* 15.2.

Sieburth, Richard. "Sentimental Travelling: On the Road (and Off the Wall) with Laurence Sterne". *Scripsi* 4.3 (1987): 197–211.

Smith, Valene L., ed. *Hosts and Guests: The Anthropology of Tourism*. Philadelphia: University of Pennsylvania Press, 1977. 2nd ed. 1989.

Stout, Janis P. *The Journey Narrative in American Literature: Patterns and Departures*. Westport, Conneticut; London: Greenwood Press, 1983.

Turner, Louis, and John Ash. *The Golden Hordes: International Tourism and the Pleasure Periphery*. London: Constable, 1975.

Urry, John. *The Tourist Gaze: Leisure and Travel in Contemporary Societies*. London: Sage, 1990.

Westerly 32.4 (1987): special issue on Australian expatriates.

Wolff, Janet. "On the Road Again: Metaphors of Travel in Cultural Criticism". *Cultural Studies* 7.2 (1993): 224–39.

UQP AUSTRALIAN AUTHORS

The Australian Short Story
edited by Laurie Hergenhan
Outstanding contemporary short stories alongside some of the best from the past. This volume encompasses the short story in Australia from its *Bulletin* beginnings in the 1890s to its vigorous revival in the 1970s and 1980s.

Writings of the Eighteen Nineties
edited by Leon Cantrell
A retrospective collection, bringing together the work of 32 Australian poets, storytellers and essayists. The anthology challenges previous assumptions about this romantic period of galloping ballads and bush yarns, bohemianism and creative giants.

Catherine Helen Spence
edited by Helen Thomson
An important early feminist writer, Catherine Helen Spence was one of the first women in Australia to break through the constraints of gender and class and enter public life. This selection contains her most highly regarded novel, *Clara Morison*, her triumphant autobiography, and much of her political and social reformist writing.

Henry Lawson
edited by Brian Kiernan
A complete profile of Henry Lawson, the finest and most original writer in the bush yarn tradition. This selection includes sketches, letters, autobiography and verse, with outspoken journalism and the best of his comic and tragic stories.

Christopher Brennan
edited by Terry Sturm
Christopher Brennan was a legend in his own time, and his art was an unusual amalgam of Victorian, symbolist and modernist tendencies. This selection draws on the whole range of Brennan's work: poetry, literary criticism and theory, autobiographical writing, and letters.

Robert D. FitzGerald
edited by Julian Croft
FitzGerald's long and distinguished literary career is reflected in this selection of his poetry and prose. There is poetry from the 1920s to the 1980s, samples from his lectures on poetics and essays on family origins and philosophical preoccupations, a short story, and his views on Australian poetry.

Australian Science Fiction
edited by Van Ikin
An exotic blend of exciting recent works with a selection from Australia's long science fiction tradition. Classics by Erle Cox, M. Barnard Eldershaw and others are followed by stories from major contemporary writers Damien Broderick, Frank Bryning, Peter Carey, A. Bertram Chandler, Lee Harding, David J. Lake, Philippa C. Maddern, Dal Stivens, George Turner, Wynne N. Whiteford, Michael Wilding and Jack Wodhams.

Barbara Baynton
edited by Sally Krimmer and Alan Lawson

Bush writing of the 1890s, but very different from Henry Lawson. Baynton's stories are often macabre and horrific, and her bush women express a sense of outrage. The revised text of the brilliant *Bush Studies*, the novel *Human Toll*, poems, articles and an interview, all reveal Baynton's disconcertingly independent viewpoint.

Joseph Furphy
edited by John Barnes

Such is Life is an Australian classic. Written by an ex-bullock driver, half-bushman and half-bookworm, it is an extraordinary achievement. The accompanying selection of novel extracts, stories, verse, *Bulletin* articles and letters illustrates the astounding range of Furphy's talent, and John Barnes' notes reveal the intellectual and linguistic richness of his prose.

James McAuley
edited by Leonie Kramer

James McAuley was a poet, intellectual, and leading critic of his time. This volume represents the whole range of his poetry and prose, including the Ern Malley hoax that caused such a sensation in the 1940s, and some new prose pieces published for the first time. Leonie Kramer's introduction offers new critical perspectives on his work.

Rolf Boldrewood
edited by Alan Brissenden

Australia's most famous bushranging novel, *Robbery Under Arms*, together with extracts from the original serial version. The best of Boldrewood's essays and short stories are also included; some are autobiographical, most deal with life in the bush.

Marcus Clarke
edited by Michael Wilding

The convict classic *For the Term of His Natural Life*, and a varied selection of short stories, critical essays and journalism. Autobiographical stories provide vivid insights into the life of this prolific and provocative man of letters.

Nettie Palmer
edited by Vivian Smith

Nettie Palmer was a distinguished poet, biographer, literary critic, diarist, letter-writer, editor and translator, who played a vital role in the development and appreciation of Australian literature. Her warm and informative diary, *Fourteen Years*, is reproduced as a facsimile of the original illustrated edition, along with a rich selection of her poems, reviews and literary journalism.

Colonial Voices
edited by Elizabeth Webby

The first anthology to draw on the fascinating variety of letters, diaries, journalism and other prose accounts of nineteenth-century Australia. These colonial voices belong to adults and children, some famous or infamous, others unknown, whose accounts reveal unusual aspects of Australia's colourful past.

Eight Voices of the Eighties
edited by Gillian Whitlock
These eight voices represent the crest of the wave of women's writing that has characterised the 1980s. Short fiction by Kate Grenville, Barbara Hanrahan, Beverley Farmer, Thea Astley, Elizabeth Jolley, Jessica Anderson, Olga Masters, and Helen Garner is supported by a selection of their criticism, reviews, interviews and commentary, to give an unusual perspective on the phenomenon of women's writing in Australia today.

Randolph Stow
edited by Anthony J. Hassall
Stow's most powerful novel, *Visitants*, is reproduced in full, together with episodes from *To the Islands*, *Tourmaline*, the semi-autobiographical *The Merry-go-Round in the Sea*, the satiric comedy *Midnite,* and *The Girl Green as Elderflower*, as well as a generous selection of his poems, many not previously collected.

David Malouf
edited by James Tulip
A well-balanced, compact selection of David Malouf's intricately connected work. Short stories, poems, essays, interviews and the classic novel *Johnno*, reproduced in full, show the range of his remarkable achievement.

John Shaw Neilson
edited by Cliff Hanna
John Shaw Neilson was the most original poet of his time, able to imbue the Australian landscape with a universal significance. This volume gathers together Neilson's poetry, arranged chronologically from his earliest work to the confidence and maturity of his last poems, his autobiography, and correspondence. It also includes an interview with members of his family.

Kenneth Slessor
edited by Dennis Haskell
This collection of Kenneth Slessor's writing — poetry, essays, journalism, war despatches and diaries, personal notes and letters — allows a fuller, more rounded view of his work than has previously been possible. Slessor emerges as a sensitive, complex and sophisticated person and writer — in any medium.

A.B. 'Banjo' Paterson
edited by Clement Semmler
This collection of bush ballads, poetry, stories and journalism reveals Banjo Paterson's remarkable versatility as a writer, journalist, war correspondent, and racing scribe. It shows that classic Australian humour — the laconic tinged with the sardonic — which is the abiding characteristic of his best-loved work.

Xavier Herbert
edited by Frances de Groen and Peter Pierce
This volume reveals the scope of Xavier Herbert's vast output, with a selection that confronts broad issues such as nationalism, the land, Aborigines, sex and gender, and the role of the creative artist. This sampling, which includes extracts from *Capricornia* and *Poor Fellow My Country*, as well as significant and hitherto unpublished material and a range of polemical and autobiographical writing, will serve as an enticement to further reading of a writer who has always generated controversy and reached a wide popular audience.

Henry Kendall
edited by Michael Ackland
This edition offers new perspectives on Kendall's work and stresses the cultural and historical context shaping his thought. Included are poems not reissued since his death, together with well-known pieces from his most significant books of verse; prose that enriches our understanding of Kendall and of colonial journalism; and letters offering insights into his early family and religious turmoil, as well as his later personal and literary regeneration.

Martin Johnston
edited by John Tranter
Glittering with Martin Johnston's erudition and wit, this rich collection reveals a life lived with literature as its highest aim. Included are his best poems, many of them never published in book form before, a selection of his translations of Greek folk-poems and modern Greek poetry, essays and book reviews, excerpts from interviews, and family photographs. Assembled by long-time friend and fellow-poet, John Tranter, the collection captures not only Martin Johnston's brilliance and love of poetry but also his gentle charm and delight in life.

Christina Stead
edited by R.G. Geering and A. Segerberg
Christina Stead is often coupled with Patrick White as the two most important Australian-born novelists of this century. This cross-section of Stead's work amply displays the range of her writing as well as her political and social views. Her fiction is represented by selections from three novels and short fiction with Australian settings and associations. Material previously unavailable in book form includes extracts from interviews and public talks.

Patrick White
edited by Alan Lawson
Patrick White is presented in this collection as a writer passionately involved in the world around him, in humour, sex and love; who, in his fiction as well as his public utterances, has a keen interest in the social and political events of his time and place. This selection of fiction, poetry, theatre pieces, speeches, letters, essays, interviews and autobiographical writing places White in his literary contexts from the 1930s to the international postmodernism of the 1980s.